BLOOD-RACE

Joe Floyd knew he was losing the footrace as the Shawnee runner—smaller and lighter—took the lead going up the hill toward the torchlights that flickered in the darkness, marking the finish line. Forcing his long legs to pump harder, Joe closed the gap, but the dim figure of the Indian swerved to block him as he tried to go by.

"Damn you," Joe gasped. Chief Black Fish had made the rules of the race clear: the winner got to split the loser's skull with a tomahawk. And, if Joe Floyd passed this test, he'd go free—to warn the people at the stockade.

Desperately, Floyd lashed out with his toe, sending his opponent sprawling. The Shawnee runner was up in an instant, clawing at his back as they reached the finish line. In one last blind lunge, Joe Floyd fell gasping across the finish line.

The tight-lipped Black Fish handed him a tomahawk, gesturing for him to do his duty. Then for the first time Joe got a clear look at the vanquished Shawnee runner.

Though brown as a berry and wearing the breech clout and leggings of a brave, it was a girl—a white girl!

The
WILDERNESS
SEEKERS

Lou Cameron

A DELL/JAMES A. BRYANS BOOK

Published by
Dell Publishing Co., Inc.
1 Dag Hammarskjold Plaza
New York, New York 10017

Dell © TM 681510, Dell Publishing Co., Inc.

ISBN: 0-440-09287-6

Printed in the United States of America

First printing—July 1979

The
WILDERNESS
SEEKERS

1

The spy reined in on the ridge, partly sheltered by a dripping hemlock, and peered down the north slope through the shimmering silver veils of a soft summer rain. It was late afternoon and both the spy and his mount were chilled to the bone by now. The spy had grown accustomed to the lesser discomforts of His Majesty's Service, but the pony wasn't going to make it back to the British lines at this rate. The poor brute had thrown a shoe on the ghastly Post Road and he didn't like the way it was breathing. The spy needed professional care for his pony, or, better yet, a fresh mount. The Quaker blacksmith at the roadside smithy down the hill was reputed to be a loyal Tory, which was good. The spy had ridden out of his way to reach him in this neck of the woods.

Yet he hesitated as he sat his shivering pony, staring down at the cluster of log buildings in the clearing he'd been searching for.

The information he had on the Quaker family was sketchy and at least a year old. Since the distressing news from Saratoga many erstwhile Loyalists were said to be having second thoughts about the probable outcome of this messy little revolution. The spy decided to play his cards carefully as he clucked the sick pony forward down the slope. Doubtless General Howe had had his own good reasons for putting to death a Yankee schoolmaster named Nathan Hale, but the Yankee Doodles had seemed dreadfully upset about it and this was simply not a good time to be captured by rebel militia.

He rode slowly into the open, keeping his free hand well clear of the saddle gun against his right thigh in case they were already aware of him down below. The Quaker family was named Floyd and he had information about the Floyds having been run out of Berks County, Pennsylvania, by their own Quaker neighbors. That the smith was said to be a King's man didn't seem good cause for him to be cast out. Most Quakers were said to be nominally loyal to their king. It was probably some religious dispute. Not that it mattered. The damned pacifist Quakers seemed to offer little help to either side, since they refused to bear arms.

No smoke rose from the smithy beside the little cabin, but a plume of whispy blue hovered over the wattle-and-daub chimney of the living quarters. Doubtless the blacksmith had shut down his forge for the evening. It was hard to see how he did any business at all this far from town and deep in rebel territory.

The spy noticed an open shed in a split-rail paddock behind the forge. There were three horses under the plank roofing, out of the rain. The situation was improving. He had vital information for Major Andre's intelligence detail in New York and with any luck one of those other nags would be fit to ride.

As the spy turned in at the gate in front of the main cabin, the door opened. A tall morose looking man of about fifty called out, "Thy brute is limping badly, friend. Thou hast thrown thy hind-off shoe, look thee."

The spy dismounted wearily. He called back, "I know. Poor thing could use a good dry rub and some oats too. I was hoping to find you open for business."

The blacksmith turned his head to call out to someone in the cabin. Then a blonde youth, a good head taller than any man really needed to be, joined the smith in the doorway for a moment, nodded and came out into the rain, saying, "I'll tend thy mount, sir. Go inside and warm up by the fire."

As the spy handed over the reins he reached in his wet pocket for some coins, but the youth shook his head and insisted, "Go inside. It's the sabbath and we do no business on the sabbath."

"But my pony . . ."

"I said I'd take care of him and I mean to, sir. Our faith forbids trade on the sabbath. But we're not forbidden to do a favor and I doubt this critter will last the night unless I rub him

9

down with dry sacking and bed him in a warm stall. I'll see about shoeing him after warming him some."

"By Jove, that's awfully decent of you, young sir."

The youth smiled. "I'm not a sir. I'm just Joe Floyd and they're waiting on thee in the cabin."

The older Floyd had already gone inside. With a grateful nod at the youth, the spy sloshed over to the cabin and ducked inside. The interior was warm and dark. The only light came from the open doorway, narrow loopholes cut in the log walls, and a huge strange-glowing fireplace at one end. He found his host, the older Floyd, seated on a bench near the fire. A woman in severe black wool knelt on the hearth, her head under the overhang of the big timber mantel-beam as she stirred the contents of a cast iron kettle with a wooden spoon. The blacksmith said, "Come sit by the fire and dry thyself, friend. Yon lass is my goodwife Margaret."

The woman looked up with a wan smile. The spy saw she was quite beautiful despite the smudge of soot on one cheek and the severe styling of her blue-black hair. The spy removed his soggy tricorn hat and bowed to say, "Your servant, mum."

The blacksmith's voice took on a slight edge. "We don't hold with worldly greetings in this household, friend."

"I assure you I meant no disrespect, sir."

"We don't hold with sirs and other worldly

titles either, look thee! I know thou art but attempting common courtesies, friend, and I ask thee to forgive us if our ways seem strange to thee. It's important we cling strongly to our faith in these parts. For we are surrounded by worldly folk here. The boy out there needs constant watching since we moved down here to the piedmont. He has not the example of proper neighbors and unless I remind him constantly he is given to speaking like the ruffians he meets in town."

"We live in troubled times, uh, friend Floyd. My name is Cyrus Marvin and I hail from Connecticut. I've been on a peddling trip as far south as the Carolinas and I'm bound home for some more Yankee notions. I sell ribbon bows, pins, looking glasses and such. As to my political leanings . . ."

"I did not ask thee which side thou were on, friend Marvin! Thou art right about these being troubled times, but I treat all men of good will the same, be they Loyalist or Rebel."

Not waiting for an answer from his guest, he turned to his young wife, "Set the table, Margaret. If that stew's not done by now it never will be."

The woman asked, "Are not we to wait for Joe, husband?"

"No. The lad has chores and he knows he must finish before he sups. It is not seemly in the eyes of the Lord to keep a hungry guest waiting."

The spy protested, "I'm quite prepared to wait for the lad, folks." But Floyd insisted, "Come, let us to table. His portion will keep in the pot and he'll enjoy it all the more for coming to table hungry after honest toil."

Suiting action to his words the smith ushered his guest to a plank table in the center of the room. Margaret began to set four places with rough wooden bowls, horn drinking cups and battered pewter spoons. The spy knew it was proper in these backwoods communities to use one's own knife.

As Margaret filled the cups with soft cider and the bowls with warm meat stew, the spy appraised the family. The woman was far too young to be the natural mother of that big son. But that did not surprise him. Women didn't live long in America. Most men buried at least two or three in a lifetime. The couple were both rather dark. Young Joe's mother must have been the blonde he'd gotten his coloring from. He could see father and son shared the same bone structure, although the son was much taller than the powerfully built smith. He also seemed just just a bit rebellious. Could that have resulted from the older man's strictness?

Despite his thees and thous there was a bitterness about the older Floyd. Young Joe had seemed pleasant enough and the stepmother thought enough of him to object, however mildly, to his eating late. That was an interesting thought. The spy could see the cabin consisted of a single room. The married couple doubtless occupied the sleeping loft down at the far end. That trundle bed in the corner was obviously where the lad slept. A bit sticky when one thought about it. The boy was old enough to be interested in country matters. There were no neighbors nearby, and had there been, with a daughter worth consideration, few piedmont Yanks would want a Quaker courting her.

The spy felt a slight discomfort in his groin as he considered what it would do to *him* if he had to lay on that trundle in the dark with the old man and this stunning wench bedded above him close enough to hear every breath. He managed not to grimace as he took a mouthful of stew and found it quite tasty. He said as much, and Margaret Floyd murmured, "Thanks to Joe, our pot is ever filled."

The blacksmith shot his young wife a sharp look. Then he shrugged and agreed, "The boy is not a bad huntsman, though I do wonder how seemly it is in the eyes of the Lord for him to be so much interested in guns."

The spy asked, "Is hunting forbidden to Quakers, friend Floyd?"

"No. Only the hunting of our fellow human beings is a sin. But it's said a lad shakes hands with the devil every time he picks up a gun. Methinks our Joe would rather be off in the woods after squirrel than at my side where he belongs."

The English officer repressed the temptation to ask what he was eating. If it was a bloody tree-rat it was tasty enough. If it was something other than squirrel, he didn't really want to know. When in Rome and all that.

Munching, he considered the blacksmith's earlier words about Loyalists and Rebels. He knew men on the side of the puffed-up Continental Congress tended to distinguish the sides as Tory and Patriot, but whatever they were called didn't trouble him. The old man Floyd did sound like a Loyalist. Yet he was surrounded by rebel neighbors. Why hadn't the pony boys or cow boys paid them a visit? The backwoods were crawling with roving bands of young toughs, who were using the revolution as an excuse to pillage in the name of either cause. Those claiming to be raping and burning for His Majesty called themselves "cow boys." The rebel thugs were known as "pony boys." This isolated smithy offered a tempting target to either group. Aside from their goods and chattels, the woman, no more than thirty, was a tempting prize. The local militia might protect their own, but hardly an outsider reputed to be a Loyalist. All in all, the spy was not satisfied that he understood the Floyds' position in the community. For now, it ill-behooved him to drop his cover story.

The son, Joe, came in to say, "Thy horse is as comforted as I could manage, friend. Thou hast rode him hard over sharp wet gravel and he stands to be fair sore for the next few days."

The spy said, "I have to get home. Have you replaced the thrown shoe, Joe?"

"No. The hoof is split and the poor brute has a tender and swollen frog. He can't be shoed until his hooves have dried and the swelling goes down. I cannot shoe him this night lest he be crippled before he is ridden many more miles."

The spy frowned.

The blacksmith said cheerily, "If my son says the brute can't be shoed this night he's doubtless right. Look thee, Joe is a fair smith. Son," he continued, "change thy shirt before thou suppeth. Thou art wet."

The spy, having given up on riding his horse that night, was suddenly intrigued by the argument that ensued,

Joe protested, "Father, I only have a few drops on my shirt and it's fair warm in here." But the older man snapped, "Do as I command, look thee!" and Joe turned from the table without a word. He moved to a corner and peeled off his slightly damp flannel shirt, exposing a young muscular torso while he rummaged in a chest for a fresh shirt. The spy noticed the woman's eyes were lowered to her own empty bowl. The father gazed at his powerfully built son with an odd expression of mingled pride and . . . envy?

The Englishman, having listened and watched intently, stared at a knot hole in the table top and pondered. These Quakers lived like livestock in a barn. The youth and the young stepmother were obviously aware of each other's bodies. The older man seemed virile enough, but the spy could see how awkward the situation could be for the younger people in these close quarters. He was trained to judge people and so he felt it safe to assume neither Joe nor his pretty stepmother entertained conscious carnal thoughts. But he was certainly glad he didn't live here.

There was, indeed, a feeling in this cabin that reminded the spy of that electric fluid Doctor Franklin had demonstrated for the Royal Society before he'd taken up his newer hobby of high treason. With one breath the blacksmith had praised his son as a skilled helper. With another he had treated the huge lout as an infant who didn't know when it was time to change his shirt.

Having obeyed his father and donned a clean but threadbare shirt of homespun grey, young Joe returned to the table and the father made no further comment as the woman served him his belated supper. The boy was slightly flushed, but if he resented his father's command he kept it to himself as he ate with downcast eyes.

The spy saw the older smith was lighting an after-supper pipe and, relieved the Quakers were not quite as strict as he had thought, took out his own tobacco while he considered his next move.

He didn't really need such information as the Floyds could give him. He already had most of the facts Major Andre had sent him down the Post Road to acquire. On the other hand, every scrap of gossip from behind the American lines could be put to good use by his clever superior. Young Major Andre had a keen Swiss mind and was a genius at putting odd bits and pieces together. The spy felt that anything at all he brought back might be grist for his mill.

Choosing his words carefully, the spy said, "I've heard some rather interesting talk about another man named Floyd. John Floyd, I think. He wouldn't be related to you folks, would he?"

Young Joe looked up brightly to say, "Oh, that's Cousin John. He's from Berks County too."

"Oh? I didn't know the famous rebel adventurer was a Quaker."

The blacksmith grimaced and said flatly, "He's not. The Society of Friends have disavowed him. John Floyd is a drunken ruffian as bad as his lapsed Quaker friends, the Boones."

"The Boones? Surely we're not talking about Captain Daniel Boone, the long-hunter?"

"We are. The whole lot are ruffians and traitors. Even before this scandalous revolt the Boones and my fallen cousin took up arms against their fellow man. They both bore arms in the Cherokee War, despite their upbringing."

The spy made a mental note that the notorious Daniel Boone had peaceful Quaker relatives in Pennsylvania. Such a detail might come in handy in the future. Young Joe said, "Father grew up with Dan'l Boone. They used to be close."

His father snapped, "Forgive me, Lord, but my son is a fool! I knew the Boones in my youth. I was never close with them. They seldom came to meeting and were given over to hard drink and worldly lusts. Our community was well rid of them when the Friends threw them out. Their father, Squire Boone, was himself a lapsed Quaker. The whole clan is useless, look thee!"

Joe protested, "Come on, father. The folk in Berks County were fanatics, as well thou know. Didn't they turn on *thee*, when thou married Margaret here?"

The older man lowered his eyes and muttered, "That was different. They simply misunderstood my motives. *We* know I did right by thy poor dead mother's bondservant. Marrying out of the faith is not the same as shooting Indians and rebeling against our king!"

The spy didn't think Major Andre would be interested in the messy domestic affairs of a backwoods blacksmith. He steered the conversation back to their rebel kinsman. "When I was down in the Carolinas," he said "folks spoke highly of John Floyd and Captain Boone. They seem to be leading a lot of people over the mountains into the Crown lands reserved for the king's Indian subjects. Not that I understand the legalities of the situation, of course."

"It's a simple act of land piracy," snapped the

blacksmith, adding, "That so-called Transylvania Company they're working for has no right to settle people west of the Cumberland Gap. The land belongs to loyal subjects of the king!"

Joe swallowed a mouthful of squirrel stew and said mildly, "I understand they bought the land from the Cherokee nation, father."

"Don't be foolish, son. In the first place, the land belongs to the Crown. In the second, those thieving Cherokee would have had no right to sell it even if the French still owned it! The Kentucky meadows are the hunting grounds of the Shawnee, and the Shawnee are faithful servants of His Majesty, look thee!"

Joe lowered his eyes but muttered, "Thou might call them that. They say Royal Governor Hamilton is paying for Yankee scalps delivered well smoked in Detroit. On the other hand, the Crown has paid for many a Tory scalp, too. The Indians seem not to make fine distinctions in the sale of hair!"

His father snapped, "That's Yankee propaganda, put out by that old lecher Franklin, look thee!"

"Was Jeannie MacRea one of Franklin's fables, father?" Joe glanced at the spy to add, "The MacRea girl was a Tory, engaged to one of Burgoyne's British officers. During the Saratoga campaign the Indians delivered her blonde scalp to her intended groom and couldn't understand why they weren't rewarded."

The spy nodded and said quietly, "I've heard of Burgoyne's problem in disciplining his Indian irregulars. It's my understanding the Yankees are having much the same difficulty with their own red friends."

Joe said, "General Washington refuses to enlist Indians. He says it's uncivilized to scalp even a Tory."

"But Tories have been scalped, Joe."

"Maybe. But the Continental Congress isn't buying hair. Some of the Cherokee seem to be on our side. Others are for the king. One never knows with Indians."

The boy's father cut in to snap, "*Our* side, Joe? Bite thy tongue! I thought we'd settled the loyalties of this house long ago, look thee!"

"My father's a Tory." Joe sighed, looking away.

The spy nodded without comment. He didn't have to ask if Joe was sympathetic to the Rebel cause. He understood the two men now. The wife remained a mystery. Margaret Floyd sat cat-like in her corner, not joining in the man-talk. But her loyalties hardly mattered. What could a mere woman do, for or against her king?

He had as much information about the notorious Yankee scout John Floyd as these rustic relatives were likely to give him. They were not in contact. Floyd and his irregulars were doubtless over the mountains as other informants had said. The older man was still loyal. The boy was at that dangerous age when youth tested itself against age and authority, but the old Quaker ruled with an iron hand and the lad was too far from the front for his foolish opinions to matter. Now all the spy had to do was get back to New York alive.

The spy coughed and said, "If what you say about my mount is true, I fear I must press you about business despite the hour of day, friend Floyd. How much would you ask me to add in silver if I were to offer my injured mount for one of yours?"

"I'm a blacksmith, not a horse trader, look thee."

"I know, but I do have to be on my way and Joe says my pony won't be fit to ride for days."

The father shrugged. He looked at his son and asked, "What say thee, Joe? Thou hast knowledge of our friend's brute. Have we one that would make an honest trade?"

Joe nodded. "The piebald mare is a pony of the same value, father. If we send friend Marvin on his way with her and wait until his chestnut mends, we'll neither profit nor lose by it."

The father said, "In that case it would not be unseemly in the eyes of the Lord, for an even trade is not business on the sabbath. When our friend is ready to ride on, see him well mounted and safely on his way."

The spy objected, "I insist you make some small profit. You've been very kind to a wayfaring stranger and I've some thoughts of my own on seemly behavior."

"We can't accept money for hospitality, friend Marvin."

"Well, see here, I've a few Yankee notions left in my peddler's pack. Perhaps a case-knife for the lad, or some ribbon bows for the lady of the house?"

Both younger people looked up hopefully, but the blacksmith shook his head. "Keep thy Yankee notions for those worldly folk who feel they need them. Joe has a knife, and my wife is not a saucy maid. She does not wear ribbons in her hair."

The spy didn't argue further, having the distinct impression that the stern Quaker seldom retreated from a stated position. He said, "In that case, please accept my heartfelt thanks and I'll be on my way. Would you like to show me the painted pony, Joe?"

The tall youth got up from the table to lead their guest outside as Margaret began to clear the table with no expression on her pretty face. The blacksmith followed them to the door but stood under the jamb, out of the rain, as Joe and the spy trotted to the adjacent forge. Inside, the spy saw the boy had already placed his dried saddle on a frisky piebald mare in the stall next to his crippled chestnut. He smiled and asked, "How did you know I'd be riding out on this one, Joe?"

The youth smiled thinly and replied, "I would have talked you into it one way or the other, sir. Can I assume this is a private conversation, man to man?"

"Oh, mum's the word, Joe. But what are we keeping secrets about?"

The youth seemed older and much more sure of himself, away from his strict father. He said flatly, "The Minute Men are looking for a British spy. He's said to be riding a chestnut pony and posing as a Yankee peddler. You'd have never made the county line had I let you ride out on that chestnut."

There was a long pregnant pause. Then the spy licked his lips and said, "I see. May I assume my chestnut wasn't really as lame as you made out, Joe?"

"I could have doctored his hoof well enough to carry you as far as you'd have gotten. But you'll get further on this piebald mare. You did say you were from Connecticut, didn't you, sir?"

"Quite. Why are you doing this, Joe? If you know who the Minute Men are looking for, you have to be one of them!"

The youth shrugged and said, "I am. How do you think my Tory father stays in business despite his views? As to the why of it, I'm still a Quaker, in my own fashion, and a guest is a guest."

"In other words, you're not a fanatic, either way?"

"That's about the size of it. I don't like the king's damned quit-rents but I'm not sure I like the idea of paying taxes to any new government we're likely to get. I'd as lief move west and let the devil take the hindmost. But you saw how my father is."

"I did, and I understand the game you're playing, young sir. I hear you sometimes, uh, forget your thees and thous. I don't suppose I could induce you to become a double agent for His Majesty?"

"No, sir, you could not. I don't want to see you hanged because you're a fellow human being. But if it comes to fighting hereabouts, I'll have to fight for my country."

"Joe, your country is England. You're an English colonist."

"You'd best be on your way, sir. I've had this argument with my father more than once and it's a waste of time. You know you're right and I know I'm right. We may both be wrong, but a man fights for the things he has to. Let's say no more about it. I wish you a safe journey to your own lines."

The spy held out a hand and murmured, "I sincerely hope we never meet again, Joe."

The youth shook hands with the Englishman and said, "So do I."

Then he turned and went back to the cabin as the spy led his new mount out, forked the saddle and rode off in the gathering darkness.

The spy knew it was his duty to add Joe Floyd's name to the growing list of rebels to be dealt with after this whole distressing mess was over. But he knew he wouldn't do it. Major Andre had enough on his plate for any worried man and, come to think of it, so did young Joe.

2

Militiaman Joseph Floyd stood at attention in the rear rank of the trained band mustered on the village green. His father thought he'd gone hunting for the family pot. Joe hadn't lied exactly. There was a fat porcupine, a rabbit and three plump squirrels in the rawhide rucksack on his back. He'd bagged them on his way to the county seat for the weekly meeting of the local Minute Men.

Despite his position in the rear rank, Joe had a clear field of vision over the shorter young men around him as the fife and drum came down the green ahead of the new colors. A village girl cried out, "Here comes the flag, and, oh, it's so pretty!" as the fife and drum passed. They were playing a tune written by a British surgeon to mock the Americans, then adopted by them as their own. At Joe's side, little Freckles Grogan softly sang, "Father and I went down to camp, along with Captain Gooding, and there we saw the men and boys, as thick as hasty pudding!"

Another Minute Man sang, "Yankee Doodle, keep it up, Yankee Doodle dandy . . ." and then the sergeant snapped, "God damn it, you boys are at *attention!*"

The song faded away as the color guard passed in review. The new flag authorized by Congress was a bit fussy to Joe's taste, but pretty enough with its little white stars and candy stripes dancing in the sunlight. At least there'd be less confusion now that every American unit would be flying the same colors. There'd been some nasty accidents in the past because of the bewildering variety of improvised banners. They said the Jerseymen had fired on the Marylanders at the Battle of Long Island when they took their red coats and Baltimore arms for British.

The trooping of the colors ended and their sergeant dismissed them for the rest of the week. Joe fell out and unpinned the blue-and-red cockade from his hat brim, putting it in the breast pocket of his fringed hunting jacket. He hefted his Brown Bess musket and strode away with its muzzle down as Freckles Grogan tagged along at his side. Joe said, "I'm going to the general store before I head back our way, Freckles."

The shorter redhead grinned and said, "I know, and I wouldn't miss it for the world. Do you really think you can whup Mister Garth and both his sons, Joe?"

"Don't know. It's not your quarrel, Freckles."

"Hell, we're neighbors, even if your pa don't know it. I heard the gossip too, Joe. If you can handle the old man and one of his sons, I mind I can lick the other."

Joe said, "I'm hoping it won't come to blows, and it's still not your business, Freckles."

"Aw, hell, can't I just watch? Tom Paine says it's a free country now."

Joe chuckled wryly and, to change the subject, asked, "When are you and Tilly Hanks figuring to get hitched, Freckles? I saw the bans posted on the church door as I passed, but you never set no date."

Freckles said, "Her pa says I can't marry up with Tilly 'cause I own no land of my own. Can you keep a secret, Joe?"

"Why not? You've kept more than one for me."

"Well, we're fixing to run off. I'm carrying Tilly out beyond the Cumberland Gap and we'll be married there."

"You sure you know what you're doing, Freckles? I know what they say about Kentucky, but . . ."

" 'Oh, Heaven is a Kentucky of a place!' " quoted Freckles with a laugh, adding, "The rivers flow milk and honey and the woods is filled with bear and buffalo. We'll clear us a hundred acres or so and . . ."

"Damn it, Freckles, the Transylvania Com-

pany *sells* new homesteads out that way. Some
lawyer named Dick Henderson holds title to all
the land from the Cumberlands to the Ohio."

"A lot you know. We're off to join Dan'l
Boone and the other long-hunters. Cap'n Boone
discovered Kentucky and . . ."

"Freckles, you're talking foolish. A cousin of
mine is with Boone this minute and you have
your facts all wrong. Boone didn't discover the
Cumberland Gap. It's an Indian trail that other
long-hunters have known and used for years.
Boone's a land agent for Henderson. All he's
done is guide new settlers through to sell the
plots he's surveyed for the Transylvania Company. How much money do you and Tilly have
between you?"

"Not a lot. But I mind I've enough for a
wagon and enough supplies to last us through
to our first harvest."

Joe shook his head and said, "God give me
strength! You can't take a wagon through those
mountains, boy! You take your girl out there,
broke, and you'll both be stranded until Governor Hamilton buys your hair! How in thunder did you ever talk Tilly into such a foolish
notion? We both know *you* were behind the
door when the brains were passed out, but
Tilly seems smart, for a girl."

"You ain't been keeping up with the news,
Joe. The Transylvania Company's been giving
land grants to men who know how to handle

a gun. They've had a little trouble with the Injuns, but us Yankees are born sharpshooters and . . ."

"And you are purely full of shit, Freckles! I've seen you at the target butts. You're as good a shot as most, but that's not saying much. Those stories about the Yankee riflemen picking off the poor redcoats at a distance are trumped up. The Royal regulars shoot better than most of us and those Indians likely shoot better than anyone, since it's all they do for a living."

Freckles looked worried but determined as he insisted, "Hell, look how we peppered the redcoats at Lexington and Concord, Joe."

"That's what I mean. Piss poor shooting if you ask me!"

"Piss poor? Why, Joe, Pitcairn's regulars lost over a hundred men getting back to Boston after the Minute Men fell in on their flanks!"

"Sure they did. And it was still piss poor shooting! Look at the odds that day, Freckles. There were about six hundred redcoats marching in formation down the road, with every man in the whole damned county who had a musket blazing away at them from cover! Let's say at least a thousand men and boys took one or two free shots at the passing column. Then add it up. If they only brought down 2 hundred men in a whole morning of constant fire, think how many of those damn fool Minute Men who were doing the shooting must have missed! I

swear to God, I don't see how such poor marksmanship was possible, but the figures speak for
themselves."

"Well, maybe they was out of practice the
first day of the war. We purely shot the shit
out of them at Bunker Hill, didn't we?"

"No. General Gage was a fool. He sent close-
packed troops up the hill marching in step. The
Patriots on the ridge would have knocked
down a thousand had they used bowling balls!
And remember the British finally took the hill,
and killed or wounded five hundred or so of our
own. The casualties were two to one. Two redcoats downed for every American, and the
Americans were firing into closed ranks from
behind a barricade. I'd say that was piss poor
shooting too! The British regulars were poorly
led, but they proved themselves damned fine
fighting men at Bunker Hill."

"Jesus, Joe, I thought you was on our side."

"I am. But facts are facts and we'll never win
this war until we face them. You don't whip
an enemy by whistling Yankee Doodle and telling yourself he's a sissy. You treat him with
the respect he deserves. The British and the
king's Indians are tough, Freckles. If I were
you I'd stay right here with Tilly. They say
when the war is over every militiaman will be
given a land grant for his services."

"Hell, we can't wait that long. You see, Tilly
. . . uh, never mind."

Joe didn't ask what Freckles meant. If he'd

gotten the girl in trouble Joe didn't want to know. He had enough trouble of his own with the village gossips. But, Lord, if Tilly Hanks was expecting, Freckles might be better off facing Shawnee at that!

The two youths reached the village store, where Morgan Garth and his two brawny sons were unloading a Conestoga wagon out front. Joe handed his musket to Freckles and strode over as the Garths eyed him warily. Joe saw one of them had just wrestled a keg of nails off the wagon bed and was trying to walk it up the plank steps of the store. Joe said, "Let me give you a hand with that," and reached down to pick the nail keg up in one hand. He placed it carefully on the plank porch and turned with a smile. The father, Morgan Garth, stared at the nail keg as if he expected it to explode. He considered himself a strong man, but hefting a nail keg, one-handed, wasn't human.

Morgan Garth nodded his thanks as the two sons fell in on either side. Joe noticed one of them had casually picked up a pick handle.

Joe said, "I'd like a word with you about my kith and kin, Mister Garth."

"Oh? I'm not sure I follow you, Joe. Your father's not too friendly, but I don't mind having words with him."

"Not to his face," said Joe, still smiling. Then he added, "My father can defend himself from scandal mongering, and you'll find out just how unfriendly he can be if something I heard in the tavern should reach his ears, Mister Garth."

"See here, young sir, I don't know what you mean to accuse me of, but if you think I've wronged you or yours in any way, suppose you say right out what it might be."

"That's fair enough, sir. And I'm willing to take your word if you deny speaking out of turn about my stepmother in the tavern."

Morgan Garth frowned in what seemed genuine confusion. Then he shook his head and said, "I don't know what you're talking about. I've never spoken to the wench!"

And then his feet were a good six inches off the ground as Joe lifted him bodily by the front of his broadcloth jacket. One of the sons made a move to help but Freckles Grogan cocked his own musket and said, "Stay out of it, Will Garth!"

Joe Floyd was still smiling as he told the man he held aloft at arms' length, "My stepmother is not a wench, sir. Would you like to try it again?"

"God damn it, Joe, I meant no offense to . . . the lady!"

Joe said, "That's better." He lowered the gasping storekeeper gently to his feet again. He said, "They told me in the tavern you passed certain remarks about a young bawd sharing a one-room cabin with two grown men. Do you deny it, Mister Garth?"

"As God is my witness, I *do*, young sir! I don't know your parents and I don't want to. I know your father's Tory opinions are not mine. But since Quakers bear no arms, and you're a Minute Man, I say live and let live. As to anything that may or may not be going on at your homestead, I deal in stores, not gossip."

Will Garth still held the pick handle ready, but he said, "Our dad never said nothing about your maw, Joe. If you tell us who's been putting words in his mouth we'll lick him good!"

Mollified, Joe said, "I'm taking your words at face value, gentlemen. I'll deal with whoever might have started the talk in my own way. Before I bid you good day though, I mean to set you straight on a few things."

Morgan Garth said, "Joe, there's no need for explanations. We're not interested in your stepmother."

"You're likely unusual folks for such a small town then. But I aim to tell you anyway. I know my father's a hard man to know. My stepmother is the next thing to a saint. When I was ten my mother bought her indenture papers and she was our servant. My mother had the consumption and could hardly lift a finger about the house. Back in Pennsylvania, Margaret fetched and carried for us all. She cooked and sewed and taught me how to read and write. To the day my mother died, Margaret nursed her tender, and when she passed away Margaret comforted me. I was only twelve then and I guess I bawled some. My father is an unbending man. If he grieved he tried not to show it. The only one who held my hand at the funeral was my stepmother. She wasn't my stepmother then, of course."

Morgan Garth's eyes softened and it was hard to tell how much of what he said came from guilt. He nodded and said, "I see, Joe. I do remember some of the old biddies talking about the difference in their ages. You know how womenfolk talk, son."

"Yes, I'm sure it was old biddies. Most men would understand my father's position. He'd just buried a wife and had a half-grown son to care for. He never has been one to cook and sew worth mention and Margaret was there. He could have just kept her as a bondservant, I suppose. He didn't have to marry up with her. But he knew how it might look. So he did right by her as the Lord saw fit to let him see the right. Maybe he was wrong to wed a young girl who wasn't of our faith. A lot seemed to think so. Some folks in Pennylvania who talk a lot about the Lord said Margaret was forced into something unseemly 'cause she had no other choice. None of them saw fit to ask her. I only know what I saw."

"Joe, we understand. You'll hear no evil talk about the lady from me or mine from this day forward."

"I hope so, Mister Garth. I'm going to say one more thing and that'll be the end of it. I'll allow I was too young to know how the folks felt about each other when they married. I'm eighteen now and I know why the Lord made men and women different. So I hope you'll take my word for it that my stepmother Margaret Floyd has been a good and faithful wife to my father. Do you have any further questions about the matter?"

"No. I'm certain she's as fine a lady as you say, Joe."

Joe nodded and shook hands with all three before bidding them good day and taking his musket back from Freckles. As they walked away, the redhead asked, "You reckon they was telling the truth, Joe?"

Joe said, "No. But I doubt they'll say it a second time. That was a fool stunt you pulled back there, Freckles, but I thank you anyway."

"Hell, three on one is poor fun. How come you let 'em off if you suspicion they lied, Joe?"

"You ever tree a bobcat, Freckles?"

"Not recently. Why?"

"If you run a bobcat up a tree you can shoot him or you can walk away. Nobody but a fool keeps any kind of critter cornered when he's offered a peace pipe. I can't shoot the storekeeper and they said they didn't aim to fight me."

"So you just let 'em off?"

"Only sensible thing to do. My aim was to shut them up, not stand trial on a hanging offense. They know now anything they might say about my folks will get back to me. They know what I'll do about it too. I'd say the war was over."

Freckles laughed and said, "General Washington should have you on his staff, Joe. I vow, you're a slippery cuss. You could likely talk General Howe into going home if you offered him a way out of a corner."

Joe laughed. "You're not far wrong, Freckles. Both sides seem to have a bobcat treed and neither has the sense to let the poor brute get away."

They walked toward their neighboring homes in silence for a time. Then Freckles asked, "How long do you mind it'll go on like this, Joe? I mean, Tilly and me can't wait much longer. But if the war was to end right soon and I was to get a military grant . . ."

Joe shook his head and said, "It's got a good four or five years to run, Freckles. We held out the first four with the British kicking hell out of us. Now that we've started winning a few battles the British will likely be as stubborn. My rough guess is that we're about halfway through this war."

Freckles sighed, "Well, it's off to Kentucky for Tilly and me then. We don't have no four years to wait. At the most, we got maybe four more *months* afore her old man comes after me with his musket!"

3

Three days later Joe Floyd was up well before dawn and seated on a damp fallen oak a mile from home. His Brown Bess was across his knees and he had one palm cupped over the firing pan to keep his powder dry. He knew the sun would burn away the morning fog by nine. The locusts singing the last two sunsets to sleep had forecast hotter and dryer weather to come. But he aimed to be back at the forge and ready for work before this neck of the woods dried out. He'd positioned himself by the game trail well before the critters would be moving into cover for the day. He could see trees nearly three hundred yards away now, and he'd know any minute whether he'd been right about that fresh deer sign he'd been spotting up this way lately.

A deer was almost too much to hope for these days. The country had become crowded since they'd first cleared their land and, thanks to the war, all sorts of blundering fools had guns these days. When they weren't at their chores or cussing King George in the tavern they were out here in the woods wasting the powder and ball the new state government had issued them. The part-time Minute Men hadn't simply shot out such game as was left. They'd frightened everything with ears a day's ride deeper into the woods. He'd seen a bluebird with its head shot off the other day. Less than a quarter mile from here. It hardly seemed possible any deer would be grazing the night pastures that close to a fool who shot up bluebirds. But sign was sign. Maybe the deer was stupid, too.

Joe wanted the venison for Margaret, but his pre-dawn hunt was as much an excuse to leave the two of them alone for a while as anything else. He figured his folks had natural feelings, since he'd heard the cautious sounds from the sleeping loft often enough. He suspected Margaret was not always pleased; the other evening, for example, he'd heard her whispers of protest when father started going at it hot and heavy. But Joe had no call to think about such matters overly much. He was respectful of their privacy. He figured to give them at least another hour before he ambled back to the cabin, deer or not. He had to be careful about his timing. Give them time, yes—but then, father would fuss if he was late firing up the forge. He'd sweat the deer out 'til just before it got light enough to make out the colors of the morning flowers. Then he'd head back and have the forge stoked and fired before they got up and had breakfast. Joe didn't eat breakfast with his elders. It was seemly for him to have his morning chores done before he thought of his creature comforts. Margaret would bring a cup of tea and crust out to the forge for him to eat while he pumped the bellows and his father worked at the anvil.

There was a blur of movement to his left in the mist. Joe stopped breathing, sat motionless and watched the critter take a few cautious steps before freezing again. It was a deer, sure as hell. An expectant doe, moving awkwardly on three legs. She seemed to be looking right at him. Many a novice threw away his shot at this stage of the game. Joe knew the faint morning breeze was favoring him and deer couldn't tell a motionless man from a tree stump unless they heard or scented human sign. The deer twitched an ear and acted like it was about to bolt. Joe knew that trick too. He stayed the way he was. Satisfied, the doe lowered her head to crop some sorrel. As her head was buried in the grass, Joe eased the musket into firing position. He didn't cock it. A serious deer-hunter had his pan primed and his hammer cocked well before any critter was close enough to hear the metallic snicks.

The deer's head snapped up as if pulled on a string, She was looking to catch a creeping catamount—or even a hunter—off guard. She hadn't caught Joe. He hadn't flinched at the sudden movement. He had silently moved his musket, but the deer's poor memory hadn't allowed her to recognize the new position of what she had seen only as an uninteresting blob at the base of a lightning-crippled chestnut. Satisfied, the doe moved closer, testing the morning air with her sniffs and ear wags before pausing again to lower her head to graze once more. Joe had her read now. The poor critter was heavy with fawn and some over-anxious tyro had put a ball in one hind leg a while back. She'd been left by her herd to fend for herself and her hurt had forced her to graze and water tight, where his keen hunter's eye had read her fresh sign. She'd likely been grazing the bottom-lands along Willow Creek and was bedding down in the alder-hell up near the ridge. If she was making for the alder-hell, she wouldn't drift much closer. Her next move would be away from him to the left.

Joe raised the sights to his eye and aimed for the angle where the doe's neck and body formed an inverted L. Then he squeezed the trigger.

As always, there was a maddening split-second between the flash in his musket's pan and the dull boom from the big muzzle. The deer's head swung up and she was gathering for her first bound when the three-quarter-inch ball slammed into her, shattering a shoulder-blade and parting the spine at the base of her neck. The deer went down, legs twitching as she voided her bowels and filled womb in the wet grass.

Joe didn't watch. The killing of critters was part of his life, but he didn't enjoy watching them die. It was more important to see to his weapon. He knew he was far from any redcoat or prowling king's Indian, but he wasn't about to fall into sloppy habits. Many a man had lost his hair as he sat congratulating himself on a good shot with an empty musket in his hands.

Joe sat the Brown Bess on its butt plate between his knees and drew the ramrod, running it down the empty tube to snuff any lingering sparks. With his other hand, he took a fresh cartridge from the pouch on his hip. He tore the paper open with his teeth as he withdrew the ramrod. He poured the powder above the enclosed ball down the tube, then palmed the ball and ran the paper wadding down before dropping the ball in the muzzle. He took the paper remnant from his mouth and thumbed that wadding in too before ramming the whole round down hard.

Replacing the ramrod, Joe placed the reloaded musket across his knees with the muzzle safely trained on a nearby tree. He put the hammer on half-cock, opened the pan and charged it with finer corned powder from the ox horn hanging from his shoulder. He closed the frizzen over the pan and slammed it with a hard palm to set the primer in the touch-hole.

His musket was ready to fire again, had any curious ears been attracted to the sound of his first shot. It had taken him perhaps thirty seconds, for he was in no hurry and liked to do it right. In a pinch he could get off three aimed shots a minute. Joe wasn't proud of this. He'd heard a well-trained British regular could get off four.

Joe got to his moccasined feet and strode over to the dead doe and her half-born fawn, musket cradled over one arm. He nudged the dead critter a couple of times with his gun muzzle before he bent over her. Sometimes dead critters surprised you, and those hooves were razor sharp.

Satisfied, Joe bent and dragged the dead beast to the base of a poplar sapling. He leaned his musket on a stouter tree nearby and cut a short sharp length of tree branch. He drove it through the tendons of the deer's hind hams, pulled the stillborn fawn and afterbirth out of the way, then hoisted the carcass up by the stake through its hind legs. He hooked the stake over a tree limb and drew his sheath knife. He drove the tip in just forward of the pubic bone and sliced down to the breast, stepping back and out of the way as the guts spilled to the ground. He cut away the connective tissues while still holding the inner organs, being careful to avoid tainting the meat by spilling the contents of paunch or spleen. The liver and heart were good eating, so he left them in place. Then he swabbed out the gaping cavity with a fistful of grass. The critter was a mite thin, but there were no worms to fret Margaret this time. He wondered what she'd say if he cleaned and carried the stillborn fawn in too. He knew it would taste like tender lamb. But Margaret was sort of silly with her tender notions about such things, so he decided to leave the poor little brute with its dead ma's guts. There was enough for them all and the raccoons too. Margaret would likely say some fool thing about the carcass being a doe. Sure it was, but everybody knew a buck deer was tough as hell in the pot and it likely hurt just as much to get shot wearing horns. But girls were funny that way.

Joe took the cleaned carcass down and folded it for carrying, with the forelimbs and head wedged between the pinned hams. He hoisted the hundred-odd pounds of fresh meat to his shoulder, picked up his musket and went home, rather pleased with himself.

As he turned in at the gate Joe saw his father was up and standing by the cold forge in the open-fronted smithy. The dour Quaker wore an ominous expression. Joe quickly said, "I'm sorry the fire's not lit, father. I did not mean to inconvenience thee. It must be later than I thought. Just let me hang this deer in the shed for Margaret and . . ."

"The devil take your deer! Put it down and attend me at once! Thou hast more than a cold forge to answer for this morning, I vow!"

Joe walked over with a puzzled smile and placed his musket and venison by the door frame. His father stepped into the light holding a small patch of red and blue in one hand, a drover's whip in the other. He said, "I found this in thy possibles-pouch, look thee! Art going to tell me it's not the cockade of the Rebel militia?"

Joe took a deep breath, let it half out so his voice wouldn't crack, and said, "I thought my personal belongings were my own, father."

"Then thou art sadly mistaken! Thou art my son, thou insolent pup! Everything thou own and art are *mine!* How long have you been sneaking off to the Rebel army, Joe?"

"Father, I don't belong to the Continental Army. I'm a Minute Man. No more. I am only pledged to defend our township at a minute's notice should we be attacked by roving Tories or the king's Indians. I have no intention of marching off to the real war in the north."

"When I get through with thee, thou shalt neither march nor sit comfortable for a week! Take off thy shirt, Joe. I haven't had to do this for some time, but I see thou needeth another lesson."

Joe shrugged and said, "Thou art my father and I'll not resist thee. But may we go off in the woods a way? It frets Margaret when thou maketh me seemly in the eyes of the Lord."

But the blacksmith snapped, "It's as well she hears the sound of my whip. For she'll feel it too as soon as I finish teaching thee the error of thy ways!"

Joe frowned and said, "Father, I do not understand. Margaret hasn't been running off to the militia musters with me. They wouldn't let her, even if she wasn't a woman. She's as Tory as thee!"

But the blacksmith threw the bright scrap of gathered ribbon on the earth between them and spat, "Dost think I don't know my own wife's needlework? What else have the two of thee been up to behind my back?"

Joe protested, "Father, thou art wrong. I don't deny I disobeyed thee. I shan't expect thee to understand I did it to protect us from the Patriots all around. But as God is my witness, Margaret knew nothing about it. My cockade was sewn by the ladies in town. I think it was Captain Palmer's wife whose neat sewing has thee so overwrought!"

"Bah! Get over there against the stalls and bare thy back to me. I will give thee five more licks for lying. To save thee more, I already have the truth from thy stepmother. She confessed while thou wert playing soldier in the woods!"

Joe shook his head and insisted, "Father, Margaret couldn't confess to a wrong doing. She has done none. Did you hit her?"

The blacksmith's face contorted with rage. "*You*, thou say? So it has come to open defiance, has it?"

Joe's eyes narrowed. "It is tedious for me to speak thee-and-thou to you now, father. I can see from your face that you have struck Margaret. I told you what I'd done and I said I'd take my beating for it. But not Margaret, father, not Margaret."

"Bare thy back, I say! As master of my own hearth I'll deal with both of thee as the Lord commands!"

Joe said quietly, "Sir, I would do no such thing if I were you."

His father gasped in disbelief and roared, "Thou wouldst not? By my very God, the lad's gone mad!"

Joe, controlling his anger, was prepared to reason with his father when the burly smith punched him full in the mouth. The older man was strong and his fist had the kick of a mule. Most men would have gone down, if they remained even semi-conscious. Young Joe just shook his head like a bull with a fly between its horns and felt his bloody lip with his tongue. He said tentatively, "Father, you'd best simmer down."

The smith swung again. This time Joe was set and warded off the blow with a forearm. He stood stock still, his cheeks flushing.

The door of the cabin flew open and Margaret came out, calling, "Stop it, both of you!"

Joe saw his stepmother's bodice was torn and that she had a black eye. His father snapped, "So it's the *two* of thee defying me, is it?" Then, hefting the whip, he tried to step past his son, shouting, "I might have known, thou shameless Irish slut!"

Joe reached out, picked his father from the ground and swung him back into the smithy. "Father," he said, choking back a sob. "Father,

I warn you—you don't know what you're doing or saying!"

The blacksmith lunged forward, slashing with the whip. Joe caught it around his upraised elbow, twisted it from his father's grasp and threw it over his shoulder. The blacksmith sobbed in frustrated rage, took a tentative step toward his now frightened son, then whirled, ran over to the anvil and turned with a weighty shoeing hammer in his white-knuckled fist.

"Please, husband!" cried Margaret, as the enraged man came forward in a fighting crouch, red-rimmed eyes fixed on Joe.

Joe mumbled, "Father, I don't want to hurt you." But as the blacksmith lunged at his head with the hammer he sidestepped and, roaring out his anguish, grabbed the man by shirt and belt. With a mighty heave, he threw him as far from Margaret as he could manage.

The blacksmith landed sitting near the cold forge, his back to the anvil stump and the back of his skull against the cast-iron base of the anvil itself.

He lay still.

Joe looked at his father, feeling his own blood running from the corner of his mouth. "Get back inside, Margaret," he said quietly then.

But she didn't move. Nor did Joe. The blacksmith seemed to be just sitting there, staring bemused at his taller son's knees. After a time, Joe said, "Father?"

There was no answer.

Margaret gasped, "Oh, my God!" and ran past Joe before he could prevent her. She dropped to her knees at her husband's side and took one of his limp hands in hers as she stared into his glassy eyes. She said nothing for a long time. When she did speak, she said, trembling, "Joe, I think he's dead."

A great grey cat got up in Joe's stomach and started running around looking for a way out. But the youth's voice was quiet as he walked over, felt the side of his father's neck and said, "I think you're right. I know you'll think I'm lying, Margaret. But I never meant to hurl him against the anvil like that. I didn't mean to kill him. You don't have to take me to law. I'll go into the county seat and turn myself in, soon as I get hold of myself."

Margaret shook her head and said, "I saw and heard it all, Joe. Most of it happened before you arrived here. He found your ribbon and made me . . . made me confess to my sins. He must have heard certain rumors in town. When he found your ribbon he just became enraged."

Joe was puzzled. "I can see he hurt you badly, Margaret. What else did he accuse you of, aside from sewing my cockade?"

"Joe, that's neither here nor there now. What are we to do about this dreadful mishappening?"

"I told you. I'll see he's laid out dignified before he starts to stiffen. Then I'll report it to the sheriff. What happens next is up to the law."

"Joe, they won't believe you didn't mean to kill him. Everyone knows he was Tory and you were Patriot and of the hard feelings between you. You couldn't always hide your feelings, despite the respect you tried to show him. People might think you killed him in a fight over the Cause and might let you off on that score. But if they were to think the two of you were fighting over . . . over *me* . . ."

"Margaret! If you're referring to the words I had with the Garths over. . . !"

"I am, Joe. You humiliated Morgan Garth in front of his sons. The lads in your militia will stand by you no matter what, but they are no match for Morgan Garth. He is a well-known and powerful Patriot and his party rules this county. If you should be charged, Garth would be able to control the selection of the jury.

Joe shook his head. "Please, Margaret, I must think."

He took his father's shoulder gently and eased the blacksmith forward, as if encouraging him to stop shamming and arise. The dead man's head came unstuck from the anvil-bolt imbedded in the crushed back of the skull and the body rolled face down on the dirt floor. Joe wept inwardly, struck by the full horror of what he'd done. Margaret put a hand on his sleeve and murmured, "Joe, perhaps we should not tell anybody?"

Joe was blinking back tears.

Margaret importuned, "If we were to bury him, respectfully but quietly, he wouldn't be sought for days."

Joe shut his eyes. It was easier for him to think with his father's crushed skull out of sight. He finally shook his head and said, "Be worse, in the end. He's the only blacksmith in the valley, popular or not. Sooner or later somebody would need a draft-ox shoed, or a tool mended."

"You could do those things, Joe. You're almost as good a smith as your father was."

"Maybe. But people would still begin to ask questions. And after a time they'd begin a search. If we were to hide his body, and it was then found out, I would be doubly damned as a murderer."

"But you're a fine woodsman too. Surely you could hide all traces of what happened and . . ."

"No!" Joe opened his eyes and looked squarely into Margaret's upturned, pleading face. "The sooner I go and tell the truth, the more likely it is I'll be believed. I'll leave out your part in it. I'll say father and I had a fight over the Cause and he fell and hit his head. Captain Palmer will side with me. I have a better than fifty-fifty chance to escape a hanging."

Margaret said quietly, "But that wouldn't be truth, Joe. Don't you see?"

Joe flushed, "I don't understand. What is it you want from me? Why do you want me to bury my father in secret? Why? Accident or not, I killed him!"

Margaret looked at him. "Oh Joe," she said softly. "Oh, Joe." She faltered. "I . . . I raised you since childhood, Joe. I'm your . . . your mother, as close to a mother as I could be." She glanced back at the barely visible body in the shadows of the forge and shuddered before she licked her lips and said, "I'm sort of cross with *both* of you. But what's done is done. Your father was as good a man as he knew how to be and I'll likely grieve over him when there's time for it. But I don't want to risk losing you now, Joe. I just don't."

Joe looked into her blue eyes, at her flushed cheeks, wet now with her pleading tears. He said nothing. Vague feelings stirred in him, troubling feelings.

"I . . . I can't do what you ask, Margaret," he said finally.

She started to agree. Then her blue eyes widened as, listening to his hesitation, new hope and a new thought struck her. "I don't mean forever, Joe, but if you put him well back in the smokehouse, with hams and curing venison and such over him . . ."

Joe swallowed. His head was in a turmoil. Putting his father's body in the smokehouse, like so much dead meat, was repugnant to him. But truly it was a safe hiding place. And a longing to satisfy Margaret possessed him. He said gruffly, "All right. I'll put him there for now and clean the anvil. You go in and do something about the way father messed you up."

"And then, Joe?"

"I don't know. I need time to think now."

But inwardly, Joe had already decided what he would do. He would leave this place in the woods. He would take Margaret and leave.

4

Captain Robert Palmer was a work-worn farmer of forty-five who'd worked for the British Army as a teamster one summer during the French and Indian War. He'd been elected captain of the militia's trained band because of his military experience. This was in keeping with other Patriot appointments. General Washington, Commander-in-Chief of the Continental Army, had had limited experience as a young militia officer in that half-forgotten old war. General Knox, who commanded the Field Artillery, had read some books on the subject as a Boston bookstore proprietor. The famous General Benedict Arnold had sold drugs door-to-door before saving the day in '76 on Lake Champlain. Most of the real soldiers were on the British side.

Joe Floyd found his captain splitting rails near his own small cabin. Palmer hit the wedge a good lick with his splitting maul as Joe walked up to him. Then he leaned the maul against the growing pile of chestnut rails and wiped his brow with the back of his hand as Joe saluted.

"I'd like a few words with you, sir, if you've time," Joe said.

Palmer nodded. "Let's go over and sit on the steps where it's shady. Ain't this day shaping up to be a scorcher?"

Joe agreed it was hot and followed his militia officer to the ramshackle porch. They sat down as one of the Palmer children came out with a jug to whisper, "Ma says you're not to bring company in whilst she's sweeping, pappy."

"Shoot, Joe ain't company. He's a neighbor. But we'll sit out here anyways. What's on your mind, Joe?"

"Captain Palmer, I come over to get a discharge from the trained band if it's all right with you."

"Aw, hell, Joe, you're one of my best shots. How come you want to quit?"

"I don't, sir. It's my father's notion."

Palmer took a swig of cider, handed the jug to Joe and sighed, "I might have knowed. That's the trouble with enlisting boys under age. You reckon it would do any good if I was to talk with your pa? I know he's a Quaker and a Tory to boot, but if he could only be made to see the political advantages of a son in the militia at times like these . . ."

"It's not his politics this time, sir. You see, we're moving out of the county. He's setting up his forge out west, past the Cumberland Gap."

"Jesus, Joe, a Quaker in the Kentuck?"

"I know. I told him there'd likely be more

fighting out there than hereabouts. But you know how stubborn my father can be. He says he's sure the Tory Injuns will leave us alone and, if they don't, I still know how to shoot, thanks to you."

Palmer set the jug aside and shook his head. He said, "You're still a soldier. Can you keep military secrets, Joe?"

"I can."

"Joe, things have been going poorly out in the Kentuck. I mean, a lot worse than the newspapers have let on. You likely know the Shawnee has come out for the Crown."

"Yes, sir. That's what I told Freckles Grogan when he talked of moving west. But I suppose between my musket and Dan'l Boone . . ."

"Joe, there ain't no Dan'l Boone no more. Him and a score of his men was took by the Shawnee months ago. Happened at a place called Blue Licks. Folks is streaming back through the gap like the devil was after them, 'cause the devil *is!* The Big Sagamore, called Black Fish, is leading at least a thousand Shawnee down from Detroit. They have brand-new Mackinaw trade guns and some white Tories with 'em. One of the whites is a Canadian who used to be an engineer for the French Army. He's been showing the Injuns siege tactics and there ain't a fort in the whole Kentuck as could stand up to a four-pound field gun."

Joe shook his head. "And Captain Boone is dead, you say? What about my cousin, John

Floyd? He was one of Boone's lieutenants, last I heard."

Palmer shrugged and said, "Dispatchers never mentioned anyone named Floyd. The Americans around Boonesburough is led by a man named Callaway. As to Boone hisself being dead, nobody knows for sure. They took him last February as he and the others was making salt along the Licking River. The Shawnee might have kilt him. They might have sold him to the British. Dead or a prisoner of war, he's not much use to our side now. They do say Callaway's not much, and if he was, it wouldn't cut much ice agin' a Shawnee army backed by the Crown. So you see you and your kin would just be going to a heap of trouble committing suicide. If your pa's so set on dying, he could just blow his own brains out here and now and be done with it. They do say it smarts more to be kilt by Injuns over a slow fire."

Joe repressed a gag as the older man's words about his father conjured a picture to his mind unbidden. But his face was impassive as he said, "Well, it's likely as bad a move as you say, sir. But we're moving anyway. Don't I need some sort of paper from you in case folks ask why I deserted your command?"

Palmer shrugged and said, "Who's going to ask? Half the men in this war seem to light out or change sides as the spirit moves 'em. Just try and talk your pa out of his fool notion. If you miss a couple of musters I'll know you've left and I'll scratch your name off my books."

"Isn't that sort of, well, informal, sir?"

"Well, that infernal Congress ain't been paying the *real* soldiers in this war worth mention, Joe. I'll just cross you off and if they ever pester me about it I'll just say you was kilt by Injuns."

He got to his feet with a morose little smile as he added, "It ain't like I'm likely to be fibbing."

5

Lying was hard work. Joe Floyd was as strong or stronger than any man in the valley, but he was exhausted with nervous strain by the time he returned to the smithy that afternoon.

The clearing reeked with smoke and as he came out of the tree line, Joe thought for a moment the cabin was on fire. Then he saw the billowing clouds from the chimneys and the lesser blue haze hanging over the bark-shingled smokehouse. Margaret had been busy and it was a hot dry day. What in thunder was she up to?

Whatever it was, she must have been watching for his return. The door opened as he approached the cabin. Margaret greeted him with red-rimmed eyes and a sooty face. She asked anxiously, "How did it go at the county seat?" and Joe replied, "As you said. They swindled me shameless. They took me for the bumpkin boy they'd rather deal with than they would with my father. What have you been burning?"

"Everything I can get to burn. Folks don't

leave much on an abandoned spread unless they're leaving with unwholesome suddenness. We have to leave this place stripped for them when they come poking about for such chattels as a moving family usually leaves behind. The rough furnishings can stay. Everything of value goes with us in the wagon or up the flue."

Joe nodded as he sank wearily to the split-log flooring. "I allowed you were craftier than I am," he said. "I'll wrestle the anvil and such aboard the wagon in a while. Right now I'm feeling poorly. It's likely the heat and the ale I had at the tavern just now."

Margaret sat beside him, her thigh against his, and murmured, "I know. I've been crying some while you were gone. But we have to steel our nerves until we're clear of this place, Joe."

Joe did not look over at the smokehouse but said, "Doesn't it make you feel strange, smoking father that way?"

Margaret didn't answer for a time. When she did, her voice was low. She said, "I was married to him for nearly seven years, Joe. We both know the kind of man he was. There was more good in him than bad and, even had he been worse, no natural woman can live with a man for years and not feel something."

"Yes, but he did become ugly since this war started. And this morning wasn't the first time he hit you, so . . ."

But Margaret took his hand and squeezed to

shush him as she said, "Stop that, Joe! We're in
a fix. We'll likely have to lie to everyone we
meet up with for a long time. But we must face
the truth with one another. We have to know
exactly what we've done and what we're doing
to get out of it. If you start trying to justify the
incident by making your father something he
never was, the next thing you know, you'll be
bragging that you killed him!"

"Margaret, that's just crazy! Who'd brag on
killing his own kin, even if they needed killing?"

"It's happened, Joe. More than one murderer
has been hanged because he couldn't let the
dead lie peaceably. A guilty conscience eats at
a man and makes him dream up reasons for the
things he's done. After a time he gets so satisfied the man he killed needed killing that he
starts to think he deserves the gratitude of the
human race. One night it all spills out over ale
in the tavern. Or he tells some girl his secret
and . . . Never mind. Just remember you're to
always lie about your father's death to everyone
but me. We were both there, Joe. We don't have
to make up pretty stories for each other."

Joe nodded. Then he sobbed, "Jesus, I wish we
didn't have to *smoke* him!"

Then he buried his face in the sleeves crossed
over his knees and, though he tried not to,
started crying again. His widowed stepmother
put an arm around his heaving shoulders and
drew him to her. Her own eyes filled with tears

as she soothed, "It's all right, honey. You don't have to hold it in right now. Meg knows how you feel."

They clung to each other for comfort there for perhaps a full five minutes, the small dark woman holding the brawny young giant's head to her breast as if he were a small child. She patted his wet cheek and comforted him with soothing words until his shoulders heaved less. Then she murmured, "Joe, we can't sit here like this in broad daylight. If anyone came by they'd take this wrong and the gossips of the township would really have something to talk about!"

Joe pulled away and sat up straight, wiping a palm across his face as he swallowed hard and said, "You must think I'm a blubbering sissy girl! I don't know what came over me just now!"

"You're wrong, Joe. It came over *me*, right after I lit the smudge in the smokehouse. I knew we had to preserve him and take him along in the wagon 'til we're well out of the country. But I'm only ten years older than you and the man was my husband."

Then she patted his hand and stood, saying, "We've both got to set aside our feelings for now, Joe. Come inside and tell me how it went in town while I put some tea and cornpone in you."

Joe rose and followed her inside the smoky cabin, but as he sat by the table he said, "I'll tell you about going to town, but I can't eat right now. I throwed up twice on the way home."

"You have to swallow some tea at least. How do we stand at the county clerk's office?"

"I told him father was moving his forge out to the Kentucky meadows and he told me my father was crazy. I asked if I could have the land rent we'd paid in advance back and he said we couldn't. I told him my father would likely come in personally and raise holy hell with him if I came home empty-handed, and he just laughed."

Margaret put the tea in front of him and said, "That was smart of you, Joe. The clerk will be bragging for months about the way he talked a Tory out of six months' taxes. The story loses in the telling if he allows the man he cheated might be dead as well as gone. What about the militia? We don't want them looking for you as a deserter."

Joe sipped some tea, surprised how dry he'd gotten, and replied, "Oh, that part was easy. Captain Palmer's just scratching my name off his list. He told me things are a mite confused out beyond the Cumberland Gap and that's both good and bad. They'll be so short of fighting men by the time we get there that I doubt they'll ask too many questions."

"You told me we have kin there too. But what's the bad part?"

"It seems there's been more fighting on the

frontier than the Transylvania Land Company has been putting out. We could be leaping from the frying pan to the fire, Meg."

Then he blushed and stammered, "I mean, Margaret. I know father called you Meg when he was in his better moods and . . ."

"That's all right, Joe. Just so you don't call me Maggy. Your mother used to call me that and it was the only thing about the poor sick woman I couldn't abide. I've always hated Maggy and . . . Never mind. How did they take our story at the tavern?"

"Well, if I didn't convince 'em the three of us were moving west they were lying better than I was. Freckles Grogan and Tilly Hanks ran off the other night and Tilly's father said if we catch up with them before they get over the mountains, I'm to tell them all is forgiven and that Freckles is to bring his daughter back. Mr. Hanks said he'd as lief his daughter lived in sin with that Grogan boy than out among wild Indians. A couple of the men asked if I'd cleared it with Captain Palmer and when I said I wasn't deserting but maybe moving closer to the war, they bought me ale and drank to my health. Morgan Garth even gave a toast for father. He said father would likely wind up a Patriot out there whether he wanted to be one or not. The Shawnee ain't particular and Governor Hamilton is buying American hair with no questions asked."

He brightened and added, "I just thought of

something, Meg! When we get out there without father, we can say the Indians did him in as we was in the mountains and . . ."

"No, dear. You're going to have to learn about telling tall tales if you mean to get good at it. When we find Cousin John we'll say your father took a fever on the trail and just died one night. Stories about folks getting killed by savages interest people. They get repeated and enlarged with the retelling. You'll be asked too many questions if you say he was killed, whereas nobody really wants to hear the tale of a middle-aged man just taking sick on the Wilderness Road."

Joe nodded and said, "I'm glad I have you to do the thinking for us, Meg. I never would have thought to go into the county seat and make a claim for our taxes. I'd have lit out like a fool and by now they'd be tracking me with hounds."

Margaret said gently, "Your father and I moved on more than once, Joe. That's how I knew the tidy moves folks expect from a family leaving peacably. You did well to ask for the money due for your father's services too."

Joe smiled thinly and said, "Will Jenkins said he'd send us the money for the plough we mended and Cyrus North paid me fifty cents on the dollar in Continental paper. I suppose they're laughing at me this very minute. But they likely won't come out here to say goodbye to father neither."

"You're sure you didn't leave any of our own bills unpaid?"

"No, I settled with the merchants and the county as you told me to. I never would have thought of that, Meg. I reckon most murderers just light out owing, huh?"

Margaret saw that Joe's conscience was still troubling him. She grew stern. "You're not a murderer. You're not a saint either. The deed, Joe, has been done. It was partly your fault and partly your father's. It can't be undone. You have covered our tracks well. Now I'm depending on you to get us through the mountains."

Joe searched her face. He was eighteen. Never had he felt more uncertain of himself. He said slowly, "You're the elder of us, Meg. I'll allow you're in charge, even if you are a girl."

"No." Margaret smiled wanly, brushed a strand of smoke-stained hair from her brow and said more softly, "I'm nearly ten years older than you and I've had experience in pulling the fangs of gossip. But you're the man of this family, Joe. I don't know how to get us through once we're out of here. I'm not even sure of our next move."

Joe thought long and hard. Then he drained the tea cup and said, "We've got the rest of the afternoon to put this place in order and load up the wagon. We'll move out well past sundown."

Margaret offered, "If we should pass a neighbor, you'll be expected to do the talking. You'll say your father's riding one of the ponies out ahead and seem surprised if they say they didn't pass him."

Joe nodded his understanding and went on. "As to the move, we can't take the wagon and our heavy goods through the gap. The Wilderness Trail is only a couple of feet wide and twists like a snake on a hot stove. We'll have to ditch the wagon somewhere."

"We'd best sell it," Margaret said, frowning as she thought. "Nobody leaves a wagon full of chattels by the side of the road unless he's in a fearful hurry. What's the last civilized place this side of the Cumberland Gap?"

"Place called Salisbury. It's on the Carolina Piedmont, just east of the Blue Ridge."

"Good. Here's what we'll do. We'll make our way down the post road so as to arrive in Salisbury early one morning. We'll ask at the tavern if your father is waiting for us there. When we're told he isn't we'll say he must have ridden on to scout the trail."

"I see. Then we'll offer the wagon for sale and . . ."

Margaret shook her head. "Not quite. Joe. Who's going to drive a team and wagon all that way just to get rid of it? This too would cause gossip and perhaps suspicion. Best to say you aim to drive the wagon up the Wilderness Road after your father ahead."

"But, Meg, you *can't* take a wagon over the mountains. Everybody knows that."

"Exactly, Joe. They'll tell us that in Salisbury.

You'll act stubborn at first until they convince you. Folks like to convince a greenhorn. If the town is like every other I've ever seen, you can count on some local trader trying to skin us on the price of our wagon and heavy goods. As your ma, I'm going to make a fuss and suggest you ride on and catch up with your pa before letting them have things at their price."

Joe grinned sheepishly and said, "Oh, won't they hug themselves for being so smart when I let them talk me out of it! I can almost hear them now. They'll say father's likely halfway over the mountains and that they haven't time to wait all summer. They'll raise the offer a mite and tell us to take it or leave it. Then, when we ride out cheated, they'll laugh at the *three* of us!"

Joe, after relishing this much of their plan, sobered. "About the burial, Meg." he said. "I know an alder-hell just beyond the county line not far from the road. We'll be passing it around four tomorrow morning and that's where we'll do it."

"An alder-hell, Joe?"

"Wet ground where thickets of alder saplings grow closer than the hairs on your head. It's almost impossible for a man or a hound to get through. I'll pull some saplings up by the roots, dig a grave for father and plant the trees back in place. Nobody ever clears alder-hells, for the growth tells the soil's too wet for corn. Sometimes they cut a few fishing poles or such from the roadside alders, but nobody pokes in far enough to matter. A hunter's blind in an alder-hell, and you can meet up suddenly with a bear or wild pig."

"I understand." Margaret paused. "It sounds like a good place to rid outselves of the anvil and heavy tools too. See how we do need one another, Joe. You'd have never thought to play the innocent bumpkin. I'd have never known about the alder-hell, and I didn't know about the Wilderness Road."

Joe frowned, lost in thought. "One thing pesters me, though." He looked up at Meg quickly. "Oh, I'm not still thinking about the fight I had with Father, exactly. I have our story memorized and when we get to Kentucky I'll know what to say. What's pestering me is after we get there. I mean, just the two of us."

"What do you mean, Joe? Cousin John will likely believe your father died on the trail, and even if he doesn't . . ."

"No, I mean what happens about, well, you and me, once we're there? I mean, you'll be a woman alone in a rough country, so we'll have to stay close together, but . . . won't it look sort of funny?"

"You mean a man your age with a woman ten years older?"

Joe hesitated, feeling uncomfortable. "I know you're still my stepmother. But we've had to deal with gossip right here, with father sharing the cabin with us."

Margaret gave Joe an odd look and asked,

very quietly, "What are you suggesting, Joe?"

Joe blurted, "Damn it, I don't know. Most of the folks we meet out there will be married up, but you have to have a man and . . . damn it, you're not all that much older than me."

"For God's sake, Joe, I'm your own father's widow!"

Joe flushed and stammered, "I know that! What do you take me for, a heathen? My father isn't even buried yet, and even if he'd been in the ground a year as decency calls for, you know *we* could never . . . oh, I don't know what I mean! It's just that we have to get you married up with somebody as soon as we make it out west and, well, it bothers me."

Margaret looked relieved. "I see. Well, we're a long way from Kentucky and we'll have plenty of time to plan for my future on the way. Is your Cousin John good looking?"

"Shoot, he's nigh as old as father was and married besides. You don't aim to make that mistake again, do you?"

"Mistake, Joe?"

"We said we were telling things true, remember? Father was too old for you. You never should have married up with him even had he been younger. You were never cut out to be a Quaker gal, Meg. I mind how you used to sing and laugh when he wasn't around. We have to get you a nice young feller who'll laugh with you next time."

Margaret turned and threw another chair-rung on the dying fire. "That would be nice," she murmured. "So far, all the men I've studied on have either been too old—or too young for me."

It took forever for the sun to go down and they were both nervous wrecks when it did. Joe had kept a fire in the forge and an eye on the road in case a late-afternoon customer came by with a critter to be shoed. They'd agreed the best way to handle such an emergency would be to do the chore quickly and send anyone who came by on their way, contented. A satisfied customer was less apt to talk about them in town.

Meanwhile, Margaret went on getting rid of as much as possible by burning. She cried softly, alone in the cabin, for while little of monetary value went up the flue, most of the things she had to burn held memories, some bitter, some sweet.

She hesitated when it came time to toss Joe's baby things on the fire. Joe's late mother, her husband's first wife, had knit the cap and slippers with her own hands, with the love and care of the bride she'd been. Margaret wondered if she should ask Joe before she burned these things. But she knew he'd say to, and it seemed needlessly cruel to remind him of his dead mother. The boy had enough on his mind at the moment.

And so the pathetic treasures of Joe's childhood were sacrificed to the present emergency and it was only after she'd thrown his mother's hair ribbon and fan in the flames that Margaret realized how a body who didn't understand might think she'd been a mite spiteful.

Rubbing her eyes with the hem of her apron, Margaret protested to the empty shadows around her, "That's not fair! I was a faithful friend and servant to her while she was alive, and I never mean-mouthed her after she passed on."

She poked the coals to make sure the charred remnants fell to shapeless ash as she sniffed and added, "Lord knows she left me saddled with enough she never had the strength to finish. Had I been a mite older and wiser I'd have never allowed my fool self to be dragooned into carrying on for her."

Margaret saw the flames were dying, so she threw another log on the hearth and crossed the cabin to see what else there was to get rid of. She opened the lid of her late husband's ox-hide chest, remembered she'd already been through it and stood there, staring down at the emptiness, her eyes filled with tears.

She murmured, "It's all gone. All we had to show for all the work and saving. A body would think a man who'd worked so hard all his life would have left something worth mention."

She went to the doorway and stared out in the gloaming, past the corner of the forge to the low squat smokehouse beyond. Then she shuddered and murmured, "Durn you, Big Joe, you tried so hard to be whatever it was you aimed for that the three of us never had shucks."

Then, as she realized what she was doing, she smiled sheepishly through her tears and sighed, "I know, poor old dear. I know you tried. I reckon we all tried."

She went next door to the forge, where young Joe was hammering a bar of hot strap iron, and said, "Well, the cabin's tidy and it's nigh dark. What are you making, Joe?"

He said, "Nothing. I figured if anybody came, I ought to look busy. I'm fixing to let the fire go out though. It's past supper time and it doesn't look like anyone will come this late. How soon do you reckon we should start loading the wagon, Meg?"

"Oh, we may as well get started, Joe. It'll be dark by the time we're ready to move out. If anybody should see us now, we can say your father just rode off to tend a few last chores in the neighborhood."

Joe nodded and started gathering tools. But Margaret shook her head and said, "Dear, I think we'd better put . . . you know, on the bottom of the load."

Joe frowned and replied, "I know you're worried about us being stopped and searched, Meg. But if we get caught at all they'll surely find anything we're trying to hide, no matter where. I'm aiming to carry off father's tools, the plough, and yon anvil. I don't reckon it would be seemly to place him under such heavy things, do you?"

She shuddered and turned away as Joe swallowed and added, "We'll be dropping him off first, so I aim to carry him out atop the load. I, uh, want to fetch him from the smokehouse after dark too."

Meg said, "I understand, dear." Then she suddenly choked and shut her eyes tightly as she sobbed, "Oh, God! I feel so awful, Joe!"

He put his work-roughened hands on her shoulders to steady her and she suddenly buried her face against his chest, trying to control her tears but failing. He held her awkwardly and wondered why his heart was pounding so hard. He'd gotten over his first fright and the terrible guilt had subsided to a small hard lump under his ribs after a whole day of reliving the fight and wondering how it could have been avoided. He knew how Margaret felt and he wanted to comfort her, but, as he found his hand against her spine, he suddenly moved it away as if he'd been about to place it on a hot stove. Margaret moved quickly away too, not looking up at him as she stammered, "I said we'd cry about it later, Joe. We've got to git!"

He nodded and left to load the tools he'd set aside in the wagon bed, his mind in a whirl. Everything was happening so suddenly and he was so mixed up about it all. She hadn't thought he was getting country with her, had she? Hell, the notion was too awful to consider. He'd just held her for a second or two to comfort her. He hadn't intended it to feel so nice!

He wondered, as he loaded the wagon, how it had felt to Meg. He was still surprised she wasn't mad at him for doing such a fool thing to father. He knew it had been an accident, but had anyone else killed father, accident or no, he'd be after them this minute with a gun. Meg purely was an understanding woman. He guessed it came from being so much older.

The first stars were out by the time he'd loaded the wagon and hitched up the team. He helped Margaret up on the seat and handed her the reins as he wiped his palms on his breeches and muttered, "Moon ball will be rising, soon. I'll, uh, get the last of the load."

He went to the smokehouse and opened the door, letting the pungent hickory fumes clear before he took a deep breath and ducked under the low jamb.

They were leaving most of the smoked meat. The neighbors would find a welcome use for it and nobody expected folks on the move to haul venison in a land filled with hickory and game. Joe moved the smoked sides out of the way, hesitated, and gingerly put his hands on the shoulders of his father's corpse. He wondered if he should say anything. He decided anything he could say would be a mite silly. So he hauled the cadaver free of the other smoked meat and lay it on the earth floor while he wrapped it in a canvas tarp. He was glad it was so dark in here. He knew he'd never forget the sight of his father's crushed skull, as it was. He didn't want to know what the corpse looked like now!

He lifted the stiff bundle by one end, hoisted it to his shoulder and carried it out to the wagon after kicking the door shut behind him. He manhandled the wrapped body under the wagon cover and walked around to join his stepmother on the seat. She handed him the reins in silence and he clucked the team into motion. As they passed through the gate he reined in and murmured, "Well, take your last look, Meg." But she shuddered and said, "Drive on, dear. I never understood what the Good Book meant about Lot's wife until just now."

He said, "I don't aim to look back, neither," and drove out on the post road to swing south.

They'd driven a little in silence and the moon was about to rise when Joe heard the sound of hooves on the gravel ahead and reined in, cocking his musket suspiciously.

The northbound rider spied the dark mass on the road and slowed his own mount to a walk as he called out in a cautious voice, "Howdy. I'm headed for the county seat. Is it far?"

Joe answered, "No. Just follow this trace and you'll be there in about an hour."

The stranger edged his pony nearer and Joe strained to make out his features. But one man on a pony looked much the same as any other in this light. Margaret said, "Our son rode on ahead, mounted on a chestnut. Can you tell us how far up the road he might be, sir?"

The stranger shook his head and said, "I didn't pass him, ma'am. Wouldn't have known the color of his mount if I had. I reckon he must have passed the fork about two miles south afore I swung on to this road. To save you further questions, I'm packing militia dispatches for a Captain Palmer. Would you folks happen to know him?"

Margaret kept her voice light as she answered, "Of course. Our son used to be in Captain Palmer's trained band."

"Used to be, Ma'am? Cornwallis is about to land in the Carolinas. Forgive me for saying so, but this ain't no time for used-to-be Minute Men!"

Joe's mouth felt dry and he wondered what on earth Meg was up to as she said lightly, "We understand, sir. Captain Palmer will tell you when you ask that our son has proper papers. We're the Floyds and we're bound for the Cumberland Gap."

The dispatch rider shrugged and said, "Well, how Palmer runs his outfit is none of my concern. It's getting late, so I'll say good night to you, folks."

As he rode on, Joe clucked the team into motion again and asked his stepmother, "What was that all about, Meg? How could you say I was up the road ahead when all the time I was sitting here like a big old bird?"

She laughed and said, "It just came to me. If we couldn't see his face in this light, he couldn't see ours. When and if he's ever asked, he'll remember meeting the elder Floyds on the road this night!"

Joe suddenly grinned and marveled, "Do Jesus! You're right! The only one of us he won't vouch for meeting up with will be me. And does anybody get to fretting about where I might be, enough to report me missing . . ."

"Of course, Joe. You'll be found alive and well with Cousin John, in Kentucky."

So they rode on, feeling better as the wagon wheels ate up more miles between them and the scene of their secret tragedy. The moon rose and illuminated the road before them. Joe's elation began to fade again as he saw they were getting near the place he'd picked out ahead.

When he reined in again, Margaret looked around and said, "There's nothing unusual about this stretch, Joe. When you said we were headed for a *hell* . . ."

He said, "The saplings up the slope to our right is the alder-hell, Meg. You hold the team steady whilst I do what's needful."

"Don't you think we should pull off the road, Joe?"

"No. The ground here's soft, which is why the alders grow so thick by the side. We don't want to leave wagon tracks leading anywheres some roving hunter might study them."

"What'll I do if anybody comes?"

"Give a holler. I'll come outten the trees buttoning up my britches."

She flushed, grateful for the darkness, but as if he'd read her mind, Joe said, "I know I'm talking indelicate, Meg. But we'll be on the road a ways and camping together too. Folks don't ask why others is in the bushes on the trail. You just hold the team steady and I'll do what I have to as quick as I'm able."

He got down and went around to the tailboard. He hauled the body out and moved up the slope with it balanced on one shoulder, a spade in his free hand. He moved up the dry ground skirting the thick growth of alder until he was nearly a quarter mile from the road. Then he lowered it gently to the grass in the moonlight, placed the spade by it and waded into the whips of thick growth.

Joe was big and strong, but the saplings fought him as he tugged them from the spongy soil, roots and all. He began to sweat, despite the cool air, and for a moment considered sort of *folding* his father a mite. Then he cursed and muttered, "Do it right, durn it!" and cleared an area a little over two by six feet, laying the uprooted saplings gently aside for the moment.

He got the spade and began to dig. The soil was sticky and heavy on the spade, but he was careful where he put his spoil heap. He hit

water a few inches down but kept digging,
standing in the water as it filled the grave. He
dug down about three feet before he had to
give up against a buried rock. He stabbed the
spade into the spoil, went back to the body and
hauled it to the soggy hole. He tried to lower it
gently, but his father had been heavy in life
and hadn't dried worth mention, so there was
a sickening splash despite Joe's effort at a little
dignity.

He straightened up, rubbing his back, and
wondered what he was supposed to say at a
time like this. He decided first things came
first and began to shovel mud on the floating
canvas bundle until he'd weighed it down,
packed almost all the spoil back in the grave,
then replaced the uprooted alders with their
trunks at the same angle he'd found them. He
used what was left of the spoil to pack in between their roots and when he tested a trunk
with his muddy palm it seemed as if it aimed
to keep growing there. He knew he'd done the
best he'd had time for. It was time he got back
to the wagon and Meg.

But he removed his hat and bowed his head
as he stood there awkwardly and knew, somehow, he had to say something. He knew nothing he could say to father would help. Father
had never listened all that much when he'd
been alive. So Joe murmured, "Lord, if you're
really there like father always said you were,
you likely know what happened here, so I'll ask

no favors for myself. What I did was wrong and if you aim to hold it against me I won't argue. You likely know my father thought highly of you, Lord. So you might think I have no call to speak for him this way. But Father vexed folks some, with his own notions of what was seemly in your eyes. I know you're pretty busy with the rest of us poor brutes, the stars, the sun ball and things. I mean, father said you marked the sparrow's fall, but, forgive me, Lord, I suspicion you can't really keep your eye on everything, or we'd likely have a nicer world down here."

He looked up at the cold uncaring stars and demanded, "You never *did* much for him, Lord. He worked twice as hard as most men and prayed so hard it made him sick in the head at times. He did his best by you, Lord, and he never had a word to say against you when he just got old and poor and mean. I reckon you owe him, Lord. I'm not asking you to bring him back, not even asking you to let him sit up there and play a fool harp for you. We both know father wasn't a joy to have around these last few years."

Joe hesitated, picked up the spade, then said, "All I ask for him now is that you leave him *alone*, Lord! He did his best, and if it wasn't exactly what you had in mind, just be a gent and let him rest in peace. We both know you never gave him a day's peace while he was toiling in your vineyards, Lord."

Joe put his hat back on, trudged down the slope and climbed up on the wagon next to Margaret.

She asked if he'd done what had to be done and when he nodded and clucked to the team, she said, "Joe, I wanted to say a few words over him before we left him. Won't you take me to him?"

Joe said, "No. In case you're ever questioned, I don't want you to know just where I buried father."

"Joe! That's a terrible thing to say! Do you really think I'd betray you?"

"No. But you might betray your ownself if some tricky lawbird got at you. Don't worry about the words, Meg. I said a few before I came back down the hill."

"Oh, I'm so glad, dear. What prayer from the Good Book did you say?"

Joe shrugged and said, "I never was one for rote larning, Meg. I just sort of had a talk with the Lord, man to man."

"Joe, dear, it's not considered seemly for us to talk that way to the Lord."

"No? Well, what in thunder is He good for, if he is not interested in anything we have to say to Him?"

Salisbury, North Carolina, was the last outpost of civilization on the Wilderness Road.

It looked it. The town was the county seat and its post office was in the tavern. The only local industry seemed to be spitting and whittling. A whole corporal's squad of loafers were seated on the tavern steps as Joe reined in, got down and tied the reins to the hitching post.

He waited for someone to say something. When nobody did, he said, "My name's Joe Floyd. The lady yonder is my ma. Is my father here at the tavern?"

There was an exchange of blank looks before a man in a greasy buckskin jacket shook his head and said, "You be the first strangers we've laid eyes on in days. They say Cornwallis is fixing to land down to the Tidewater."

"We're Patriots, and we've been on the trail too long to know the latest news. My father was mounted on a chestnut pony. He's maybe a few inches shorter and a few years older than me."

"We ain't hiding him in the woodshed, son. How'd you git that red stuff on your britches? You look like you've been lost in an alder-hell."

Joe's heart skipped a beat as he realized the man in the hunting shirt wasn't as simple as he looked. They'd considered getting rid of his stained britches since discovering, at daybreak on the post road, how the stain from wet alder bark had dyed his clothes with streaks of rusty red. In the end they'd decided he'd draw even more attention in spanking new clothes, even if they'd been able to buy any. The stain had faded some since then. Most people might not have noticed.

Joe pasted a smile across his numb lips and said, "I can see you've hunted hogs, mister. I went after a big old razorback a day or so from here, but the rascal lost me in the alders."

The hunter spat and said, "You're lucky he didn't geld you, boy. I never chase a critter past the first alders. You say your dad was to meet up with you here?"

"Yep. He rode on ahead to make a side trip to some folks he knows here in the Carolinas. Said he'd leave a note for us here in town if he decided to push on west ahead of us."

Once more there was a blank-faced exchange. Then the hunter asked, "You folks is headed for the gap with a wagon, with the Shawnee on the prod?"

"That's why my father rode ahead. His friends have been over the mountains and . . ."

"You got a name as goes with these friends of your'n, son?"

Joe nodded and said, "Our cousin, John Floyd. He's said to be on one side of the gap or t'other. He's a long-hunter, working for the Transylvania Company."

"Oh? Your dad knows Dan'l Boone?"

"Just to say howdy. They grew up together in Penn State."

He could feel the relaxation in tension as the

hunter got to his feet, putting his barlow knife away as he said, "Fetch your ma from the wagon and we'll share some ale or porter, Joe Floyd. They calls me Cherokee Slim, but I'm mostly Scotch-Irish. You said the magic words when you allowed you was kin to John Floyd. Big John shot an Injun offen my back during Lord Dunmore's War, couple of years back."

Joe asked, "What about our wagon? I have to put the brutes to livery and . . ."

"Shoot, Windy there will be proud to lead your team to the livery and see they're tended, won't you, Windy?"

A shy-looking boy nodded silently and got up as Joe smiled and walked with him to the wagon. He helped Margaret down without any explanations, knowing she'd heard the conversation and was better than himself at improvising.

They entered the tavern with Cherokee Slim and he led them to a corner table. A tavern wench with a nice figure and a harelip took the hunter's order for three porters and Joe told her to bring three more and something to eat, on him.

Then he excused himself from the table and went to the landlord's cubby-hole near one end of the bar to go through the motions of asking if there was any mail for them.

While the tavern-keeper postmaster pawed through a box of letters Cherokee Slim smiled at Margaret and said, "Keeping in mind I know your man's likely to bust in on us any minute, ma'am, I just has to allow you're a right handsome gal to have such a big kid."

Margaret dimpled and said, "I thank you for your gallantry, sir. Joe's my stepson. His mother and I were close friends."

"Oh? I'm sorry to hear the other lady's no longer with us, ma'am, but it relieves my mind to know my eyes ain't going. A long-hunter who gets to seeing older gals as young fillies has been hunting too long, if you takes my meaning."

Joe came back in time to save Margaret from further sparring with the grinning Cherokee Slim. He made his voice sound worried as he told her, "No letter from father. You don't reckon he's gone on ahead, do you?"

She said, "Well, dear, you know he told us not to tarry here in Salisbury more than a day. We'll just have to push on without him if he doesn't join us here today."

"Gee, I don't know, Meg. He's likely to be worried if he's been held up this side of the mountains."

Cherokee Slim sipped his drink and suggested, "You could leave word here, folks. I'd be proud to tell him where you was headed. But, you can't take your wagon any further."

Joe frowned and asked innocently, "What do you mean we can't take our wagon?"

The hunter explained, "The so-calt Wilderness Road ain't no road. It's just an old Injun trail over the mountains. It ain't more'n two yards wide at best, and there's places it narrows some. You got streams to ford where the water runs wild and white. There's grades too steep for a pony to make with a rider aboard. You'll have to pack your gear on a mule. There's no way you'll git a wagon through to the Kentuck."

Margaret said, "Oh, dear, what are we to do, Joe?" and Joe tried to look downcast too as he answered, "We'll just have to wait for my father. He'd skin me alive if I showed up without his wagon!"

The tavern wench came with more drinks and a rasher of bacon and eggs. She said the round of drinks was on the house, and they'd no sooner thanked her than the landlord joined them with an innocent smile on his face.

Cherokee Slim went through the motions of filling him in on the discussion about the wagon and Joe realized they'd played this little drama before. He'd been wondering if he'd have to fight Cherokee Slim over Margaret. It was good to see the locals were only out to swindle them.

The landlord agreed it was impossible to take a wagon through the mountains, but he was too shrewd to make any direct offer himself. He and the hunter let the newcomers fret back and forth about the "bad news" for a time. Then, about the third time Margaret asked her stepson what they were to do, the landlord said, "Well, we could ask about and see if anybody here in Salisbury wants to buy a wagon."

Cherokee Slim nodded and said, "There you

go, Joe. I'd sell the durned thing and such gear as you can't pack on a mule."

Joe said, "I dunno, it's not for me to say. I reckon we'd best wait 'til my father gets here."

The two locals exchanged veiled glances and the hunter said, "It ain't my business, Joe. But there's no telling how long that could take. For all we really know, your dad's halfway to the Kentuck right now and wondering what's holding you up."

"I know, Cherokee, but he's still the man of this family."

"You're over eighteen, ain't you, Joe?"

"Just about. But that doesn't give me the right to sell my father's property."

"Sure it does, Joe. We've agreed you can't use that wagon no more. Seeing you're kin to a friend of mine, I'll tell you what I aim to do. I'm going to ask around and git you the very best price there is. Your father couldn't do half as well his ownself."

The landlord nodded and said, "Cherokee Slim is right, folks. If he allows you around town as friends of his, the boys will treat you right. Your dad wouldn't git a better price with old Ben Franklin advertising for him in Poor Richard's!"

Joe looked at Margaret and asked, "What do you think, Meg?"

She lowered her eyes and murmured, "I'm only a woman. It's up to you menfolks to talk out business deals. But I will tell your father you were looking out for his best interests, as I'm sure you are, dear."

Cherokee Slim got to his feet and punched Joe playfully on the shoulder, saying, "There you go, Joe. You got your ma's say-so. I'll mosey over to the livery and see what sort of a deal I can make for you and your'n."

Joe said, "Well, I'll listen, but I got to study on this some. What sort of a commission are you expecting, Cherokee?"

"Aw, hell, son, who said anything about a commission? I'm selling your fool wagon out of the goodness of my pure Christian heart!"

6

They rode out of Salisbury, North Carolina, with the two ponies and pack mule the owner of the livery stable in town hadn't swindled them out of. Joe wore a modest amount of Continental currency and a few shillings in silver around his waist in a money belt. Margaret rode behind Joe's pony, leading the mule, carrying another musket he'd bought across her skirted knees as she rode side-saddle. It was said some women had taken to riding astride like a man on the frontier, but it wasn't seemly and she was a good horsewoman in any position.

Margaret had never fired a gun, let alone a loaded one. But Joe had shown her how to cock the worn flintlock and it was charged with buckshot. He'd said to fire from the hip and trust to the Lord if the need arose. The folks in Salisbury said Shawnee hadn't been raiding this side of the gap this summer, but the Cherokee had a reputation for treachery and it wasn't too clear which side they were on. It seemed doubtful the Cherokee knew for certain either. For them, much depended on the latest dispatches from the fighting fronts to the north. After Saratoga, the Cherokee had sent a delegation to Congress asking for powder and ball from their white brothers. When the British took Princeton back, they'd collected some scalp money from Detroit. Down on the Tennessee a Tory-allied Chief had joined the half-breed Mackintosh and his Creeks in open warfare against the Patriot settlers. It was not a time for female notions about letting the menfolk do all the fighting.

The young couple passed Sycamore Shoals, the northernmost Cherokee town, by swinging wide through the woods. They forded forest streams whose names sounded like beating tom toms: the Watauga, the Mumchung, the shallow treacherous Hobbamock where the Indians said evil spirits waited in the quicksand shoals. They crossed the Holston and the Cinch, with brooding pine-clad mountains looming over them on every side and the forest still as the grave. And still the famous Cumberland Gap retreated from them into the sunsets of the trail.

At Long Island, where the parted roiling waters offered a safe campsite for the night, they decided this was where Joe's father must have died of the ague. Long Island was deserted when they got there. But the rocky island had been nearly stripped of firewood and the trash and abandoned gear between cold campfires told of many others who'd passed this way. There was a row of stark wooden crosses by the riverside. Few had inscriptions. One was marked with a pine board on which someone had penciled, "Here lies a man called Stark. He drownded. 4/17/77."

Margaret pulled the marker out and threw it in the river. Then, as she prepared a fresh one, she explained to Joe, "The man was buried by decent folk who hardly knew him. I doubt anyone will ever see fit to dig any of these litches up, but should they do it for some fool notion, they'll find the bones of a man in your father's grave. Since this stranger drowned, there'll be no arrowheads or bullets to make liars of us."

"You're likely right, Meg. You think we ought to say some words? It feels strange to me the way we keep putting father to rest."

"Joe, he's got to stay to rest."

"Maybe. But he was my father. I know you never really loved him, but he tried to be a good father to me and . . ."

"Joe, we all tried. It's not fair to say I wasn't fond of him. I know I married him because I had to choose between being his wife or being a bondservant again when he sold my indenture. But there was more to my feelings than that. You remember him only as a stern parent. I remember times when he was quite tender, even, when we first married up, almost boyish. Folks simply didn't understand his ways or the way he felt about his king . . ."

"I wasn't putting you down as a mean-hearted wife, Meg. I know you were decent to us both.

I reckon I keep saying foolish things 'cause my head won't set words to the feelings in my heart. I was pure mixed up about the man while he was alive."

She handed him the new marker and he drove it into the earth at the head of the old grave. They both walked back to the fire and Meg sat on the bedroll. Joe sat beside her and stared into the coals of his small smokeless blaze for a time before he said, "Well, we've buried him for sure this time. I'm going to say one more foolish thing and then I'm going to try and forget what happened."

Margaret put a hand on his wrist and said, "I know you loved your father, Joe."

He said, "I loved you both. I loved my real ma, too. But she was sick for so long and hardly ever spoke to me. I reckon you're the ma I'll always think of when I remember being a child."

He saw her wipe a furtive finger to her eye and asked, "Did I say something wrong again, Meg?"

"No, dear. It's about the nicest thing anyone has ever said to me. We'll always be friends, won't we?"

"I hope so. Even if you marry up again and stop being my stepmother, I'd like to stay kin to you. You reckon that's lawful?"

"Of course it is, dear. It's getting dark and I'd best see to feeding us before we turn in. Are you sure we're safe here? The Indians must know this is a regular stop for folks moving west."

"I studied on that before we made camp, Meg. This island's cut off from the mainland by deep rapid water on most every side and we've got a field of fire on the only ford for a few miles. They could get on this island further up or down, but they'd have to move in across a mess of dry brush. The moon will be full tonight and the brutes will nicker if they smell folks they don't know. But I'll lay awake for a spell. I been having trouble sleeping lately anyway. It's sort of cramped in that bedroll with the two of us sharing space meant for one."

"I'm sorry if I've been crowding you, Joe."

"Can't be helped. It's right cold in these hills at night even if we had two bedrolls. I'll hold out as long as I can. Then I'll nudge you awake and maybe catch forty winks afore sunup if that's all right with you."

"You're to wake me by midnight, Joe. I have to do my share if we're to make the gap with our hair. Why don't you see to the brutes while I make supper?"

Joe knew the ponies and mules were tied securely. But he went to check anyway. Meg likely wanted to be alone for a spell too. Traveling alone with a girl made for complications when nature called. They hadn't discussed it, of course, but he knew she must be relieving herself some darned way in the few moments they had apart from one another.

He walked past the ponies and got a tall stump between himself and the fire. Margaret was sitting with her back to him. He could do it here, but he walked on until she was out of sight. Then he opened the flap of his breeches and urinated against another stump, knowing he wouldn't get another chance before they went to bed.

He shook his penis dry and was aware it was misbehaving again as he buttoned up. It was uncomfortable sleeping on his belly on the hard earth, but it couldn't be helped. The last two mornings he'd woke up with his fool pecker hard as a rock and Meg snuggled close beside him. Jesus, they could feel each other's heartbeats in that bedroll and if she was to somehow brush against it she'd likely think he was crazy. He knew it was a mortal sin to masturbate the way some boys did, but it was sure getting to be a problem. How in hell could a man explain a crazy old pecker to a girl? They didn't have the durned things to pester them.

7

Joe reined in and sat his mount, staring up at the big wedge God had sliced out of a sheer wall of white granite. The pass was a deep saddle in the otherwise impassable ridge. The trail rose gently perhaps three hundred feet before dropping off beyond the blue horizon. Margaret drew up beside him and asked, "Is that the Cumberland Gap, Joe?"

"Has to be. There's no other way through."

"Then why are we waiting here, dear?"

"I'm not looking at the Gap. I've been studying the peaks on either side. I wouldn't want to have to sidestep arrows coming down."

"My God! Do you think Indians may be lurking up there, Joe?"

"It's where I'd be if I were collecting hair for the British. Every party coming or going has to pass through that natural ambush. It looks all right, though. The ridge on either side is bald as well as steep and it isn't likely we were expected this morning. You fall back and keep your flintlock pan-up as I carry us on through."

Joe waited until they were lined up single-file, then heeled his mount forward with an anxious eye on either rock wall. He led them over the slight rise at a trot and didn't pause midway. Only a fool stayed against the skyline longer than it could be helped. Going down into the unknown lands ahead, Joe danced his pony around and swept the ridges behind them before moving on. Nobody up there seemed set up for a shot at his fool back, so he waved to Margaret and led them out of the gap. He rode them off the trail to the shelter of a cottonwood thicket and reined in once more, telling Margaret, "Let's just set a spell and study what's ahead. From here on we're in Shawnee country."

Margaret stared with him down the long gentle slope to the hazy dove-grey horizon. Below them, as far as the eye could see, rolled a park-like expanse of knee-high emerald green, dotted with scattered clumps of forest and occasional lonesome oaks. She said, "Oh, isn't it ever so pretty, dear? It's nothing like I imagined."

Joe said, "The Shawnee call it Ken-ta-ke. Cousin John wrote it means Big Meadow. That's what it is, all right. A whopping big meadow sloping all the way to the Ohio River. You can't see the river from here, of course. It's days from here."

"There sure is a lot of it. I thought Kentucky meant the Dark And Bloody Ground in Indian."

"I heard that too. It's some fool notion somebody wrote without asking the Injuns what their words really meant. It looks like the trail is clear and we got some riding ahead."

"Are you sure it's the trail to Boonesburough, Joe?"

"I hope so. There's other towns. Harrodsburg is older and bigger than Boonesburough, but that's not where Cousin John is. He wrote there's a fork in the trail near the headwaters of Dick's River. First we have to ford the Rock Castle, about a day's ride from here."

"Oh? I thought we'd reach settled territory just a few miles past the gap."

"Not hardly. Boonesburough's a good forty-odd miles down the slope. We're going to spend at least another night in that infernal bedroll before we have a roof above our heads. And if we don't get cracking, it may be more like two."

They rode on over the limestone swells of the Cumberland plateau as Joe studied their new surroundings with a pleased, albeit puzzled eye. The land was rich and well watered. Even this late in summer the grass grew rank and green. They passed place after place where one would expect to find a family homesteading. The land lay clear enough for plowing with plenty of timber and water all around. Joe wondered why was it all so empty. You'd have thought anyone with a lick of sense would have gotten here by now. The Atlantic slope of the mountains was far less promising, as Joe well knew. There was enough rich land here to feed the whole new nation. What was everybody doing on the wrong

side of the Blue Ridge? Hell, if Washington had
sense he'd march the whole country out here and
let the durned redcoats *keep* the rocks of New
England and the sandy pine barrens of the South
Atlantic states!

As if to answer his question, a line of dots
came up the trail toward them from the west.
Joe reined in, rode back to Margaret and said,
"Looks like white folks leading a pack train."

"Joe, do you reckon we should hide?"

"No. If we've spotted them, they've spotted
us, and there's no cover near enough to mention. We have two guns and they're not acting
skulky. See there? One of 'em just waved at us.
Feller in a wool cap."

Joe waved back but stood his ground as the
others approached. The party consisted of two
men, two women and a mess of ragged children
who looked like a warm meal and a bath couldn't
harm them.

The leader paused on the trail near Joe and
Margaret, but the others plodded on, barely
nodding howdy. The man in the wool cap said,

"We don't mean to be surly, folks, but we
want to make it through the gap afore sundown. My name is Kip Bryan and my party is
Continental."

"We're Patriots too. This is my stepmother,
Margaret Floyd, and I'm Joe. We're kin to John
Floyd of Boonesburough. You know him?"

"Met him. He's all right. But he ain't at
Boonesburough right now. Nobody left but a

few stubborn fools and some niggers who has no say in the matter."

"You folks are packing it in, huh?"

"That's for damn sure, Joe. They say Simon Girty's with the Tory army headed this way. I'd sooner face old Black Fish and his Shawnee with a stick of stovewood than meet up with Simon Girty. You know who he is, don't you, son?"

"Yep. White American who's turned Injun and gone sort of savage. What's the latest news about Captain Boone and the others on our side?"

"Hell, Boone's been dead or worse since winter. There ain't all that many left on our side. Rebecca Boone herself has given up. We'uns is kin to old Rebecca on her ma's side, and we'll be joining her soon in the Carolinas. If you has any sense worth mention you'll be heading back with us."

Joe glanced at Margaret, who looked as if she was about to be sick. Then he shrugged and said, "We're going on, I reckon. How safe does it look this side of the fort?"

"You know as much as I do, son. Some say the Shawnee are still on the other side of the Ohio. Some say they've sent scouting parties on ahead. We ain't hanging about to find out."

"Well, we'll say good day and good luck to you then."

Bryan looked uncomfortable and said, "I know what you'd be thinking, son, but you don't know these parts, so you've no call to mark me down as a coward."

"I never said you were, sir."

"No, but I can read what you're thinking. You're young and you look like you know how to handle that Brown Bess. But you and your ma are riding into a hornet's nest! I've whupped my share of Shawnee and I've left bones buried in the Kentuck. But enough is enough. They've took our leader and the damned Continental Army refuses to help. We sent us a delegation to Congress, asking to be made a fourteenth state, but they said they had enough states for now. They said we was squatting on Crown lands they might want to give back to German George if there's ever a peace treaty. So you see, even if them fools further west should whup the Injuns, which ain't possible, they don't even hold clear title to the lands they're fighting for!"

"You're likely right. Your folks are sort of far off now, Mister Bryan."

The older man nodded, said, "Keep your head down, boy," and rode off after the others.

Margaret asked, "Do you think it's as bad as he says, Joe?"

Joe said, "Don't know. We'll find out when we get there. It isn't as if we had other parts to head for."

8

The other party must have passed the place, but they hadn't noticed the carrion crows, or hadn't wanted to find out what the big black birds were fussing over a quarter mile north of the trail.

Joe told Margaret to stay put and loped his pony over for a look. The crows rose in an angry dark cloud as he approached and his pony suddenly shied. Joe steadied his mount and said, "Easy, boy. I smell it, too."

He dismounted and tied the pony to a sapling before walking on, gun in hand. Then he stopped and gagged as he saw what the crows had been squabbling over in the trampled grass.

The two bodies lay across the remains of what must have been their own campfire. They were mangled, charred and badly bloated. One was a man. He'd been castrated. The other was the still obscenely spread-out corpse of a young woman. Their belongings lay scattered about, as if some boisterous naughty children had rummaged through an attic before going out to play. Joe bent to pick up an all-too-familiar sunbonnet. He muttered to himself, "Damn it, Freckles, I told you not to carry Tilly out here!"

He saw Margaret was coming over on foot and he waved her back, calling, "Don't come closer, Meg! The Injuns jumped some folks I know and is isn't pretty."

"Oh, God, are they dead?"

"Yep. They likely welcomed it too. Let's go back to the pack mule. I have some digging to do."

She fell in at his side, asking, "Was it that young couple you told me about? The boy and girl who eloped?"

"Freckles Grogan and Tilly Hanks. I aim to put Mr. and Mrs. Grogan on the marker. I don't know if they ever married up lawful or not, but it seems more seemly to allow they might have."

"Joe, I want to help. They should be buried properly."

"I know what you want, Meg. But there's no use two of us getting sick. I can roll 'em in with the shovel. There isn't much left to pretty up. You can stand at my side and we'll say some words over them once I get them under the ground. I'll want you to write the letters to their kin too. You're better with words than me."

It didn't take Joe an hour to bury his young friends and mark their resting place in the waving green meadow. They prayed a bit. As they turned to leave a redwing fluttered to the simple pine marker and began to sing. Joe said, "You might write how pretty and peaceful this place looks, Meg. It might comfort them to know their children are sleeping together under wildflowers and birdsong."

She started to cry and he said gruffly, "Now what's the matter? You never met up with either of them, Meg."

"I know, dear. But I never had a son or daughter of my own. You were right—it's better that I didn't look. Now I'll be able to remember those young strangers in my mind as a smiling happy couple. The boy will be tall and clean-limbed. His bride will be a lovely little blonde girl with pretty ribbon bows in her hair and they'll just be sleeping. They'll never get old and . . ."

"Meg, Freckles was a likable but goofy little runt and Tilly had buck teeth."

"Don't spoil it for me, Joe. I want to remember them as I'm sure their own poor mothers will."

"You sure are given to poetic notions. But I reckon they'd like to be remembered like that, now that I study on it."

Then he asked, soberly, "How do you remember father, Meg?"

She didn't answer for a time as they strode through the tall grass back to the ponies. Then she said, "Like a strong and handsome man that Time's cruel teeth had been worrying some.

Let's fancy him in his best clothes with a Loyalist cockade in his buttonhole. And, for God's
sake, Joe, let's *leave* him that way!"

They camped for the night in the shelter of
a limestone outcrop. Joe made no fire and they
supped on jerked venison and pure water from
a nearby spring. Joe allowed they were less
than a hard day's ride from Boonesburough
now. He didn't mention his worriment about
whether the forted town would *be* there when
they arrived.

Despite the season, it was cold after sundown
without a fire. The prevailing west wind swept
up the great meadow, cool and moist from the
wetlands along the Ohio beyond the horizon.
Joe figured the grass stayed green all summer
because of this. But it made sleeping in the open
cold wet discomfort.

They turned in shortly after dark, more to
keep warm than with any hope of sleeping much
with who knew what-all about them in the
darkness.

Joe pulled the blankets over them as he said,
"Moonrise is due in a couple of hours. We'll be
all right as soon as I can see far enough to matter."

Margaret snuggled against him and asked,
"Would you move your arm out so I can lay my
head on your shoulder right? I'm cold as well as
scared."

He did as she asked. They lay there quietly for a time with her dark parted hair against the angle of his jaw while he stared up at the stars. After days and nights on the trail they both needed a bath and he could smell her body odors strong. She didn't smell all that bad. Girls smelled different from men. He wondered if the smell of his own sweaty buckskins offended her more delicate nose. But he reckoned it didn't, or she'd have been over on her side with her back against him, like that first night on the trail. She'd sure slept stiffly the first few nights, her back all straight and waking up every time he moved. They were likely getting used to sleeping together.

He wondered if it would be like this with whatever girl he ever married up with. Joe knew a little about sex. Sometimes the idea of it excited him more than he thought seemly. But he'd never considered how sweet it felt just to lay still with a girl, not doing or saying anything. Meg slept well against a man. He wondered if the girl he married someday would smell like this and be so warm and soft, snuggled up.

He thought about that Hawkins girl he'd had in the hayloft a mite back and wondered what it would have been like to sleep all night with her afterwards, instead of parting, shame-faced, and never speaking to one another again. Jesus, he'd sweat powder and shot for a month after. She'd gone with him into the loft after a militia muster. Thank God he hadn't got her in trouble.

She was just mad at him. Women hated men who trifled with them when it wasn't lawful, even if they'd enjoyed themselves. Joe couldn't understand that.

He became aware of a turgidness in his groin and willed himself not to dwell on the Hawkins girl. He was flat on his back and this was neither the time nor place to be getting a hard pecker!

Margaret murmured, "Joe?"

"Yes?"

"This time tomorrow we'll be in Boonesburough."

"I hope so."

"Don't you reckon we should study some on what we're to do once we get there?"

"That's all I've been doing. You go ahead and catch some sleep. We have most of the day ahead to talk about it. Won't make it in before late afternoon."

She didn't argue and, after a time, he sensed by her breathing she was asleep. It wasn't hard to fall asleep after a long day on the trail. But he knew he had to stay awake for both of them.

It sure was tedious, but they did say Simon Girty liked to strike at night.

He wondered what made men like Girty so ugly. He understood the British officers who thought they were doing right by King George, but Simon Girty had started out fighting for the Cause. He'd scouted and scalped Canadians on the northwest frontier until General Washington came out against using Injun irregulars or paying for British hair. Then he'd taken his squaw's tribe over to the Tory side and gone on killing as if he enjoyed the trade. Some said he did. Simon Girty's bloody ways were said to disgust even the Injuns and a lot of British officers refused to drink with him, though they seemed willing enough to use him against American settlers. That French Canadian engineer he'd heard about was likely De Quindre, another queer fish. The French officer had fought the British during the French and Indian Wars. You'd have thought he'd like a chance to get back at King George when the revolution started. Yet there he was with the renegade Girty, showing Injuns how to reduce frontier forts for the same redcoats who'd licked him back in '63. Folks sure changed sides a lot these days.

One thing you had to credit father for: once he'd made up his mind which side he was on, the old man had stuck to it through thick and thin. A boy could almost take pride in a father like that, even though he'd gotten mean about it towards the end.

Joe had no idea, of course, how much of his dead father's ramrod determination had been passed down to the son who'd killed him. Yet the memory of his grim father's stubborn pride and loyalty to his own concepts of justice was oddly comforting and, so comforted, Joe fell asleep.

And then, in his dream, he was back in the hayloft with the Hawkins girl and she wasn't

mad at him after all. They were both half drunk
on hard cider, for Captain Palmer had read them
a grand speech by General Washington and
they'd all been toasting the revolution at the
tavern. Even the younger boys and girls had
been served; it wasn't every day they got to
hear how important the local militias were to
the Cause. And the Hawkins girl had allowed
he'd likely be as brave as those other Minute
Men who had been at Bennington when Captain Stark's trained band had shot up those infernal Hessian foragers so Burgoyne's army
couldn't get anything to eat. When Joe had put
his hand on her breast, she'd giggled and kissed
him instead of yelling for her brothers as she'd
threatened. And here they were again and she
was only putting up a feeble little fight and she
kept kissing him even while she kept telling
him to stop and . . . Yes, by Jimmies, she was
letting him go all the way and it felt ten times
better than he'd thought it might. She was
telling him to stop even while she kept bumping
and grinding her body against his and, Jesus,
he was all the way in and he was purely coming
and she was clawing at him and sobbing, "Joe,
we can't! Please take it out!" Only her breasts
were pressed hard to his shirt and she had both
arms around him and was hugging him like anything and . . . and then Joe woke up.

The moon had risen and he stared in confusion down at Margaret's wide staring eyes.
He gasped in dismay, for it hadn't been just a

dream. He was still inside her and she was still meeting his thrusts even as she sobbed, "Oh, God, Joe, oh, God!"

And then her eyes closed and she turned her head to hiss, "Oh, oh, it's . . . Yes! God, yes!" as she shuddered in his arms and suddenly went limp.

Joe lay atop her, more astounded than aroused as he came back to reality. His britches were open and her skirts were up around her waist and he was still deep inside her and she was crying like a baby. But as he started to withdraw she clung to him and sobbed, "Don't move, Joe. Don't say anything either. I have to get myself back. I'm so confused."

He lay atop her, aware of the feel of her wool-clad breasts against his buckskin shirt and the thrilled pulsations of the moist naked flesh he was still imbedded in. After a time he said, "Meg, if I don't take it out right now I don't reckon I'll ever be able to!"

She kept her eyes closed and her face turned as she answered, "I know. I feel it too. Joe, what are we to do? I don't understand how it happened, but I don't want you to *stop!*"

He tried not to move, but found himself gently thrusting again even as he said, "I was dreaming, I reckon. I didn't mean to start this, Meg. I'm sorry I made you cry."

"It's all right." She twisted under him. "What's done is done, but we've got to stop, dear."

"Meg, I don't want to stop."

She said, "It's wrong, Joe." But her hips were moving in a way that made her out a liar. And then she sighed, "Oh, what difference does it make?" and kissed him full on the mouth as she responded fully. Joe had never been kissed that way. It drove him wild and this time he thought he was going to die from the pure pleasure and wonder of what was happening.

When they'd finished a second time, Margaret didn't speak and Joe couldn't think of a thing to say. After a while he said, "I must have fallen asleep. The Shawnee could have lifted our scalps. You must think I'm awful."

"Joe, we've started something I just don't know how to finish. We just seem to be getting in deeper and deeper."

Then she suddenly laughed and added, "I mean, deeper in *trouble!* I think we'd better stop, Joe. And this time I really mean it."

Joe withdrew from her and rolled off, fumbling his breeches back up. He said, "Uh, if I've gotten you in a fix . . ."

"That can't be, Joe. I'm barren. Your father and I tried, but the surgeon said I can never bear a child. Not that it makes any excuse for . . . what we just did."

Joe thought about it for a time before he said, "I guess we did do a sinful thing, Meg. And I'm sorry if I made you mad at me. But I don't feel ashamed. I know I'm supposed to feel ashamed. But I don't."

She snuggled closer as she murmured, "Nor

do I, Joe. It was wonderful. But nobody's going to understand this, dear. I'm old enough to be ... well, at least your aunt."

"Hell, General Washington married up with a woman older than him and nobody says he did wrong. Of course, they weren't *kin,* but ..."

"Joe," Margaret smiled tenderly. "I don't expect you to marry me because of what just happened."

"You don't?" Joe looked at her in disbelief.

"Oh, my poor little Joe. You're six-foot-six and such an innocent. In the morning we'll go on to the fort and when your Cousin John asks about us we'll just have to stick to our original tale."

"You mean you want to go on being father's widow and my stepmother?"

"We have to keep it that way, Joe. Can't you see how it would look if we turned up with your father missing and us living as man and wife?"

He thought of the father he had killed and buried. He thought of Meg helping him to do it. He thought of the gossip back home. He grew confused.

"But, what we just did? Are you saying tonight has to be the end of it?"

"I don't know, dear. My common sense tells me we should put this down to an accident. A natural thing that just happened in our sleep. A thing that should never happen again."

"I'm likely to be weak again, Meg."

"I too," Margaret said helplessly. "But until we see how things go out here we're going to have to be very careful. We're certainly not going to be able to sleep together openly in Boonesburough."

He shyly put a hand on her breast again as he asked, "What about tonight, Meg? I sure don't feel like sleeping."

She said, "Neither do I, dear. I wish tonight could just go on forever." Then, as he started to run his hand down her wool dress, she said, "Wait. It'll be better if we take our clothes off."

9

Late afternoon, when they were riding through stirrup-deep daisies, Joe spotted movement ahead. He reined in and Margaret rode up beside him, asking why he'd stopped. He said, "Critters up there on that wooded ridge ahead. They look like cattle, only bigger."

Joe thought it odd that they'd fallen right back into their former comradeship once on the trail again. He had expected Margaret to act differently, after what had happened back there the night before. He'd thought folks were supposed to get all red-faced and ashamed to meet each other's eyes after being wicked together. But that hadn't happened. Had he really had her like that, bare breasts gleaming in the moonlight as she crooned love words up at him, eyes soft as a tame fawn's? It hardly seemed possible she'd just got up and fixed breakfast for him the same as always before they rode on.

The strange animals were headed their way, moving fast and unaware of them. Joe marveled,

"I do believe they must be buffalo! I didn't know they roamed this far east!"

He dismounted, moved off to one side and raised his Brown Bess without thinking. Meg called, "Joe, don't do it! We've no need for that much beef and the sound of a shot might bring Indians!"

Abashed, Joe lowered the muzzle. He realized Meg was right, as usual. For a gal, she thought good as well as sudden. He'd clean forgot the Shawnee at the sight of this game. He'd just never seen buffalo before and it had overly excited him.

But if Joe didn't want a buffalo, someone else did. A musket boomed up ahead. Joe spied the white puff of smoke under the sycamores as one of the running buffalo went down head over heels. The rest ran on a hundred yards to Joe's north and he could see three figures running down the slope toward him. He held the musket at port. As they spotted him, the three men slowed to a walk but kept coming.

One stopped by the fallen buffalo. The other two walked over to Joe and he saw they were a white man and an Indian. Joe called out, "Just stop where you are and we'll talk some. We're the Floyds from Berks County, Pennsylvania, and we're headed for Boonesburough if it's all right with you."

"We're Patriots," replied the white man, adding, "This fool Injun's on our side, I think. He calls me Wide Mouth and I call him Many Jackets and we're hunting meat for Boonesburough."

"Do you know John Floyd from Boonesburough?"

"Yes, we're friends, but he's off scouting the Shawnee."

"If you know him, where does he hail from?"

"Pennsylvania, same as you. He's been long-hunting out of the Carolinas for a spell. Works for the Transylvania Company."

Joe grounded his musket and said, "I reckon we're on the same side then. I'm Joe Floyd and this is my stepmother Margaret."

The man called Wide Mouth doffed his floppy wool hat and said, "Your servant, ma'am. Just let us clean and quarter yon buffalo and we'll be pleased to guide you into the fort. You folks shouldn't be out here alone."

As Wide Mouth came nearer, they could see he was about forty-odd with a big generous mouth and the innocent eyes of a born bumpkin. The Indian at his side wore a dark blue cotton suit embroidered with floral designs and a twisted red calico turban. As if in answer to Joe's unspoken question, Wide Mouth said, "He's a Cherokee, mostly. His daddy was a half-breed trader from Georgia and he claims he's kin to Big Chief Attakullaculla. You can't prove it by me."

Many Jackets nodded soberly and said, "Wide

Mouth thinks his little jokes are funny. Have the two of you seen any Shawnee sign along the way?"

Joe said, "Yes. Found two folks somebody killed slow and dirty over their own campfire. About halfway back to the gap."

Many Jackets looked at his white companion and asked soberly, "Simon Girty? Shawnee should have taken them prisoner if there were only two of them."

Wide Mouth shook his head and said, "No. Girty doesn't lead small scouting parties. In the second place he's not with Black Fish. I keep telling you that rascal can't be everywhere at once. It's just folks thinking they see him ever'-where these days. And Black Fish don't need help at fighting dirty. Sounds like the work of his ornery sachem Wo-Kan, the one who's started calling himself Corn Burner. There's one bad Injun who don't need lessons from any renegade. We'd best help Wolfgang with that buffalo yonder and get us all back to the fort."

With Margaret following, mounted and leading the other critters, the three of them walked over to where a pale man in a tattered green jacket was skinning the dead buffalo. Joe looked the big beast over with interest as they approached. It was much bigger than he'd been led to expect and looked like a bear crossed with a cow. The man called Wolfgang stood up, knife in hand, and said, "Such much meat *ist*. A fat cow. It will dress out to feed us all, *nicht wahr?*"

Wide Mouth introduced Joe and Margaret and said, "Old Wolfgang's one of them Hessians who come over with Gentleman Johnny Burgoyne."

Wolfgang nodded with a grin and said, "*Ja,* I was at Saratoga by General Arnold captured. But I got away."

Joe looked startled and Wide Mouth said, "It's all right. He's on our side now. He's sore at King George too."

Wolfgang grimaced and said, "*Nein,* the Prince of Hesse I am cross with. From *mein* father's farm near Frankenberg they dragged me and said I had to fight for the British. They said to America we had to go fight, and when we asked where America was they hit us. But it is all right now. I have the English learned, and now I know what the fight is about. Now I fight for the *right* side! I do not like kings and princes who think their people cattle are!"

Wide Mouth said, "Tom Paine couldn't put it better, old son. But let's quarter this critter and get back to Boonesburough. I'm gonna start right now with these folks. That shot might have carried and the lady is riding sidesaddle. You two catch up when you're done here."

As the Cherokee and erstwhile Hessian mercenary went to work, the man called Wide Mouth led Joe and Margaret in a northwesterly direction.

The innocent-looking man made small talk as they went and a duller mind than Joe's might not have caught the way he tried a few trick questions only kinfolk of John Floyd might have known.

At last he seemed satisfied and suddenly changed course, saying, "The fort's over yon ridge. We seem to have strayed a mite to one side."

Joe laughed and said, "I figured you might. Isn't Wide Mouth a funny name for a white man?"

The other chuckled and replied, "Wide Mouth is my Cherokee name. The Shawnee call me Big Turtle for some fool reason."

"Don't you have a Christian name?"

"Sure. My name is Boone, Dan'l Boone. I'm a captain in the Kentucky militia."

Joe, startled, said, "Are you funning us, mister? Folks keep telling me Captain Boone was taken by the Shawnee last winter!"

The older man laughed and said, "They told you true. The rascals took me all the way up to Detroit and introduced me to Governor Hamilton in the hair-buying flesh. I acted so dumb the British let Black Fish, the Shawnee sagamore, keep me as some sort of pet. They kept me over four months afore I was able to slip away. Just made it back a few weeks ago."

"But, Captain Boone, everybody thinks you're dead! Your wife is living as a widow woman back east!"

The man nodded. "We've been letting ever'-body think the Shawnee lifted my hair. Makes for mebbe a little surprise when that Tory column reaches these parts. They think Boonesburough is commanded by Dick Callaway and some other idjets. You see, Black Fish knows poor Dick ain't worth spit in a fight, so he's counting on an easy victory. You any good with that English musket?"

"I'm considered a tolerable shot."

"We'll likely get to know soon enough. Old Wolfgang back there has a German rifle and shoots impossible. It's too bad rifles take all day to load. I could hold them pesky Injuns off 'til doomsday if I had a dozen rifles like his that could get off more'n a shot a minute."

"I heard Morgan's Virginians carried rifles at Saratoga, captain."

"They did, but they mostly clubbed folks with 'em once they got off the first volley. Black Fish is leading too many folks agin' us for fancy shooting. He's got Mingo, Wyandots and Cherokee along with his durned Shawnee. Got some redcoats and French Canucks, too. We figure to have us a real hoe-down hereabouts. Old Hamilton issued them a full six hundred pounds of war paint this spring. So that'll give you some idea about numbers."

Joe frowned and said, "Cherokee? I thought the Cherokee were mostly on our side."

"Some are. Some ain't. Many Jackets' half-brother, Dragging Canoe, seems to think he'd do better if he wiped us out and sold Kentucky all over again to whoever wins."

"My God! How can you be sure of Many Jackets if his brother's on the other side?"

"Hell, my wife's family are mostly Tory. Family don't mean much these days. Ben Franklin's son Will is fighting for King George. That's why I had to ask you some questions afore I led you the right way to Boonesburough. Being kin to my friend John Floyd don't cut as much ice with me as you might think."

"I know. My father was a Tory."

"Tell me something I didn't know, son. I knowed your father back in Penn State. What ever happened to him anyways?"

"Uh, he died just the other side of the gap. Took a fever on the Wilderness Road and we buried him on Long Island."

Boone turned to Margaret and touched the brim of his hat, saying, "I'm sorry to hear that, ma'am. Your man and me fit a couple of times when we was Quaker lads in Berks County, but I sort of liked the cuss."

Joe, surprised, asked, "You say you fought my father, sir? May I ask who won?"

Boone laughed and said, "It was even. One time he'd whup me and the next time I'd whup him. We was both stubborn kids and you likely know your dad wasn't easy to scare. If you're half the man he was, the two of us figure to give them Tory rascals a hard row to hoe."

Joe felt a lump in his throat even as his chest swelled with pride. Then Boone hit him with, "How come your pa was headed out this way,

Joe? Boonesburough ain't the best town for a Tory smith to set up shop."

Joe said, "We heard the settlers out this way tended to be uncaring about politics, sir."

Boone smiled crookedly and said, "That was last year. You just met Wolfgang. That damn fool Hamilton has managed to make rebels out of retired British officers and some Spaniards from across the Big Muddy who were just passing through. You start paying redskins for white scalps, no questions asked, and you breed rebels faster than a dog breeds fleas. You hear what Hamilton did up in the Mohawk Valley last summer?"

"No, sir. Didn't know we had many American settlers up that way."

"We didn't. They were Germans. King George owns Hanover, some place in the German states. He allowed his German subjects to settle Crown lands along the Mohawk. Bunch of derned furriners who don't read or write word one of English, let alone Tom Paine."

"What happened up there, sir?"

"What happened was a mess of whoopin' and hollerin' Iroquois under a Tory sagamore named Brant. Fell on those poor, ignorant German settlers with trade muskets and scalping knives. The survivors were converted to Yankee rebels afore half of 'em knew enough English to read the Declaration of '76! Right now King George's Iroquois are getting the liver and lights shot out of 'em by the meanest maddest mess of German folks you ever saw! It's like that all along the frontier. You don't have to read *The Rights of Man* to be converted after you've swapped shots with Hamilton's Tory Injuns! Had your old man made it this far, son, he'd have likely wound up singing Yankee Doodle."

They topped the wooded rise and Boone led them through the trees to a saddle in the ridge, free of sycamore and pine. He said, "Rest your brutes a minute, folks. From here we got a field of fire down both slopes. That's Boonesburough down yonder. We're close enough to make her in a sudden downhill run. I want to cover the boys as they bring in the meat."

Margaret saw Joe was unimpressed by the little settlement they'd come so far to reach. It looked more like a log fort than a proper town. It nestled in the valley bottom, sixty-odd yards from the little Kentucky River, and was dominated by wooded ridges north and south. There was a log blockhouse at each corner, connected by ramshackle walls of upright posts. One of the blockhouses was roofless and unfinished. The walls enclosed thirty-odd cabins, cheek-by-jowl around a small open square.

The bottomlands and some parts of the sloping land had been cleared and converted to an irregular patchwork of rail-fenced fields. None were more than five acres in area, and tree stumps stood among the growing corn. Joe commented that an enemy could judge the numbers of the garrison by the extent of cultivated land and Boone said, "Had some scouting lessons, huh? Well, so have I. Half them fields are fallow. Just fenced to make folks think there's more'n the thirty families there is." To reassure them he added, "I aim to have the boys plough up some more fallow land. Right now we're working harder at stocking the smokehouses. Damned game's sort of shot off since we first come out here. You know how critters spook when folks move in."

He looked wistfully at the rolling country to the north and seemed to be talking mostly to himself as he went on. "When I first saw this country there was more game than you could shake a stick at. You could nail a deer or elk almost anywhere along a tree line if you hunkered down afore sunset. Now you have to roam some to flush a deer. Not many buffalo left either. Used to be big herds of 'em in nigh every valley, so many they'd shake the ground when they ran past you. And there was bear and wolves and catamounts. Just going for a walk was mighty interesting. But civilization sure sneaks up on a man."

Margaret smiled and said, "My late husband told us you and your family have always been a few years out ahead of civilization, captain."

Boone shrugged and said, "Tried to be. My daddy, Squire Boone, used to say it was time to move when you could see the smoke from a neighbor's cabin. I've wandered some myself. Got all the way to Florida and long-hunted the swamps along the Gulf of Mexico. Hunted up Canada way for a time. Like these parts the most. But it sure was prettier when it was more open."

Margaret laughed, thinking of the miles of empty country she and Joe had just crossed. She said, "It was my understanding you were mainly responsible for bringing the settlers in, Captain Boone."

Boone answered with a trace of an embarrassed grin. "Ma'am, there was lots of folks here afore me. Why, Harrodsburg ain't much more'n twenty miles from here and it's bigger'n Boonesburough. There's Logan's Station, Bryan's Station, Limestone and places folks ain't got around to naming yet. I never would have led folks out here if us long-hunters could have kept it to ourselves. But a man has to go with the times. The Transylvania Company pays more for scouting and surveying than I was ever able to make off hides and furs."

Joe said, "I see Many Jackets and the German now. They just topped a rise back yonder."

Boone frowned and said, "I know. I been watching. You'd best take your ma down to the fort, son. Uh, you'd best trot downslope sudden. The boys ain't lugging meat."

Joe nodded, grabbed the reins of Margaret's pony and heeled his own mount into a trot without answering. As they jogged down the slope

Meg gasped, "Joe, what's happening? Why are we in such a hurry?"

Joe snapped, "Injuns!"

"Indians? I didn't see any Indians when those men appeared on that other ridge."

"You don't see Injuns, Meg. You move when you see sign! The Hessian and the Cherokee didn't abandon all that buffalo meat because they suddenly lost their appetites!"

Joe led Margaret's pony and the pack mule to a gap in the village stockade. A pair of men with muskets stepped casually out from between two cabins. Joe slapped his companion's pony toward them and shouted, "Boone's up yonder covering his friends. I haven't time to jaw about it. This lady can fill you in."

Then he was off his pony and legging it back the way they'd just come. Slapping the side of his Brown Bess to make certain of the primer, he ran up to where Boone still stood on the ridge, smoking a pipe as he seemingly enjoyed the view. As Joe fell in at his side, Boone pointed with his chin at the two men now legging it up the opposite slope and said, "Many Jackets and Wolfgang are all right. Neighborly of you to be so thoughtful, Joe Floyd."

"Just wanted to carry Meg to cover. Don't see anybody chasing your friends, captain."

"Watch that far rise just to the left of that lonesome pine, Joe."

Joe did so, but didn't see anything. He became aware of someone coming up behind him and turned as a man almost as tall as himself joined them. Boone said, "Joe, meet Simon Kenton. Joe's kin to John Floyd, Simon."

Kenton, a tanned muscular man in his late thirties, nodded at Joe and said, "His lady said you were up here standing off the Shawnee nation, Dan'l."

"Likely just a scouting party. The lad here said he buried a couple who'd been tortured ugly."

Kenton nodded and said, "Sounds like Corn Burner's band. Likely no whites with 'em. Black Fish likes to pretend he's a British officer and the only white Tory who'd stand for slow torture would be Girty."

"Girty's up around York State this summer. I'll go with Corn Burner for now."

Joe asked curiously, "If he was Wo-Kan, why's he calling himself Corn Burner?"

"He burns corn, son. And that ain't all he burns. He's a mean one."

Joe saw a sudden flash of light near the lonesome pine Boone had pointed out. But he didn't mention it. He knew they'd seen it. The Cherokee and his Hessian comrade came up to them, quite calmly.

Many Jackets said, "We had to leave the meat. I pissed on it before we left it to the Shawnee."

Wolfgang added, "I still say we could have fought them. No more than five of them I saw. But you say I must obey this Cherokee."

Boone smiled and said, "That's for sure. He just saved your hair. What was their play, Many Jackets? The old one of exposing a small force, all painted and feathered on a rise?"

Many Jackets looked disgusted as he nodded and replied, "Of course. And they could see I was an Indian."

Wolfgang looked honestly puzzled. So Boone said, "This lad has some militia training. I'll bet *he* can tell you more than you ever learned in that Hessian regiment."

Boone nodded at Joe, who hoped he was right as he explained, "They likely had eight or ten others moving in around you, Wolfgang. When men spot the enemy, they generally run directly at them, or directly away from them. I wasn't there, but since you both got here, I'd say Many Jackets led you out at right angles. I noticed you came in walking, not running. So you stayed in open country and steered clear of the natural cover they'd be expecting you to fort up in."

Boone grinned at Kenton and said, "I told you he was kin to John Floyd, Simon. Try for some numbers, Joe."

Joe thought and said, "Roughly fifteen. Five showed themselves. Five circled around to cut these fellers off if they bee-lined for the fort. Five more were held back in reserve in case you two went crazy and charged up at the five on the ridge."

For the first time since they'd met, the Cherokee stared at Joe with respect. But Wolfgang asked, "Why five in each bunch? Why not ten, or two, or a hundred?"

Joe explained, "Five is about the right size for a patrol. Leader in the middle. Followers out to all four compass points. They could see the two of you were armed with a rifle and that Mackinaw musket. So no less than five would want to swap shots with you or jump you man-to-man after everyone's weapon was empty."

"Very well, I will allow you a five-man patrol swinging wide to cut us off. Why the reserves behind the five on the hill?"

"Any two men who rushed five Injuns across open ground would have to be crazy or mean as hell. Five against two is fair odds if you're after most ordinary men. Ten to two is better when they're as confident as you two appear to be. I could be off a few Injuns either way, but I'll stick with a fifteen-man scouting party out to lift some hair and raise a bit of commotion."

Wolfgang shrugged and muttered, "Bah, such a way you people fight over here!"

Boone asked Joe, "Who trained you, Joe? Sounds like an old Injun fighter."

"Our militia captain was a farmer, sir. His name was Palmer and he said he drove a team for Braddock in the French and Indian War."

"He likely did. Dan Morgan of the Virginia Rifles had the same job and *he* learned some tactics that weren't in the book. While you're helping me teach Wolfgang here, I'll toss another question."

"Am I taking an examination, sir?"

"You are, Joe. You just brung us two more mouths to feed and I like to know who I can count on and who's likely just to be in the way. By now, most men would be asking why the five of us are just standing here instead of running down to the fort."

Joe laughed and said, "That's easy, sir. We've got them spotted. So they have us spotted. You're letting them know the settlement's been warned and at least one patrol is out looking for them."

"Close. Take your time. Look around and try again."

Joe frowned, then, since he couldn't see anything to the east, swung his eyes to take in a complete circle of the bottomlands. He spotted some dots driving other dots toward Boonesburough and said, "Now I see. While the Shawnee are keeping an eye on us, wondering what we're up to, your folks are getting the livestock in from the pastures."

"Natural mistake, Joe. We agreed it was a small scouting band but you don't know Corn Burner. Most Injuns don't trouble much about cows when they're too far from camp to drive 'em home. Corn Burner's mean enough to snipe at milk cows and scalp stray hounds. But I didn't want to let them close enough to see us drive the stock in. Don't want 'em to carry back word we're scared of a few feathers on a rise. Injun fighting's more like a checker game than the stand-up fight old Wolfgang here is used to. They feel us out, we feel them out. Sometimes a whole summer passes with nobody hurt. We just stay nervous."

"So I've gathered," Joe said. "We met some of your folks over by the pass who said they'd had enough. I think their name was Bryan."

Boone nodded and said, "They're kin. Settled over by Logan's Station. Black Fish figures to whittle us down by scaring folks away afore he attacks us later this summer."

"He sure had those folks frightened, sir. How come they thought you were still dead if you've been back a spell?"

"We ain't been gossiping about it much, Joe. Nobody but my own friends down there in the fort know I got away. I told you before I aimed to surprise Black Fish. He figures to be plenty angry when he finds out I'm still alive."

The Cherokee Many Jackets said, "I still say you should let me spread the word among my people, Wide Mouth. There are Cherokee in the Tory column. If the Indians knew they'd be facing both you and Kenton, many of them would lose heart. They might not attack at all."

Boone shook his head and said, "Black Fish has to attack. He's made his brag and those white Tory officers will insist on pressing forward as long as they have any Injuns left."

"True, but we can deal with a smaller force, Wide Mouth."

"We can. But it would mean a whole summer-

and-fall hunting season of bushwhacking and sniping 'til they head home for the winter. We're not here to play hide-and-go-seek, Many Jackets. The land company wants me to show a profit on the books and I can't do that until the rascals learn to leave us alone! I want to send Black Fish home worn out and thoughtful." His normally bland eyes went cold as Boone added, "I mean to kick the shit out of them Shawnee this time."

10

The next few days and nights, especially the nights, passed pleasantly for Joe and his young stepmother. They'd been given quarters in an abandoned cabin near the stockade wall nearest the river. Nobody seemed to find it unusual that a boy and his recently widowed kinswoman shared a tiny one-room cabin. Whole families shared similar quarters. Besides, the people of Boonesburough had other things to occupy their minds.

The village sheltered less than a full platoon of fighting men and their families. By now, there were fewer than two hundred guns left in all Kentucky to defend the Great Meadow. Seven settlements had been abandoned, leaving only Boonesburough, Harrodsburg and Logan's Station. The Shawnee had been flitting between the trees and doing prankster-like damage since the year before. Clothes hanging out to dry were stolen. Children picking berries would suddenly look up to see a painted warrior grinning at them and run screaming for home, leaving a bucket of berries to be nibbled by a chuckling savage. Abandoned barns were burned. Smoke signals hovered mysteriously on the far horizon. Some of the mischief was ugly. A woman Margaret met going down to the stream for water told her of the young mother who'd had her baby snatched from her and killed before her eyes within sight of the fort. A hunter had heard what he thought was a turkey gobble in some brush and, moving in to put meat on his humble table, lost his scalp.

People simply vanished in Kentucky. Nobody could say for certain if they'd been taken by the Shawnee or had simply given up and gone back east.

A flaming arrow had come out of the night at Harrodsburg and set a roof on fire. That was all. After putting out the fire the men of Harrodsburg waited and waited, losing sleep and neglecting their chores until it became clear there wasn't going to be an attack after all.

Margaret met Jemima Boone, the captain's daughter, and found her a vapidly pretty young matron married to one of the many Callaway boys. Half the folk in Boonesburough seemed to be named Boone, Callaway or Bryan. They'd intermarried, fought Indians together, and feuded savagely with one another when there was nobody else to fight. Richard Callaway, a self-styled colonel and a rather stuffy man, was Boone's bitter rival. It was one of the Bryan girls who confided to Margaret, with a snicker, that Jemima Boone was not Old Dan'l's real daughter but the illegitimate child of his absent wife Rebecca. Their captain's wife wasn't there to defend herself and Margaret refused to gossip about her. What she heard, however, was that Rebecca Boone was a middle-aged snuff-dipping bawd who'd birthed a baby or two when her long-hunting husband had been away from home more than nine months, and that she had been more than neighborly with Dan'l's brothers, her own brothers and just about everybody else's brothers.

When Margaret giggled this tale to Joe in bed one night he laughingly agreed that, if true, it made their own bizarre relationship seem almost wholesome. But by then, Joe was a bit more interested in the defenses at Boonesburough than he was in scandals of this nature. The settlers had erected stout blockhouses at the corners of the stockade. But, Joe saw, the wall around the little settlement looked flimsy and there were gaps in it. One morning he found Simon Kenton sitting on his own steps cleaning his musket, and he commented on the fort's weaknesses.

Kenton nodded and said, "Can't be helped, Joe. Each head of a family was to erect his own stretch of palisade. As you see, most of 'em at least threw up a few logs. But some men are just born shiftless."

"But why don't you or the captain just order them to do better?"

Kenton spat and said, "It's not that simple, Joe. It's a free country, they keep telling us, and Dan'l isn't a real captain. We're not a state and the Kentucky militia isn't backed by law. Dan'l sent a letter to Patrick Henry and we're expecting some real Virginia militia most any day now. But the boys here know Dan'l can't shoot or even whup 'em. And, like I said, some men are just born shiftless. You've met Dick Callaway. What did you think of him, Joe?"

"He talks pretty good about Injun fighting."

"Yep, I think he's just a talker too. But he claims he's a militia colonel and some of the men side with him. It's easy to side with a leader who doesn't drill you too hard."

Joe glanced at the open gate facing the river and said, "I noticed there's no village well. Where are we to get water if the Injuns hole us up in here, Simon?"

Kenton shrugged. "Don't know, son. Dan'l ordered a well dug, but the men hit limestone a few feet down and gave up. We told 'em we could drill to the water table through that soft rock, but Dick Callaway said it was too hard. Wonder if he'll be the first to volunteer to fetch water from the river once Black Fish gits here."

"Do you think this place can stand up to an attack, Simon?"

"No. Not to a strong attack. Not unless Virginia sends us troops. North Carolina already said they're not interested."

Joe shook his head and said, "I hope you'll

forgive a foolish question, but what in thunder are we doing here if nobody's willing to settle down and soldier?"

Kenton peered critically at his new flint and tested the edge with a thumb as he answered, "Don't know what you're doing here, Joe. I'm here 'cause I'm stupid, most likely. Dan'l Boone is a friend of mine."

"All right, what's he doing here? I know they say he's King of the Frontier and all, but little around here seems to be working well. They say Dan'l's own wife lit out to get away from the Injuns and now you say half the men here don't do a thing he tells 'em."

Kenton rested the musket across his knees and spat again before he said, "Dan'l Boone is a friend. But I think highly of you and your ma, Joe. This country is going to need smart folks like the two of you if it's ever to amount to much. Why don't the two of you light out while there's still time?"

"Are you lighting out, Simon?"

"No. I'm going out with Many Jackets to do some scouting. Be back in a few days. If you have sense enough to pour piss outen your moccasins, I won't find you here when we get back."

"I reckon we'll be here, Simon. Got no place else to go and I'm hoping Captain Boone knows more about this fix than it seems."

"Joe, I wouldn't want this to get around. Dan'l Boone is a good man in a scrap, a tolerable hunter and a total fool."

"But he's . . . well, almost a legend!"

"He is that. But I've knowed him for a long time, Joe. He's a fighter and a dreamer and the dreams keep getting him in trouble. He's good at one thing and one thing only. The ornery cuss is nigh impossible to kill! But he ain't got a lick of sense otherwise. He's been cheated out of every dollar he's ever made. He trusts anyone he meets up with—that goes for card sharps and people who want to sell him a map to Captain Kidd's treasure. I've seen him robbed of a whole hunt's profits by some smooth-talking jasper he met in a tavern. He's lost farm after farm and paid off mortgages he never owed. Right now he's betting our lives on that fool letter he sent to Virginia. He won't shoot Dick Callaway like I told him to. No, he wants folks to like him and he wants Jemima married up with a Callaway boy."

"But Simon, if that's the kind of man Dan'l Boone is, why do you and his other friends follow him?"

"I've often wondered, Joe. It ain't like it's safe to side with Dan'l. *He* seems to be immortal, but it don't rub off. His oldest boy Jim got kilt by Injuns at Wallen's Ridge afore we ever got out here. His daughter Jemima got kidnapped along with Fanny Callaway two years ago and we had a time getting them back from the Shawnee. Right now he keeps writing to poor Becky, asking her to come on back, saying things out here will be just fine once the troops get here."

"But you're not sure they'll send the troops?"

"With Washington facing Clinton in the north and Cornwallis about to open a new front in the south? Not hardly, Joe. Why do you think the British are sending Injuns to ravage the frontier? Governor Hamilton ain't some sort of crazy cannibal. It's a three-pronged attack and Washington only has one army."

Kenton spat again and added, "Washington's a good soldier. The British are trying to make him break up his Continental lines and fritter away the men he managed to train at Valley Forge on a lot of bitty fights. But Washington's too smart for the rascals. He'll send militia here and there to harass the redcoats, but he'll hold his army together, waiting for a chance to use 'em where it can mean something. And, Joe, a Yankee victory out here in the middle of nowhere won't mean spit."

"But we're not asking for real troops. Just a few militia."

"True. But they'll need all the few militia they can get when Cornwallis invades the settled southern states. Dan'l ain't worth a company to Patrick Henry and ever'body but Dan'l seems to know it."

Many Jackets came around the corner and said, "I am ready when you are, Simon. Wolfgang said he wanted to go along, but I told him we were going scouting, not picking flowers."

Simon Kenton got up with a nod. He started to say something more to Joe. Then he shrugged and told the Cherokee, "Let's get cracking. Dan'l wants us to see if the main Shawnee column is this side of the Ohio."

Many Jackets snorted, "I know what Wide Mouth wants. I told him I know they're not more than a day's march from here, but he said to make sure."

"Let's go pick up some hair then. Take care of your ma, Joe."

Then Kenton hesitated, stared soberly at the younger man, and added, "She's sort of pretty, Joe. You likely think of her as an old lady, but men my age think she's a handsome woman."

"Meg's all right, I'll allow. I'll take care of her."

"Right. You'll, uh, know enough to save a couple of last bullets, won't you?"

Joe swallowed the green taste in his mouth and said, "Of course. I saw what they did to the Grogans."

11

Joe didn't mention anything about saving two bullets for Margaret and himself as he held her in his arms that night. He didn't think he had to. They'd made love once and neither was sleepy. Joe knew she'd want him to do it again before they went to sleep and he knew he would do it. But right now he felt like talking.

He wanted to talk about what living with Meg meant to him. It was hard to remember she was so old, almost thirty, when they lay together in the dark, her nude body cuddled against his and her sweet-smelling hair against his shoulder. Maybe she was too old for him, but she sure had the Hawkins girl beat a country mile, even in daylight.

He'd repeated some of the unflattering comments Kenton had made about Boone and Margaret said it might be just envy on Simon's part. She'd never met so many back-biting people in her life, she said, adding with a giggle, "You know, if I were to say I was your *real* mother and we were sleeping together like this I don't reckon it would shock them all that much? They'd just have more fodder to chew on."

"That part don't worry me for now," Joe said absently. "Simon Kenton is a friend of Boone and I'm worried he's telling the truth about Dan'l. I've been watching and Dan'l sure is easy-going for a man getting set for a siege. He told one of the men it might be a good idea to gather in all the stock and keep 'em in the fort at night. But when the man refused and said his critters were grazing fat on clover, Dan'l gave in. I mean, he knows the rules but he's sort of wishy-washy about enforcing 'em. By now, Captain Palmer back home would have been cussing and banging heads together, and he's miles from the nearest enemy."

"Those were young farm boys. I think I understand the captain's problem with these older, rougher men."

Joe frowned up at the ceiling and muttered, "I wish you'd stop bringing up how young I was, Meg. I reckon I'm old enough for you when we're going at it hot and heavy."

"Don't be crude, dear. Besides, it's not men your age that's giving Captain Boone a problem. The other men are the ones being foolish about it. They think because they're husbands and fathers they know all they have to. There's no sin in being young. It's refusing to keep growing that causes half the problems in this world. Sometimes I think folks chose General Washington just because he's older than most of our other officers. Men hate taking orders from anyone younger than their fathers."

"Simon Kenton says Washington knows what he's about. Old George fought seven years in the French and Indian War. He likely knows the British Army, since he used to be in it."

"I'm sure you're right, dear. But they'd refuse to follow him if he were younger, or if he gave the impression of being ignorant, like poor Boone. Did you know he can barely read and write?"

"Kenton said he sent a letter to Patrick Henry."

"Oh, dear, I hope he got somebody to spell for him. It's hard to take a message seriously from a man who spells bear b-a-r."

Joe held her closer and chose his words before he said, "That's something I've been meaning to talk to you about, Meg. Kenton doesn't think we're likely to get help. I don't see how we can hope to hold this place against a hundred Injuns."

"What do you think we should do then, Joe?"

"I was hoping you'd tell me. I'd have never got this far had not you told me what to do."

She kissed his throat and sighed, "That was on the other side of the mountains, dear."

"I'm still looking up to you for wisdom, Meg. I mean, just because we've sort of become more neighborly of late doesn't change things. You're old and smart. I've still got a heap of learning to do."

Margaret sighed, "That's for certain." Then

she added, "Joe, I really don't have the least notion of what we should do about this fix we've gotten into. I don't mean us sleeping together. I mean the Indians."

"I know. We've got the sleeping part figured pretty good. The girl gets on the bottom and the boy gets on the top, most times. I've studied the Injun part 'til my head's worn out and no matter what I come up with, I can see it won't work."

"Suppose you tell me what you've planned for us, Joe."

Joe shook his head. "I don't have plan one! It's not safe to stay here. It's not safe to go. I've lost faith in Boone's leadership, but we know the Shawnee advance skirmishers are just outside the fort under a mean sachem called Corn Burner, so . . ."

Margaret interrupted him. "What's a sachem, Joe?"

Mildly irritated, Joe said, "Everybody knows what a sachem is, Meg. A sachem is a sub-chief or captain. The sagamore is the big chief, and the warriors are called pinesee. You want me to tell you what a squaw or a papoose is too?"

"No. Even we womenfolk know that. But you see, Joe," Margaret said quietly, "you do know more than I do about Indians, so I'm counting on you to take care of me now."

Joe looked at her suspiciously. "You're just funning me. You're trying to make me feel grown up, because we've sort of stopped acting as if you were my ma."

She laughed softly and said, "It's partly that, dear. But I do trust you to decide about the Indians. Whatever you think we should do is all right with me."

He kissed the part in her hair and patted her shoulder before he said, "Well, it's suicide for the two of us to try and make a last-minute run for the Cumberland Gap. We might be safer in Harrodsburg, but it's a hard day or more from here and they'll likely have some scouts watching the trail to keep the two towns out of touch. I figure the only hope we have is sitting tight right here and hoping the captain is right about help being on the way."

"So you've made a decision, Joe. And yet, you still look troubled."

"I've got to tell it to you true, Meg. I can't promise you I can keep you from getting hurt. I'll sure try, but you may as well know I might be making the wrong move."

"Joe Floyd, I'm likely safer with you than many a woman in Kentucky right now."

Joe swallowed. "Like I said, I aim to try. I hope it turns out right. But I want you to know, no matter how it goes . . ."

She waited before she kissed his throat again and murmured, "Yes, Joe?"

"I'm sort of mixed up, Meg. You're wiser than me. Do you reckon we're in love?"

She stared at him and said slowly, "I don't think you're in love with me, Joe. But I thank you for wondering."

"Aren't we supposed to be in love? I mean, the way we've been acting in bed and all?"

Margaret smiled. "There's that, yes, dear. But I just don't think you know what love is yet."

"Damn it, Meg! You're treating me like a baby again! You don't talk to me like that when I'm pleasuring you! You seem to take me as a grown man and you a bitty girl when I'm on top of you!"

She put an arm across him and murmured, "I know. I want you right now, darling. I want to make love and forget about who's older and wiser. I just want to be here in your arms. As long as they let us."

Meg's breath had caught. Joe looked at her face. She looked sad in a way she never had before. He wondered why.

12

The Indians forded the Kentucky River at dawn and marched behind the ridge to the south of Boonesburough. They appeared as if by magic from the direction the settlers had expected help.

There were at least five hundred of them under fluttering flags. Nominally they were led by the Shawnee sagamore, Black Fish. The powerful leader behind Black Fish, however, was the oddly twisted French Canadian, Dagneaux De Quindre, with a small detachment of whites.

Some wore the red coats of Britain. Others, like De Quindre, wore the buckskins of their red brothers. Above them flew the Union Jack and the Lily Banner of France. For though France itself was allied with the American cause, De Quindre was a soldier of fortune who did things his own way. His superior in Detroit, Governor Hamilton, had given his Tory agents a free hand. The sardonic Frenchman was reputed to be as cruel and ruthless but much more clever than his Yankee counterpart, Simon Girty.

Black Fish was a benign-looking man with a

ready smile, vermilion paint on his face, and a reputation for emotional instability. Like his Shawnee followers, he shaved his head bald, save for a taunting scalplock. At his side marched his black interpreter, the runaway slave, Pompey. Like the Shawnee, Pompey was streaked with war paint. A blonde scalp hung at his belt.

The main force was made up of Shawnee. There were others. Wyandot, in fringed deerskin and the feathers of the great white owl, the Brother-Bird of Death. Sullen Mingo warriors, some streaked with the vermilion tears of Those Who Cry Blood, others with the half-black faces of the dreaded Contrary Society. And there were Dragging Canoe's Cherokee, who wore no paint or feathers, for, unlike their Algonquin-speaking allies, they made war for profit and scorned dramatics.

Young Moses Boone, Captain Daniel's nephew, was watering horses at the riverside when he spotted the enemy among the sycamores up the hill. A steady lad, Moses whistled to another boy and the two led the horses toward the open gate as if they had seen nothing. Boone met them, gun in hand, and the three drove the ponies inside. They went about it as if the five hundred Indians on the hill were fixtures of the usual scenery.

By now a sentry on the wall had also spied the enemy. He was about to shout a warning when the captain called up, "Simmer down, old son.

Just walk your post in a military manner. The lads can wake folks up."

The boys started going from door to door, giving a short rap and murmuring, "They're here," when anxious faces peered out at them.

When Joe Floyd joined Boone and a handful of others atop the stockade catwalk, the long line of Indians were simply standing there, as if they'd paused during a morning walk to enjoy the view of the valley below.

Dick Callaway muttered, "My God, there must be a thousand of 'em! What are we to do, Dan'l?"

Boone said, "Don't know. Next move is up to Black Fish."

Joe asked, "Shouldn't I close the gate, captain?" But Boone shook his head and said quietly, "The gate's on the far side. Simon and Many Jackets are still out there, if they're alive. If they come in at all, they'll likely be moving sudden."

Someone said, "Alex Montgomery is out there too," and Boone replied, "There you go. We'll just leave the gate open and go on about our morning chores. No reason why us two or three hundred men down here should be spooked by a few Injuns, is there?"

Callaway gasped, "Dan'l, there ain't fifty men in this fort!"

Boone's eyes narrowed. "Black Fish don't know that. He's sitting up there trying to scare us into giving something away by our actions. If we don't do nothing, he can't find out nothing."

Another man asked, "How long can this go on, Dan'l? Sooner or later don't something have to happen?"

"Yea, but I'd rather it was later. Longer we hold out, the more likely it is help will arrive."

"But what if help don't arrive?"

"It's still better later than sooner. You can go on up there right now and hand Black Fish your hair if you're in a hurry. Rest of us will just sit and see what the old rascal has in mind."

Boone looked at the sun and said, "It's about time for our morning drill. We can run up the Stars and Stripes and have the piper play us a marching tune. They can see down into our village square from up there, and if the boys marched up and down some . . ."

Joe Floyd interrupted to ask, "May I make a suggestion, captain?"

"Speak your piece."

"I was thinking of what you said about looking like there were a mess of us down here. Most of the men must have extra clothes. What if the womenfolk were to dress like men and join in the morning muster? We could give them broomsticks to hold like muskets and if they didn't try to drill but just lined up for roll call . . ."

"By Jimmies, that's a good one!" Boone beamed. "You men heard Floyd. Start getting your women in pants. I want half the men on the wall at all times. The rest can chore for now."

Some of the men dropped down inside to carry out Joe's suggestion.

Richard Callaway stayed and said, "Maybe we could parley with 'em, Dan'l."

"Parley what, Dick? There ain't a thing here I can think of that I'd like to give Black Fish except a musket ball in his head. We can't surrender. The way they've chose to fight out here has made heroes of us all whether we'd like to be or not."

And so the morning wore on as smoke rose from cooking fires on both sides. Boone sent Joe around to make sure the loopholes were manned on all four flanks. As he finished giving an order to the Hessian, Wolfgang, and a black slave named London, both armed, Joe met young Jemina Boone Callaway and Margaret with empty wooden buckets in their hands. Jemina asked where her father was and Joe pointed up at the blockhouse. Margaret said, "Joe, we have to fetch in all the water we can. We've just come from the other women and there's only a day's supply in the whole place."

Joe thought about how they'd had all summer to lay in a store of water. It wouldn't help to mention it now. Jemina added quickly, "Meg and I figured we could slip down to the stream and fetch some while the Injuns are still far up yonder."

Joe worried about Meg, about both women. "Too dangerous," he said. "Besides, there wouldn't be enough in all four of those buckets to matter, even if you both got back."

Margaret said, "I think we should try it, Joe. Last night you asked me for suggestions. I still don't know Indians. But I do know we need water. We've a clear view of the stream and we could run back if anyone came down the hill at us."

Jemina said, "I've ducked Injuns afore, Joe Floyd."

"Jemina, I can't give you permission to do this. I'm not in charge."

"Would you if you were?"

"Don't reckon so. But maybe I could take a watering party of men and boys down to the bank."

Jemina shook her head and said, "That'd set them off for certain. I savvy Injuns, Joe. They're like growly dogs. You make an unexpected move around a growly dog and he'll start for you for sure. My father said we're to go on acting natural. Ever'one knows it's the womenfolk who fetch the cooking water."

Meg said, "It makes sense, Joe."

Joe looked from one to the other. Finally, he nodded and said, "Your point's well taken, ladies. I'll mention it to the captain as soon as I meet up with him again."

The two women exchanged glances and walked off together, still in close discussion. Joe went about his rounds and, when he'd completed them, joined Boone and two others on the catwalk. He told Boone at least a few guns were guarding all four sides and Boone said, "They're coming in under a white flag. Looks like that slave of Black Fish's. I'd best see what he wants."

As the black Pompey and two Shawnee came within hailing distance, Boone shouted down, "That's close enough, Pompey. State your business!"

"Is that really you, Big Turtle? Black Fish will be pleased. He thought you might have died when they left you, wounded, in the woods."

"Well, tell him I'm glad to see he's still breathing too. What do you want, Pompey?"

"I have letters from Lieutenant Governor Hamilton in Detroit."

"You just come a mite closer, alone, and run 'em round to the gate on the far side."

One of the other men suddenly gasped and Joe turned to see what he was upset about. His own jaw dropped in dismay. On the far side of Boonesburough, the womenfolk were walking down to the river carrying water buckets. *All* the womenfolk. Even the little girls!

Boone saw them at the same time. Unmoving, he called out, "Just leave the letters here next to the wall, Pompey!" But the black was already rounding the corner. It was too late. Joe raced the length of the catwalk, leaned over the palisade with his Brown Bess trained on the Negro messenger, and shouted, "Stay where you are! Don't move a muscle, Pompey!"

Pompey stared up at him reproachfully and

said, "I am holding a white flag as well as these letters."

"I won't shoot you and you won't signal to the others up the hill, agreed?"

"Ah, I see what you mean. You cowards have sent the women out to fetch water, knowing Black Fish is a gentleman."

"They're just fixing to make tea, Pompey. Let's leave things that way and all act like gents."

And so, as Pompey and the Indians on the hill watched silently, Jemina, Margaret, and the other brave women and girls filled their buckets and trudged back through the gate.

It only took a few minutes, though to Joe it seemed like forever. As he stood under Joe's gun, Pompey spotted his fellow African, London, covering him with another gun from a loophole in the stockade.

Pompey called out, "Howdy, brother. What are you doing with these whites. You like being a slave, boy?"

London called back, "I'll boy you, you sassy nigger! What you doin' with them Injuns?"

"I'm a Shawnee warrior. A free Shawnee warrior, if you take my meaning. What's your name, brother?"

"My name is London and I ain't no brother to a fool in feathers and paint. I'm a *Yankee* nigger, nigger!"

"Shoot, you a slave. I'll tell you what though. Soon as you gets the chance, slip out and ask for me, Pompey. You bring that musket and they'll likely make you a chief, like me."

Before the conversation could go further, Joe saw the last woman was safely back. It was Margaret, lugging a big washtub filled with water.

He raised the muzzle and told the black Shawnee to run around, drop the letter packet and move on. As Pompey moved to obey him, Joe looked down at London and said, "You knew what he was trying to do, don't you, London?"

London laughed and said, "Sure I does. I'm supposed to just walk out there with this musket and hand it to the fust Injun I meet, like a melon-eating coon. Then it's bye bye, London, howdy, scalp and musket! I'll stay Yankee if it's all the same to you, suh."

"You're a smart man, London. Are you really a slave?"

"I ain't sure. I works for the Bryans, but the Continental Congress said all men is created equal, so maybe I won't be after the war."

Joe didn't know the answer either. He saw Pompey moving up the slope after dropping off the letters. So he moved back to Boone along the catwalk and arrived just as the packet was being handed up.

Boone was still ashen-faced, but his voice was calm as he muttered, "Damn that Jemima. If she wasn't a married woman now, I'd take a hickory to her behind! How come you didn't stop them, Floyd?"

"It couldn't be helped, Captain. I figured I'd throw down on Pompey. I don't know if the women got away with it because of that or because the Shawnee were as surprised as we were. But it's over, and they got a lot of water."

"Damn wilful, just the same. Let's see what Hamilton wants. You want to read it for me? I don't seem to have my specs with me this morning."

Joe had trouble reading the letters too. They were written in the copperplate hand of a clerk, but the words were long and fancy and took a long time to get to the point. He finally looked up and said, "Near as I can make out, sir, Hamilton guarantees our lives if we surrender peaceably and let the Injuns make us prisoners of the British Army. He says if we hurt any of his pets, all bets are off and we have to deal direct with Black Fish."

"Hell, I'd trust any Injun I know afore I'd take that rascal's word the sky was blue! We'd best gather the other leaders, though. An offer is an offer and they have the right to know I'm turning it down."

A short while later the other family heads were assembled and the British offer was read to them. A man named Gass just spat. Big John Holder said, "I say Henry Hamilton can go straight to Hell, and take his king's mercy with him!"

To Joe's surprise, even Dick Callaway, Boone's

rival, nodded and agreed. "My boys and me will go down fighting afore we'll hand our kids and womenfolk over to Black Fish and his braves."

Boone thought and said, "That's the way I feel. But fair is fair. I lived with the Shawnee for four months and, fact is, Black Fish treated me pretty decent after I'd run the gauntlet and took a few lickings with a grin. The Shawnee don't eat folks, the way some say the Mohawks does. If they take us afore they've spilt blood us men will likely be mistreated, but the kids will likely be all right. Injuns like kids."

"And they'll like our wives even better! My Bess would rather die than be raped by some greasy buck!"

Boone shrugged and said, "Mebbe. Gals talk that way, I know. It's funny, though. They never seem to kill themselves when the Injuns capture 'em. They might get raped. They might not. Depends on how an Injun feels and what a gal looks like. The point I'm making is that we can save their lives if we give up without a fight. Once the battle is joined, it'll be too late."

Callaway sneered, "So the great Captain Boone is ready to surrender, eh?"

Boone said, "No. I've been captured by Shawnee once. Can't see my way clear to let it happen again. I just wanted to set the record straight so none of you cuss me, when and if they run us over."

While they were still discussing Hamilton's

terms a sentry on the blockhouse called down, "That nigger's back with his fool truce flag, captain!"

Another said, "Look at the puffed-up bastard in his feathers. He struts like a grenadier guard in a whorehouse. He thinks he's a big Injun chief. He looks more like a durn cannibal if you ask me."

Boone took the comment in and remarked, "Well, the man has a lot to ponder on. No matter how wild and woolly he acts, he can't get the Shawnee to treat him like anything but a useful servant."

Joe frowned and asked, "You mean they think he's a Negro too?"

Boone nodded and said, "Hell, he *is*. Creek and Seminole can't seem to tell the difference, but Pompey run off to Shawnee. They treat him well enough, but they still call him Pompey. Injuns like to give folks Injun names if they think they're the least bit important. Hell, they call *me* Big Turtle and they ain't that fond of me! Pompey would lay down his life for Black Fish if he could be Buffalo Hair or Black Eagle or something. But the sagamore just feeds him, issues him powder and ball and calls him the same name his white master did."

Pompey stopped at a half-built rail fence a hundred feet from the stockade and called out, "Hey, Big Turtle, they want a parley with you. You want to come out or can they come in?"

"We'll meet you halfway. Out of range from

both sides and nobody armed. Who's coming to the powwow, Black Fish or his Canadian master?"

•   "Black Fish has no master. He is brother to the Great White Sagamore in England. The French engineer is here only as an observer and to show you we are British soldiers, not wild savages."

"Shoot, don't make a speech about it, Pompey. Tell Black Fish I'm willing and I'll come without my gun. But I'm likely to kick his ass good on the way home if there's any tricks."

The black nodded and turned to trot back up the slope to the Indian lines on the crest. Boone turned to Joe and said, "We still ain't run the flag up. Would you see to it, Floyd? I'd surely appreciate it."

Joe nodded, and dropped down from the catwalk and trotted over to the log armory near the flag pole, which rose bare above the village square. As he came out with the folded flag, Margaret and a girl of thirteen or fourteen met him. They were both wearing breeches, shirts too big for them, and hats. Margaret wore Pa's old tricorn. The girl had borrowed a coonskin cap from one of the boys. They were carrying brooms.

Margaret said, "The other women are busy getting dressed like menfolk, Joe. This is Mercy Bryan."

Joe smiled at the girl and said, "Pleased to meet you, mister. Would you two fellers run this flag up for me? The Captain and me are going out to powwow with Black Fish."

"Joe, you can't! What business is it of yours?"

"It's everybody's business, Meg. Some of the men here can't seem to get that straight yet. But we have no choice in the matter."

He saw Boone walking toward the gate unarmed, so he handed Meg the Brown Bess and added, "While we're out there, see if you can get the women to sort of mill about looking military."

"Joe, we don't know anything about militia drills."

"That's all right. I'll show you when I get back. They can see down here to the square from the tree tops up yonder. But they won't expect us to be holding a parade while the parley's going on. Just have the girls stand around where the Injuns can count 'em. I've figured out why nobody got around to taking charge of you new recruits after Boone told 'em he liked my idea. But we'll talk on it later."

He wondered if it would be all right to kiss Meg goodbye and decided it wouldn't look seemly. Aside from her being his stepmother, what would the Shawnee think, seeing two fighting men kissing?

Joe ran after Boone and caught up with him near the corner of the stockade. Boone said, "I take your notion kindly, Floyd, but I see no need for both of us to risk our hair."

"I'm not being a hero, captain. Simon Kenton hasn't made it back yet."

"I suspect he's skulking somewhere with Many Jackets. I doubt they'll catch Old Simon."

"Be even harder to catch 'em if they're not looking, sir. Kenton and me are about the same size, a head taller than most of the men here."

"I follow your drift. Yes, they could very well mistake you for Simon—they've likely heard my second in command is a tall drink of water. So they see my big sidekick is still with me and they won't be poking into bushes for him. I admire a man who thinks on his feet, Floyd."

They reached the rail fence, legged over it, and had gone a couple hundred feet when Boone said softly, "Look at the Shawnee coming down to meet us. You see the painted one in the red officer's coat? That's Black Fish. The taller man with his face striped black is the one I want you to keep an eye on. That's Corn Burner, who used to be Wo-kan. He's as slithery as a copperhead and twice as likely to strike."

Joe eyed the approaching Indians warily. There were at least a dozen, and while they didn't seem to be carrying trade muskets, some of them had scalping knives tucked in their waistbands. He commented on this with some trepidation to Boone, who nodded and said, "Too late for either of us to show squaw thoughts now. Just act like you're at a friendly tea party and let me do the talking."

One of the Shawnee spread a blanket on the grass and, as Joe and Boone approached, many crowded in around them. One felt Joe's bicep and the youth flinched. Boone said, "Steady, boy. Remember you ain't scared."

The sagamore in the British officer's coat had taken a seat on the blanket. The surly-looking Corn Burner and the black Pompey remained standing. So Joe remained on his feet too as Captain Boone sat down on the blanket with Black Fish.

Pompey began to make a welcoming speech, but Black Fish waved him off, saying, in English, "We don't need to pretend with my son Big Turtle. He knows I speak his tongue."

Then he stared coldly at Boone and added, "His tongue is forked in any language! Shame on you, Big Turtle! When I gave you the freedom of my town you promised to behave yourself. But you ran away. I am very cross with you, Big Turtle. I treated you as a son. I gave you tobacco. I gave you the girl Pretty Baskets. You said you were happy with us. You said your heart was Shawnee. Then, the moment you had the chance, you ran away."

"My father knows I wanted to be with my wife and children, Black Fish."

"Was that reason to run away? Why didn't you ask me, if you wanted your old white woman with you? My young men would have brought her to you. Pretty Baskets would have made her a sister. I am very annoyed with you."

"Well, I got spanked plenty before I run off, Black Fish. You say you made me your son, but did your young men let me have my gun back?"

"Of course not. Do you take me for a fool?"

The sagamore suddenly grinned quite boyishly and asked, "Big Turtle, how did you do it? They told me your tracks just ended in mid-air, as if you'd sprouted wings and flew across the snow. Corn Burner there is angry with you too. You made him look foolish and he is very proud of his tracking."

Boone glanced up at Corn Burner and said, "Howdy, you murdering son-of-a-bitch. Kilt any babies lately?"

Corn Burner didn't answer. Joe noticed he was powerfully built for an Algonquin. Joe knew the American Indian was not a homogenous breed. Tribal groups differed in appearance as much, say, as an Italian might differ from a Swede. Most Algonquin-speaking tribesmen tended to be slender and fine-boned. Corn Burner was big-boned and rugged, more like a Mohawk. He likely had some white blood, too. His shaven head was square enough for a Dutchman and the wolf-like eyes staring hard at Boone were a pale amber shade.

Black Fish was saying, "We didn't come to trade bad words, Big Turtle. We have come to take your fort. If you give up before blood has been shed we will take you all to Chillicothe, across the Ohio, and you will all be treated as prisoners of the Great White Sagamore in England."

"I know how we'd be treated, Black Fish. If it was up to me, I'd tell my folks how nice things are up in Chillicothe. But *my* Great Father in Virginia says we're not to surrender 'til the army he's sending gets here. They likely want to use the fort too."

"Hear me, Big Turtle. I am not a bad person. You know I have been trying to act as an officer and gentleman. The sagamore Brant, of the Iroquois nation, thinks he's more civilized than I because he's been to a school called Oxford and some Englishman painted his picture in a British officer's clothes. But I am just as civilized as Brant. I do not like to torture prisoners. I do not want to hurt women and children. You know this to be true."

Boone nodded and said, "You was decent enough, for a Shawnee, when you had me and them other fellers tied up. What's a few cuts and bruises among friends?"

"I am still speaking. My young men think I am weak because I try to make war the white man's way. I offer you good treatment if you surrender peacefully. But if we have to storm you, I can't make you and your people my children. The men will run the gauntlet. The women will be given to my young men. If any of my young men are killed, their squaws will insist on revenge. I think you would be wise to accept my terms. I think you should do it now!"

Boone said, "My father's words are wise. But it's not up to me. Maybe when the other soldiers get here they will tell me I can come back to live with you."

The tall sachem Corn Burner muttered something in Shawnee and when Black Fish nodded, threw something on the blanket near Boone's knee. He said, in a surprisingly pleasant tone, "I wanted you to have this, Boone. I think it belongs to you. It's the letter you sent to Governor Patrick Henry. I am sorry about the blood on the paper. Your runner didn't seem anxious to let us return it to you."

Boone picked the tattered blood-stained envelope up casually. He said, "Oh, one of the runners lost his hair, huh? Was it the young boy with the raggedy pants, the old man in buckskins or the colored man I sent?"

Corn Burner frowned and said, "The boy. He cried when we took our pleasure with his nose and ears."

"Oh, that'd be the Culpepper boy. His brothers will likely remember, Corn Burner. But as long as the others got through . . ."

"You are bluffing. No message got through. No soldiers will come."

Boone shrugged and said, "You may be right. We'll know in a day or so, won't we?"

Black Fish interrupted to insist, mildly, "Big Turtle, do you or do you not accept my terms?"

"Like I said, I have to get permission. This war can't last forever. Even if we all live, the

Great Fathers in the east might punish us for disobeying 'em. You got to give us time to study on it, Black Fish."

Black Fish reached inside his red coat. Joe stiffened warily but the Indian only took out a deerskin packet and handed it to Boone. He said, "I brought you some smoked buffalo tongues, knowing how you liked them when Pretty Baskets prepared them for you. We have plenty of food and water. We can wait while you persuade your people I merely wish to be a father to them."

Corn Burner smiled down crookedly and added, "We have driven off many of your cattle and helped ourselves to your green corn, Boone."

"That's all right, old son. You can shove corn cobs up your ass for all I care. We got most of the harvest in afore you got here."

"You lie. Few of the fields have been harvested and Pompey says you have no well. Your squaws were seen going down to the river for water."

"Oh, that was for the laundry. You know how hard well-water is in limestone country. . . . Though, now that I think on it, you likely don't wash much. If you knowed what soap was, Corn Burner, you'd know lime water leaves an awful curd around the washtub."

Black Fish chuckled and said, "Damn me, Big Turtle, it's fun to have a war with you! You remind me of the tales we tell about Raven, Turtle and the other tricksters. I can never tell when you are lying or telling the truth. It makes fighting you interesting."

"My father Black Fish has given me a chuckle or so too. How long a truce do you reckon we have? Not that I'd take your word on the sun coming up on Friday."

Black Fish said, "We will attack when we wish to. If we see a white flag first, we won't."

"Don't reckon you'd consider any other terms? I mean, I know you has to look good to your young men, so I wouldn't like to send you home empty-handed. You've already stole everything outside the fort. If I was to say it was tribute to the Great Shawnee nation and mebbe throw in some play pretties for the squaws . . . ?"

"I am an officer in the army of the Great White Sagamore, not a young pinesee on his first raid. You can surrender with honor or you can die. I have spoken."

"Could I talk to them white officers up yonder under the flags?"

"No. I am leader here. The Frenchman and the redcoats came along to help us take your fort. They are not my masters. I am their master! Even Governor Hamilton calls me his brother and treats me as I deserve to be treated. Why is it Big Turtle never treats me as I deserve?"

"Ain't had the chance, Black Fish. Never had you in my gun sights long enough to matter."

The sagamore laughed, slapped Boone on the knee and got to his feet. Before he turned away, he said, "Try not to get killed when we storm you, my son. I am looking forward to taking you alive."

Boone rose too. As they walked down toward the fort, Joe asked, "Did he mean that about taking you alive the way I think he meant it, captain?"

Boone said, "I don't know. Likely he don't, neither."

"The two of you acted liked you were almost friends, captain."

"I know. I had a cat like that one time. Used to play half the morning with a mouse, enjoying the game too much to end it."

13

Nothing happened all morning. The Indians up the hill feasted on green roasting ears and the settlers' beef. Or they strolled around as if they were puttering in their own backyards. It made the newer pioneers nervous. It was supposed to.

Inside the walls, men suddenly remembered Cap Dan'l had suggested more than once that they finish their own stretch of stockade. Poles and cordwood were wedged hurriedly into the gaps as, in the open center of the little fort, the women drilled with broomsticks and the men made ready for the first attack.

Joe Floyd had a little trouble getting Boone alone, but when he did, he said, "I've been trying to figure a better way to put it, captain. But I've figured out why little ever gets done around here until it's too late."

"You has? Well, share the secret with me, son. I know the boys can be counted on to do what's right sooner or later. Like you can see, it's later."

"Captain, you don't give orders."

"Of course I gives orders. I just can't seem to get nobody to carry 'em out, damn it!"

Joe hesitated. "Remember captain when we decided to run up the flag and have the women dress up like men? You said it was a fine idea, but you never told nobody to do it! Wait, I know you said to do it, but you just said it sort of to yourself, grinning sheepish. You never pointed to, say, Dave Gass, and ordered him direct."

"Well, they're doing it now, ain't they?"

"Yessir, an hour later than they should have started. My stepmother and Mercy Bryan got dressed and then they waited for *me* to tell 'em! Your daughter Jemima likely knows you well. She didn't wait for orders. Like you, she knows when things have to be done. So she does 'em. But most folks aren't like that, sir. They wait for their chosen leader to give them a direct order. Folks are scared of making mistakes and looking foolish. So they hang back, sort of shy."

Boone nodded and said, "Reckon you're right, Joe. I've had this same conversation with Simon Kenton. Even that Cherokee rascal, Many Jackets, says I'm a piss-poor hand at ordering folks. I know all of you are right. I've just never been no good at being bossy. I know how I hate to be bossed, and it feels mean-hearted to treat folks like I thought I was better than they was."

"Captain, you *are* better than they are! Better at staying alive around Injuns anyways."

"Hell, Joe, I've never been all that much. I

ain't never had no education. My daddy had an itchy foot and we moved around a lot."

"They don't teach what you know in schoolbooks, Captain Boone."

"Joe, fact is I ain't all that big a boo at pioneering, neither. I wouldn't want this to get around, but I miss a shot ever' once in a while, and right this minute I'm scared skinny. I ain't too sure what orders I should give, even if I could give 'em in a bossy tone."

Joe wet his lips and swallowed. "Sir, I did drill the trained band when Captain Palmer was busy. Would it be all right with you if *I* sort of told folks to do something, if I saw it needed doing?"

"Well, sure, Joe. If you think they'd do as you say. What did you have in mind?"

"I just want the authority, sir, to shore up the defenses. I keep seeing things that aren't seemly. I point 'em out to you and you agree. Then you stare up at the sky and say it should be done, like you're expecting some angels of the Lord to come down and get right to it."

Boone laughed and said, "You know, you're right? Give it a try, son. Make that lieutenant. Lieutenant Joe Floyd. Shore the defenses, lieutenant. I'll stay up here and keep an eye on the ridge. If you need me, I'll be here."

Joe saluted happily. As Boone just stood there smiling, he got down off the wall and went over to the gate. He moved it partly closed, still leaving it ajar in case Kenton or another scout should break cover on the far side of the stream. He picked up the locking beam and leaned it beside the gate post. Then he pointed at a youth lounging on a nearby barrel and said, "You there, what's your name?"

"Martin McBride. What's it to you?"

"I want you to stand here in the opening until I relieve you. If you spy any Shawnee coming, you're to slam the gate and bar it while you yell like hell."

McBride didn't move. He said, "You do, huh? What if I was to tell you to go shit?"

Joe walked over to the youth and grabbed the front of his shirt. Then, one-handed, he picked him up bodily and carried him off the ground to the opening. There, Joe sat him gently on his feet and told him, "Remember some of our own are still out there. I'll send someone to take your place in about an hour. I'm Lieutenant Floyd. Are there any questions, Private McBride?"

"Jesus Christ, no!" the youth gasped. "Not now that you've pointed it out, lieutenant."

Joe turned to walk away. A burly man was blocking his path. The man said, "That's my son you just laid hands on, mister."

Joe repeated, "I'm Lieutenant Floyd, Kentucky militia. You are purely in my way. I didn't hurt your boy. I don't want to hurt you. But I lack the time for friendly brawling with an Injun army about to rush us. So do you aim to stand aside, or do I have to kill you?"

The man stepped hurriedly out of Joe's path, muttering to himself.

Joe cut across the square. Waving Margaret over, he said, "That's enough drill, Meg. They've had time to count us all and they likely make it over a hundred men in here. I want you gals to slip inside a few at a time and get back into dresses before some smart Injun wonders where the womenfolk went. Boone told 'em you all went to the river for wash water. So hang some clothes up to dry. It doesn't matter they haven't been laundered. The Injuns won't be able to tell from up there."

"I understand, dear. The other women are so worried. We all feel so helpless. Jemima says when they attack it will be the women's job to load the muskets, but half of them don't know how."

Joe nodded and handed her his own Brown Bess, saying, "Take mine and get her to show you how to double-shot. Get a few more of you older gals good at it, then teach the young wives and daughters. Teach anyone big enough to lift a gun."

"I already know how to load and prime a gun, Joe. You showed me on the trail."

"Jemima can show you how it's done in a serious hurry. There's loading and then there's loading. Most men are rotten shots. So it is not important to seat each ball particular. Double-shotting sends two bullets out with every discharge. It's wasteful, but the more lead we throw their way the better."

"I'll get Jemima to explain, dear. You'll come for me when it starts, won't you? I want to be the one loading for you."

"I'd like that, Meg. But I won't have time to look for you and I'm likely to be moving about some. We'll talk on it some more when I take that musket back in a while. I've got to tend to my rounds, Meg."

"Take care, Joe. I'll be with Jemima and Mercy Bryan when you have the time."

Joe moved on, shifting an awkwardly placed bale that was blocking a loophole, moving a wagon tongue someone was sure to trip over in any real confusion.

He found the young Hessian, Wolfgang, seated on a box with his back to the stockade's inner wall. The slave, London, knelt beside Wolfgang, cutting apart a deerskin with a hunting knife. Joe saw dozens of little deerhide patches on the box between Wolfgang's knees and asked what they were up to.

Wolfgang patted the German rifle leaning against the logs beside him and said, "Herr London *ist* for me to load. I will my rifle and two trade muskets be using. These patches only for my rifle are. Herr London understands."

The black nodded and said, "Corporal Wolfgang says he can get off two rounds a minute even without help. But if I feed him loaded muskets between rifle shots . . ."

"Damn it, Wolfgang. Nobody can fire a rifle that fast. That's why you see so few of 'em. I'll admit they shoot pretty, but by the time you hammer the ball down the tube for a second shot . . ."

"You are talking about British rifle-drill, Joe. In the hills of my Fatherland we do it better. You understand the ball must in the tube fit tighter than in a musket, *Ja?*"

"Of course. The twisty grooves put a spin on the ball and make it fly true. But you have to use a ball tight enough for the grooves to bite in and grip the lead. That's why the few soldiers who use rifles are issued hammers with their steel ramrods."

"Not Hessian soldiers, Joe. We drop the powder. Then we place over the muzzle a leather patch. We nest the ball in the oily leather. Then we drive it home. It is not much harder than loading a musket. A little, maybe, but a man can push, *nicht wahr?*"

"Hmm, I can see how it might work. The patch seats the ball on the charge with no need for separate wadding. Time it hits bottom the rifle lands have gripped the leather, not the lead, but the leather's holding the ball tight and . . . By Jimmies, why didn't *I* ever think of that? You likely could fire a rifle nigh as sudden as a musket with that German notion. How far can you hit tolerable with your rifle, Wolfgang?"

"A man-sized target, every time? Three hundred of your English yards. Farther than that I can put a ball, but I can't promise every time a hit."

Joe whistled thoughtfully. His Brown Bess was effective out to a quarter mile. But he couldn't hope for accuracy a third of the distance. The three-quarter-inch musket balls were terrible things to get hit with. You could hurt a man just by throwing them like rocks. But if you could hit *every* time, at greater range . . .

"How many of the other men among us have rifles, Wolfgang?"

"At least five or six. Boone has one for hunting deer, but, of course, he with a musket fights Indians."

"Have you ever showed him that trick with patched balls?"

Wolfgang shrugged and said, "They say I must learn from them. I think it is the way I English speak."

"You say you were a corporal in the Hessians?"

Wolfgang nodded. "Eight men I had under me at Saratoga. I only lost two. We would have kept fighting, but our officers gave up when the Americans started at officers to shoot. General Burgoyne complained of this when we surrendered. He said in Europe gentlemen did not each other shoot unless they were a duel having. He said he was a letter to the Continental Congress writing because one of Arnold's rangers shot Lord Lovett off his horse."

"Never mind. Saratoga was last summer and you're a Yankee now. I want you to be a corporal for me, Wolfgang. Captain Boone just said I was his lieutenant. Are you willing?"

Wolfgang got to his feet, snapped his heels and shouted, "Corperal Wolfgang Heger Rodenau, *mein herr!* What are your orders, *mein herr!*"

Joe was aware of others turning to stare slack-jawed at them. So he said, "Stand easy, corporal. I want you to show the few riflemen that trick with the patches. I'd put it to 'em a little less formal. But if they josh you, say it's orders from me and Captain Boone."

He looked at London and said, "I'm making you Wolfgang's lance corporal, London. You stick with him and help him carry out my orders."

"Yessir. Does that mean I ain't a slave no more?"

"I don't know. We'll ask when this is over. Right now you're a Kentucky militiaman until I say different."

"But what if my mistress asks me to fetch and carry, sir?"

"You tell her I said she could do her own chores whilst the Shawnee are up there fixing to make a squaw out of her. She'll likely see it our way."

Turning back to Wolfgang, Joe said, "You get as many shooting straight as you can while there's still time. When the fighting starts I'll want you near with that rifle of yours. I might have some targets picked out for you. I won't have time to look for you. So you'd best look for me."

"I understand. It is good at least we have three soldiers in this crazy place."

Joe nodded and started to turn away. Then he thought and asked the Hessian, "Have you any suggestions about our defenses, corporal?"

"Many, but they are all too late."

Joe nodded. "How did you get to Kentucky, Wolfgang?"

"I walked. After I was captured, there was talk about selling us back to the British for some captured Americans. I was tired of being sold. I took pack and rifle and just started walking."

"The Continental Army let you keep your gun?"

"Honors of war, General Burgoyne called it. Your General Gates *ist* also a European gentleman. Burgoyne gave his word I would fight no more or try to get away. But nobody asked me. So I am here. I came over the mountains with some settlers who asked no questions from another white man with a gun. This place is almost as pretty as Hessia and you don't have princes here!"

"We sure got a mess of Shawnee though."

"*Ja, ist* so."

"Well, you both know what to do."

Joe climbed the nearest log ladder and walked the catwalk to the corner, where he found Boone smoking his pipe. He told Boone some of the orders he'd given and the older man said, "You're doing fine, son. Things is looking up."

Joe looked doubtful. "Except that the Injuns are holding the high ground and the initiative. Soon as we can figure how, I'd like to clear those rails betwixt us and them."

"The fence Gass built out there? It figures to slow the charge, Joe."

"I don't think so, sir. They'll come down that long slope fast and likely just vault that fence. Or they'll use it for cover. Any one of those rails would make a tolerable battering ram too. And look at the way the weeds have grown up along the fence line. They're summer-dried and could burn like hell."

"Hmm." Boone puffed on his pipe, then pointed with it. "I reckon if they do set them weeds aflame and do it after dark, we'll be lit up like we was on the stage of an opera house. They could stand off, up the slope in the dark, and pepper us, hoping to drive us to cover while others took a long run, hop, skip and howdy, neighbor!"

Joe didn't answer and Boone kept staring morosely down at the danger his young lieutenant had pointed out. "You know, Joe," he said slowly, "this is my first crack at siege warfare, the first fort I've ever tried to hold. It's not like playin' hide-and-go-seek in the woods." Then he brightened and said, "But then, Black Fish ain't never took no fort afore. So I'd say we was even."

"Sir." Again Joe hesitated. "Didn't you say that Frenchman in the Injun camp's a military engineer?"

"De Quindre? Yes. So he is. He's a sissy frog who likely sits down to pee. But he is an engineer."

Neither man had much to say for a spell. They weren't quite even with the Indians and Boone knew it. Black Fish, no doubt with De Quindre giving him orders, had already cut the settlers off from Harrodsburg and the Cumberland Gap by taking the high ground before the settlers had known Indians were about.

Joe said, "What lies north of us, sir, across the river he's pinned us against?"

"North across the Kentucky, Joe? Nothing much. It's just Injun country, all the way to Canada. We can't expect help from that direction."

"Nossir, we can't. We can't even run that way ourselves."

14

Thirty men and sixty-odd women and children waited and waited. A million years later, it seemed, the sun went down.

The night was longer. The defenders of Boonesburough took turns on the ramparts or at the loopholes, staring into the inky darkness and straining sleepless ears. From time to time a bird would call out in the Shawnee-haunted night. The bird calls might well have been from birds. One didn't know. There were no taunting war whoops, no flaming arrows. Up on the ridge they could see the dull glows of Indian campfires and sometimes someone moved across the light, as if a Shawnee were heeding nature's call. Or getting ready to attack.

Joe shared his watch with Dick Callaway, who soon got on his nerves. When he wasn't hearing Indians, Callaway was complaining about Boone. But Joe had heard it all before. How Boone and his salt-making party had surrendered at the Blue Lick without a fight. How Boone had been friendly with the other side while he was a prisoner. How Boone had oddly gotten away, though the others were still prisoners, if indeed they were alive.

Joe thought calling Boone a Tory was putting it a mite strong. He asked, mildly, "If you reckon the captain's on the other side, Dick, what do you suppose he's here for?"

Callaway said, "To talk us into giving up, of course."

"But he's been voting to hold out. He says if we can just keep it like it is until Alex Campbell's Virginia militia gets here . . ."

"Boy, there's no militia coming and Dan'l knows it. Have you noticed how the Shawnee keep holding back?"

"I have. Been watching for 'em to attack all day and half the night. Black Fish doesn't want to lose more blood than he can help. He's likely hoping to wear us down or talk us into giving up without a fight."

Callaway grunted, "Him and Dan'l are in on it together. He'd have hit us by now if he didn't know he had at least one friend among us."

"You're talking like an old woman over a backyard fence, Dick Callaway. I don't see you attacking them."

"Are you mad, boy? It'd be suicide for us to charge up that slope agin' them rascals!"

"On that we're agreed. Don't you reckon Black Fish knows we're set to pepper his braves when they charge us? Use your head, Dick. The sagamore knows he's got us in a fix if he just sits tight. We can't hold out without help for much more'n a week, and he's got the whole fall and Injun summer ahead."

"Injuns don't fight that way, boy. His warriors will start getting restless and telling him he's a sissy if he just lays siege much longer. They got no quartermaster corps and their women are sleeping up in Chillicothe. Likely with some other braves. He's got to take us or give it up. And if he gives it up, the new sagamore will likely be Corn Burner."

"I met Corn Burner. Didn't like him."

"Neither does Black Fish. But the others will follow Corn Burner if Black Fish don't win. So he's got to win and Dan'l is a friend of his."

"Yep, they both got the same problem with junior officers after their job. You took over here while the captain was a prisoner this spring, right?"

"That's got nothing to do with it, boy. I'll follow any man who can show me he's a better fighting man than me and not a spy for the other side."

"I could prove I'm a better fighter, I reckon. But even if I whupped you, it wouldn't prove I wasn't the Crown Prince of England in disguise. So why don't we just quit discussing it? Nothing I can say will make you like Boone. Nothing you can say is going to convince me he's a turncoat."

"I reckon I got a right to state my opinions all I want, damn it."

"Just like I got a right to swing my arm right

where your mouth is flapping. You ought to pack your head in salt and ice, Dick Callaway. Your brain's been dead for some time and I don't like the stink that's coming out."

And so it went. Up on the hill, the Indians were quiet and still.

Dave Gass and the self-appointed Major Smith climbed up to relieve Joe and Callaway. Joe was glad to be off-duty.

He went back to the cabin, where he found Margaret awake in bed and waiting for him. She was undressed.

He peeled off his moccasins and hunting jacket but no more, saying, "We'd do better to stay dressed, Meg. I'd hate to have to man the walls in my birthday suit."

She looked hurt and asked, "Are you sure that's the only reason, Joe?"

"Only reason for sleeping with my duds on? It's not as if I like feeling sweaty flannel on my hide, Meg. I'm hoping to get a few winks before we have to swap bullets with the Shawnee."

"Oh, I thought you might be . . . Well, I saw the way you smiled at Jemima and little Mercy Bryan."

Joe stared at her, astounded. "God damn it, Meg, that's the dumbest thing I've heard all night and I've been standing watch with an idjet! Jemima Callaway's a married woman and little

Mercy isn't old enough for a seemly man to look at."

"My, yes, she must be four or five years younger than you, Joe."

"If you're trying to get my britches off, you're choosing poor words, Meg. I told you I didn't like to be twitted about being too young for you."

"I'm not twitting you. I'm twitting me. Joe, I'm confused and scared."

"Well, you got reason to be scared. All of us are scared. But saying mean things to each other isn't going to drive the Shawnee back across the Ohio."

Meg hesitated, unsure of herself in the face of Joe's own uncertainties, "Are you sorry you brought me out here with you, Joe?" she asked.

"I sure as hell am, Meg. Had I known how it was going to be, I'd have headed for almost anywhere else with you. We purely do appear to have jumped from the pan to the fire. But Cousin John was supposed to be here and he never wrote the Injun trouble was this bad."

"You mean we'd be together no matter what?"

"We're friends, aren't we? Since having time to study on it, I can see we made a dumb move heading out here, even if Kentucky wasn't crawling with Injuns. Folks run for their own kin without thinking. Had not I had kin out here, we wouldn't have needed to tell folks you were my stepmother. Had we just kept going down the post road, say, to Georgia, we could have changed our names and told everybody we were married up."

"Joe! Do you mean that?"

"Just said so, didn't I? We were almost here before we started going all the way with each other, and so when it came to me, it was too late."

"Oh, darling, come to bed. You don't have to undress. I just want you to hold me. Being held is sort of important to a woman, Joe."

He got in beside her and got an arm under her head as he said, "I know. That other stuff is fun, but it's over before you know it. I like the holding and talking part too. I don't remember ever having a comrade as good as you to talk to, Meg. Sometimes it's like you were another feller. Not that you're not a handsome gal and a damn fine lay, you understand."

"I do understand, better than you imagine, dear."

"Well, now that we quit fussing, would you like to have at it? I'm a mite tuckered, but . . ."

"Just hold me, Joe. I'm so scared. I know I'm being a ninny, but I can't help it. I keep telling myself other women have more to be afraid about, but it's more than the Indians. It's that whole big world out there, Joe. Even if we come through this siege alive, what's to become of us?"

"I dunno. This war can't last forever and Tom Paine says when it's over we'll all be free and life will be easy."

"Life is never easy, Joe. We can't just go on like this."

"'Course not. We'll claim us some land further west and build us a cabin and live off the fat of the land."

"Joe, you're still thinking like a boy running off to play Robinson Crusoe. Sooner or later we all have to grow up. No matter who wins the war there'll be laws and papers and taxes. You can't just run wild across the country like an Indian brave. Sooner or later you have to settle down and make something of yourself. Do you want to end up like poor old Dan'l Boone when you're his age?"

"You really reckon I could? I'd admire being a man like Boone. I don't see anything wrong with it, Meg. What's wrong with being a man like Boone or Kenton?"

"Nothing, if a boy could stay a boy forever. But it's hell on the womenfolk and kids. Rebecca Boone has left her man after birthing baby after baby like a squaw and seeing them grow up to starve or be scalped. Little Mercy Bryan is an orphan, thanks to her folks being in-laws of Boone's wife who followed him out here. Right now Jemima Boone Callaway is likely sobbing herself sick with worry on her pillow and she's never seen a play or worn a decent pair of shoes."

"I can see being in-lawed to old Dick Callaway can't be all that much, but I don't see why she'd still be blubbering about it. She must have known her man was kin to the rascal when she married up."

"Oh, didn't you know? Her husband, Flanders Callaway, is one of the scouts still out there, cut off by the Shawnee. Jemima's putting up a brave front, but I know she's sick with worry. And Joe, even if her man gets back to her this time . . ."

"She's a frontier woman, Meg. She's likely used to living rugged."

"I'm a frontier woman, Joe. My folks settled on the Pennsylvania frontier when they came over from Ulster. They settled just in time to be massacred in the French and Indian War. I was raised by kind neighbors, who sold me as a serving wench to your parents. You know the rest. So don't tell me we get used to it, Joe. I never have. I've never had a nice dress or been to the sort of gentle home I used to read about. I've never even met a fine lady or been to a concert. I've never seen a grand city like London or Philadelphia. So I suppose I should be used to this life by now. But I'm not, Joe. A woman wants a home, not a one-room cabin in a clearing and a grinning boy for a husband."

"Well, you married up with my father. Are you saying he was just a boy?"

"I think he was, in a way. I think all you men who choose life on the frontier are some odd race of big rough children."

"What do you figure to do then? Go back east when this is over and marry up with some tidewater planter in a powdered wig?"

"No. I'm stuck with the education and breeding of these other women. God help us all. I reckon we'll just have to make our own civilization out here somehow. God knows our men will never tame this wilderness."

Joe laughed and said, "Well, if the Shawnee don't take our hair, maybe someday you and Jemima or Mercy will have curtains in the windows and Kentucky will be all gussied up with opera houses, libraries and such. But let's get some sleep. It ain't likely to happen 'til the Shawnee give up on their own notions of civic improvement."

She laughed and said, "I doubt a Shawnee would have any ideas on improving Boonesburough with an opera house, Joe."

"You're right. Their idea of improvement is burning every town out here to the ground."

15

Joe was manning the wall the next morning when Pompey came in under his white flag to invite Boone to another parley.

This time the captain decided to take "Major" Smith along. Not because William Baily Smith wanted to risk his hair, but because he'd served in the Virginia militia in '76 and still had his blue-and-buff uniform. The ladies improvised a black cockade of the kind they'd heard General Washington wore. Dick Callaway contributed the officer's epaulets from his fringed jacket. Little Mercy loaned a blue silk sash, the girl's most treasured memento of her dead mother, because important officers on both sides wore blue sashes across their chests. When they'd finished, Bill Smith was a rather shabby imitation of a staff officer. But it was the best they could manage and, as Boone said, shrugging, "What the hell, we're *saying* he come all the way across the mountains!"

Joe followed Smith, Boone and the obstinate but brave Dick Callaway as they walked under their own pillow-case flag up the slope to the bower of sycamore branches the Indians had erected for the meeting.

This time Black Fish had brought the sardonic De Quindre and some of his white aides, along with other chieftains. One was Moluntha, whom Boone introduced as the "sort of Pope" of the Shawnee without translating the meaning of his name. The powah Moluntha sat wrapped in blankets and grave dignity, staring through rather than at the visitors. Corn Burner wasn't present. Joe didn't need to be told the sachem and his roving killers were out scouting for Simon, Many Jackets, Flanders Callaway and the other scouts from Boonesburough.

Boone introduced Bill Smith to De Quindre as an American officer who outranked them all. But the Frenchman replied, "I am honored, M'sieu, but I am only here as an observer for Governor Hamilton. Please do not consider me part of this parley."

Black Fish nodded at Bill Smith and said, "Big Turtle, I have decided to be gentle with you even though you ran away like a bad boy. I have over forty ponies just for your old people and the smaller children to ride. I wish to make the trip north pleasant for your people. I am not a bad person."

Joe couldn't look at the three others he'd come with. He was afraid what the Indian had given away would show in his own eyes. The ruse of drilling the women in men's clothing had worked. If Black Fish thought they had that many weak or sickly dependents, he had to be judging their strength much greater than the thirty men and perhaps twenty strong boys inside the walls!

Boone nodded and said, "Forty ponies would not be enough. But I thank my father for the notion."

"We could get more. How many mounts do you need, Big Turtle?"

"Well, before you go to all that trouble, I'd best tell you my superior officer here wants to fight you. I've told him not to fire off his field piece at my Shawnee brothers until we see if they really can't work something out with us."

De Quindre smiled thinly and said, "You have a field piece down in that little outpost? *Trés curieux, non?*"

Boone smiled thinly at the Frenchman and said, "I thought you was staying out of this. If I was you I'd think twice afore I risked my own hair urging these folks to charge into grape shot, if I didn't know for sure the other side was bluffing."

"M'sieu has a point. Please forgive my interruption and, pray, continue."

Black Fish looked at Bill Smith with a raised eyebrow and, to Joe's surprise, the ignorant looking lout proved himself a born actor.

"Hear me," said Bill Smith pompously, "I have orders to drive every Indian out of the new State of Kentucky. Captain Boone, however, now tells me you showed mercy to him when he was your prisoner."

"That is true, but you are talking like a child, colonel. You are not driving us anywhere. I have many young men with me. Many."

"Perhaps, but you are here, threatening these people. Have you no fear for the safety of your own women and children in Detroit or Chillicothe? The Great White Father, Washington, is angry with his red children. Very angry. Even as we speak, George Rogers Clark is on the Ohio with many Yankee long knives. Sullivan and Bloomfield are ready to march up the Mohawk and the Iroquois will pay dearly for what they did at German Flats last summer."

De Quidre said, *"Merde alors!"* But Boone suggested, "Careful, Frenchy. If you're guessing wrong it's a long walk back to Canada, baldheaded."

Bill Smith smiled expansively and said, "Captain Boone tells me you are a good man who's been misled by the redcoats, Black Fish. I'll tell you what I've decided to do. I offer you a truce until you can send a runner home and back. Your fellow sagamores may be having second thoughts about the side they chose and I wouldn't want to make your squaws and children unhappy by wiping you out over a simple misunderstanding. I'll give you a week or so to come to your senses and go home. But after that I might get surly."

Black Fish didn't answer for a time and his

thoughts were well hidden, whatever they might have been. Finally he held up two fingers and announced, "Two days truce. Your young men will not come out of the fort with guns. My young men will not go within musket range of your walls with weapons. For two days we shall live as brothers and you will ask your people to consider what a good person I am. At the end of two days, you must give yourselves up and come home with me as my children, or I will know you wish me for your enemy and will crush you forever. I have spoken. Would you like to eat supper with me, Big Turtle?"

Boone smiled and said, "I'd like to. But I can't. Have to make sure the folks in the fort understand my father's words."

"Perhaps another time, Big Turtle? The wild geese will be flying soon and we could go hunting together if you would be my son again."

"Maybe when the war is over, my father. I reckon I'd really enjoy a long-hunt with you, if things was different."

The next two days seemed incredibly strange to many of the settlers. As Corn Burner and his followers ranged the surrounding territory with their scalping knives for possible victims, Black Fish sent fresh-picked fruit down to the fort for the people he said he wanted as his children. Boone had explained that the Shawnee considered the taking of captives a great honor. If the

sagamore returned to Chillicothe with even a
few living captives he'd impress the other chiefs
more than by simply reporting Boonesburough
destroyed and the settlers wiped out. Captives
could be and often were tortured to death by the
Indians, but they gloated more at converting a
white than they did at the most ingenious death
they could devise.

Boone claimed many of these conversions were
sincere and that many whites had brought great
honor to their adoptive Indian parents. Just as a
white missionary delighted in saving souls, the
Indian leaders delighted in having white followers. Men like Simon Girty fought as hard or
harder for their new red brothers than many a
born Indian warrior. In Boone's opinion, based
on his own observations, the life of an Indian
seemed to appeal to many people born into
tightly restrictive Christian societies. It had freedom and beauty. He himself, Boone said, had
fond memories of the time he'd been a captive of
Black Fish.

The Shawnee were simple folk with simple notions of behavior. When a man was your enemy,
you killed him and took his hair. Surprise and
what the white man called treachery and atrocity
formed part of the warrior's code. When told a
man was not his enemy, the Shawnee was a generous, warm and open man. And Black Fish had
said the people of the settlement were to be their
friends for the next few days.

And so on the first morning of the truce a

Shawnee walked up to the gate of Boonesburough leading a milk cow. He called out, "Heya, I am Painted Knife and I think someone should milk this cow. She has not been milked and her udder is swollen. Maybe some of your little children would like her milk."

Then, as worried frontiersmen watched, he drove the cow through the gate for them, stopping as ordered just outside the gate post and accepting a gift of tobacco with a gracious nod.

Jemima, Margaret, and little Mercy Bryan witnessed the exchange. Before anyone could stop them, they stepped gingerly outside with their water buckets. A trio of Shawnee were fishing nearby on the river bank, but Jemima pointed out they weren't wearing paint, they carried no weapons, and in any case they were within musket range of the walls all the way to the stream.

The three of them pretended to ignore the Indians as they filled the buckets. But as they started back, one of the Shawnee walked over to them, smiling. He reached for one of Mercy's buckets, saying, "Let me help you, pretty little squaw. You do not look strong enough to carry so much water."

Mercy drew back, saying, "I'm likely strong enough to snatch you totally bald if you *touch* me, dang it!"

The Shawnee seemed genuinely puzzled. He protested, "I do not want to hurt you, little squaw. I am Red Club. I am not an evil person."

Jemima murmured, "Let him carry for you, Mercy. Margaret, don't try to get betwixt them like that. It's all right. Keep it friendly!"

So Red Club helped the three young women fetch water to add to the meager supply inside the fort. He waited politely outside until they came back for more and strolled with them down to the river. As he got a closer look at Jemima's face under the sunbonnet, Red Club grinned and said, "Heya, you are Big Turtle's daughter, Jemima Boone! Do you remember the time we captured you and that other girl?"

Jemima nodded and said, "Yes, it was a good fight. Did those men my father wounded live?"

"No. Big Turtle put too many bullets in them. Are you well, Jemima Boone? Green Snake, one of the others with us that day, will be pleased to hear I met you again. You are still very pretty and you seem in good health."

"I'm married now, Red Club. Will you tell your friend I'm glad to hear he still lives?"

"His heart will soar. Why don't you and these other squaws come with me up to our camp on the ridge? We often speak of the fun we had with you and Fanny Callaway that time. You could stay for supper and we could talk of old times."

"I'd like to do that, Red Club, but my father won't let me go that far from the fort. I'll be pleased to talk to Green Snake if you bring him down for a visit."

"That will please him. We will bring some

buffalo tongues for you when we come. Perhaps your father will join us. Big Turtle is a grand enemy. It would be good to meet him again."

Margaret listened in wonder as the grotesque conversation continued up from the river bank. She noticed the other two Shawnee had given up their fishing and were ambling over to join them. She looked at Mercy with a nervous smile and murmured, "Maybe we should have brought more buckets." The young girl's face was pale, but she grinned back as she nodded.

And then they heard a shout from the lookout and stiffened. The lookout was pointing upstream at a distant figure running their way. It was a white man clad in buckskins and moving as if his life depended on it. It did. Three Shawnee were right behind him, wearing paint and carrying war clubs!

As the three women gaped, undecided whether to run for the gate or not, Red Club said, in a conversational tone, "Heya, it must be one of your scouts with some of Corn Burner's band chasing him. I wonder if he's going to make the treaty line."

And so the three women, their unwanted Indian escort and the men on the wall of Boonesburough watched together as the exhausted white man ran toward them for his life with the others in hot pursuit. Men on the wall were shouting encouragement now. Red Club grinned and called out, "Heya! You can do it, white brother! Run! Run faster or they will have you!"

Joe Floyd came out the gate, musket in hand, but Jemima called out, "Don't mix in it, Joe! Leave that fool musket out of this!"

Then, as she recognized the oncoming figure, she suddenly gasped, "Oh, my God!" and ran forward to meet him. As Joe left his musket on the grass near the gate and trotted over to Margaret, Mercy and the nearer Indians, Mercy cried, "It's Flanders Callaway, Jemima's husband!"

Flanders was staggering now, out of breath, with the painted men behind him gaining. One of the Shawnee near the fort shouted something in his own language just as Flanders stumbled to his hands and knees and his young wife threw herself on him as if to ward off the blows of the upraised war clubs.

Suddenly, the three warriors chasing Flanders slowed to a walk, clubs lowered. One of them, his face painted red and black, put his weapon in the grass and walked over to help Jemima get her husband to his feet. The painted Indian was grinning boyishly as he helped Jemima walk her semi-conscious man toward the gate. The unpainted Shawnee who'd been talking to the white women were laughing and pointing taunting fingers at their comrades. Joe went to meet them and saw Flanders was just barely aware of his surroundings. Jemima was sobbing as the painted Shawnee let Joe take the exhausted young man from him. The Indian said sheepishly, "I thought we had him. He runs like a deer."

Joe nodded grudgingly and said, "I see you are a man of honor and I thank you, mister."

"My name is Running Wolf. Are you Simon Kenton, the tall one Corn Burner wants so badly?"

"That's close enough. You and the others ran this boy pretty good, Running Wolf."

"Wait until you see the way our Two Hearts runs! Two Hearts would have caught this one before he reached the treaty line."

"My brother Running Wolf must let me bring out tobacco for him and his two honorable friends."

"No. We are wearing paint. Corn Burner would not want us to share tobacco with white men, even now. Maybe after we take your fort, we will share a smoke. I have to leave now. Corn Burner wants to make sure no messages pass between this place and the other forts. Our sagamore's peace does not protect your people beyond the treaty line."

As Running Wolf and his companions went off to hunt again, Joe helped Jemima get her husband to the gate. Flanders was coming to his senses now as Jemima sobbed love words in his other ear. Joe said, "You've time for mush inside, Jemima. Can you hear me, Flanders?"

"Sort of. Who are you?"

"I'm Joe Floyd. What happened out there?"

"Hell, didn't you see? I been trying to get back for days. I thought I was hid good, but the rascals tracked me, and I been running since dawn. What in thunder's going on here? I thought I was dead for sure when I spied these other Shawnee betwixt me and yon gate!"

"We got a two-day truce off Black Fish. These boys are neighborly. Do you have any word about the others? Simon and Many Jackets are still out there. Montogomery, too, if he's alive."

"I been alone. I never been so alone in my life! Is that really you, Jemima? For a minute there, I suspicioned I'd been kilt and gone to heaven."

Jemima said, "You're home, alive and well, and do I ever see you pull such a fool stunt agin' I'll flay you alive, Flanders Callaway! I'm carrying our baby and I'll not hear of you running no more foot races with Shawnee, you hear?"

By now Margaret and Mercy had carried their bucket to the gate, where wary hands relieved them of the precious water. The smiling Red Club half-barred Joe, Jemima and her young husband as he held out a hand and said, "I wish to shake the hand of Jemima Boone's man. He runs well, pretty Jemima. Does he treat you well?"

"He's a tolerable husband, Red Club. And I thank you for shouting to them others about the treaty line."

"I had to. It would have been wrong of my brothers to kill anyone so close to your father's fort. If this man ever beats you or fails to provide, you must come and live with us again."

Flanders, partly recovered by now, growled, "You touch my woman and you'll die, redskin!"

"Why are you so unfriendly? Your woman knows what is in my heart. I was not speaking evil thoughts to her. I have a fine fat wife already. When we capture you all, Jemima Boone will be our little sister. I don't know about you. You are not friendly. Maybe we will just kill you when the fort falls to us in two days."

The two-day truce ended all too quickly, as the patient Black Fish had known it would. The settlers had gained some few advantages in the gathering of food, water and firewood. Captain Boone's older brother, Squire Junior, made it in from an outlying settlement to saddle them with more mouths to feed and not much else. In all the years he followed his younger brother, Squire Junior was seldom recorded as doing anything important or even helpful. He assumed a doglike devotion to the chosen head of the Boone-Bryan clan but, as even Dan'l noted, Squire Junior had a few weaknesses. One of them was sloth and the other was corn likker. Some of the others allowed Junior might fight an Injun who tried to take his jug away, but wouldn't be much on the wall in an attack worth mention.

Joe found it almost impossible to keep track of all the Boones, Bryans and Callaways intermarried and breeding like rabbits around him. So he didn't try. He noticed the captain's orphaned niece, Mercy Bryan, had apparently decided Margaret was her mother or at least a big sister. He made no objection to the way Meg fussed over her. Mercy was a friendly little gal and she gave Meg something to think about.

There was a nip to the late summer nights now. This was both good and bad for the settlers. It meant the Indians would be thinking of returning to their own families for the fall hunting. It also meant the settlers had lost the harvest for the year whether the Shawnee spared them or not.

In the cool of evening on the last day of the truce, Black Fish and De Quindre came to the gate under a white flag and demanded an answer. Joe went out with Boone and listened as the laconic captain told the sagamore he was still trying to talk the garrison into a surrender and needed more time.

Black Fish said, "I can give you no more time, Big Turtle. My young men say I am afraid."

"You mean Corn Burner, don't you, my father? My folks is reasonable and your folks is reasonable. Corn Burner's the one who wants blood and slaughter. He likely wants your job too."

"My naughty son knows the ways of my people, but what am I to do? If many of my young men are killed, their squaws and mothers will reproach me. But if I have to tell Governor Hamilton I could not take this fort for the Great White Sagamore in England, he will shame me.

The British have given me many muskets and trade goods. Corn Burner says we will be disgraced, mere beggars, if we do not return the British gifts with gifts of our own. All Hamilton wants is this fort. He is not an evil person. He said we were not to kill any more of you than we have to."

Boone said, "I know. The British Indian policy has sort of backfired on 'em. Burgoyne would have made it down the Hudson to Albany had not his scalping St. John Algonquin handed Ben Franklin a made-to-order broadside. Men who'd never studied taking sides at all come out that summer agin' Burgoyne. Green Mountain Boys from Vermont fit side by side with the York Staters they'd always hated. Albany Dutch who'd said they wanted no part in the war on either side found themselves trudgin' up toward Saratoga alongside Yankee Doodles they'd never have invited for supper in a hundred years. The Schuylers of New York was Tory 'til that pretty little gal, Jeanne MacRea, had her scalp lifted by Injuns in the pay of England. Now General Schuyler is on Washington's staff."

The Frenchman, De Quindre, said, "M'sieu has made his point. It is true that needless savagery is not in the best interests of His Majesty, King George. May I offer a possible solution to both you gentlemen?"

As Boone and Black Fish nodded, De Quindre said, "The objective here is not the taking of scalps or prisoners. It is the reduction of a rebel outpost. You know, of course, George Rogers Clark and Sullivan are preparing a pincers movement to isolate Britain's western holdings from Eastern Canada. Boonesburough commands the route between the Ohio and the Cumberland Gap."

Boone said wryly, "I know. That's likely why the Virginia militia will be here any minute."

"Let us have no more of these ridiculous stories, captain. I see a possible compromise. You and your people here are no danger to the Loyalist cause, provided only that you do not offer help to the king's enemies and we can be assured of certain things."

"I'm listening."

"Good. Suppose we were to draw up a treaty of total neutrality, with assurances to Hamilton in Canada."

"What sort of assurances?"

"You and your people must promise not to bear arms against your king."

"He ain't our king no more, and what if we're attacked by his pet Injuns?"

"I have not finished. In return for your promise not to take up arms against Loyalists, we will assure you no Indians will attack or even hunt on the same land. We will honor your purchase of Kentucky from the Cherokee. After the war, you will of course be expected to pay taxes and quitrents as any other subject of Britain must."

"Well, since there's no Tory army out here and your side figures to lose in the end, I can live with not shooting at folks who don't shoot at me. And if King George wins I'll likely pay his durned taxes. What's the catch? You sure paint generous terms for a man who walked all this way to pester folks who was just minding their own business."

"Ah, m'sieu must continue to, how you say, mind his business? We must control the routes along the Mississippi and Ohio rivers. You must promise to move no closer to the Ohio than you are at present. You must promise not to serve as scouts for Clark's expedition which we expect to move up the Ohio valley. None of your men and boys are to join the Continental Army or to offer it any military help of your own free will. You must also surrender any heavy guns you may have. Oh, and you will, of course, lower that ridiculous little rebel flag. We can accept harmless settlers here. But a garrison is unacceptable as well as ridiculous, don't you agree?"

Boone looked at Joe and, eyes twinkling, asked, "What do you think, lieutenant?"

"Those are mighty generous terms, sir, if anybody means 'em."

Boone turned back to Black Fish and his white aide and said, "Hell, all you have to do is head on home and leave us be, gents. We can put the flag away if it's fretting Governor Hamilton all that much."

De Quindre said, "We must take your flag to Governor Hamilton, along with your signed surrender. Wait. I mean an honorable surrender giving no more than you just agreed to. I will tell you frankly, Hamilton wishes to present at least a token victory to London. There has been much bickering in Parliament about the conduct of this unfortunate conflict. M'sieu is right about certain clumsy brutalities having prolonged the argument needlessly."

"In other words, you'll leave us be for a scrap of paper and a tattered homemade flag?"

"For a diplomatic victory, M'sieu Boone. Please don't trouble your head trying to understand these things. I find the delicate part of politics most fatiguing myself."

Boone thought and said, "Well, what if we just sent you home with a handshake?"

"We can't permit it. Black Fish and I would have to confess failure. Before we'd do that, depressing as it may be to us all, we would simply accept the bloodshed and no doubt a scolding for another nasty little massacre."

"All right. I reckon the boys and me would rather see you off with honors of war than have to wipe you out. You write your fool surrender and if we don't see nothing in the fine print you ain't mentioned, we'll throw the flag in too."

16

The face-saving agreement was to be signed at Lick Spring, just out of musket range from Boonesburough but in plain sight. The soggy patch of meadow was northwest of the fort, so Wolfgang and other rifle hands went up in the northwest blockhouse with orders to fire "into the whole damn lump" if it looked like treachery.

The nine leading family men of Boonesburough had agreed to sign the treaty with Black Fish. Only eight agreed to go out, but Boone excused the frightened man by placing him on guard duty.

Since they'd agreed to meet with the enemy unarmed, Boone suggested they wear light clothing in case they had to move sudden. Joe tagged along, wearing only moccasins, breeches and an open shirt. Dick Callaway began complaining before they got to the table Black Fish had improvised between the spring and river bank. He insisted the captain was giving away too much and suspected it was a trick because the enemy was being so generous. Callaway was one of those men who could think in two directions at once.

But even Joe was wary as Boone led them toward the assembled Indians. There were twice as many Shawnee around the table as they'd agreed to meet with. Boone stopped within earshot and called, "How come you brung so many, Black Fish?"

The Indian called back, "I lead the young men of eighteen villages. A sachem from each band must sign."

Callaway said, "Let's run for it. I think it's a trap."

Boone shrugged and said, "We've come this far, Dick. I'll signal if I see it's time to light out."

As they drew nervously closer, the black Pompey picked up the scroll from the table and began to read the surprisingly generous terms. The Ohio River was to be the boundary neither side would cross while armed. Kentucky was recognized as a Royal Colony, subject to future discussion with Washington and the Continental Army. As long as Hamilton remained Governor in Detroit the people of Boonesburough were to recognize him as the rightful representative of His Majesty. No flag at all had to fly over Boonesburough, but the Stars and Stripes were totally forbidden.

Boone walked up to the table and said, "Put her on the planks, Pompey. I'll sign, if that's all you rascals want!"

One by one, the family leaders stepped forward to sign the seemingly meaningless document. Joe was not invited to, so didn't offer. He noticed an Indian standing on either side of him now. One was Corn Burner. The sachem wore no paint, but he wasn't smiling either. Dick Callaway edged back as two other Indians hemmed him between the table and the fort. Joe murmured, "Captain Boone?" and Boone said, "I noticed. Black Fish, tell your young men not to crowd us so close."

Black Fish stood up with a lighted calumet in his hand, holding it out to Boone as he orated, "Hear me, my white brothers! Together we shall smoke to the peace. From this day forward we shall live as friends and brothers. Beside my mark on the paper I have drawn hearts. Now all of us must shake hands. Each of you should shake the hands of the man on either side."

As the whites began nervously to submit, Joe found his right hand tightly gripped by one Indian as Corn Burner put out a hand for his left. Outnumbered two to one by their seeming well-wishers, each white found himself gripped by both hands.

All but Richard Callaway. In times to come it would be argued the Shawnee had plotted treachery from the start, or that Callaway had destroyed the last hope for peace. To the day he'd die under an Indian tomahawk, Callaway would remain convinced he'd saved them all by drawing back and yelling, "Not hardly, damn it! I'm not about to be held fast by no infernal Injuns!"

As Callaway broke free and ran for the fort, all hell broke loose. The two men holding Boone began to draw him toward the river bank as the captain dug in his heels. Bill Smith tore free and was jumped by a burly Shawnee with a contraband tomahawk as he bulled his way toward the fort. Up in the blockhouse a youth they'd laughed at squeezed the trigger of his German rifle and the Indian attacking Smith went down. Wolfgang quickly reloaded.

Another tomahawk swung at Boone's head but glanced off his shoulder as he upended the table and sent Black Fish sprawling. Both sides were shooting now, and it was every man for himself. Joe Floyd saw the gleam of steel in Corn Burner's hand and swung, smashing the sachem flat as he whirled and threw the other Indian holding him head over heels at black Pompey.

And then something smashed into the back of Joe's head. His world exploded in a cloud of pinwheeling little stars and empty blackness.

As Joe went down, the other men from the fort were running for the gate through a two-way hail of bullets. Boone, bringing up the rear, paused long enough to shout at the nervous men on his own walls, "Hold your fire, damn it! We're on *your* side!"

But nobody heard or cared. As the betrayed treaty party ran on, their friends in the fort began to close and bar the gate. Behind them, Indians who'd crept along the shelter of the river bank sprang into view to follow, whooping wildly in their paint and feathers.

A Wyandot swung his tomahawk at Boone's head, but the long-hunter sensed it and ducked his head between his leather-clad shoulders. The instinctive reflex saved him as the tomahawk glanced off the thick oiled buckskin. Once again Boone had earned his name of "Big Turtle." The Shawnee had noticed the way he protected his head that way, the time they'd made him run the gauntlet.

The Wyandot grabbed the skirt of Boone's shirt and raised the tomahawk again. Then the Indian's head exploded in a cloud of bloody froth as Wolfgang the Hessian showed only his speech was comical. The German reloaded his rifle and a Cherokee went down near Big Bill Smith.

Dick Callaway made it inside and, to his credit, shoved the panic-stricken men aside and held the gate open for his comrades. Dick's kinsman Flanders Callaway knelt in the gateway firing round after round as his wife Jemima handed him fresh weapons as fast as she could reload.

Captain Boone was last. Covered with his own and Indian blood as a result of his running fight, he dove headfirst through the opening as the two Callaways shut and barred the gate with bullets and thrown tomahawks thudding into it. The air was blue with gunsmoke and filled with the war cries of the Indians and the screams of frightened women and children. Inside the little fort, ponies, goats, and milch cows stampeded madly between the cabins and the stockaded wall. Dogs howled. Guns roared. A white man fell from the parapet as a Shawnee bullet found its mark. Another leaped down, screaming he'd been killed, only to discover later theey'd just shot his hat and jacket to shreds without leaving a mark on his flesh.

The northern wall of the little stockade quivered to the hail of Indian bullets and it sounded, from the shouting, as if they were coming over the wall. But the defenders of Boonesburough were rapidly separating the men from the boys now. As some hid in corn cribs or knelt praying in the dust, others manned the loopholes and began to punish the attackers with a savage drumfire of their own.

Men fired, tossed their smoking guns aside, were handed fresh ones from the braver boys and womenfolk. The Indians, driven back, howled like demons as the ground was littered with their painted dead.

As suddenly as it had started, the savage ten-minute battle stopped.

An eerie silence fell across the valley as the smoke clouds slowly drifted away.

Daniel Boone sat shirtless as his daughter Jemima cleaned his superficial wounds. He saw

Bill Smith was on his feet, militia uniform in tatters, and he asked Bill how many they'd lost.

Smith said, "Your brother took a bullet in the shoulder, but his woman is tending him. Jim Collins was knocked galley-west by a spent ball, but he's all right. We didn't lose a man, once we made it back. But they got the boy, Joe Floyd. I seed some Injuns draggin' him off as I lit out. I think he's still alive."

"Jesus, we'd best not tell his stepmother. It's better if she thinks he's dead."

"I know. Corn Burner was the one who drug him off."

Dick Callaway came over, red-faced with anger, and shouted, "Now look what you've done, Dan'l Boone!"

"Dick, I never done nothing. It was the Injuns as jumped us!"

"God damn it, I told you they would!"

"I know, Dick. What do you reckon we should do now?"

"What can we do? They want a war, let's give it to the bastards!"

Boone laughed and said, "We do agree on some things, don't we? Let's run the flag up and nail her to the staff."

"Now you're talking. No more parleys. Fight to the goddam finish!"

"I ain't arguing, Dick Callaway. We got us no other choice!"

17

Joe tried to go back to sleep. He knew pa expected him to get up and fire the forge before breakfast, but he felt stiff from a restless night in his hard little trundle and maybe his head would stop hurting if he caught a few more winks. He tried to turn over, but his body was tangled in the blanket and, damn, pa was shaking him to wake up. He ducked his head to avoid the slap he had coming for laying slug-a-bed. Then father rose, and a voice said, "Listen to me, Joe Floyd. You are going to die. But you can still be of service to your friends."

Joe opened his eyes and stared up into the face of an Indian, glowing red in the flickering firelight of the camp on the ridge. The man who crouched over him was Many Jackets. The Cherokee slapped him softly and warned, "Don't let them see you know me. I will pretend to tease and taunt you. We have to talk while there is time."

Joe tried to sit up, saw he was bound hand and foot and raised his head to take in his surroundings. He was stretched out on bare earth under a sycamore. The nearest campfire was a few yards off and other Indians sat around it, paying little attention. Many Jackets said, "Listen to me, Joe. We can't get you out. You're in the middle of the campsite. There's nothing you can do to save yourself. It won't matter how you talk to them or plead with them. They lost young men today and failed to take the fort in their first rush. They're very angry. Do you understand?"

"Tell me something I don't know."

"I will. They think they've captured Simon Kenton. You all look alike to us, too. You and Simon are about the same size."

"I've got that part. You said there was something I could do about it, Many Jackets."

The Cherokee said, "Then listen. I am taking a great risk in telling you this. You may gain a few moments of comfort by telling them. But I think you are a man. You are going to die, Joe Floyd, and it will not be pleasant whether you talk or not. When they make you run the gauntlet, there is one trick you should know. Don't try to avoid the clubs by veering away from the man swinging at you. That is what he will be expecting. It is better if you lunge toward him as he swings. Sometimes you can get inside his swing so that he hits you with his forearm instead of the club. Watch for the end of the double line. The ones who want to brain you will be there, hoping to get you as you stagger confused from the earlier blows."

"I understand. What's this I'm not supposed to tell 'em? I don't' know a thing I could say to make up with Black Fish."

"The real Simon Kenton is out behind their lines, picking off their runners and warning other whites away from this place. We have intercepted messages meant for Detroit. The messages are on their way to General Washington. De Quindre has asked for supplies. Hamilton doesn't know this, so he won't send them. Do you understand our problem?"

Joe nodded. "The Injuns think I'm Simon, so they're not looking for him out in the pines. They know Flanders Callaway is bottled up in the fort. What about Montgomery?"

"He made it to Harrodsburg. The Shawnee know this. They don't think any scouts are operating behind their lines."

"Right. So if they kill me as Simon, Simon can keep killing them and picking up their dispatches on the sly."

"Will you do it, Joe Floyd?"

"I will. Long as they aim to kill me anyway, I may as well have the last laugh on the rascals."

"You are a man, Joe Floyd. I would shake your hand, but I see one of the Shawnee coming this way, so I must appear to be your enemy as I leave you."

"I understand. No chance of your coming back sometime to cut these thongs, is there?"

"No. I have to slip away before one of the Tory Cherokee recognizes me. I was only able to

get to you for these few moments. You are surrounded by Shawnee. They can't question my
movements because our people do not speak the
same tongue. When Shawnee speaks to Cherokee
they must use English, and I pretend not to
speak English. Farewell, Joe Floyd. We will remember you as a man."

The Cherokee suddenly shouted something
that sounded like a jeer as he slapped Joe's face
hard. Then he got up to dance away, laughing.

The second Indian came over and squatted at
Joe's side, smiling. It was Running Wolf, one of
the men who'd chased Flanders Callaway to the
treaty line.

Running Wolf said, "Pay no attention to that
Cherokee, Simon Kenton. Cherokee are not real
men. He had no right to hit you. You were taken
by Shawnee. How are you feeling?"

"Not so good. Was that you who hit me on the
head down there?"

"Yes. I saw you were too much for Corn
Burner. I hit you with the flat of my tomahawk.
I am very proud tonight. They say you are Big
Turtle's friend who fought us so well on Licking
River that time. I wasn't' there, but they tell me
it was a good fight."

"Well, I can't say I think much of your manners at the peace meeting, Running Wolf. Didn't
your mama ever tell you it was wrong to fight?"

"I do not know what happened. Nobody told
me we were going to have a fight. Black Fish is
very cross with Corn Burner and Corn Burner

keeps calling Black Fish an old squaw. I think something went wrong. But we have you anyway."

"That's for damn sure. What happens now?"

"I do not know. I told them I wanted to take you back to Chillicothe as my captive. But I am only a pinesee and Corn Burner says you belong to him. He is a very selfish person, but what can I do? He is a sachem."

"Well, it was nice meeting you, Running Wolf. I don't reckon I'll be around much longer."

Running Wolf shugged. "I wanted to take you home to show off before we had a Death Race. But they will probably burn you here. Are you hungry?"

"No. What's this Death Race notion of yours?"

"You saw me beaten at running and I am very proud of my running. In a Death Race, two men run for a finish line. The man who crosses the line first is handed a tomahawk. He kills the loser."

"You mean, even if the winner is a white captive and the loser is an Injun?"

"Of course. A Death Race is run fair. I do not think we will have one, though. Corn Burner says it's foolish to play games with captives. I sometimes think Corn Burner acts like a squaw. Helpless captives are given to the squaws to torture when their men have been hurt. Most Shawnee men like to give the man they kill a sporting chance."

"I don't reckon you ever just turn folks loose, huh?"

"Now you joke with me. I like a man who can joke when he's facing The Owl. You have some time before they come for you. Are you sure I cannot bring you something to eat? You'll bear up better under torture on a full stomach."

Joe shook his head and said, "It's a funny thing, Running Wolf, but I don't feel like eating just now."

Running Wolf nodded, then frowned. "If that Cherokee comes back, just shout to me. The Cherokees did not capture you and have no right to tease you."

Running Wolf got up and went back to the fire. One of his comrades passed him a bottle and he took a healthy swig. He was not permitted to offer the captive whisky. It dulled the senses to be drunk and Corn Burner would be angry if the captive was not fully aware of his fate.

Joe experimented with his bindings as he explored his surroundings with his eyes. There were other scattered fires on every side. He saw no avenue open for a surprise run for it, even if he could free his hands and ankles. The leather thongs had been oiled. The Shawnee likely knew a captive could stretch leather if he could manage to wet it with his own urine. Despite the casual way they seemed to be holding him, they were holding him good.

After a time some other Indians came and hauled Joe to his feet. One of them cut the thongs binding his ankles with a scalping knife and they half-led, half-dragged him across the clearing. Running Wolf tagged along. None of the others they passed seemed particularly interested in the captive.

They took Joe before Black Fish. The sagamore was seated on a blanket. Pompey and De Quindre stood nearby. Joe wondered where the other white Tories were. Maybe the Canadians and English irregulars had delicate feelings and didn't like to watch.

Black Fish looked up at Joe and said, "Well, Simon Kenton, we have you now. What have you to say for yourself?"

"Doesn't seem hardly likely anything I could say would matter."

"I am very cross with you. You have made things hard for me. You should not have let them take you alive."

"It wasn't my idea, Black Fish."

"Hear me, these white friends of mine say the Great White Sagamore in England will be cross with me if I let the young men torture you. But Corn Burner will say I am an old woman if I don't. The Great White Sagamore is far away. Corn Burner is here. Right now he is leading an attack on Boonesburough. You had better hope he returns victorious. Big Turtle has taunted us with the Yankee flag. Corn Burner will be very angry if he loses any more young men and fails again."

De Quindre said, "M'sieu le Sagamore will forgive me if I seem Machiavellian, but all in all, I would not be distressed if Corn Burner failed to come back at all. He is a most fatiguing young man."

Black Fish held up his hand for silence and said, "Hear me, Simon Kenton. I am not an evil person. I think it would be best if we were to finish you now, before Corn Burner comes back. I will give you a good death. Not the slower one Corn Burner plans for you. But you must understand my young men expect at least a bit of entertainment. Even they would say I was weak if I simply shot you. Can you think of an entertaining way to die?"

"Well, I could maybe stand on my head while you shot me."

Black Fish smiled and said, "They told me you were a man. You look big enough to live through running the gauntlet. We must think of something better."

Running Wolf stepped forward and said, "Hear me, Black Fish. I want to have a Death Race with this man. I will beat him to the finish line and kill him with the winner's tomahawk. It will be the manly way for both of us."

Black Fish considered. Then he shook his head and said, "He has longer legs than you, and I have been told the great Simon Kenton runs even faster than my old friend, Big Turtle. He would beat you and be alive when Corn Burner returned. I would have lost a good man for no reason."

Running Wolf said, "I am sure I can beat him. I run almost as fast as Two Hearts, and Two Hearts has beaten every young man I know."

Black Fish smiled again and said, "Heya, that is it! We shall let Simon Kenton have a Death Race with Two Hearts instead of Running Wolf. I do not want Two Hearts to die either. So before we let them race we will make him run the gauntlet. How do we all feel about this?"

Pompey nodded. De Quindre shrugged and said, "I would say it does not seem just, but it would make no difference and at least the man will die in a manner less distressing to Governor Hamilton, yes?"

Running Wolf said, "I wanted to have the Death Race with him. But Two Hearts is my friend. My sagamore's words are wise."

Black Fish nodded to Pompey and the black began to call loudly in high-pitched Shawnee. As the Indians all around began to get up, grinning, Pompey looked at Joe and said, "You gonna run the gauntlet, boy! It's the Shawnee way of saying howdy. If you got a lick of sense you'll just walk down the line and take you' lumps. Gittin' clubbed to death ain't the worse way to go, you know."

Joe didn't answer. The other Indians began to form a long double line running along the crest of the ridge they were on. Some were swinging tomahawks to limber up. Others stretched leather thongs and started knotting them. De Quindre grimaced and said, "If M'sieu le Sagamore will excuse me, I should like to rejoin my companions. This is no place for a white man."

As De Quindre walked away, Running Wolf took Joe's arm and led him to the gauntlet lines, hands still bound. He murmured, "Start the moment I let go. Sometimes a man gets part of the way before the first men near him are ready to swing."

Joe didn't wait for Running Wolf to let go. Taking a deep breath, he pulled away from the helpful Shawnee and started running, head up to see where he was going not making the mistake of trying to bull his way through head down.

Running Wolf had been right. He got between the first four or five on either side before they'd been set. A howl of merry laughter rose on both sides as a Mingo swung a club and missed. The next club hit Joe's left shoulder, staggering him. He saw the upraised gleaming steel of a tomahawk and ran into the Indian about to swing it, sending him sprawling. He zigzagged across the narrow corridor into another, taking the blow of the club wielder's arm atop his head.

An Indian put out a foot to trip him. Joe kicked under and up, setting the prankster on his breech-clouted rear as he ploughed onward.

He didn't avoid all the blows aimed at him. Nobody could have. But his sudden moves and dancing footwork carried him down the gauntlet at least fully conscious. Bloody but unbowed, he saw the last man ahead with an upraised nail-studded club and, lowering his head for the first time, rammed into his mid-section as the club came down across his back. He went down with the Indian in a confused tangle. Still bound, Joe rolled off and tried to struggle onward. But hands were helping him to his feet now, and the man he'd just flattened was grinning and patting him on the back.

Laughing, they dragged him back to Black Fish. Running Wolf spoke English for Joe's benefit. He called out, "Oh, didn't I tell you he was good! And remember, it was I who captured him!"

Black Fish said, "Pompey has gone to get Two Hearts. You did well running the gauntlet, Simon Kenton. I see Big Turtle told you how it is done. They hardly weakened you. Would you be willing to run it again?"

Joe licked his split lip and asked, "Do I have a choice?"

"You have a choice. Do you take us for Mohawk? Our customs say a captive can be forced to run the gauntlet only one time, unless he wants to show us how brave he is."

Joe grunted, "I know how brave I am. So if it's all the same to you, I'll just take my chances on having you boys think I'm a sissy."

"Heya, the bravery of Simon Kenton is well known to all. I am surprised you are so young. I thought you to be near the same age as Big Turtle. But you are just a boy."

"Clean living, I reckon. Who's this feller I

have to race, one of your heap big sachems?"

Black Fish smiled and repeated his words in Shawnee. The Indians around them seemed to think it was funny too. Black Fish said, "Our Two Hearts is younger than you, but a very good runner."

Running Wolf suggested, "Let us make it a three-way race, Black Fish. I believe I would cross the line second."

Black Fish shook his head and said, "You are not thinking clearly, Running Wolf. If Two Hearts came in first and you second, I would have one Shawnee killing another while the white man laughed at us. No. It must be Simon Kenton against Two Hearts, with the loser killed by the winner. I have spoken. You will take him down the far side of this hill, so he won't play a trick and run for the fort. I will stand here waiting. They will run up the hill toward me. The winner will be the first between those two trees over there. Do you understand my terms, Simon Kenton?"

Joe nodded and said, "First man crossing the finish line gets to brain the other. Untie my hands and give me a tomahawk."

"I will be waiting here with the tomahawk for the winner. Your hands will be untied at the starting line. If you run anywhere but up here to me, you had best get away. I am not as fond of torture as Corn Burner, but I can be very cross with a man who cheats."

It was dark in the bottom of the valley and the ground was soft and soggy underfoot. Joe stood with Running Wolf, Red Club and the other warriors guarding him. As another party approached, Running Wolf cut the thongs binding Joe's wrists and said, "Hear me. I do not think you are going to win. But if you do, it would be dishonest of you to take advantage of your unbound hands at the finish line. You must take the tomahawk, strike once and hand it back to Black Fish. If you fight with anyone else, you had best win. Black Fish spoke true. He is a better torturer than Corn Burner when he wants to be."

Joe stared up at the line of flickering lights on the ridge as he massaged life into his stiff arms. He glanced over at the silent figure he assumed to be their champion, Two Hearts. The Shawnee runner was shorter than he but tall for an Indian. Running Wolf seemed to be explaining the rules in their own language as Two Hearts stood impassive.

Then Running Wolf said, "I will stand between you, like this. When you feel me slap your back, start running."

Joe bent his knees and got set as, from the corner of his eye, he saw Two Hearts do the same. Then a hand slapped Joe between the shoulder-blades and he was running as hard as he could. But not moving as fast as he wanted to. The grass was rank and his feet bogged in the marshy meadow as he moved his legs.

The damned Shawnee runner was pulling ahead of him as Joe cursed himself onward. Two Hearts was lighter and sank less in the mud. Joe knew they'd planned it that way. A Mohawk would have raced him fair and square. But the Shawnee were smaller and slyer men than their big Iroquois cousins and considered trickery common sense.

Two Hearts was well ahead of him as they reached the bottom of the drier slope. Joe's feet, on firmer ground, were carrying him faster now, but he was already half-winded from the struggle through the bottomlands, and from here on it was all uphill, with Two Hearts carrying less weight!

Joe ran as if his life depended on it, which it did, but he knew Two Hearts felt the same way. His chest was filled with fire and little fireflies were swimming before his eyes. His temples throbbed and his head hurt badly from the drubbing he'd taken in the gauntlet run. The damned Two Hearts was fresh and rested up for such occasions. The son of a bitch was going to beat him to the top. Joe knew he was licked, but he kept on running. The bastards were going to hand him over, all worn out, to be toma-hawked by a grinning Two Hearts. By jimmies, he'd make the Shawnee rascal work for his little joke!

So Joe bulled on, out of breath and not bothering to try sucking fire into his tortured lungs. But then, as they got closer to the glow ahead, Joe saw he was gaining, and hope put steel into his wobbly legs.

Two Hearts sensed he was gaining too, and the Shawnee runner swerved in front of him to block him from passing. Joe gasped, "Want to play it that way, do you?" and, as he overtook Two Hearts, lashed out with his toe at a flying moccasin.

Two Hearts fell sprawling with a high-pitched gasp of dismay as Joe thundered on. The Indian was up in the instant and running even faster, but now Joe was out in front and the two trees he had to reach were outlined by the fire of Black Fish.

Two Hearts tried to trip Joe the same way, but the lighter ankle lost as it collided with Joe's heavier bones and hardly threw him off his stride. Joe was now blocking the Shawnee and he aimed to keep it that way if he didn't black out, dear Lord, for just a few more yards.

Two Hearts tried to grab Joe's shirttail to get past, but Joe was inches too far out front. He *was* blacking out. He felt he wasn't going to make it as the glow ahead faded in his vision. But then a tree flashed past on either side and Joe fell sprawling near the sagamore's fire. Astounded to be awake, but angry as hell.

He struggled to his feet, gasping for breath,

and when the tight-lipped Black Fish held out the handle of a tomahawk, Joe took it.

He turned, eyes narrowed with rage, as Two Hearts staggered into view and fell forward on hands and knees, sobbing for breath.

Then Joe saw Two Hearts clearly for the first time and muttered, "What in tarnation—?" He lowered the weapon to his side.

Two Hearts was a girl. A *white* girl! She was wearing the breech clout and leggings of a brave and her body was almost tan enough to be an Indian's, but her hair was sunbleached blonde.

As she recovered from the race she'd lost, Two Hearts raised her head to face the man who'd beaten her up the hill. Her face was calm and her brown eyes were defiant as she said in English, "Strike, Simon Kenton. I will not flinch."

Joe turned and said, "Black Fish, you must be crazy! I can't hit no lady with a tomahawk. Not even an Injun lady!"

Black Fish said, "She would have struck *you* had she won." And, looking down at Two Hearts, Joe decided he was likely right. The white girl's bare firm breasts still heaved with her efforts to recover her breath, but Joe saw she neither expected or extended mercy in those wide unwinking eyes watching him. Joe remembered the time he'd found a wolf in a trap back home. It had been waiting for some time with its forepaws caught in the steel teeth. And as he'd raised his musket to finish the poor brute, it had stared up at him the same way. Not understanding or expecting any favors from the man-thing about to finish it off.

Joe threw the tomahawk to the earth between them and muttered, "I don't hit gals. You folks do what you have to. I can't stop you all from killing me, but, by jimmies, I can die like a white man!"

Two Hearts took the tomahawk and got to her feet. She handed it to Black Fish and said, "If he doesn't have the courage, father, I put my life in *your* hands."

Black Fish didn't answer for a moment. He stared at Joe, his face like stone but his dark eyes warm and moist. The other Shawnee waited silently. Then Black Fish said, "Hear me! Simon Kenton has given me back my daughter's life. When a man gives a gift, it must be returned. Simon Kenton is now my son as long as he stays with us. If he tries to go back to Big Turtle, any who see him doing it should kill him. If he behaves, he is to be treated as your brother. Do we have to tie your hands again, Simon Kenton, or will you be a good boy?"

Joe frowned and said, "Well, I'm no renegade. So you can forget about me turning Tory. If I can get away, I will. But I'll give my word not to choke or punch anybody hereabouts, if that's what you mean."

"That is all I ask. I am not a fool, Simon Kenton. I know what is in your heart, and we are enemies outside my camp. Inside my camp, I adopt you as a brave son. You will eat with the people of my lodge. I have spoken."

Two Hearts smiled and held out a hand, saying, "Come, Big Brother. I will show you to my father's wigwam and we will eat together."

But before anyone could move a voice cried out, "Stop! What is the meaning of this?" Corn Burner stepped into the light. The sachem was oily with sweat and his paint was running. His amber eyes were filled with hate as he snapped, "We had to give up for the night. The moon is rising and Boone has some kind of medicine gun. It sounds different from the other muskets and every time it fires someone gets hurt. I have just lost four young men, yet I find my father smiling at a captive. The man is mine, and there are now many of our people to pay for."

Black Fish said, "Simon Kenton has run the gauntlet and lived. He has run a Death Race with Two Hearts and he gave me back my daughter's life. If you want to kill him, you must kill me first."

Corn Burner looked dismayed, but recovered quickly. He said, "Hear me. I am not afraid of any man. But I will not fight my own sagamore in the middle of a war with the Yankees. My father's words are not wise and I do not think he means them. I think he knows his son Corn Burner would not fight an old man he respects. The threat means nothing."

There was a murmur of agreement from some of the others. Then Running Wolf walked casually over to stand at the side of Black Fish. He smiled thinly at Corn Burner and said, "I will fight you in our sagamore's place, if his rank stands in the way of a good fight. I am only a pinesee. You would not be killing a leader if you killed me."

Then, staring quite pleasantly into Corn Burner's angry eyes, he asked mildly, "Do you think you could kill me, Corn Burner?"

"Do not be foolish. I would not kill any brother over a white man."

"Then we have spoken."

Corn Burner licked his lips. "What is this white man to you, Running Wolf?"

"An enemy. I do not care if he lives or dies. I offer merely to fight any man who fails to heed the wishes of our sagamore Black Fish. If Black Fish says to kill Simon Kenton, I will do it. As long as he wants the captive alive, I will fight any man who tries to kill him."

As the Indians glared at one another in the flickering firelight, Two Hearts took Joe's hand and murmured, "Come away with me, Big Brother. We will eat while they talk."

"Don't we have to wait until it's settled, Two Hearts?"

"No. Nothing is ever settled between Black Fish and Corn Burner. They will argue half the night. But my father has spoken, and while he lives his words will be obeyed. He told me to take you to his wigwam and feed you. That is where we must go and what I must do."

As the strange white girl led him down the line of campfires, she made short explanations to those few Indians curious enough to comment on a captive walking freely through their camp. None seemed inclined to challenge the odd situation.

Reaching the canvas wigwam. Two Hearts said, "Sit on the blanket in the opening. I will call for food and tobacco for you, Big Brother."

Joe sat gingerly on the Hudson Bay trade blanket as Two Hearts called over to a quartet of Shawnee by a nearby fire. Joe waited until one of them came over with a bowl of corn mush and a twist of jet-black trade tobacco before he asked the girl, "Are you a captive, like me?"

She shook her head and said, "No. I was once English. Now I am Shawnee. They didn't capture me. They rescued me from the Huron, when I was a white child of six or seven. The Huron were ordered to stop fighting for the French when that war was over, but the Huron are evil and there was much to steal at my father's trading post."

"Your folks were the Hudson Bay Company?"

"Yes. My parents came to trade for furs after the French gave Canada to England. We were living by the Great Waters when the Huron killed my parents and carried me away. Black Fish found out they had a little English girl in their village and sent word he would fight them if they didn't let me go. He said it was wrong to kill Englishmen. The Great White Sagamore in England was a friend of the Shawnee. The Huron sent me to him with gifts. Black Fish said I was his daughter. I have lived with the Shawnee ever since."

"But can't you see you're a white girl, Two Hearts? And what sort of a name is that for a girl? It sounds like some fool buck's name!"

"My people name each other for what they are or for their totem spirit. Black Fish is Black Fish because the Black Fish is the medicine of his clan and he is its leader. I am called Two Hearts because I have a heart that is red and a heart that is white. At first I cried for my mother. Then, as I learned to speak Shawnee, I saw they were my brothers."

"I see. What's your real name?"

"I told you. I am Two Hearts. When I was a white child it was either Joan or Jane. I don't remember. It was all so long ago."

"Haven't you ever tried to get away?"

"Why should I want to leave the people I love? You speak very strangely, Big Brother."

"Maybe. I've been getting hit on the head some lately. Are you saying you could just walk out of here any time you felt like it?"

"I could. But where would I go?"

"Hell, back to your own kind, of course!"

"You mean, the white people? I don't think I'd like that. I have met white women. I met some of the British officers' wives when we were in Canada. They were very silly women. They clucked at me like hens and said I should wear clothes like they had on. They said I should go to the funny big wigwam with the cross on the roof and learn to pray to some powah called Jesus."

"Well, I don't agree with many Tory notions, but I'll go along with them as far as the clothes. It's not seemly for a gal to expose her, uh, upper parts like that."

"Why? Don't you think my body is pretty? Many of the young men have said they liked the way I looked. More than one has asked me to be his squaw."

"Jesus, you didn't let no redskins trifle with you, I hope."

"I'm not sure what you mean, Big Brother. Running Wolf teases me and Corn Burner has asked for me to be his squaw. But I don't think I'd like to be the squaw of either. Running Wolf can't beat me in a race and Corn Burner is not nice."

"You mean you can't marry up with a man unless he can whup you at fool games?"

"I can marry anyone I choose, but a woman would like to think her man was stronger and better than she was. My real parents must have been big and strong. I can outwrestle most of the boys I know and beat them all in a foot race."

"Well, you came close to beating me tonight.

Would you have tomahawked me had you won?"

"Of course. Those are the rules of a Death Race."

"You mean you've done that sort of thing before?"

"Not a Death Race. It's very unusual for a woman to take part in warriors' games. I think my father must have wanted you beaten very badly and he knew I was the fastest runner in the Shawnee nation."

"That's for sure. I notice you're dressed like a pinesee instead of a squaw. How come? Are you some sort of Amazon?"

"I do not know what an Amazon is, Big Brother."

"A woman warrior. I never heard of Injuns having woman warriors, but I never expected a lot of notions they seem to have. I reckon your daddy wanted you to be a boy, huh?"

"Oh, Big Brother, you are so silly. We are on the warpath. When Shawnee girls follow warriors on the warpath they dress as men. It makes the enemy scouts think there are more men in the party. I suppose you white warriors never heard of that trick, eh?"

Joe glanced away and said, "Not hardly. How many of you fierce braves up here are really gals, Two Hearts?"

"Just a few dozen. No women who are carrying or tending children could follow their men from Chillicothe. If a squaw wants to come along she must be able to keep up."

"But you don't fight like men, right?"

"We fight if we have to. We are Shawnee."

"But you've never really kilt anybody, huh?"

"I can't count coup as a pinesee. I am a woman. But I have killed two Iroquois and a Huron. The Iroquois were raiding us. I shot them. The Huron was a captive. Black Fish told me I should light the fire, because the Huron owed me a blood debt for killing my parents."

"Jesus! You ever trade shots with white folks?"

"Not yet. This is the first time I have been on the warpath. How many men have you killed, Big Brother?"

Joe stared at the ground and muttered, "Only one. I don't count coup on it."

"I know what is in your heart. I still don't like the Huron, but I did not enjoy it when they let me burn one. The Huron died well and only screamed a few times at the end. But I couldn't help feeling his pain in my heart. Why are you not eating your food, Big Brother?"

"Not hungry, I reckon. I notice you're not packing a knife or tomahawk. Aren't you supposed to be guarding me, Two Hearts?"

"Guarding you? Nobody in this camp will attack you while you are under the protection of my father."

"I figured that. But you're supposed to be keeping an eye on me, right?"

"My father said I was to make you comfortable. But if you don't want to eat and don't want to smoke I can think of nothing else I can do for you. I don't lie with men yet. My father has not given me to anyone."

"Oh? I heard you Injuns or whatever lived sort of easy. I didn't know Shawnee were so, well, proper in their ways. They told me Captain Boone had a Shawnee squaw while he was with you all last winter."

Two Hearts grimaced and said, "That was Pretty Baskets. She is not very particular in such matters. I think you white people call women like Pretty Baskets whores."

"Then there are Shawnee whores?"

"Of course. Don't you white people have whores? Pretty Baskets lies with any man who gives her presents, or to entertain guests for my father. I told you I met white women in Canada. They asked the same questions. From what they told me of their customs, our women are the same as yours. Some are easy, some are not. Do you have a white squaw back at the fort, Big Brother?"

"Not exactly."

"My heart soars to hears this. You are safe in my father's camp and we won't kill anyone important to you when my father takes the fort."

"Those people in Boonesburough are my friends, Two Hearts."

"I understand, but it was your people's idea to have a war with us. Black Fish has always been a man of peace. The Shawnee are brave, but they never fight with nice people."

"Two Hearts, your fool Shawnee lit into us

the minute we came over the mountains! *Our* side wasn't looking for a fight."

"Then why did you come over the mountains? Did my father's people move their wigwams to the shores of the Great Bitter Water? Has any Shawnee gone to Virginia to say, 'Hear me, this land is mine and you must tear down all your homes to make room for our deer and buffalo?'"

"It's not the same thing, Two Hearts. This land out here was empty in the first place and we bought it off the Cherokee in the second."

She laughed and said, "Oh, Big Brother, you speak so foolishly about first places and second places. Big Turtle told us much the same joke when he was with us last winter."

"I don't see as it's all that humorous."

"Then you must be very foolish people. The land was not empty. *We* were here, since before the Grandfather Times. The Cherokee sold you hunting rights to lands they had no claim to. Even by your white man's laws this land was ours. My father and the other sagamores fought for the English against the French and the men in London said this land was ours forever. They still say it is ours forever. The English sachem, Hamilton, has given us many guns and white pinesee to help us hold what is ours by law. both red and white. It is the people in Boones-burough who are evil. They had no reason to come over the mountains. They had no reason to start killing us and driving us from the Great

Meadow. Why are the followers of Big Turtle so quarrelsome?"

Joe thought about what Meg had said about overgrown rough children. But he said, "We're Americans, fighting for our freedom from the English."

"I have heard these words. They make no sense to me. The Great White Sagamore in England has not taken any freedoms from the Shawnee. Have the redcoats fenced us off from any springs or salt licks? Do the English drive away our game? The Great White Sagamore in England says the Crown lands to the Mississippi shall be Indian forever. The Continental Congress says they belong to white Americans. Who is trying to take away our freedom, Big Brother?"

"Well, I've never heard things put that way. I don't know too much about the politics. I just want folks to leave me alone."

"Then you should stay with us and be a white Shawnee. You want the same thing we do. Perhaps when we get to know one another better we will decide to share the same blanket. You are pretty and the only man who can beat me at running. Our children would be strong as well as pretty."

Joe laughed and she asked what was so amusing. He shook his head and said, "Less than an hour ago you were fixing to brain me with a tomahawk. Now we're sitting here jawing about getting hitched. Things sure happen sudden hereabouts."

"I too am glad we are no longer enemies. Have none of the women in Boonesburough considered you as the father of their children?"

"Well, sort of. I reckon you're right about white and red gals not being all that different. When they're not fussing at a man, it seems all they can think about is getting him hitched up."

18

Joe spent a sleepless night. It would have been difficult for him to sleep in the wigwam of Black Fish even had he wanted to.

The wigwam was large enough for perhaps six people to have slept in without touching one another. But Black Fish was a most friendly man, and it was an honor to share the wigwam of a sagamore. Two Hearts had first shown Joe to a pallet near the canvas wall. Soon, however, friends and dependents of Black Fish's began to drift in, and Joe, though tired, willingly gave up the pallet to stretch out on a smoke-scented blanket. Then other people piled in on top of him. Many other people. Two Hearts was bedded down across the wigwam. A squaw Joe didn't know lay with her head across his waist. A brave who'd been drinking heavily sprawled across his legs.

After that the wigwam started getting crowded. Indian after Indian crept in to grunt a greeting and be greeted by all in return. The place was dark as well as stuffy. Joe couldn't tell if or when Black Fish himself came to bed. He heard sing-song Shawnee murmurs. A pair of moccasined feet were gently placed across his chest -as, somewhere in the crowd, an Indian began to softly sing himself to sleep. The song was atonal and monotonous to Joe's ears, but two more Shawnee liked it well enough to join in nasally and harmonize.

Joe considered trying to slip out and make a run for it. But even if he could have rolled out from under a half-dozen Indian bedmates, he could see the flickering orange lights from outside had neither dimmed or died out. Some Indians were clearly up outside tending the night fires, even if he felt as if he had the whole Shawnee nation in the wigwam with him. He doubted very much they hadn't been instructed to watch for sudden moves. He began to see how Boone's odd story of his own captivity was probably truer than Dan'l's detractors allowed. Since Black Fish's mood toward him had changed, with almost childlike suddenness, the Shawnee hadn't made a single obvious move to place him under guard. Yet he was as securely held as if he wore leg irons. By now a fool would have made a break for it, and probably died before he reached the edge of the camp. Like Boone, Joe would have to wait for a chance, knowing one chance and only one was all he was likely to get.

It had taken Boone four months to escape, and Boone had been at this game before Joe was born. It hardly seemed he was going to get away the first night. So Joe gave up. He didn't remember sleeping, only twisting away from under Indians. But he must have slept because, despite the discomfort, the night passed quickly and the wigwam was almost empty when Two Hearts called him out to breakfast.

Joe joined her at the nearest fire. She sat with Red Club, De Quindre and two of the British agents with the Indian forces. As Two Hearts fed him succotash with jerked venison, De Quindre smiled at Joe and said, "Your Captain Boone is a very impressive marksman. What is that medicine gun he's using, a German rifle?"

Joe nodded as he chewed his food. If the Shawnee wanted to credit the legendary Big Turtle with Wolfgang's Hessian training, he saw no reason to disabuse them.

"We were wondering about your water supplies, M'sieu Kenton. At the moment Black Fish is not inclined to allow your women to draw water from the river."

"I know. They'll likely have to put off washing 'til you rascals give it up. Our well water's hard as hell."

"Ah, yes. I have noticed there is a lot of lime in the local soil. How deep is the water table under the fort, M'sieu Kenton?"

"What's it to you? You're not likely to be drawing water from our well in Boonesburough, unless you're fixing to surrender."

"Now, M'sieu, is that any way to talk? I only wish to make harmless conversation and you behave like a suspicious boor."

"I don't know what a boor might be. But I suspicion you, all right. If you aim to tunnel a sap under the walls from the shelter of the river bank, you can find out where the water level is for your ownself."

"Now, did I say anything about a sapping operation, M'sieu Kenton? These people are, well, not the sort one would consider military engineers."

"That's why Hair-Buying Hamilton sent you to show 'em how it's done, De Quindre. There's plenty of timber for props, and that spot near the river you picked for your first sly trick is where you figure to start your tunnel, isn't it?"

"*Merde* you are so melodramatic. It would take days to run a sap that far. As we speak, Corn Burner prepares his final assault. Your fort will be in our hands by noon, I'll wager."

"Put your money where your mouth is. I got two shillings and eight pence in silver and ten dollars Continental in my pocket. I'll bet you even money that you and Corn Burner are full of shit. You got plenty of time for a sap tunnel, Frenchy. You won't take us by frontal assault in a month of Sundays."

"We shall see. Meanwhile, would you like to share our provisions, M'sieu Kenton? We whites have British Army stores. Brandy and real Virginia tobacco."

"I'm happy enough with succotash and trade tobacco. Two Hearts here doesn't ask me for treasonous answers to fool questions when she feeds me."

One of the Englishmen muttered, "Why are we fencing words with this lout, De Quindre? I could get the information you want from him in five minutes, given a free hand."

"Ah, but we do not have a free hand, M'sieu le Capitaine. Our little red brothers have for some reason made another of their pets of the great Simon Kenton. The Princess Two Hearts may mention your crude threats to her foster father as it is, so may I suggest a more civil tongue when you speak of our uncouth fellow white man?"

The Englishman shrugged and muttered, "Lot of bloody rot. Ridiculous way for gentlemen to make war, what?"

"I quite agree, M'Sieu le Capitaine, but, alas, neither our hosts nor Boone are gentlemen."

Joe frowned and snapped, "I reckon Boone and the other men you tried to take under a parley flag could teach the British Army a thing or two about honor, De Quindre. It wasn't us who broke our words!"

De Quindre looked pained and protested, "That is not just, M'sieu! I understand your dismay at the way you were captured. None of His Majesty's officers were present at that unseemly brawl."

Joe turned to Two Hearts and asked, "Are you

taking this all in, honey? The man just said your pa wasn't a British officer like Brant, after all."

Two Hearts said, "I do not understand. If the Mohawk Brant is an officer, my father Black Fish is an officer."

De Quindre bowed his head gracefully and said, "But of course, Princess Two Hearts. I assure you I consider Brant and Black Fish to be of equal rank and esteem to the British Army."

Joe said, "He means they're both savages the English can use."

De Quindre smiled pleasantly and said, "My, but I would like to turn you over to le Capitaine Moore's tender mercies. You are a very annoying young man. I can see why you are Boone's second in command. But your waste your powers of persuasion, Simon Kenton. Boone had four months to subvert these people to the Rebel cause. As you see, he was no better at it than yourself."

As if to lend truth to his words, the crackle of small arms drifted to them from the distance. De Quindre cocked his head and said, "Ah, I do believe the battle is joined again at your fort."

The sardonic Frenchman rose and nodded to his fellow officers, asking, "Shall we observe the morning festivities, my friends?"

As the others followed De Quindre away, Two Hearts asked Joe, "Would you like to watch the battle, Big Brother?"

"Are you sure your folks won't mind?"

"Why should they? Come. We will walk to

the tree line together and I will speak to anyone who asks what you are doing among us."

As they got up she took his hand and led him through the wigwams under the sycamores to the edge of the ridge. From there they had a clear view down the slope to Boonesburough.

Joe's heart sank as he gazed down across the river valley. The fort seemed even smaller and more pathetic than when he'd first glimpsed it from up here, so long ago, it seemed. His bird's-eye view gave him a perspective the defenders couldn't have. The Indians moving from one clump of cover to another had their backs to Joe and were more visible to him than to the men at the loopholes of Boonesburough. But none were close enough for a safe final rush. A distant figure in Cherokee costume rose from a clump of tattered corn stalks and a cotton-blossom of gunsmoke from the nearest blockhouse made him drop for cover. A Mingo made a rush from a fence row to a tree stump. Though he made it, Joe saw the gouts of dust chasing him to cover and knew the Mingo was pinned down as close as he was going to get in daylight.

But Joe wasn't sanguine about the battle's outcome. Boone's men were shooting fast and shooting well, but there were many Indians down there and thirty guns shooting four rounds a minute added up only to a hundred and twenty bullets in the time it would take four hundred men to run a quarter mile. If all of the Indians rushed at once, the battle would be quickly over. Joe felt the settlers' only hope lay in any Indian's reluctance to be one of the first hundred or so who'd go down in any all-out charge.

A man in buckskins with the royal cockade pinned to his felt hat joined Joe and Two Hearts as they watched the skirmishing below. He was white and spoke English as he observed mildly, "Regulars would simply be over the wall with butt stock and bayonet by now. I doubt if your fort will fall today, Mister Kenton."

Then he lit a pipe and added, quietly, "By the way, you must have relatives on the other side of the gap, Mister Kenton. I spoke with a lad named Joe Floyd who looked a lot like you not too long ago."

Joe tried to keep his face blank as he shrugged and said, "Well, it was a good try. I see you got back to your family in Connecticut, Mister Marvin."

The British officer chuckled and replied, "I made it to Canada, thanks to Quaker hospitality. I trust your father and charming stepmother are well, uh, Mister Kenton?"

"My father died, of a fever. Margaret is down there in the fort. I reckon by now you've told De Quindre who I really am, huh?"

"Aren't you Simon Kenton, the famous scout?"

"I'd like to think so. What's your game, Marvin or whomsoever?"

The spy smiled and said, "I really am Lieutenant Cyrus Marvin, albeit my home is Great Bentley, Essex, rather than Connecticut. You see, it saves guarding against a slip if an agent on His Majesty's business uses his real name whenever possible. Fortunately, there are a lot of Connecticut Yankees named Marvin. They're doubtless distant cousins of mine. There seem to be dozens of Marvins between Old Lyme and Hartford. You probably have some Kentons on your mother's side, eh?"

Two Hearts didn't seem interested in their odd conversation. She tugged at Joe and said, "Oh, look, they're bringing Red Club up the hill. I think he's wounded."

Both white men looked down at the two Shawnee dragging a third up the slope between them. But Joe said, "I asked what game you're playing, Marvin. You just allowed you know who I am."

Marvin said, "Let's say I'm playing a waiting game, uh, Kenton. You probably know there's been some discussion back in London about the way Lord North has been putting down your rebellion. I'm here more as an observer than a fighting man."

"You mean you're spying for the opposition party in Parliament?"

"Loyal opposition, young sir. I owe you my life. But don't expect me to pay you back by treason to my king."

"You mean, if I were to make a break for it, you'd try and stop me."

It was a statement, not a question. Marvin nodded and said, "Yes. On the other hand, I see no need to pull the Tory party's chestnuts from the fire for them. My Whig friends are not too pleased by the way things have been handled over here. Should this distressing Indian policy prove to be the fiasco my friends predicted . . . Well, Lord North won the last vote of confidence, but that was before Saratoga."

"In other words, if folks on our side make a horse's neck out of Governor Hamilton, your party stands to win the next election over in England?"

"Another frontier disaster can hardly help Lord North and his party. You and I have a rather interesting situation here, don't we?"

"Hell, if you want these rascals to lose, just help me to get back to Boone and watch my smoke."

"I can't do that and you know it. You're in no danger at the moment, even if you feel I owe you for past favors."

"But you said you wanted De Quindre and Hamilton to lose."

"I said nothing of the kind. I said my faction thinks they're wrong and that we're expecting them to fail. I have no intention of doing a thing to make them fail. That would be against my code."

"But you don't aim to bust a gut making sure they win, eh?"

"Ah, now you're starting to grasp my position. May I offer you some suggestions you may feel advantageous to both of us, Mister, uh, Kenton?"

"Keep talking."

"I'm not sure just why you've decided to be Simon Kenton, but since De Quindre seems to know all the answers, I see no need to suggest he may have confused you with somebody else. You seem to have made some other friends on this side. If I were you, I'd stay here and work on that. If you make a break for it, and I know of it, I'll be as honor bound as any other British officer to stop you. Working together, we might persuade the Indians this nonsense is neither in their best interests, the king's best interests, nor, of course, the interests of your rebel friends. Do you follow me?"

"Not hardly. If you're a Loyalist, I can't see what you have to gain by our side winning."

Two Hearts was moving down the slope away from them now, to join the Shawnee bringing in the wounded warrior. Marvin took advantage of their moment of privacy to say, "Listen, Joe. This is a rotten mess for the Crown and your friends alike! That damned little fort means nothing in a strategic sense. When the Shawnee overrun it, we'll just add grist to Franklin's propaganda mill with another sordid frontier massacre!"

"Maybe. I don't see them running up the white flag down yonder just yet."

"True, Joe. You won't believe me, but I honestly hope the fort holds out until Black Fish gives up. A victory by Royalist Indians will make Lord North look good in Parliament. On the other hand, a clear-cut Yankee victory would not be in England's interest."

"Hell, it's got to turn out one way or the other, Lieutenant Marvin."

"No it doesn't, Joe. I'd like to be able to report a stalemate to my friends in Parliament. We Whigs don't want the Tories to win and we don't want the Rebels to win. We want this mucking war to drag on, undecided, until the king is forced to hold new elections."

"I see. Then after your party wins, you figure to kick the shit out of us and smell like roses to King George, right?"

"The Whigs will offer your Congress a just peace. We'll forgive a few incidents like Saratoga and the French Alliance and the thirteen colonies can go back to being properly run, as well as British."

"I'm not sure I like the last part. But I'd like to see the last of these fool Injuns. What's our play?"

"Stay a friend to Black Fish and that white daughter of his. She likes you, I can tell. De Quindre says you've been working at it already and he's peeved as the devil. Stay friendly with Two Hearts. If you can, make love to her. Whatever you do, don't make a break for it and don't let Corn Burner's faction get you alone."

They saw the girl approaching with the wounded Indian and Marvin said, "We'll talk about it some more later."

Two Hearts and the unharmed Shawnee carried the wounded man into the tree line and Joe saw it was Red Club under all that paint and blood. They lowered him to the grass and Joe went over to see what he could do. There wasn't much. Red Club had taken a ball under the floating ribs and was breathing unnaturally. Two Hearts knelt beside the wounded Shawnee as Red Club looked up at Joe and sighed, "Heya, that medicine gun of Big Turtle's is good!"

Two Hearts asked, "Do you know any white medicine, Big Brother? Our friend is bleeding badly."

Joe knelt by her but shook his head silently, not knowing what to say. He sort of liked Red Club, but he liked Wolfgang too. It sure *confused* a man at times like these!

Red Club stared up, through and beyond Joe and Two Hearts. Softly, he said, "I told them they were risking their lives for a dead man. These two pinesee don't speak English, but I have told them what is in my heart. Will you tell your father how brave they were, Two Hearts?"

The girl murmured to the two youths in Shawnee before reverting to English to say, "I will back their coups at the council fire, Red Club. They did well. You did well. My big white brother knows this to be true too."

Red Club smiled up at Joe and said, "I am proud to die well before an enemy. Did you see me, Simon Kenton? I got closer than anyone to your fort before Big Turtle shot me with his medicine gun."

Joe said, "I saw you, Red Club. You're a hell of a fighting man."

"I am that. The others took cover when Big Turtle started putting his balls close. I kept going, singing my death song, to the end. I think when Big Turtle saw these other brave ones coming to carry me away he held his fire. Will you thank him for me if you ever meet him again?"

"I sure will, Red Club. But don't you folks have a medicine man or such to fix you up?"

"No. Our medicine is no good against Big Turtle's. I am dying. But hear me, I count coup! No ordinary man could kill me. I am Red Club. I am a wonderful fighter. It took Big Turtle himself to kill a man as great as I am!"

Then he frowned and said, "I see a cloud in your eyes, Simon Kenton. It *was* the mighty white man, Big Turtle, wasn't it?"

"Of course it was, Red Club. Nobody else in the world shoots like Captain Boone."

"I know. I want my people in Chillicothe to know this when they keen the mourning tunes for me. Tell them to remember I was mighty. Tell them I was killed by Big Turtle, greatest of the Yankee long-hunters. I have spoken."

Joe saw other Indians moving back up the slope. Feeling less worried now about his friends below, he suggested, "Shouldn't we carry Red

Club into camp and make him comfortable, Two Hearts?"

The girl shook her head and said, "If he dies in a wigwam they will have to burn it. I think he is almost dead already."

Joe stared soberly down at the man in the grass and nodded. Red Club was still breathing, but his eyes were closed and his face was too relaxed for a man with a bullet in his side if he could still feel it.

Joe looked around for Marvin, but the spy had slipped away as other Shawnee approached from every side to stare morosely down at the dying Red Club. None of them were looking at Joe, but the youth felt very white all of a sudden.

Black Fish came out of the trees with Corn Burner and De Quindre. Two Hearts looked up at her foster father and said, "He's stopped breathing. Big Turtle shot him. These two, Crow Foot and Grey Stick, took him from under the guns of the fort."

Black Fish nodded at the young Shawnee and complimented them in their own language. But Corn Burner glared at Joe and spat, "They have killed one of your young men and I find your daughter Two Hearts with Boone's second in command, Simon Kenton."

Black Fish shrugged and said, "I am tired of my brother's words. They buzz in my ear like a fly and say nothing I have not heard before. Red Club was not shot by Simon Kenton. It was the medicine gun of Big Turtle."

"Yes, and we have Boone's friend here to pay back the spirit of Red Club in blood."

Two Hearts got up to stand between Joe and Corn Burner and began a tirade in Shawnee. But Joe drew her back and took a step toward Corn Burner as he said, "You talk a lot for a man I didn't notice within musket range of the fort. If you're so anxious for a set-to with a white man, I'm ready any time you are."

Joe turned to Black Fish and added, "How about it, chief? I'll give him a fair crack at all the blood he wants if you'll let us have it out right here and now."

Black Fish said, "No. There is fight enough for everyone down the hill. You will not hurt Corn Burner. Corn Burner will not hurt you. I have spoken."

De Quindre caught Joe's eye and murmured, "Good try, Yankee. But perhaps a little obvious, no?"

"While I'm on the subject, Frenchy, I'll fight you too, any time you have a mind to."

"My, we are most testy, are we not? Your dramatics are no doubt meant to impress Princess Two Hearts. They fail to impress me. We both know our prowess can't be put to the test at the moment. Save your swaggering boasts for the tavern wenches, if you ever live to see any."

"Some other time, then?"

"But of course, my young friend. I would be most amused to have it out with you, under more serious conditions."

Corn Burner had been following the sinister Frenchman's byplay. He was more sophisticated than the simple Black Fish or the innocent Two Hearts. He stuck out his chest and shouted, "Hear me! I accept the white captive's challenge! I think Black Fish should let us fight with tomahawks!"

Black Fish ignored him and began to instruct the Indians in Shawnee about the disposal of Red Club's body. But Corn Burner was dancing in a little circle, shouting threats and taunts at Joe. The watching Indians seemed most impressed, so he repeated them, loudly, in Shawnee.

De Quindre muttered, "*Merde,* I am surrounded by children," and strode off to plot further destruction with his Tory companions.

Black Fish told his foster daughter, "Take your new white brother to my wigwam and see to his comfort, Two Hearts. I am very busy. We must attack again, and this time my young men must be properly led."

Two Hearts said, "If my father is leading the charge down the hill I wish to watch. If he is wounded by the medicine gun I will come to him."

Black Fish slapped his own brow and roared, "Hear me! I am weary of giving commands nobody seems to obey! Corn Burner, you are acting like a papoose! Stop that dancing and gather some young men who are not afraid to die. Two Hearts will take Simon Kenton where I said to take him and she will keep him there. I do not want a white man watching our movements as we attack again."

"But my father, if you are hurt . . ."

"If I am shot by Big Turtle it will pain my heart less than a disobedient child! Go!"

Two Hearts sighed and led Joe away. They'd not gone far when they met the black, Pompey, carrying a rifle. The long gun was decorated with brass tacks and squirrel tails. Pompey said, "Howdy, Miss Two Hearts. The powah just blessed this English rifle for your daddy. Now he got a medicine gun too!"

The girl said, "Show it to my new brother. I want him to tell me if it is good."

"Miss Two Hearts, he's a captive, no offense, and this here gun is loaded!"

"I said to show it to him. I do not think he will shoot us. He knows about the medicine gun of Big Turtle. I want him to tell us if this one is as good."

The Negro handed the weapon gingerly to Joe, who hefted it and said, "Hessian. I don't know what good the tacks and tails do, but it should put its ball in a deer's eye at a hundred yards if you aim it right."

He checked the flint and priming, wondering if there was some way to make sure it never fired. He asked the black, "Where's the ramrod?" Then he saw the slender length of steel projecting from the muzzle and marveled, "Jesus! Who loaded this fool piece, Pompey?"

The ex-slave seemed sincerely puzzled as he answered, "Corn Burner. The English gave it to him in Detroit. He said a mighty sagamore deserved a mighty gun."

Joe pulled at the ramrod and grunted, "It's jammed solid. It's been hammered into the lead, likely with a double charge."

He turned to Two Hearts and said, "This isn't my business, gal, but the sachem's trying to murder your daddy."

"Murder? I don't understand!"

"You see, you folks are used to trade muskets. You can fire damn near anything out a musket barrel. But this present is a bomb, not a gun! If Black Fish puts it to his cheek and pulls the trigger, he'll blow his own fool head off!"

"You mean the medicine gun is no good?"

"Oh, it's a fine fancy rifle, but it's bore-packed with solid steel. Corn Burner knows he can't kill your father man to man. But he'd be sagamore if Black Fish blew his own brains out."

"I don't believe you. You are trying to make me have a bad heart toward Corn Burner. You know I am not fond of him, but I can't believe he is my father's enemy."

Joe said, "Let's find out." Still holding the rifle, he turned and retraced his steps to where the Indians were lining up for another charge down the hill.

Corn Burner saw him first and cried out, "Look, Black Fish! Your daughter has armed the captive! I told you her white blood would tell in the end!"

Black Fish scowled, but as a warrior raised his own musket he snapped a command in Shawnee. Then, speaking English, he said, "What is the meaning of this, my daughter?"

Before Two Hearts could answer, Joe swung the rifle butt-first and held it out to Corn Burner, saying, "I aim to shoot nobody, Black Fish. Pompey here just showed me the medicine gun your sachem gave you. I purely admire the way they loaded it for you."

Mollified, Black Fish said, "Yes, it is a fine rifle. Give it to me."

Joe shook his head and said, "Just bear with me a minute, chief. Before you rush down there against the fort with it, I'd like to have Corn Burner show us how good it shoots."

Corn Burner said, "I have given the weapon to my sagamore. Black Fish should shoot at Boone with it."

"I said I only wanted a minute. You just got through saying you weren't all that fond of me, old son. Why don't you show these folks how good a gun it is by shooting me with it?"

Black Fish frowned and asked, "Has my daughter's new white brother been drinking? I told Corn Burner he was not to kill you."

"I know, but I don't mind. I'll just stand here and give him a free shot at me to show him there's no hard feelings."

Joe shoved the butt stock at Corn Burner, who

backed away from it as if it were red hot. Joe grinned and insisted, "Come on, Corn Burner, show us all how mean and brave you are. Shoot a white man for luck before you charge my friends down yonder."

Corn Burner shook his head and said something in Shawnee.

Two Hearts told her foster father, "My white brother says the gun is no good. He says it will kill the man who fires it instead of his enemies."

Corn Burner shook his head again and protested, "He lies! If the gun is as he says, it would have killed me by now. I have fired it many times since I took it from the English in Detroit."

Joe said, "Why don't you prove it, then? I'll stand right here and you just fire at me. If I'm not telling the truth, I'll be dead as a turd in a milk bucket. What have you to lose?"

Pompey was translating the exchange for the Indians watching. Joe didn't understand Shawnee, but he knew some of the suggestions from the onlookers were backing Corn Burner into a box.

Black Fish nodded gravely and said, "I think you should shoot him, Corn Burner. I gave him back his life last night, but if he is not telling the truth he deserves to die."

Corn Burner suddenly snatched the gun. But he didn't point it at Joe. He held it over his head and shouted, "Hear me, we waste time with this foolish talk! If my father does not want the gun, I will lead the attack with it."

And then, before anyone could object, the sachem broke cover and was running down the slope, chanting his death song.

Black Fish snapped, "Wait for me at my wigwam," and turned to follow, with others in his wake whooping cheerfully.

Two Hearts took Joe's hand again and led him away before he could see how the attack was going, though he heard the crackle of musketry from both sides as they reached the quiet clearing by her wigwam.

They sat by the entrance. Two Hearts was very quiet and didn't look up when Running Wolf and Pompey joined them. Joe noticed both men carried muskets as well as tomahawks. He nodded and said, "I noticed no more than fifty or so followed Black Fish and Corn Burner. You really need so many here to guard me?"

Running Wolf said, "We attack in turns, so they get no rest in the fort. Pompey has told me what you said of the rifle Corn Burner wanted to give Black Fish. If I ever have to kill you, you will feel no pain. Black Fish is my friend."

"Do you boys understand what Corn Burner's plan was?"

Pompey said, with a gesture of impatience, "Ever'body knows Corn Burner desires to be sagamore."

"You're closer to him than me, Pompey. Can't you explain it to him?"

"I done that a dozen times. Black Fish don't believe it. Maybe he don't want to believe it.

You likely noticed he's a trusting cuss. Injuns don't lie as much as black and white folks does. He ain't used to folks like Corn Burner. He figures they's on the same side."

Running Wolfe nodded and said, "This black Shawnee is wrong about my people, but he is right about Black Fish. Some of our people lie as much as any white man. Black Fish has too good a heart to understand this."

Two Hearts looked up, her eyes as puzzled as they were hurt, to exclaim, "I am said to have two hearts and neither understands. Why would Corn Burner want to be sagamore? He is not as old and wise as my father."

Pompey said, "He thinks he knows where the honey-tree grows. But old Corn Burner ain't the danger. Not by his ownself. Running Wolf here could likely lick him, and if he can't, I can. I'm a mean nigger when folks tries to blow my friends up!"

Two Hearts nodded and said, "I know you both have counted coup. Why can't one of you fight Corn Burner if you think he's bad?"

Pompey explained, "We don't think he's bad. We *know* he's bad. If you can't see it, you just ain't been brought up right. But Corn Burner won't fight any of us, and he ain't alone. There's Standing Elk and Blue Dog to back him and both of them is mean. But it ain't even the pinesee running with Corn Burner we got to worry about, Miss Two Hearts. It's the powah faction."

Joe frowned and asked, "You mean the medicine men are down on Black Fish?"

Pompey nodded. "They don't like his new notions. Black Fish is trying to be some sort of British officer, like the Mohawk, Brant. He keeps carrying prisoners alive to the redcoats in Detroit and talking 'bout treaties, land-title deeds and such. Up in Chillicothe, him and some others who think his way is starting to build cabins and live half white, like the Cherokee. The powahs don't cotton to the notion of learning new ways. They liked it better before there was any white folks hereabouts, be they rebel or redcoat. They figures Corn Burner is their sort of Injun."

"Can't they see he's a fool with a yellow streak to go with his mean one?"

"I 'spect they does. They likely reckon they can control him with spirit talk. You know how you gets to be a powah? You lives long. Most Shawnee die young, unless they're special good at fighting. Most old Shawnee got that way same as how Corn Burner figures to. By talking a good fight, taking safe hair but not taking many real risks. By the time a man is oldest in his band, the others starts to figure he knows something or has good medicine."

Running Wolf leaned forward to murmur, "Black Fish comes. We will talk more of these matters later."

The older Indian joined them at the wigwam, his shirt damp and his paint running. He flopped down and grunted, "Another of my young men got hurt. I'm getting very cross with Big Turtle."

Joe asked, "Have you given up for now?" The sagamore shook his head. He said, "Standing Elk is leading another skirmish line. We will keep them busy down there until Big Turtle gives up the fort."

Two Hearts asked if he was hungry. Black Fish shook his head and said, "No, but fill my calumet and I will smoke as I think of a better way. It was safe once to stay just at musket range, then rush in when they were reloading. That Big Turtle has more than one medicine gun. They shoot very far and it is dangerous to taunt a man with a gun like that." He looked at Joe and asked, "How many of those new guns do they have in the fort, my son?"

Joe said, "Not more than twenty or so. Have they fired the cannon yet? I didn't hear it."

"De Quindre says they have no cannon."

"He does, huh? I notice he stays up here in the trees while he's handing out advice. How did Corn Burner make out with that rifle he aimed to give you, Black Fish?"

"Corn Burner is eating at his wigwam. I still do not understand what you were saying before. Corn Burner fired the gun more than once. He hid behind standing corn and shot it at the fort. He says he thinks he hit some of your people."

Joe snorted. "He likely had a time pulling that ramrod out of whatever was holding it in the barrel."

Two Hearts said, "Explain about the way those guns blow up." But Joe shook his head and said, "I'd do better jawing with a tree. Is it all right with you folks if I go over to have a talk with the white man, De Quindre?"

Black Fish nodded and said, "Have you decided to help him take the fort, after all?"

Joe got to his feet, saying, "Well, I got some information he might find interesting."

De Quindre and the other white Tories had an improvised table set up by a pair of British Army tents in another part of the sprawling camp on the ridge. Running Wolf and another Shawnee had followed Joe politely, doubtless to keep him from getting lost, but he was beginning to grasp the layout of the camp. When he made a break for it, he'd have to head northeast. The wigwams and cooking fires tended to thin out in that direction.

De Quindre and the mysterious spy, Marvin, were having a snack at the table and asked Joe to join them. He sat across from them, but ignored the commissary biscuits and trade whiskey on the table but accepted a cigar. He lit up, leaned forward, and told the officers, "I'm not on your side about most things, but there's something you ought to know. Corn Burner is after the sagamore's job. He just tried to kill Black Fish. He'll likely try again."

De Quindre shrugged and asked, "What is that to me and mine, m'sieu? The internal bickerings of the Shawnee are of no concern to His Majesty."

"That's likely why he's losing this war. Old German George paid no attention when the first Continental Congress was just sending friendly letters about his fool governors on this side of the water."

Marvin asked, "What is your point, Kenton? We know about the rivalry between the various Indian factions. I believe it's called divide and rule."

"You'll have yourselves a time ruling Shawnee led by men like Corn Burner," Joe said. "He's dumb as well as mean. Black Fish think he's a Tory officer of King George. Corn Burner's just out to lift white scalps."

De Quindre sniffed and said, "And you, no doubt, have come to us out of the goodness of your heart and loyalty to your king?"

"No. I come over here to talk sense to you. I figure to live no more than two minutes longer than Black Fish if Corn Burner's faction takes over hereabouts."

"True, but that is your problem, *non?*"

"Just the part about my own scalp. You other white boys are a long hard walk from Canada, and they'll have your powder, jam and whisky as well as some easy hair to lift."

"*Merde!* What you suggest is ridiculous. I

have no fear of Corn Burner turning on us. He knows, how you say, which side his bread is buttered on?"

"You might be right. He and the old powahs might go on fighting for the king as long as they get paid for it. But at best, they'll be downright pesky to control. Black Fish takes you at face value, being a trusting jasper. Corn Burner will want to fight his own way. Like those other Injuns fought for Burgoyne, near Saratoga."

"Perhaps. But again I ask what concern this may be to me? We did not come down here to make life pleasant for you Yankee rebels. What do we care if perhaps the fighting is a bit more brutal?"

Joe shook his head wearily and said, "With friends like you, poor German George sure don't need enemies. I thought you boys were out to win this war against us."

"We shall win, have no fear of that."

"You're sure going about it backwards, De Quindre. I'm going to tell you something Captain Boone would likely say I was wrong to tell the enemy. I might be committing treason, but, Jesus, you Tories can't seem to figure nothing for yourselves."

Lieutenant Marvin's voice was quiet and bemused as he nodded at Joe and asked, "Just what is it we don't know, Kenton?"

"What you're doing here. Kentucky isn't a state. Boone's folks aren't real American militia 'cause the Continental Congress isn't sure where Kentucky is and likely don't care."

"We know that. Boone is bluffing about Virginia sending troops to help."

"You mean he thinks he's bluffing and you think he's bluffing. Last year Burgoyne marched through the Green Mountain country, where half the folks or more were Tory and most didn't give a damn one way or t'other. Then Burgoyne's Injuns got out of control and started killing any white folks they met up with."

"We know the unfortunate results of Burgoyne's march. Make your point."

"My point is that you fool Tories have done it again. Those folks down the hill never came out here to join the Continental Army. Hell, Boone's own wife comes from a Tory family."

"I see. You're trying to tell us we're turning less than enthusiastic rebels into Patriots, eh?"

"Trying to tell you, hell. You've *done* it! Boone was ready to lower the Stars and Stripes and keep Kentucky neutral. Now he's blistering mad at you."

De Quindre conceded, "The breakdown of negotiations was unfortunate. But we shall reduce your pathetic little fort in any case, so . . ."

"I'm not finished. You might take Boonesburough, you might not. The mistake you're about to make is more important to your side. You say it doesn't matter whether Black Fish or Corn Burner leads the Shawnee and I say you're a fool. Black Fish aims to take my friends alive to turn over to Governor Hamilton. Corn Burner will kill every man, woman, child, and likely the cats and dogs."

"It was Boone's idea to resist.."

Joe kept shaking his head from side to side. "You *can't* be that dumb! What do you reckon Carolina and Virginia will do when they hear about white women and children getting butchered by Injuns out here beyond the gap? Right now you have a private little war. Let Corn Burner take over and you'll have Campbell's militia boiling through the gap before you can spit!"

Marvin looked at De Quindre and said mildly, "He has a point, you know."

De Quindra shrugged and said, "Perhaps. But what do you suggest? I hardly feel it would be wise to step between two fighting Shawnee."

Marvin turned to Joe and asked, "If you could get back to Boone, do you think he'd resume negotiations? Black Fish was quite sincere at the last parley. We still don't know just how its unfortunate conclusion occurred."

Joe said, "The men down there will never come out unarmed for another powwow. But they'd likely lower the flag and toss a fool paper out to you if I could tell them you were fixing to march off and leave them be."

Marvin said a few words in French to De Quindre. The Frenchman nodded and replied, "I have no objections to letting M'sieu Kenton try. He is only a complication for us here in the Shawnee camp. But the matter is not up to us. He is a captive of Black Fish. Only the sagamore can set him free."

Joe said, "I'll see what I can do to get my ownself loose. If I can't talk Black Fish into it, there are other ways to get back to the fort. What sort of deal are you boys offering Boone?"

De Quindre said, "The fort must be disarmed and neutralized, as I said before. I am not concerned with what happens to the inhabitants."

Marvin said, "Meanwhile, we'll work to strengthen the hand of Black Fish and discredit Corn Burner and the conservatives. I suggest you don't attempt to make a break for freedom if you have difficulty talking Black Fish into letting you go. Wait a day or so. He's inclined to change his mind rather unpredictably."

"I'll worry about his fickle notions. You boys see if you can keep him alive. We'll all be in a fix if Corn Burner winds up in command!"

19

Joe waited until evening to broach the subject to the sagamore. The day's skirmishes had ended indecisively, with no serious losses to either side. Joe waited until Black Fish had eaten and smoked a pipe, hoping he'd be in a good mood.

He wasn't. Joe sat with him and Two Hearts as the sun sank in the west and tried to explain his plan. But the sagamore's face remained stony. "Big Turtle must be taught a good lesson," he said. "He has made me look weak. He has made me look foolish. Red Club is dead. Other young men have been hurt. Blood must be paid for in blood. I have spoken."

Joe tried once more. "Black Fish, I can put an end to the fighting if you let me go. Maybe some of the men in the fort have been hurt. Didn't Corn Burner say he'd shot a couple this afternoon?"

"I said I had spoken, Simon Kenton. I am very cross with Big Turtle. I am very cross with Corn Burner. Do not make me cross with you!"

Joe stared into the coals of the fire for a time

before he asked, "Have you figured out what Corn Burner was trying to do with that medicine gun he loaded up so nice for you?"

"I think you lied about that gun. He shot it and it did not hurt him."

"But you said you were cross with him."

"He taunted me. I said it was time to halt the attack for now. Corn Burner said he thought we should fight on. I think many of the others agreed with him. They think I do not know how to lead men."

"Why didn't you tell Corn Burner he could lead all the attacks he wanted to, if he figured he could do it better? That would have taken the wind out of his sails."

"All of you young men talk foolish. I am saga-more. As long as I draw breath, nobody shall lead but I."

"But don't you see how Corn Burner's using that against you, Black Fish? *I* could promise to take the fort, bare-handed, if I knew nobody would let me try!"

Two Hearts nodded and said, "I understand my new brother's words, my father. I think you should fight Corn Burner if he says bad things about you."

The sagamore snorted and said, "You are a woman. You do not understand the ways of men. My people follow me because I am a father to them. What father fights his own son?"

Two Hearts said, "What son says bad things

about his father? If I spoke out against you, would I not be punished?"

The Indian's eye were fondly and sincerely puzzled as he looked at her and asked, "What are you saying, little Two Hearts? Have I ever punished you? I have heard the white men beat their children. They are very cruel people. But when was Two Hearts beaten by any Shawnee?"

"Never, my father. But I have always been respectful. Corn Burner is not a good son. He has a bad heart."

"He is young," sighed the sagamore, adding, "Perhaps in time he will learn to be good. Meanwhile, I am still sagamore, and when we take the fort the others will see I know what I am doing."

Black Fish tapped out his calumet and said, "I am tired. I think I will feel better after a good night's sleep. Corn Burner too will feel better after he has rested. Are you children coming to sleep with me?"

Joe said, "I'll just sit out here for a spell, sir. I haven't been running up and down the hill all day like you folks."

He noticed Two Hearts wasn't moving from the fire, either. He kept his eyes lidded as he casually took in their surroundings. There were other Indians all around at other fires. None seemed interested in him at the moment. They'd apparently become used to his being there.

Joe stared into the flickering coals and when Two Hearts spoke to him he answered in a deliberately sleepy voice. Others were drifting in to bed down in the crowded wigwam. Nobody insisted Joe join them. After a while, he stretched and said, "I reckon I'll go over and see if that Marvin feller will share some likker with me."

Two Hearts said, "I'll go with you."

He'd been afraid she would.

But Joe nodded agreeably and got to his feet, his heart pounding in his chest as he fought to make every movement casual. The girl tagged along as he strolled over to the Tory tents. The surly Captain Moore was up, smoking by the table. He said the others were out on patrol or asleep and asked what Joe wanted. When Joe asked him for a drink, the Englishman muttered, "Not bloody likely! I've no whisky for a rebel."

Joe shrugged and turned away. When they were out of earshot, Two Hearts said, "He has a bad heart. But why do you want to drink if you are already sleepy?"

Joe yawned and said, "I don't know. I likely should turn in, but I'm sort of restless. I'll just take a walk along the ridge and study some before I turn in with you all. You go ahead and bed down if you want."

"I am not very tired. Besides, I do not think you should walk about my father's camp alone."

He noticed she carried no weapons. So he smiled as he asked, "Are you still guarding me? I thought you was supposed to be my little sister."

"I like being your sister. But my father does

not want you to run away as Big Turtle did."

He strolled on, not answering. She said, "I think you must think me very foolish. We have passed my father's wigwam. You mean to run away, don't you?"

"Would you try to stop me if I did, Two Hearts?"

"Of course. I am Shawnee and you are a captive."

He kept talking to distract her as he walked on, scoffing, "You're not Shawnee. You're white, the same as me. You'd make a right handsome white girl with more seemly clothes and some ribbon bows in that long blonde hair."

He remembered some of Margaret's complaints about frontier life. He told Two Hearts how much fun it was to go to the opera and wear real silk petticoats. He noticed the fires were spread farther apart now. They had almost reached the saddle in the ridge where the trees opened out.

Two Hearts tugged at his sleeve and said, "We must turn back. I do not think my father would want you to go so far from his wigwam."

Joe said, "I just want to have a look down the hill. I want to see what's going on down to Boonesburough."

She protested softly but didn't try to stop him as he walked out of camp to the clearing on the ridge. Down in the valley, a single lonely light gave away the position of the little fort. Otherwise it was black as pitch by now. Two Hearts said, "Hear me, you have seen your people are still there. Let us go back now. I have spoken."

Joe turned as if to follow her. He saw there were no Shawnee in sight. He took a deep breath, turned, and started running.

He didn't run down the hill toward the light. He knew there were Indians skirmishers skulking in the fields around the fort in case some fool tried just what he was doing. Joe ran across the saddle and into the trees beyond, following the ridge to the northeast, trying to put some distance between himself and the camp before Two Hearts could give the alarm. A branch whipped his face as he bore on, listening for shouts behind him. But the girl hadn't shouted. The night stayed silent save for crickets as he loped along the ridge and he grinned to himself as he felt himself getting a second wind. He had a good start and was running fast and, by jimmies, he was *free!*

Then, as he slowed a bit, a good mile out of camp, Joe heard the sound of running moccasins behind him. He gathered speed and ran on, not looking back until he came to another clearing.

It was Two Hearts. She was right behind him. Running strong and silent and alone. Joe cut down the slope at an angle until they were both in the open. Then he stopped and turned around.

Two Hearts stopped a few paces away, breathing hard. Her voice was reproachful as she said,

"You said you were only going for a walk. You lied to me."

"I know. Listen, honey, I don't want to hurt you. You just go on home and tell them I ran off, if you've a mind to."

"I won't. You are my captive. You must come back with me."

"Two Hearts. I'm bigger than you and you're not armed. You're not taking me back and we both know it."

She walked over to him and grabbed his arm. Joe stood, more puzzled than alarmed as she tried to tug him back the way they'd just run. He planted his feet firmly and just let her tug, knowing she couldn't budge him. He said, "Honey, I have to get back to my own folks. I'd like to take you with me. It's tempting."

"Big Brother, you are making me very cross with you. If you do not behave I will have to hurt you."

"Let's keep it polite, then. You don't want to come with me and I sure as hell won't come with you. Let go my arm and we'll just part friendly."

She kicked his legs out from under him and as Joe sat down, surprised, Two Hearts leaped on his chest.

He laughed as he rolled her off and pinned her flat on her back in the grass, her naked breasts against his damp shirt and her eyes filled with angry tears. She protested, "This is not fair! You are bigger than I!"

"And you're as pretty as a picture in the moonlight." He grinned. Then he kissed her.

She struggled. She was as strong as many a boy, but helpless in the arms of a man Joe's size. As he explored her face with his lips he found his free hand wandering over her nearly nude form. He told himself to stop. This was no time to trifle with a girl, even had she been willing instead of trying to knee him in the groin. But his heart was pounding wilder than it had the first night he'd had Margaret and, hell, he didn't know *how* to turn her loose!

She stiffened as Joe's hand slid under her breech clout and gasped as his fingers entered her. She twisted her face from his lips and pleaded, "Please, I don't want to!" and he saw her face was glistening with tears in the moonlight.

Joe removed his hand from her writhing groin and murmured, "It's all right, I understand."

"Am I going to have a baby?"

"What?"

"You . . . you *touched* me! That was a terrible thing to do in the middle of a fight!"

Joe laughed and kissed her wet cheek, soothing, "You're not going to have a baby, Two Hearts. I'd show you how it's really done, but I lack the time. I don't reckon it would be right, if I did."

He got off her and stood up, saying, "I've got to go. I purely wish you'd come with me."

She rose too, but kept her distance as she adjusted her breech clout and replied, "I feel so strange. My heart is beating like a tom-tom and my legs are trembling. Are you sure I will not have a baby?"

"Come away with me and we'll maybe have a dozen. I felt it too, and there's some sort of magic going on hereabouts. I don't want you to go back to the Shawnee, damn it. I want you to come with me."

"I can't. Your people are not my people. I should try again to take you captive. But you won't fight fair."

He hesitated, trying to put words to what he felt, wondering if he knew himself. Then he nodded and started running again. He ran hard and far without looking back. He ran down the slope at the same angle until he reached the banks of the river, a good four miles upstream from the fort. Then he stopped and turned.

He was alone. The girl hadn't followed. He strained his ears for distant sounds and it didn't seem as if she'd given the alarm, either.

Joe slid down the bank and waded knee-deep into the Kentucky. He moved along the bank until he came to a sawyer, or half-floating tree, in the shallows. He braced his heels in the muddy bottom and pulled the sawyer clear of the mud and other debris holding it near the river's edge. He hauled the brushy little tree out to where the water ran swifter and lowered himself in the cold current until only his head showed above the surface, hidden among the soggy twigs and branches. Then he let himself and the sawyer drift west with the current.

It took over an hour and he was chilled to the bone before he and his improvised driftwood screen reached the vicinity of Boonesburough. He let the sawyer go as he slid up the bank facing the fort's closed gate and listened keenly for a time. No Indians were risking the sixty yards of shadow between the landing and the fort. He hadn't expected them to be.

He rose and started to run for the gate. A musket flashed and Joe yelled, "Hold your fire, damn it! It's me, Joe Floyd!"

Somebody else fired but missed. Then orders were shouted and the gate opened a cautious crack. Joe dashed through, soaking wet, to be grabbed and thrown to the ground until a lighted torch appeared above him and Boone's voice said, "It's him, all right. Where the devil have you been, son?"

"Where do you reckon I've been, to the moon? I'm getting tired as hell of folks sitting on me."

The men hauled him to his feet, laughing and patting him on the back. Then Margaret was plastered against his wet chest, sobbing fit to bust and not caring if folks thought it seemly to carry on like that with her own kin.

Joe patted her, uneasy in his mind, and murmured, "I'll come to you directly, Meg. I hope there's a warm fire waiting in our cabin. Uh, right now we got some man-talk to take care of."

Boone laughed, "That's for sure!" Even Dick

Callaway seemed cheered to have Joe back. They hauled him to their ward room in a block-house and gave him a pipe and jug as he filled them in on his adventures.

Boone asked him if he knew where Simon Kenton was and Joe said, "No. The Injuns thought I was him. They don't know Simon and Many Jackets have been picking off runners between here and Detroit."

Another man asked about Montgomery and Joe said, "Many Jackets said he made it safe to Harrodsburg. The Injuns are fighting amongst themselves. De Quindre's likely worried about no messages coming down from Hamilton. If we can hold this here fort for a week or so they'll likely give it up."

He saw the uncertain looks around him in the crowded room and insisted, "We can hold out that long, can't we?"

Boone said, "We'll have to." But Callaway said, "We're running low on water. The damned livestock drink more than we do."

"Why can't we run the critters out to fend for themselves?"

"Two reasons. The Injuns will eat 'em, and we won't be able to. Going thirsty is hard enough. Going hungry is worse."

Joe disagreed, privately. He knew a man could last a month without eating but only a few days without water. But the livestock were owned by these dirt-poor farmers, and he knew he'd only waste breath telling them to give the brutes to the Indians. Nobody on either side, it seemed, wanted to listen to him.

He repeated De Quindre's offer and what the more reasonable Marvin had said about a token surrender. This time even Callaway agreed when Boone snorted, "The hell with the double-dealing sons of bitches! This time the flag stays up and we fight to the last round."

Boone saw Joe was shivering and added, "I'll carry you to your cabin, Joe. You need warming and some shut-eye. Them rascals will be coming down the slope at us come morning, and you won't be able to aim much if you don't throw off that chill."

Boone led him outside. As they walked toward the cabin Joe shared with his stepmother, the older man asked anxiously, "Did Many Jackets say if Campbell's militia is on its way, Joe?"

"He didn't know. The whites up there don't think so, and one of 'em is a master spy for the Crown."

"They might have been bluffing you, son. I'm sort of counting on us getting help."

"I can see that. They think there's more of us here than there is. I lied like a trooper about the water. The Injuns have some squaws in men's duds too. Did you meet up with that white squaw, Two Hearts, when you were their captive?"

"Little blonde gal? I did. She's a right pretty little thing, and still a virgin unless Corn Burner's been at her. Old Corn Burner has been

pestering Black Fish for her. Has he had her
yet, or would you know?"

"She told me she doesn't like Corn Burner."

"That's no surprise. Corn Burner is one mean-
hearted cuss, even for a Shawnee. He still after
the old man's job?"

"Yep. Tried to kill him with an overcharged
rifle while I was sort of socializing with 'em. I
put a stop to it, but . . ."

"What the hell did you do that for, boy? Don't
you like your hair on top of your head?"

"I figured Black Fish was the lesser of two
evils, captain."

"You figured wrong, then. I could hold this
fort with two girls and a mean rooster agin' a
yellow bastard like Corn Burner. Black Fish is
one fighting son of a bitch."

"But Corn Burner aims to torture us all to
death if he's in charge when we're overrun."

"Joe, none of them Shawnee aim to play hop-
scotch with us if we can't hold out 'til Campbell
comes. You got to understand something about
warfare, son. It don't matter how polite an
enemy acts. It's how good a soldier he is, and
Black Fish is the best."

"He thinks you're good too, captain. Every
time Wolfgang picks off a brave with that Hessian rifle of his, they credit it to Big Turtle."

Boone laughed and said, "I hope you didn't
give my medicine away?"

"No. I figured the more medicine they reckon
we have, the less anxious they'll be to make an

all-out attack. Even if we allow for some of the men up there being squaws, we're outnumbered about thirteen to one and, at best, none of us can drop more than three or four before they're over the wall and stomping us."

They'd reached the cabin door. Boone glanced around before he murmured, "I'd sort of like you to keep them figures to yourself, Joe. Some of the others has been talking about white flags and such."

"I don't reckon we should surrender neither, captain."

"Good. Get some rest and be ready to stand your watch come sun-up."

Joe let himself into the cabin. There was a low fire on the hearth and Margaret was on the bed, stark naked. She got quickly to her feet and met him in the center of the room saying, "Get out of those wet things and let me warm you right, darling! My God, I was so afraid I'd lost you!"

He grinned sheepishly and said, "I was looking for a library and some street lamps for you, but . . ."

"Tell me about it later, dear. They didn't hurt you, did they? What you must have gone through among those howling savages!"

She literally stripped him as she hauled him into bed, kissing him all over as she fretted over his bruises. He lay beside her and felt his flesh responding to her caresses. As he automatically ran the same hand over the same places he had on Two Hearts, he was surprised how different two women could feel. Margaret's soap-scented flesh was softer than the smoke-perfumed and harder flesh of Two Hearts, but he couldn't decide which felt best. His heart began to throb again as he ran his fingers between Margaret's thighs. It didn't seem possible they'd been anywhere else just a short time ago. She moaned in pleasure as he entered her and, as her more familiar body enveloped his, he wondered if it would have been as good up there on the hillside in the moonlight.

It likely wouldn't have. The little Shawnee gal had been a frightened virgin and Meg was a skilled lover. But as she pleasured him he wondered if he'd been a fool. He knew taking any gal against her will was a mortal sin. But, damn, he'd never get another chance with Two Hearts now!

And even though he liked old Meg, there was something missing. Something magic he'd never known existed.

"Oh, God, I'm coming!" Meg was gasping as she chewed his collarbone. Joe knew he was going to come too. It felt good. Real good.

He wondered why he couldn't seem to lose himself in her tonight.

He'd likely caught a chill, after all.

20

War was certainly a funny thing. It wasn't like most hates. When men had fights over something personal they went on hating one another all the time. But war was crazy. They put decent men and rascals on both sides. It was sort of like a serious game of checkers, where the loser wound up dead.

Joe found himself talking about it to the Hessian, Wolfgang, as they stood lookout on the tallest, roofless blockhouse the next morning. Joe said, "When I was a captive up in them trees I found myself feeling neighborly to some of the folks I met. It was like you folks down here were, I dunno, *off* somewheres."

Wolfgang nodded and said, "I, too, have a soldier been. It seems so long ago I shot an American at Bennington. And now I am here waiting to put a bullet in the next redcoat I see."

"Well, you Hessians wore green coats anyways, so it isn't like you'd be shooting at friends."

Wolfgang laughed. "Forgive me, Joe, but wrong you are. At this moment, if my old Frankenberg brigade from those trees marched down toward us, I would aim for the sergeant major. Now *there* was a man one could love to hate!"

"What about the others? The German farm boys you grew up with?"

"I would have to shoot them. As they would me. War for old friends makes no allowances."

Joe sighed and opined, "You're likely right. Now that I'm down here, the folks up there on the hill are the ones who seem . . . off somewhere. Like they're not human."

Wolfgang was silent for a moment, reflecting. "*Ist* so, Joe," he said then. "And yet human they are. When I deserted my captured comrades I asked a friend to come with me along. He said it was his duty to stay with the regiment. We grew up together. Together we would hunt the forests as far as Dreihausen. We learned of women together with some naughty sisters who lived near the beer garden. We pledged *Broderschaft* together and called one another *Du,* a thing you would not understand but important to a Hessian."

"I had a friend like that called Freckles. The Injuns killed him."

"My friend Karl was named. If we meet in this war, one of us will surely die. We both shoot good."

"But you don't hate him?"

Wolfgang shrugged and said, "I love my friend Karl as much as one man another *ist* allowed to love. I hope he through this war lives.

As I know he hopes for me also. But if we meet in battle, we will fight. This is the way of all good soldiers."

"I met a couple of Injuns up there. One of 'em was more like a colored man, but I reckon he's Shawnee too. Feller named Running Wolf took my side and treated me right. I sure hope I don't get him in my gunsights."

"If you do, you will shoot. Trust me, friend Joe. I have been there."

"Does it make you feel funny, changing sides the way you did?"

"Why should it? I was on the first side because the prince sold me like a cow. I am on this side because I chose it. I told you all this when we met first, *nicht wahr?*"

"I remember. I reckon I'm slow to understand some things. I got into this war sort of by accident. I don't understand a lot they've written about Rights and Taxation and such. I just want folks to leave me be. I figured the Continental Congress pestered folks less than the fool Tories. But some folks take it all so *serious.*"

"Joe. A bullet kills you, even when you laugh."

"Oh, I'm serious my ownself about that part. I met a . . . another captive up there. I tried to get her to come back with me. I still can't see what's so important to her about the other side."

Wolfgang grinned and said, "Ach, a Shawnee *mädchen.* I know that feeling also. Once they sent us to occupy some little Balkan state and there was this *mädchen.* Her name was Sophia.

When we were paid off to return to Hessia, she told me she would write to me. But she never did. After we marched away, her people must have reminded her we the enemy were after all."

"You're likely right."

"Cheer up, friend Joe. There are always other ladies in another place. Did you get any of your Shawnee *mädchen?*"

"Hell, no! I was only with them two days and a night!"

"So slow you move for an old soldier, friend Joe! In time you will learn such little chance we get for such things."

Joe smiled and said, "This is my first war. How old a soldier did you say you were, Wolfgang?"

"I will soon be four-and-twenty. I have a soldier been since I was fifteen. So you must listen to me about such matters, even when I funny English talk."

"I'm learning. Do you ever think about that Sophia gal?"

"Often. She was beautiful and I was in love that spring. By now she is of course married to some fat peasant. These things happen in any war."

Joe grimaced as he thought of Two Hearts in the arms of Corn Burner.

He knew he had no right to think of her at all. Old Meg would cry fit to burst if she knew he was thinking of some other girl. It was just as well Two Hearts had balked at coming along. He'd forgotten all about Meg for a few minutes, but there surely would have been some feathers flying by now had Two Hearts tagged along all the way home.

He chuckled and said, "I never understood how them Turkish rascals can marry up with more than one gal. I mean, it's not seemly to marry up with a gal 'less you love her. But suppose a man feels the same way about two gals at once? What's he supposed to do?"

Wolfgang shrugged and said, "I am not the one to ask that. I am not a Frenchman. It takes a Frenchman or a Turk to take two women at once. I slept with two whores once. My poor back!"

Joe laughed. "I don't reckon two gals would like it, neither."

The slave, London, came up to join them with a jug of water and two crusts. He looked past Joe up the slope and asked if they'd seen anything.

Joe said, "We'd have fired if we had, London. I thank you for the water. It's warming up some. Be a scorcher by this afternoon."

London said, "Try to make your ration last, suh. Captain Boone says the food's holding out all right, but the water's a mite low."

"How are we fixed for powder and ball?"

"Better. They done stored up ammunition for the fall hunt afore the Shawnee got here, so we can pepper the rascals some before it gives out. Did you meet up with that sassy renegade nigger Pompey in the Injun camp, suh?"

"Yep. He wasn't all that sassy with me, London. I met other folks up there I'd rather take a shot at."

"Well, just let me git that sassy Pompey and I'll mind his manners for him good. Miz Mercy Bryan says I's to forget about bein' her serving man and jest shoot Shawnee."

Joe frowned and asked, "That little orphan gal owns you, London?"

"Yassuh. 'Course, I belonged to her daddy first, but he's daid. I been lookin' out for the chile since then. You let me know if you see that sassy Pompey, hear?"

Joe smiled at Wolfgang as London left and the Hessian nodded and said, "*Ja*, strange bedfellows war makes. You get used to it in time."

"It's pure crazy to see a slave fighting for freedom."

"*Ja*, but nobody said war must sense make. What is it, Joe? What do you see?"

Joe had stopped ruminating. He pointed with his chin and said, "Cornstalks, over there by that busted-down fence. They're waving."

"*Ja*, I have been watching them. Wind, I think."

Joe shook his head and said, "The wind's not strong enough to move the thicker stalks."

Wolfgang looked more closely, nodded, then said, "Over to our right, that stump behind. A Shawnee hides there. He forgets he casts a shadow. We let them creep into range closer, *Ja*?"

Joe nodded and moved over to the inner side of the lookout post. He called down in a deliberately jovial tone, "Skirmishers coming in, boys. Man the loopholes quiet and wait for 'em to get within musket range."

But someone immediately shouted, "Injuns!" at the top of his lungs, and someone else began to beat the alarm triangle. The fort below exploded in a clamor of shouting men and women, crying babies and barking dogs.

The first man to the wall fired his musket blindly up the slope. Joe sighed, "Shit!" and trained his own muzzle on the nearest movement.

A long ragged line of sixty-odd Indians materialized two hundred yards out and started shooting back as they retreated, knowing they'd been sighted. Joe fired at a polka-dotted Mingo and his ball fell short by yards. He snatched up another loaded musket as Wolfgang fired. A Shawnee spun around like a big awkward bird to flop out of sight in the corn.

A bullet thunked into the log in front of Joe. He fired back at the cotton ball of gunsmoke and again his round fell short, but the gout of dust between them seemed to speed up the Indian who'd fired on the run.

The Shawnee didn't run all the way back to the tree line. They knew they didn't have to. They fell back five hundred yards and stood their ground, firing a ragged volley at the futile gunsmoke from the fort. Joe heard Captain

Boone shouting, "Hold your fire, damn it! We ain't got powder and ball to give away!"

The settlers' guns crackled to a ragged silence. By now, the Indian leaders had their own musketeers under control. Joe saw Black Fish moving up and down the line, giving orders. A few yards closer to the fort, Corn Burner pranced up and down in fresh paint and feathers, yipping like a cur-dog.

Joe nudged Wolfgang and asked, "Any chance of putting a rifle ball in that gent making all the noise?"

Wolfgang shook his head and said, "He out of range *ist*. I think he must know this, *nicht wahr?*"

Margaret called Joe's name and he turned to see her and little Mercy Bryan climbing up to join them. Joe said, "You gals better stay down behind the walls." But Margaret said, "The other women are loading for their men, Joe. We thought you could use some help."

Joe started to protest. Then Mercy grabbed a musket by its warm barrel and bit a paper cartridge open as she drew the ramrod. He watched, bemused, as she loaded and rammed like an expert infantry regular. That changed Joe's mind for him. As Mercy leaned the loaded musket against the logs he said, "Stay then. But keep your heads down. Meg, you scrooch over here by me. Mercy, you help Wolfgang with his spare rifle. You know about rifle patches, honey?"

Mercy nodded and picked up the spare rifle

near Wolfgang. The Hessian gave her a sidelong glance, then handed her his cartridge pouch.

Margaret raised her head above the logs and said, "Oh, my, they're closer than I thought!"

Joe put a hand on her shoulder and said, "I told you to keep down! They're not close enough to shoot, but they're not far enough to get careless, neither."

Wolfgang said, "Ach, if only they would charge! They are not enough in number now to overcome our thirty guns. Where are the others?"

Joe said, "I heard 'em talking while I was up on the hill. They aim to keep us on edge with small skirmish parties round-the-clock. I figure the plan was to creep in close as they could, fire a volley, then light back up the slope. Had not we spotted 'em, they might have picked one or two of us off before we came unstuck. Black Fish aims to whittle us down some before he makes an all-out attack."

Wolfgang shrugged and said, "Such a way you fight in this country! By now regular troops would have had their battle won or lost."

"Lost, probably. What would you Hessians and the British regulars have done to Gates and Arnold at Saratoga had they marched toward you in a well-dressed line?"

"Ach, we would have cut them to ribbons! But around us in the woods they hovered, Gates up on a high bluff where we couldn't charge with bayonets, Arnold and Morgan's Virginia Rifles moving to flank us from the hedges and fence rails along the tree line. General Burgoyne was so mad he threw his wig on the ground and. kicked it when your General Gates began down into us to lob cannon balls."

"Yep, I heard they fought you frontier style. And won. Keep that in mind about yon Injuns. Even when I was in their camp, I was never able to count more than a dozen in any one place. There has to be at least four hundred of the rascals, but Black Fish has 'em spread from hell to breakfast."

"Let us hope he keeps them that way, friend Joe. Any hundred of them could be over these walls if a charge they made."

Joe, knowing that to be true, said nothing. Of the thirty guns they had, fifteen were in the hands of farmers and inexperienced young boys. He was counting heavily, however, on the ruse he'd tried in dressing women up as men. If it had worked, Black Fish had them down as a hundred-odd militia.

The slave, London, stuck his head up to call out, "So there you is, Miz Mercy! What is you doing up here, chile? You got no call to be up here fretting me!"

Mercy Bryan shook her head determinedly. "You go on about your chores, Uncle London. I'm out to get me a sassy Injun!"

"Miz Mercy, you come down like a good chile and leave them Injuns be."

Joe smiled and said, "She's safe enough here,

London. Where's your musket? I thought I told you to back up Wolfgang here."

The slave shrugged and said, "Colonel Callaway said I had no call to play soldier, suh. They took my musket and gave it to a boy."

"Damn it, Wolfgang told me you know how to handle a gun. I'll have a talk with Callaway about it when I go off watch."

London shook his head and said, "Please, suh, I'd just as lief you wouldn't. Some of the white gen'men say it ain't right for me to act so uppity."

Joe nodded. He would have let the matter drop, but Mercy scowled and said, "Well, I'll have something to say to puffy old Dick Callaway and that's a fact! You ain't his nigger, London! You're mine! If Lieutenant Floyd wants you to have a gun, you shall have one! Didn't I tell you not to be a slave no more 'til the Injuns went away."

"Yass'm. But you is still a chile. I ain't sure a chile has any say-so about niggers."

Mercy turned to Joe and asked, "Is that true, Lieutenant Floyd? It 'pears to me I can order my own slave as I please, even if I am young."

Joe said, "I'll talk to Captain Boone about it later, Miss Mercy. I don't know much about law and they've changed the laws of late, in any case. The Continental Congress says all men are equal now. Maybe they mean colored people too."

Mercy grinned in delight and said, "You hear

that, Uncle London? You might not be a slave no more, once we win this revolution!"

"Yass'm, I been studying 'bout that. But meanwhile, I'd best do as Colonel Callaway says."

Despite Joe's warning, Margaret had raised her head for another peek. She said, "The Indians seem to be moving back up the hill."

Joe nodded and said, "They'll likely be coming back as soon as they smoke and powpow about it up in the trees."

Wolfgang looked up at the sky and said, "At high noon they will come back."

"How can you be sure, Wolfgang?"

"They know white people eat at noon."

"Hell, Wolfgang, they'll know we have a lookout. They can't hope to catch us napping over dinner."

"No, but they will want to keep us from enjoying it. Your Washington does this. He always attacks on holidays or while the British eat. I think Black Fish is as good a general."

21

Smith and Gass relieved them at ten. Joe told
Meg and Mercy to wait at the cabin, where the
three of them would be eating that day, then
went looking for Boone. He found the captain in
the ward room with young Flanders Callaway,
his son-in-law. They were hunkered on either
side of a rusty socket-bayonet, which was stuck
in the earth floor. Boone looked up and said,
"Howdy, Joe. Flanders larnt this trick in the
militia back in '76."

Joe looked blank and Flanders explained,
"They was teaching us about sap-works. Do you
put an ear to a blade druv in the ground, you
can hear things."

Joe squatted and placed his ear against the
steel blade. There was a slight grating tingle,
almost too faint to hear.

Boone said, "You told us De Quindre wasn't
in camp when you lit out last night, Joe."

Joe nodded and straightened up before he
said, "They're tunneling at us, sure as hell.

Where do you figure they started the sap, over by the river bank?"

Boone said, "Has to be. They're mebbe a quarter mile away, upstream or down. We have the banks too well covered, closer in."

Flanders said, "I had a look-see afore I called the captain, Joe. The river would be running muddy iffen they was digging upstream. But she's running clear, so I figure they're coming at us from below, working hid below the bank and letting the current carry off the spoil. They'll likely float timbers up, hugging the bank."

Joe speculated, "So that's why they've been whooping and hollering on the hillside all morning. Trying to distract us from the river side."

Boone said, "Yep. I got somebody watching the river. But there's nothing to see over there. I'm betting on 'em coming from the north, across the river, when they gits to coming serious."

Flanders said, "They won't have to ford the river under our fire if they run that tunnel under our walls, Dan'l."

"How 'bout it, Joe? You reckon they'll dig under our walls?"

"Not sudden, captain. I sort of forgot to tell De Quindre we were sitting on solid limestone when he asked me about the well."

Boone laughed and said, "There you go, boys. Let the fool Frenchman dig his durned old tunnel 'til he butts into the bedrock. It'll keep the rascals busy and out of mischief."

But Joe frowned and said, "Captain, I reckon

we ought to try and drive 'em from that tunnel, anyways. Or better, cave her in. He might not be able to tunnel under us, but we surely don't want him to find out we have no well, do we?"

Boone looked at Flanders and whistled silently before he said, "I told you Joe Floyd was kin to Big John. That's good thinking, Joe. But how do you mean to stop them from tunneling to bedrock and catching us in a fib?"

"Don't know. I'll study on it. Wolfgang's done some soldiering too. He says he figures they'll hit us at noon to spoil our appetites."

Boone nodded and said, "About that he may be right. I've told ever'one they're to eat in shifts, a few families at a time. When they wardance just outten range we'll be ready with ever' rifle in the place. Who knows, we may get lucky."

Joe said casually, "Wolfgang tells me that slave, London, is a fair shot. Dick Callaway took his gun away and gave it to one of the young boys."

"He did? Well, Dick never has thought much of niggers."

"Captain, Mercy Bryan is your niece by marriage and London is her property. The girl says she don't mind him having a gun."

Boone said doubtfully, "Son, you're stepping in the mire. I know where you're headed, but I got enough on my plate with Dick and his friends."

Flanders said, "I'm his kin, so I can say it. He's

muley. And he's sore about the rest of us taking orders from Dan'l instead of him."

Boone sighed and said, "Don't be too hard on old Dick, Flanders. He means well and he's brave enough. He just thinks having a militia commission makes him smarter than us elected officers. I sort of like to let Dick have his way, when he makes any sense at all."

Joe insisted, "It makes more sense to have a proven man shooting Shawnee than a half-grown boy, captain."

Boone shook his head and said, "Don't be pre-judging the Collins boy, Joe. Tom Payne says we ain't supposed to do that no more."

"Pre-judging, captain? London is the one who's black, and I just said he was a good marksman!"

"I know, Joe, but maybe you're pre-judging Sam Collins because he's a boy, and white. This pre-judging works both ways. Do you know Sam Collins? Have you seen him shoot?"

"No, but . . ."

"But me no buts, lieutenant. You know Dick Callaway ain't fond of niggers and you know he don't like me much better. You know London is a growed decent man. So you've pre-judged the Collins boy must be a foolish little rascal. Tell Joe about Sam Collins, Flanders."

Flanders shrugged and said, "Sam is about fifteen, stands six-foot-two, and can whip his pappy. He's one of the best pot hunters in the settlement. With a rifle in his hands, he'd be dangerous to get near, wearing feathers."

Joe smiled sheepishly and said, "Guess you're right. I figured they'd handed London's rifle to a sassy eight-year-old. But London can still shoot and he wants to help. Can't we even issue him an old trade musket?"

"Leave it lay for now, Joe. I need Dick Callaway agreeing with me partways more than I need another musketeer. Mebbe after we swap a few more shots with Black Fish nobody will notice or care if London has a gun. Right now I'm more worried about De Quindre and them red moles of hisin. We can't rush his tunnel entrance in broad daylight. There'll be a hunter's moon tonight, though."

Joe said, "I'm going to start counter-mining. I'll get London and kill two birds with one stone."

"That sure sounds good, Joe. What in thunder are you talking about?"

"London's hurt 'cause he can't be useful. I'll help him start drilling for the well again before I go back on watch."

"Damn it, Joe, it'd take a week to drill to the water table through that limestone!"

"Maybe. But for all we know we'll have a week before the Shawnee leave us be. Meanwhile, even if we never hit water, De Quindre in that tunnel will hear London digging. He won't know it's for a well, or what we're digging through. He'll think we're running a second-tunnel to counter-sap his."

"Hmmm, ought to make him thoughtful enough to slow him down."

"And if he does dig into rock, and still hears London digging, he'll think he's just run into an outcrop, not solid bedrock."

Boone laughed and said, "By jimmies, I like it! Fancy French engineer playing hide-and-go-seek underground with a poor old nigger slave!"

"I'm going to tell London it's more important than that."

"Well, yes, the boy will work better if he thinks he's important."

"He is important, captain. We don't have enough men in here to hold any of them unimportant. I want London to treat me with respect, so I aim to treat him the same way."

"I follow your drift, son. But keep notions like that to yourself around folks like Dick Callaway. He's already said it ain't fittin' for a bitty white gal to be living alone with a nigger buck. You get him to dwelling on London and little Mercy, and he'll try agin' to auction the boy off on her."

"Jesus! Could he do a thing like that, Captain Boone?"

"If he put it to a vote and won, he could. We're what they call a dee-mocracy out here in Kentucky. Folks put anything they has stuck in their craw to a vote at Sunday meeting, and we go by majority rule. I talked Dick outten it last time he wanted to auction London off. I said the 'little gal needed him and that Jemina and the other ladies was keeping an eye on her."

"I didn't know you folks was all that interested in each other's affairs, captain."

There was a slight twinkle in Boone's eye as he said, "It ain't like the gals has books and such to occupy 'em. They don't miss a thing that's going on in the cabins at night. They surely don't, Joe." He gave Joe a meaningful look. "But it's live and let live, right?"

Joe nodded, dry-mouthed, and said something about getting a bite to eat before starting on the new well with London. He left, face flushed, and walked across to the cabin he shared with his stepmother.

So they knew. Damn it, he'd told Meg not to carry on so loud when he was pleasuring her at night.

He passed Jemima Boone Callaway and another young wife. When they smiled hello at him Joe ticked his hat brim and passed quickly on, staring at the ground. Meg said they'd told her Jemima was an illegitimate child, born to Boone's wife and God knows whomsoever. Jemima likely knew he'd been rutting with his own ma too. Right now, she and that other gal were likely talking about it. Folks never let on what they thought of you, to your face. He didn't jeer at Jemima for being what she was, and she didn't jeer at him for what he must think he was. Yet they both knew each other's shameful secrets. It was almost as if they were sharing the same seat in the privvy or bathing in the same tub, while pretending not to notice one another. It surely made a man feel funny. Like he was naked in church in one of those fool dreams where nobody seemed to notice.

Joe was scowling frightfully as he stepped inside the cabin. Mercy was seated at the table with Margaret and they both looked startled when he barged in. Margaret asked, "What's wrong, dear?" He couldn't say in front of company. He growled, "Nothing. I'm just hot, is all. It's hot as hell outside."

Mercy Bryan dimpled and said, "Aunt Meg said I could sup with you all, too."

Joe nodded, but his voice had an edge to it as he said, "You ain't to call her your aunt. She ain't your slave."

Margaret gasped, "Joe, what's got into you? What a terrible thing to say!"

"Maybe! But if London is her uncle, I sure don't want her calling you her aunt! They've been saying enough about us as it is."

Mercy got to her feet, eyes brimming, and said softly, "I'll just run along, then. I don't mean to be where I'm not wanted."

But Joe put out an arm and swept her back to her seat, saying, "You just set, honey. What I said wasn't aimed at hurting you."

"You ain't riled with me?" Mercy asked hopefully.

Joe said, "No, I'm riled at my own fool self, I reckon. You took me by surprise, calling Meg your aunt like that. I hadn't studied on it and I'd just been talking about your slave and . . . other things."

"Oh, heavens, I know London's not my real uncle, Lieutenant Floyd. I know Miz Floyd ain't my kin, neither. I 'spose I call all you older folk aunts and uncles, if I like you."

"You call *me* your uncle, girl, and I'll make up some awful names for you!"

"Pooh, you're nice enough for me to call my uncle if I want to."

"All right, Princess One Sock In the Wash."

"Princess *what*?"

Joe grinned and insisted, "Princess One Sock In The Wash, last of the Cherokee royal family. You were stolen by gypsies when you were a baby and raised as a white child, but now that your old uncle has found you . . ."

"Stop! I surrender, Lieutenant Floyd!"

The three of them laughed and he said, "You can call me Joe and old Meg is Meg. We'll call you Mercy, if you're very good."

Margaret served them as he went on gently teasing the girl. There was little enough to eat and the three of them ate quickly, in the business-like manner of most country folk. Joe finished first and leaned back to have a pipe. He noticed Meg was looking at him thoughtfully as she cleared the table. Mercy wiped her face and said, "My, that was nice, Aunt . . . I mean Meg. Do you reckon them Injuns is fixing to hit us at noon like that German boys says, Joe?"

He said, "They might. Your kinsman Flanders has their next few moves figured out for us. Figuring a mess of shovel work in a sweaty hole in the ground, we have us a day or so before they really start trying."

"Flanders says the militia might come from Virginia. He says we'll be saved if Colonel Campbell gits here by the end of the week."

"Flanders might be right. Would you fetch London for me, Mercy? I've got a chore for him, if it's all right with you, of course."

The girl got up and said she'd be pleased to fetch her slave. As she left them, Margaret said, pouting, "She'll be back any minute with her colored boy. I was hoping we could be alone, darling."

Joe said, "Meg, it's seven times hotter than it ought to be."

"I don't mind a little sweat. It's exciting when we get all slippery."

"Damn it, we'll have plenty of time for that after we drive the Injuns off. I'd like to catch a few winks, but I dasn't take my duds off and, anyways, it's broad daylight."

"The door has a bar to it, darling."

"Just leave that fool door alone. I have to put London to work and be ready for other callers. If there's time after dark, we can maybe get more friendly. Right now, rutting is about the last thing I got on my mind."

"Oh? I noticed you were interested enough in Mercy Bryan's low-cut bodice just now."

"Have you gone crazy from the heat, woman? Mercy's just a little girl, even iffen I was feeling randy."

"I noticed she's filling out nicely in that too-tight hand-me-down. You couldn't take your eyes off her, all the time we were eating."

Joe reached across the table and took her hand, saying, "I'll say this once and that'll have to hold you. There's not a gal in this here fort I'm horny for. Present company excepted."

"Are you sure, Joe? I know you think I'm a jealous fool, but when I saw the way you got all flustered with Mercy . . ."

"Shoot, I was flustered 'cause I'd just passed Jemima and another gal, and before you have me leaping at Boone's daughter, I was flustered 'cause I think they know about you and me. In bed at night and all."

She looked relieved and sighed, "Oh, is *that* all you're worried about, dear?"

"No. I'm worried more about the Shawnee. But it's sort of spooky to think of folks whispering about your sleeping habits. And you *are* my stepmother."

"For heaven's sake, Joe, that was years ago. At least, it seems that way."

"They're still likely laughing at us."

"I don't care. Next to some of the gossip I've heard I feel pure as the driven snow. Did you know they caught London with a goat?"

"You mean, he was . . . ?"

"Yes, Miz Collins saw him down behind the

pen. She said he was going at it hot and heavy, but when she told her husband he just laughed."

Joe found himself grinning, but he felt sorry for the slave as he said, "Well, they'd kill him if they caught him doing it with a white gal, and the poor cuss has to have *somebody*. But you and me are white folks, Meg. I don't want them talking dirty about us."

"I don't want it either, but what can we do? Half of them know and the rest have likely guessed. What's another slice once the loaf has been cut?"

"Another slice of gossip, I reckon. But I follow your drift. They figure to talk about us dirty whether we go on the same way or not."

Margaret said impulsively, "When you finish with London, let's get into bed."

"You want me to pleasure you right after I've had my way with a nigger?"

"Oh, Joe, you're so funny. That's about the only dirty thing nobody here's been caught at. Even the little kids are sort of horny. Miz Collins says she saw a couple of the boys playing with themselves one afternoon."

"Miz Collins sure is interested in other folks' private parts. I wonder what she does when nobody's about to catch *her* at it."

"I don't know. We're so crowded here, folks know when you have to pee. That used to bother me when I was married to your father, Joe. Do you remember how small our old cabin was?"

"Yep. Not much bigger'n this one."

"I used to think of you, sleeping right under us when we . . . you know."

"I know. I used to go outside when father was at you. I didn't know then what you were fussing about, but I knew it was something you didn't want me to hear."

He puffed his pipe and stared morosely at his own smoke before he said, "I've been meaning to mention that to you, Meg. You make an awful lot of noise when we're in bed at night. Sometimes I wonder if you want folks to know. About us, I mean."

"Joe, that's an awful thing to say."

"Well, the whole damn settlement seems to have heard us going at it. A thing like that could make a man wonder."

"Wonder about what, dear?"

"About you, well, sort of putting your brand on me for all the other gals to see."

She stiffened and said, "Oh? I thought you just said you weren't interested in any of the girls in the fort."

"I'm not," he answered truthfully enough, adding, "I've been trying to figure the future, allowing the Shawnee let us have one. I've been wondering what you aimed to do, once we were outten this fix."

"I thought you said we'd clear some land and maybe settle down for a spell, Joe."

"I know what I said, Meg. I just don't see how it's likely to work out. I mean, in the years to come."

She suddenly seemed to age ten years as she lowered her eyes and said, "You mean you need a young wife who can bear your children, don't you?"

Joe shook his head. "You're young enough for any man with hair on his chest, and I'm not planning on raising a trained band of Kentucky militia for a while. But turn it about and look at it from what's best for *you*, Meg. You're a handsome woman and not all that old. There's a mess of older men out here with land and position. Captain Boone's old woman has left him. It'll take me years to rise as high and . . ."

"Damn you, Joe Floyd, I don't want Dan'l Boone or any other man I've met out here. You know who I want. I want you all the time, so bad I can taste it!"

"I understand, Meg, but . . ."

"No you don't understand, God help me! I know you don't love me. I know I'm mad to love you. But I do, the more fool I! I don't know why I feel the way I do. God knows you're not too bright and it's not just your body. When we started up I just thought it would be a way to keep a man to protect me until I could make other plans."

"You mean, the way you married up with father?"

"Don't you mean-mouth me, Joe Floyd. I was a good wife to your father and I meant to be a good mistress to you. A woman takes as much pleasure from the flesh as any man and what's

sauce for the goose is sauce for the gander!
You've got no call looking down on a woman
who gives herself to a man when she's alone and
needs protecting."

"I never said I looked down on you, Meg. I
like you. I'm trying to study on what's best for
you."

"I *know* what's best for me. If I had a lick of
sense I'd set my sights on some older nice-look-
ing man with mayhaps a quarter-section of bottom land and a herd of cows."

"That's what I just said, Meg."

"I know. And I'm fool enough to want a silly
child like you! I think it must be some nasty spell
some mean old witchy-woman hexed me with.
Sometimes, looking at you sleeping, I feel like
I'm in a fairy dream. Sometimes, when you touch
me, Joe, the air gets all tingly with, I don't
know, mayhaps it's the little people my mother
used to tell me about. I feel five years old, and
it's like I'm about to discover some magic secret
nobody else knows about."

Joe thought back to a moment on a hillside,
maybe a million years ago, and mused, "You
reckon that's what love is supposed to feel like,
Meg? Sort of a magic something in the air?"

"I know it feels like that, Joe. Are you saying
you've felt it too?"

He nodded. Then, since he didn't want to hurt
her again, he said, "I felt it last night," and left
out the where and who of it.

She brightened and came around the table to

sit in his lap, sobbing, "Oh, I knew you felt something more than usual when you came home to me last night! When was it, Joe? When we were making love? After, or before?"

"Uh, I reckon it was a mite afore."

"Oh, darling, I'm so happy! Was the air filled with fairy dust for you too? Or did you only hear the far-off music when you took me in your arms?"

He frowned and said, "I don't remember music. I just felt all sort of weak and strong and I wanted it to be tender and maybe sort of hurtful at the same time."

Before he could elaborate, there was a knock on the door and Margaret leaped off his lap, albeit smiling triumphantly.

Joe went to the door and opened it for London. The slave said, "Please, suh, my mistress say you wanted to see me."

Joe waved at Margaret and, stepping outside, told London about the Tory tunnel and his plans to throw De Quindre off-stride by some digging sounds on this side of the stockade wall. He said, "We'll get a sledge and a star-drill and every time you whop it into the limestone they'll suck at their teeth and get set for a cave-in."

London laughed and said, "I understand, suh. Do Jesus, I hope that sassy Pompey is digging from the other side."

Joe led him to the storage sheds. It was even hotter now. He looked up at the cobalt blue bowl of sky and said, "You'd best wait until about three, when there's a mite more shade."

"Shoot, Lieutenant Floyd, I don't mind a little sweat. I've been feeling like such a useless . . . critter. I reckon I can do a man's job, does someone give me one."

Joe nodded and got the tools from the shed. He gave London a hand at getting started and they dug down through soil a few feet as some of the other men and boys stood around watching. Joe struck hardpan or rock and reached for the star-drill. He said, "Give the rod a lick with the sledge, London," and a boy called out, "You're fixing to lose your fingers, Joe? He's only a house nigger, not a field hand."

Joe grunted, "You want to help, pick up a tool. You want to stand there braying like a jackass, stuff a sock in it. I told you to hit it a lick, London."

The slave gave the star-drill a tap. Joe said, "Come on. You can drive steel, London."

"Yassuh, but if I misses . . ."

"If I didn't think you could do it, I'd have never asked. Let's go, London!" This time the slave swung hard and the air rang with driven steel. London swung again and again. As the tool drove deep enough to stand by itself in the soft rock, Joe stood up and picked up another sledge. The two of them hammered in unison and young McBride said, "Look at that steel go! Let me in there with a hammer, fellers. We'll drive her down to China."

Others moved to help and when someone muttered, "Shit, I don't work with niggers!" another growled, "Go play with the gals then. We'uns got man's work here."

Joe saw it was going to be all right. He handed his sledge to an eager boy as Flanders Callaway came over. Joe asked if he felt like digging and Flanders said, "No. I got something to show you."

He led Joe to the north wall, where Boone was waiting on the fire step. Joe joined him and stared north across the river. The Kentucky was running mustard-yellow from shore to shore.

Flanders said, "I was wrong. They wasn't digging downstream. They was digging *careful.* The sound of our digging has seeped 'em up instead of stopping them! They're up yonder, where we had that peace meeting and the bank is steeper. They must have a dozen men in the tunnel, digging fast as badgers with their tails on fire!"

Joe said, "Well, I can stop our own noise, if you reckon it would help."

Boone shook his head and said, "I got a better idea, boys. We'll run a shallow trench along the north wall and fill her up with water. If they dig this far, the water will flood their tunnel."

Joe and Flanders exchanged looks. Then Flanders asked, "Where do you figure we'll *git* water, Dan'l? Our barrels is half dry and it sure don't look like rain!"

Boone said, "Joe's digging a well. Sooner or later, there's got to be water down there somewhere. Ain't that right, Joe?" He winked at Joe, who winked back and replied, "I'll put some men to work on your trench, captain."

Flanders followed him down off the wall and murmured, "Joe, this is crazy! We won't reach water for a week, if then. What's the sense of putting them to useless chores?"

Joe said, "We have to keep 'em thinking about something and hoping about something. Dan'l knows that. You notice how the bickering stopped as soon as some of the men started helping London? I'm going to have some others erect a lookout tower even higher than that flat-topped blockhouse. Why don't you ask Jemima to put the gals to work on rifle patches? We have to keep everybody busy. Busy and not thinking in circles 'til they snap at one another for want of other targets."

"I see your meaning," Flanders said slowly. "But I ain't sure it'll work."

"It has to work. Another few days like this and Black Fish won't have to take the fort. We'll likely start killing each other."

22

The Indians, contrary to Wolfgang's prediction, didn't attack that noon. They didn't even show a feather as the long hot afternoon wore on. The settlers watched the sky for signs of thunderheads. It was so hot and muggy that they looked for an evening cloudburst. But as the sun went down the stars winked on in a clear and empty sky. The moon rose, grinning like a big round skull, and the watchers on the walls stared intently out across the silvery fields for any sign of movement.

Distant fires gleamed on the ridge above, but the Indians were apparently banking on De Quindre's tunnel now. By midnight, even Joe was sure there'd be no attack that day. He went to the cabin and made hasty love to Margaret, not removing all his clothes. He told her of Boone's latest scheme, once his odd shallow-water trench was finished. Margaret complained, "He wants to drive holes through the walls between all the cabins? Whatever for? We've no privacy as it is, darling!"

Joe smiled. "I know. But the Injuns hold the high ground. They can lob bullets into the fort. If we have to, we can move low along the walls and keep undercover by running from cabin to cabin."

"But they haven't been shooting down into the village square."

"That doesn't mean they can't, Meg. I was up there on the ridge. You'd have to waste a heap of ammunition, but plunging shots can be a bother even if they don't hit you."

Joe kissed her and stretched out to steal forty winks. But there was a timid knock on the door and Joe swung off the cot, buttoning his shirt as he went to open it. Young Moses Boone, the captain's nephew and the son of Squire Junior, said his father wanted to see him.

Puzzled, Joe went with the boy. The elder brother of the Boone clan hadn't gotten out of bed since the first day of the siege put him there with a flesh wound, a book of common prayer and a jug. It was said he kept a broadax by the bed for any final action. His nine-year-old son had the family musket.

Joe came inside and sat near the foot of the bed as Squire Junior stared owlishly at him and announced, "I've been praying for guidance from the Lord, Lieutenant Floyd. They tell me you're a young man with an education."

"I can read and write some, sir."

"You get good ideas. My brother Dan'l is set in his ways. He's respectful to me, you under-

330

stand, but I don't think he takes my notions serious."

Joe didn't answer. He'd heard the sneering whispers about the elder Boone. They said he thought he was a preacher at times, at other times a budding inventor who just needed a little capital for his ideas for steamboats, canals through the mountains and other fool notions everyone knew would never work.

Squire Junior said, "They tell me you told Black Fish we got us a cannon down here."

"I did, sir. I don't reckon he believed me."

"Joe, what if I was to tell you I knowed how to make a cannon?"

Joe didn't answer. Even a drunk old fool was entitled to respect under his own roof. Squire Junior said, "I told my brother, but he just laughed and told me to go ahead. I ask you, can a man build a cannon flat on his back and wounded mortal?"

"No, sir. I can see you're in no shape to cast a field piece. But I'm sure your brother thinks it's a fine idea."

"No he don't. You see, I really do get fine ideas. I've done it all my life. Our father allowed I had a vivid imagination. That's what he calt it, a vivid imagination. He was an educated man."

"I know, sir. They told me you preach a fine sermon too."

"Well, there's times for praying and times for doing. You see, Joe, I've always had this problem between the thinking and the doing. When

Dan'l and me was younger, I had this idea for a steam engine, like that Newcomen feller over in England built."

"I think his name was Watt, sir. I read about it in the Pennsylvania *Gazette*."

"Bah! Watt's only been at it lately. I read where this other feller built a steam engine years ago, only it didn't work so good. I thought I'd improve on it. Anyway, I drawed up some plans and me and Dan'l built a model. I still think it was a grand notion, but when it blowed up on us and shattered all our windows, Dan'l sort of lost interest."

Joe stared at the floor and murmured, "Yes, sir. You were talking about a cannon?"

"You go ahead and grin if you want to, son. I'm used to it. But I've been giving the matter some thought and, damn it, I don't think it's all that hard to build a cannon."

"If you say so, sir."

"You need a barrel with mebbe a four-inch bore. We got powder. We got all sorts of iron scrap. We can use old rags for wadding."

"Yes, sir. Let's get back to the barrel part."

"Well, what if we was to bore out a hardwood log with red-hot irons?"

"It'd likely split into kindling the first time you fired her."

"I know. That's what I mean about getting from the thinking to the doing. I thought mebbe you could help me work out a safety valve or some other way to hold the durned thing together."

Joe wondered how he was going to get out of there gracefully. More to humor Squire Junior than with any hopes for the mad plan, he shrugged and said, "Well, if we wrapped some rope around a hardwood cannon . . . Wait a minute. Rawhide. Wrap wet rawhide thongs around her. Four or five layers. When the rawhide dried and shrank . . ."

"Damn it, son, they *told* me you was bright as a tack! By thunder, that would do it! We'll get a four-foot log of hard maple, bore her out and wrap her like you said! I can see it now! We'll name her Martha Washington and blow them redskins to Kingdom Come!"

Joe stood up and said, "It ought to work, sir. It's worth a try. I got to get back to my rounds."

"You run along then. How soon do you figure to start my cannon?"

"Me, sir?"

"Well, you can see I'm in no shape to build a cannon."

Joe understood now why the poor Squire Junior's grand notions tended to peter out. But he nodded and said, "I'll see if I can detail some of the lads to it, sir."

"You promise? You ain't just funning me like Dan'l and the rest of my family?"

"No. I said it was worth a try, and Lord knows we have to keep 'em busy. I'll let you know how it's coming. Maybe your boy Moses would like to lend us a hand."

He went outside. As he walked away, young Moses caught up with him. Moses said, gravely, "That was neighborly of you, sir. I know what folks think of my dad, but I sort of like him."

"You're right to like your dad, Moses. It wasn't such a bad idea, once you get over the first shock."

"You don't mean you aim to do it? It isn't just another one of dad's wild notions?"

"We're in a wild neck of the woods, Moses. Mebbe it'll take new notions to tame this land. You run along and get some shut-eye. Come morning, I want you to rustle up a good log of rock maple, hear?"

He got rid of the boy and was intending to go back to Margaret, but he heard a shout from the lookout and ran over to the nearest ladder. He climbed to the catwalk and met London and Wolfgang, both peering anxiously over the wall at the growing circle of fire. It was only a few yards out from the wall and spreading fast. The wind was sweeping smoke and flames their way!

Other men were joining them now. One was Captain Boone, who cursed and said, "You were right about the underbrush along that fence line, Joe. The Shawnee must have gathered drying flax from yonder field and piled it up afore they lit her. I remember the gals had spread some retted flax to dry out there. Look at the damn stuff burn!"

Wolfgang said, "We must put it out." He handed London his rifle and said, "Cover me. I am over the wall going!"

Boone grabbed the Hessian and snapped, "No you're not! That's just what theyll be waiting for! They got at least a dozen muskets trained on that blaze from the dark beyond. They'll make a sieve outten you afore you reach that fence line."

"But, Herr Boone, the fire out must be stamped! In minutes this wall in flames will be!"

Boone nodded and said, "Follow me, boys. There's more'n one way to bell the cat!"

He led them down to ground level and found a place where the hastily erected wall had been plugged with bales of hide. He hauled at them, explaining, "We got to do this sneaky. Wolfgang, run and fetch some spades from the shed. Help me with these bales, Joe."

Joe did as he was told. As they crouched in the narrow gap, he stared out at the approaching flames and said, "We hug the ground and sort of dig our way close enough to throw dirt on the flaming straw, right?"

Boone nodded. "Yep. With plenty of gun flashes to distract 'em from up above."

London, holding Wolfgang's rifle, asked what he could do. Boone said, "You're to hold this gap with that fancy gun. We'll crawl out and . . ."

Joe said, "Captain, you stay here and cover me and Wolfgang."

"Hell, son, I never ask anyone to do what I ain't willing to."

"These folks need you, captain. You and that flag up there are all that's keeping this fort fighting. Me and Wolfgang will douse the fire."

"Dammit it, Joe, I'm in command here, ain't I?"

"Yessir, and you're to stay alive and commanding if I have to bust you one! I mean it, sir. You stay put or you and me will be headed for a fight!"

Boone swore. But as Wolfgang joined them with the entrenching tools, he ran for the ladder, yelling, "All right, boys. Fire into the dark for luck and keep firing!"

As the rattle of arms filled the night, Joe and Wolfgang started on their bellies for the fire line, half crawling and half digging, hidden in a cloud of dust. A bullet hummed like an angry hornet over Joe's head and a man above nailed the Indian who'd exposed his position with a muzzle flash.

Joe figured they were close as they were going to get. He lay on his side, throwing dirt with his spade at the flames. Wolfgang did the same. As the fire grew dimmer they rolled closer and beat out the embers with their tools, ignoring the war cries and shots from the darkness until the last glow of smouldering flax had been killed.

Wolfgang muttered, "Here they come!" They heard the sound of drumming moccasins. Joe grunted, "Run for it!" and, as the Hessian got away, swung the sharp edge of his spade at a shadow looming over him. There was a sickening crunch and Joe was spattered with wetness as the Indian split open like a melon. Then Joe was up and running too. He dove through the narrow opening with the Shawnee right behind. As he rolled to one side, London leveled the rifle at a blur of motion and pulled the trigger.

There was a flash in the pan, but the rifle refused to go off as it should have. One of the Indians out in the night fired at the sound and useless flash. London gave an odd little grunt and fell back, a musket ball in his chest. Joe shoved the bales back in place against a hail of lead. By the time he'd blocked the opening, the fire from above had sent the attackers packing, screaming ghastly threats.

Joe found Wolfgang holding London's head on his knees. The Hessian said, "The touch-hole fouled with powder was! I . . . I . . ." He was close to sobbing, blaming himself for the faulty gun.

Joe knelt to feel London's pulse and the Negro opened his eyes. He said weakly, "I got to git back to my mistress if them rascals is attackin', suh."

Joe said, "We beat 'em off this time, thanks to you, London."

"Did I do right, suh? There was somethin' wrong with the gun."

"You did fine, London. You drove 'em back from your post. You'll likely get a medal, once the militia gets here."

London winced and said, "I don't 'spect I'll be

here that long, suh. It's funny. I ain't feared of dying. But I did so want to see how it all turned out."

"Just rest easy while I have a look at you. It's going to turn out fine, London. We're going to win, sure as hell."

"I purely hope so, suh. But I wanted so to *be* there! They said when us Americans was free, we'd all be equal, like they wrote on that declaration paper. You reckon it'll be that way, Mister Joe?"

"I'm sure of it, London. It's what we're fighting for, isn't it?"

"I know. I just wanted to see . . . if they meant us colored folks too."

Joe found the gaping wound and blinked the sudden moisture from his eyes. London was breathing funny, but he was still half consious. He muttered, "Do Jesus, I hopes they meant what they said that day."

Joe said, "They did, London. We hold these truths to be self-evident; that all men are created equal . . ."

But London was dead. Joe hoped he'd heard the last part, whether it was true or not. Wolfgang sniffed and said, "Well, so now we bury our first dead."

Joe asked, "Do you know how a military burial goes, Wolfgang?"

"*Ja.* But I don't know if the others will permit it, for a colored."

Joe stood up and growled, "They'll permit it.

They'll permit it or I'll whup every mother's son of 'em."

There was no objection to the military funeral of the dead slave. Little Mercy and some of the other women cried and even the surly Dick Callaway stood at attention as the body was lowered into the shallow grave near the place London died. It was generally allowed London had been a decent enough cuss, for one of *them*. The red-skinned enemy all around seemed to make it less important that a fallen comrade in arms had been a mite darker than most folks.

The sun rose, but there was no sign of activity until nine or so. When the lookout did spot movement, it made little sense. Joe, Boone and Flanders Callaway watched from the east wall as a long line of Indians filed past, far out of range and ignoring them. Some were riding ponies. Others drove stolen cattle. Most just trudged on by, crossing the river at the shallows a half mile upstream. Boone sucked on his unlit pipe and mused aloud, "It purely looks like they're headed home, don't it?"

Joe watched for a glimpse of blonde hair, failed to see any and swept his eyes over the muddy river before he said, "I don't think they mean it."

Boone nodded and said, "I got eyes, son. I can see they're still digging that fool tunnel. Black Fish is trying one of the oldest tricks in the book.

If he really meant to give up and go home for the fall hunt, he'd be down here making a speech about it. You see that spotted pony just fording the river? I've seen it twice in less'n fifteen minutes. They're fording where we can see 'em, then doubling back around the river bend. Black Fish must be getting old. He should have carried the Tory tents and De Quindre's banners past us. But he takes us for fools."

Flanders asked, "How long do you figure they'll carry on like that, Dan'l?" and Boone said, "Oh, they'll let us count heads for a while, then lay low for a spell in the woods all around. They know I'm a sort of suspicious cuss. So they'll wait mebbe a day and a night to see if we fell for it. If we don't go out to salvage our crops and round up any strays they left, it'll take Black Fish at least a day or so to figure we ain't buying his wooden nutmegs. He'll likely be mad as hell about it too."

Flanders said, "The sounds of digging are louder now. I think they've hit rock, from the sound of it. They're sort of worming their way along, searching for a soft vein under us."

Joe asked, "Do they have any chance of finding a way under our walls?"

Flanders shrugged and replied, "Don't know. Limestone's funny rock. It's like wormy cheese. Hard in some parts. Soft and crumbly in others. Them hills all about is riddled with bat caves. They could hit solid rock for miles and bust into a chamber big enough to build a house in. You ain't hit soft rock at the well, have you?"

"No, damn it. We're down a good eight feet and it's dry and hard as solid bone. We're nearly out of drinking water too."

Boone looked at the sky and sighed. He said, "Black Fish knowed what he was doing, hitting us so late in the season. The logs are tinder dry and it sure don't look like rain. If he knowed how low we was on water he'd have put some fire arrows over the walls by now. We'd be in a fix if we had to put out a real fire."

Then he brightened and said, "Hell, let's eat. There's no use watching that charade. They'll be at it all morning and after they finish convincing us they've left for good, we'll have at least the rest of the day afore they come whooping and hollering again."

Leaving a couple of boys to watch the Indians' mock withdrawal, the older men of Boonesburough used the unexpected break to catch up on long-neglected chores, a little loving and, in some cases, a spell of loafing.

Joe found Moses Boone and the Collins boy working on Squire Junior's grand invention. Wolfgang, as a professional soldier, refused to consider a wooden cannon. Captain Dan'l couldn't take anything his elder brother dreamed of seriously, and Joe didn't have the time.

But at his suggestion, the boys had experimented with variations on the theme. Nobody knew if it was better to shrink the rawhide around the log before or after they bored it out with hot irons. But there was plenty of wood and green leather, so they decided to do it both ways. Two cannon seemed better than one. If one blew to matchsticks on the first try, maybe the other wouldn't. It was generally agreed no settler would be anywhere near the fool things when and if they went off.

A couple of cows and a pony had died inside the compound, either from panic or neglect. The carcasses were skinned and cut up to dry to sun-cured jerky on the rooftops. Meanwhile, a work team chopped through the cabin walls to form a corridor around the perimeter of the fort, while others criss-crossed logs into a tall rickety look-out tower on the roof of one blockhouse.

Flanders had moved his listening post to the trench scooped out inside the wall facing the river. When he put his ear to the old bayonet he could hear the sound of picks and crowbars ring-ing against soft limestone. De Quindre seemed to be drilling at them with brute force, or, as Flanders suggested, wedging out the rock by taking advantage of the natural faults and fis-sures. The work crew trying to sink the frustrat-ing water well inside the fort would find a huge chunk of the stuff loose enough to crowbar out, but then they'd be hammering again at solid bedrock. The natural suggestion was made that they try another well, some other place. But Boone said, and Joe agreed, there was no sense turning the town square into a pock-marked mess of craters, since they were as likely to break through to water where they were as anywhere else.

By afternoon, the last of the Indians had apparently crossed the river and trekked north for Chillicothe. The sun blazed down on the quiet valley and the settlers stared wistfully out at their trampled fields and torn down fences. One of the settlers had planted little peach whips a couple of hundred yards out, and his hopeful-someday peach orchard had been shabbily treated by the Indians. He was sure he could save some of his saplings by resetting them in the soil and was quite put out when the captain wouldn't let him. He insisted he'd be almost in gunshot range and could run back in time if the Indians re-appeared at the tree line. But Boone was adamant and, to Joe's mild surprise, the unpleasant Dick Callaway backed Boone when the man appealed to him.

Callaway was neither a fool nor a craven. Joe had that straight now. He simply hated to play second fiddle to a man he considered his social inferior, and while the erstwhile "colonel" was prone to hastier judgments than Boone, even Joe admitted Boone's procrastination and sometimes hasty last-minute changes could be unsettling. Callaway would have made a good officer in the regulars, Joe thought, leading soldiers who followed rule books. Boone was a natural survivor who thought on his feet and shifted with every breeze in the uncertain world of the frontier. They were both a mite right and both a mite wrong. Joe wished they could see fit to work together better. Shoulder to shoulder under fire, they made a good team. But the moment things got quiet, the back-biting started again. Boone dismissed Callaway as an idjet and Callaway muttered dark suspicions behind Boone's back.

Late in the afternoon, they watched as wild geese flew south overhead and men spoke wistfully of the coming fall hunt. The summer's hard-won harvest had been ruined. They faced a long hard winter even if they never saw another Indian. But there were nuts and berries in the woods all around and the deer and bear would be fat this time of the year, after a summer of foraging. Some were sure the Indians had given up for the same reason and gone home to gather food stores for the coming winter. But the river still swirled brownly by and as the sun went down the patches of brush and woodland surrounding them were quiet, too quiet, for the night critters seldom stirred when the scent and sounds of mankind hovered near.

There were no campfires gleaming on the ridge lines now. Some of the men suggested a scouting patrol to see if it was possible the Indians had really given up. But Boone and Callaway agreed the idea was simply foolish. No white man born of woman was going to sneak up on a Shawnee trying to lay low, while the reverse might not be true.

The sounds of mining stopped after dark. Flanders wondered aloud if De Quindre's crew had followed the others off a ways after giving up on hard rock. Boone said it didn't matter. Wherever they were, it wouldn't be far.

At midnight, as Joe lay stretched out fully dressed in the cabin he shared with Margaret, he heard excited talk outside and swung his legs off the cot. Margaret muttered in her sleep. She'd been sullen that evening because their privacy was marred by the blankets over the openings in either wall and because of Joe's reluctance to make love to her under such public conditions. Joe went outside to find others gathered around the Cherokee, Many Jackets. Part of the excite- was occasioned by the fact the Indian had come in over the wall, unspotted and unchallenged by the men who were supposed to be on guard. But they were more excited, and dismayed, by the news he'd brought them.

Many Jackets said, "All of you are dead. A man named Patton was out hunting on the north side of the river when the Shawnee first attacked. He made it to Logan's Station, very frightened. He told them you'd been overrun by the Shawnee. He said he heard the screaming as the Indians scalped you all. He said the sky was red behind him as he ran. He said Black Fish killed you all and burned the fort."

A man said, "Jesus, if they think we've been massacred, they won't be sending help!"

Many Jackets said, "I know. At Logan's and

Harrodsburg everyone is holed up, waiting for the Shawnee to hit them in turn. Shawnee scouts were spotted near Harrodsburg. A fire arrow was sent over their wall, but they put it out. I think they are very worried, but not about you."

"What about Colonel Compbell and the Virginia militia?"

"We have heard no word about a relief column. Washington is calling for more men. The British are said to be ready to land in the Carolinas. There is heavy fighting up north. Simon Kenton says he does not think we'll get any help out here. He sent me in to tell you the Shawnee have not gone away. They have been joined by more men from Chillicothe and Hamilton has sent them ammunition. We think Black Fish plans an all-out attack."

Boone shifted his weight and asked, "How far out are they right now?"

"A mile or so each way. They have you circled, but they are thinly spread. That is how I got through to you. Simon Kenton says he can do more good if he stays behind their lines. We have had good hunting."

One of the men said soberly, "Good woodsman could likely slip out right now and mebbe make it to Harrodsburg or Logan's."

There was a murmur of agreement and another opined, "Tonight may be the last chance we're likely to git! We're fixing to lose our hair for sure if we just sit and wait for the rascals to hit us agin!"

Boone snorted, "Hell, we got the womenfolk and small 'uns to think on! You aim to creep betwixt the Shawnee pickets with a crying baby or a gal about to birth one and walking like a cow?"

One of the single men said, "That's all right for you married gents to say. But I've only got my own hair to worry about, and I'm fond as hell of my fool scalp."

Callaway blustered, "Any man who tries to desert will be shot!"

But Boone said, "Oh, shut up, Dick. Nobody's deserting at the moment, and if anybody here tries it later on, there's no way we're likely to stop him. We don't need anyone that worried about his own hide anyway. A man who'd desert at a time like this would likely eat shit."

There was a general round of agreement and the meeting broke up as Many Jackets said he had to rejoin Kenton out in the Indian-haunted darkness. Joe went back to the cabin and found Margaret wide awake. He sat on the edge of the bed and told her about the conversation.

When he got to the part about slipping away, she asked how he felt about the notion. He lit his pipe and pondered some before he said, "I don't know. It'd be a mean-hearted thing to do, but I got you to study on. We got no children to hold us back, and I know you're as good on the trail as many a man. We got the guns and we got this one chance before they circle us tight again. If we were to just slip out and start walking we'd be miles from here by sun-up. The folks we'd leave behind would purely mean-mouth us some. But it is not like they figure to live long enough for it to really matter."

Margaret said softly, "I'm ready to chance it if you are, dear. Can we make it?"

"Just the two of us? The odds are in our favor. We'd have a right good chance if we left right now."

"I don't suppose we could take Mercy Bryan along, could we? The child has nobody to look after her with London dead."

"She's kin to Boone. If she heard we were fixing to light out, she might tell him."

"I see. But if we leave her behind . . ."

Joe nodded. "That's the part I don't like to think about. I'm sort of fond of some in Boonesburough. I'm going to feel bad, leaving them to face the Shawnee without my gun."

"But you want to leave, don't you?"

"Not hardly. If it was only me I had to worry about, I'd stick her out to the last musket ball and go down slashing with my knife. But it isn't just me. You're depending on me to keep you alive, and I don't see how I can do it if we stay."

"Joe, I'm frightened."

"I know. I'll get you outten this, somehow. I promise that."

"Please let me finish, dear. I'm so scared I'm about to wet my drawers. But all of us are scared. If I let you play the coward just to save myself, I know you'd hate us both later."

"Well, I'll likely hate my ownself. But it's a

man's job to take care of his womenfolks. Don't you want to go?"

"Oh, I want to go so bad I could scream! But womenfolks have a reason for being too. I know I can never bear you a son. I know I can never be a real wife to you. But I love you too much to let you hate yourself, and you *will* hate yourself, Joe. I know you better than you think."

"I'm going to tell it true, Meg. I want to stay. But you have to understand this is no story book and there don't figure to be a happy ending. If we don't light out tonight, we'll never get another chance. This fort figures to fall if they hit us again."

"You men have beaten back every attack, dear."

"Maybe. But that was before the water run out. Black Fish has more men and ammunition. He's a stubborn old cuss and his job is on the line. He'll hit with ever'thing he's got, and we haven't got shit. You have to understand I'm not talking about a snowball fight, Meg. They're out to kill us, serious. If we stay, we'll likely die and, I dunno, you're sort of pretty. "

Meg sat up and put her arms around him. She said, "I wouldn't mind if we could die together, darling."

"You mean that, Meg? You're really willing to stick it out, knowing we got hardly a chance?"

"I mean it, Joe Floyd. I'm your woman and you're a man and a man has to do what he thinks right."

He kissed her and said, "By jimmies, Meg. You're a good old gal and that's a fact. I wish they hadn't busted through our walls like that. I'd show you just how much I think of you right now, if some damn fool boy or hound dog wasn't likely to come through the blankets to see what all the fuss was about."

She clung to him, softly sobbing, and he said, "What's the matter?"

"Nothing, darling. I'm just so happy."

"Happy? Woman, you are a caution when it comes to funny feelings. I figured you were a good sport, but this ain't a laughing matter."

"Joe?"

"What are you doing with my britches, Meg? We're as good as in the public square and there's folks just beyond."

"We could be very quiet, couldn't we?"

"Well, if you promise not to holler this time. I'm sort of feeling friendly my ownself."

He lowered her to the mattress with a hand on her breast and kissed the tears from her cheeks. And this time, when she asked if he loved her, it didn't feel like he was just saying it to please her.

23

By the following afternoon Black Fish knew his
ruse hadn't worked. Dropping all pretense, the
Indians rushed the walls from every side. Some
ran down the slope, singing their death songs
and dying bravely as they ran. Others splashed
across the river from the north to sink in billowing clouds of blood or huddle against the bank,
pinned down by fire from the fort.

Boone was everywhere at once as every man
and many of the boys manned the walls, firing
as fast as their women could reload their guns.
The air was filled with gunsmoke and war cries
and a little sparrow of a woman named South
ran about in circles, crying, "Oh, stop it! Stop it!
You'll make the Indians mad at us!"

Moses Boone and some of the younger boys
scooped up rocks from the diggings inside the
fort and began to throw them over the wall for
luck. A Wyandot was hit with a rock and
screamed curses at them in broken English as
he danced in an angry circle, holding his head.
One of the boys shouted a dreadful thing about

the Indian's mother and Mrs. South cried out, "Oh, heavens, you musn't cuss like that!"

A laconic marksman blew the side off the Wyandot's head and muttered, "Sorry, Ma'am. He likely wasn't brung up right."

The first attack was broken off when the smoke got so thick nobody could see a target from either side.

The Indians drew back just outside musket range. One of the Shawnee turned his back on the defenders, removed his breech clout and thrust his bare rump out at them, shouting, "Kiss it, white man!"

A couple of men wasted shots at the impossible range as the Indian kept jeering and wiggling his naked rump at them. Then Wolfgang rammed a double charge in his Hessian rifle, took careful aim and fired. The Indian leaped high in the air and crashed down with half his rump shot away. The settlers cheered as he bled to death, writhing in the grass.

On the north wall, a man spotted a feather above the rim of the river bank. He called out, "I see you, Shawnee! What you doing, soaking your feet?"

The Indian called back, "Digging, white meat. Digging to blow you all to the Great Father In The Sky!"

The settler fired and though he only blew some straw and feathers away in the breeze, the hidden Indian did not see fit to make further comment.

Some clever Cherokee up the slope put their gun butts on the ground and began lobbing balls into the fort with plunging fire. Settlers ducked for cover as the heavy lead balls hailed down. On the wall a man shook his fist and yelled curses worthy of a muleskinner while the flighty Mrs. South held her hands over her ears and pleaded, "Oh, you mustn't cuss like that!"

Mrs. South suffered a slight lisp. Her obvious lack of common sense made even the other women laughed when she wailed, " You mustn't say such tewwible things! The Indians will weak a tewwible wevenge on us!"

The others seized on her words, which became a tag-line to be shouted back and forth along the wall. A man or boy would nail a screaming warrior and his comrades on either side would gaily shout, "Look out, boy! They'll weak a tewwible wevenge on you!"

The men sincerely tried to keep more earthy curses down as the skirmishing continued, but even women could forget their manners when a musket ball slammed down to spatter them with dust and shattered stone. Pretty little Jemima Boone Callaway contributed her own unseemly words when a bullet tore through a rotten stockade log and knocked her off her feet.

"The fuckers!" yelled Jemima, "They've shot me in the ass!" Her husband and Mercy Bryan dragged her to cover, cursing like a trooper, and rolled her on her stomach. Mercy pulled Jemima's skirt and the bullet came out of her but-

tock with the bloody cloth. Jemima rubbed her
wounded rear, got up and snatched her husband's gun. Before he could stop her, she ran
over to the nearest loophole, blew a prancing
Mingo off his feet and muttered, "That'll larn
you, you sons of bitches!"

Above her on the catwalk, Dan'l Boone
grinned fondly down and shouted, "That's my
daughter, sure as hell!"

While Jemima was having her undignified
wound dressed, Dick Callaway's wife, a fat formidable woman, caught one of the men hiding
in the potting shed, frightened out of his wits.
She hit him with a broom and, although a praying woman, shouted, "Matthias Prock, you come
out here and do your duty, you son of a bitch!"

Then she chased the poor Pennsylvania
Dutchman with her relentless broom until he
risked a peek through a loophole, shuddered,
and collapsed in a helpless ball of quivering
flesh. Mrs. Callaway grabbed him by one ear
and dragged him to the unfinished well. She
shoved him in the hole and commanded, "Dig,
you bastard! If you can't fight Injuns you can
dig for water!" Then she left him to return to
her post, reloading for her husband. Later, Joe
would find the poor old Dutchman curled up in
a ball at the bottom of the wall and send him
back to his potting shed while the formidable
dowager wasn't looking.

The Indians were using plunging fire from the
ridge across the river now. Though the three-

quarter-inch lead balls were spent as they came down, they landed with lethal momentum. Some of the remaining livestock were hit and either died at once or had to be shot as they stampeded in the confined space in pain. The carcasses were set aside against the future. But the corn and other staples had been used up and the water barrels were empty. As the sun sank low once more the defenders prayed for rain, but the sky remained a bright blue they no longer found pretty. The grit of dust and the taste of gunsmoke filled the air as the blood from the butchered livestock was carefully set aside for the smaller children and the wounded. Bathing a bullet wound with ox blood made for sticky dressings indeed, but they had nothing else. The well was given up. It would be sheer suicide to go on working in the open with the enemy on the high ground.

That night the Indians kept up the pressure, moving closer under the cover of darkness. Only an early moonrise saved them when a lookout spied skirmishers crawling within musket range.

A flaming arrow came over the wall as the men on the catwalk drove other Indians with torches back with well-aimed shots. The fire arrow thudded into the door of Dick Callaway's cabin, where he was trying to catch a few winks with his stout wife. Their son-in-law, John Holder, ran over with a half-filled bucket of precious drinking water and, using it carefully, doused the flames that outlined him vividly for the Indian marksmen up the hill. Ignoring the bullets plucking at his life, young Holder bravely put the fire out, but he was swearing a blue streak while he did it.

The door opened and his befuddled mother-in-law stuck her head out to yell, "You're going to hell for using such language, John Holder! I've a mind to wash your mouth out with soap!"

John Holder muttered, "Shit." When the woman came out at him with her ever-ready broom, he danced away, grinning. "Hold your fire, old woman! If you won't forgive me, the Lord will! He's a man, and likely understands."

But if Holder's in-law troubles provided comic relief, it was only for the moment. The Indians tried again and again to set the dry logs afire. A man named Boudrin was manning a loophole when an Indian bullet hit the hunk of limestone holding the logs apart. The stone shattered like glass and a chunk was driven through his forehead into his brain. They dragged him, semi-conscious, to his cabin, where his distracted wife kept bathing the ghastly wound. She kept repeating, over and over, how lucky it was they hadn't put his eye out. David Boudrin remained conscious to the end, holding his own brains in with his hands as he rocked back and forth in agony, until he muttered, "It's getting better," and fell forward dead, his shattered head in his sobbing wife's lap.

They buried him near London, just before sunrise.

24

The siege dragged on. Later, it would be remembered as having lasted all summer and be
inflated into family legends and hastily written
frontier sagas. In fact, only ten full days of battle
took place at the Siege Of Boonesburough. But
one day would have been long enough to the
men who died on both sides, or to the sleepless
women and children who huddled in the tiny
fortress, wondering if they'd live to see another
dawn.

Pompey, the ex-slave fighting with the Shawnee, made the mistake of taking cover in a thick
clump of green as the sun rose over the little
battlefield after another hard-fought night. Pompey had the medicine gun from Detroit and
meant to prove himself to his red comrades.

But another wanderer far from home spotted
Pompey in the screen of green. When Wolfgang
fired, his medicine was better. The Hessian's
rifle ball hit Pompey in the eye and blew his
brains out the back of his feathered head. As
the black rolled into view from his sniping posi-

tion, the lookout on the tower yelled, "Hot damn! We got the nigger!"

Two brave Shawnee darted out to carry Pompey's body away. Later, when a settler yelled out to a skulking Indian, "Hey, redskin, where's old Pompey?" the English-speaking Shawnee taunted, "Gone to get more Indians, white man!"

The whites laughed and sent the Indian back up the hill, taunting, "Hear that, boys? Now they got to recruit 'em from hell!"

The Indians got their revenge when Boone himself was hit by a nearly spent ball as he ran across the square. The bullet knocked him flat and a joyous shout rose from the Indian lines as others dragged Dan'l to cover. The wound in his muscular neck was superficial, but the Indians had seen him fall and as his daughter Jemima patched him up a man in a porcupine head-roach prancing just out of range yelled, "Heya, where is Big Turtle? Why don't we see Big Turtle? Has he followed Pompey to the Jesus place?"

This went on for some time. Even Wolfgang missed shot after shot at the jeering Shawnee. Then Boone came out, borrowed a small-bore French rifle and blew the roach and scalp off the jester, who ran screaming up the hill holding his bloody head.

Boone called out, "Here's Big Turtle, damn your eyes! Big Turtle's been to hell and back for a visit with your friends!"

Joe Floyd didn't join in the slanging match

as he moved from place to place around the walls. He didn't think it was all that funny. Sometimes it was easier to pick off a feathered head or exposed rump by just laying low and biding one's time.

Then, as the sun was once more sinking, the lookout spotted movement in the peach whips, just out of range. A clump of Indians were gathered there, as if to make a determined twilight charge, and the men on the wall knew what the tell-tale plumes of woodsmoke meant. They were planning to attack with guns and flaming arrows.

Wolfgang moved over to that wall and said it was no use. They were too far out for his German rifle and too close in for comfort. As the shadows lengthened, men had to be warned to man the other positions. The men with Wolfgang would break up the rush before they got within archery range, or, if they couldn't, there wasn't much anyone could do about it.

At that moment, Squire Junior rejoined the defenders. He walked rather grandly, his arm in a sling, carrying himself with the dignity only the drunk can hope to manage gracefully.

Behind him trailed a gang of boys with Martha Washington and Doctor Franklin. The two wooden cannon had been braced with wagon tire as well as rawhide. Both were loaded with a pint of powder, shredded blanket wadding and all the junk they could scrounge at short notice. The improvised guns were hoisted to a rooftop and trained on the peach orchard. The boys lit the fuses and scattered for cover as everyone held their breath.

Martha Washington exploded with a thunderous roar and filled the air with kindling wood and flying splinters as her maple breech blew up. The Indians were astounded at the noise but cheered by its harmless results. Some stood up to see what was going on. At that moment, Doctor Franklin cleared its throat.

The wooden barrel held. A good ten pounds of nails, horseshoes, hammer heads, a whirling crowbar and at least one flatiron cut through peach whips and human flesh alike with horrendous results. The cover was flattened. A dozen Indians were ripped to bloody hash and twice that many rolled in agony with ghastly, shredded wounds. The survivors scattered, screaming in terror.

There was a long moment of silence across the entire valley as the echoes faded away. Then Captain Boone stared in wonder at his elder brother and marveled, "Well, I'll be damned! It worked!"

And so Joe Floyd's boast about a cannon in the fort was made good, no doubt to the considerable discomfort of Black Fish's Tory advisers.

Unfortunately, the next time they fired Doctor Franklin, it split. The Indians, however, maintained a more respectful distance for the moment. Squire Junior and the boys went back to work. The next time he said someday there'd be steamboats on the Ohio, nobody laughed.

The Indians retired for a time. But in the darkness Flanders Callaway heard the scrape of shovel and pick at his listening post and reported De Quindre was still at it and getting closer. The moon set and the stars were obscured by a sullen sticky overcast as men fired at imaginary attackers in the ink-black darkness all around.

Then, in the wee small hours, a fire arrow cometted down on a rooftop. There was no water left to fight the flames. So men exposed themselves to muzzle flashes all around as they tore the burning shingles off with their bare hands, even as more fire arrows landed around them. In moments the whole southeast side of the fort was burning brightly. And the Indians came whooping in from every quarter.

The defenders tried in vain to douse the flames with dust and the contents of drinking jugs, and a man rolled off a burning rooftop with a flaming arrow in his back.

From high on a distant hilltop, Simon Kenton watched and groaned, sure that the little fort and all his friends were done for.

Inside the burning fortress it seemed so too. The settlers were saved as much by their madly milling panic as any efforts they could think of, as the Indians pumped lead and arrows into the chaos of smoke, firelight and screaming.

Men fought one another to reach their women and children, some to simply gather them in their arms as they stared, stone-faced, into the flames. Others dragged their families to the northwest blockhouse for a final stand. Indian faces were appearing above the walls now, grinning red in the flickering light and stopped more by the heat and choking smoke than by the few aimed shots in their direction.

Flanders Callaway and Jemima backed into a corner and the girl loaded her man's musket with a knife gripped between her pretty teeth.

Fat Mrs. Callaway stood between her children and anything brave enough to come at her and her broom. Her husband Dick rammed a double charge in his musket with a terrible expression on his pale face.

The lisping Mrs. South still twittered like a bird, but as a Mingo came over the wall she put a bullet in his middle.

Captain Boone stood in the open between his people and the Indians, as if to bar them with his flesh and the empty musket in his hands.

Wolfgang Rodenau fired round after round, reloading, presenting and firing as if he stood on the fields of Saratoga facing Morgan's Virginia Rifles. Behind him, the Dutchman Prock prayed mindlessly on his knees, his pants wet through with terror.

Joe Floyd and Margaret were holed up behind a bale of hides with little Mercy Bryan and Moses Boone. The boy didn't know where his father was, or if he was still alive. When last seen, Squire Junior and his wife had been near the wall, the woman loading as the old man fired, his grievous wound forgotten. He was scared sober as a judge.

Mercy and Margaret charged the spare muskets as Joe and the nine-year-old Moses made their stand. Determined to go down fighting, they were down to their last few cartridges, but little Moses allowed he still had his dad's broadax.

A Cherokee in a red turban ran across the open clearing at them, to be folded in the middle by the boy's musket. Joe held his fire for the next target, knowing there'd be more than he could hope to stop.

And then, as everyone knew they were dead and wondered why they seemed to be still breathing, there was a tremendous noise and the whole area lit up with chalk-white light. For a moment Joe thought Squire Junior had fired off his cannon again. The Indians must have thought so too, for they hesitated before their final rush.

Then the rain came down in a good Kentucky cloudburst the heat had been saving up for days. Within moments the night was plunged into a deep pit of utter blackness as the rain put out the flames, wet everybody's powder and turned the battle into a muddy wrestling match.

Someone ran into Joe in the dark. When he grabbed, he felt painted oily flesh and feathers. So he started tearing whoever it was apart with his bare hands.

The Indians didn't like to fight this way. The Shawnee were a supple small-boned breed and, unlike Mohawk, had little chance in a test of brute strength with the brawny northern Europeans they encountered for the most part in the dark. As quickly as it had begun, the battle was broken off. The Indians retreated to dry their powder and fire arrows. The settlers staggered, weak with relief, to count the bodies and make such hasty repairs as they could in total darkness by feel alone.

The rain settled down to an all-night steady drizzle, chilling the battered survivors to the bone but filling the rain barrels to overflowing.

As dawn crept grayer than any cat from the east, men manned the walls with knives, hatchets and tools. They knew their muskets were useless in such weather.

The Indians knew their own powder couldn't be kept dry in the downpour either. So as light stole across the battlefield, the settlers saw they'd retreated to dry themselves around the fires visible on both ridges.

A lookout called out cheerfully. When Joe joined Boone and the others near the gate, he saw what seemed to be a long muddy trench running in a zigzag to within twenty yards of the wall. De Quindre's mine-sap had caved in. The counter-sap inside the walls was filled with muddy rainwater but draining in a whirlpool at one end. Someone asked if Boone thought the cave-in had buried the French engineer and his crew alive. Boone spat and said, "I hope so. But the Lord was neighborly last night. I wouldn't want to press Him for more favors!"

It kept on raining. A cold fall rain that just kept coming as if the sky was trying to make up for the dry spell it had put them through for the last few weeks.

It rained all day and it rained the next night. The water leaked through the charred roofing and ran down the log walls in cindery cold rivulets until the earth floors were a quagmire. It was impossible to keep dry or to get warm and while the wet spell seemed to have kept the Indians around their own fires, it began to get on everyone's nerves. Squire Junior stood in the doorway of his charred cabin and stared up at the grey-wool sky to announce, "We thank Thee, Lord, for Thy evidence of Divine Providence. But the rain barrels are filled, Lord. These logs is soaked so good you couldn't light 'em again with the brimstones of hell. Dang it, Lord, enough is enough!"

Others tended to agree by now. Some of the

children were starting to sniffle and the men on guard were chilled to the bone. As the old familiar grumbling began again, the men more sensible of their plight took advantage of the lull to shore up the defenses.

Badly charred logs were pried loose and replaced by fingers blue with cold and too numb to feel a splinter or a gash. Some of the cabins were roofless ruins, so they were salvaged for useful timbers and the defenders crowded into such shelter as was left. The crowding helped to warm them but added fuel to the mutterings. The old forgotten feuds resumed. Dick Callaway blamed Boone for the weather now, saying Dan'l could have thought about how easy shingles burned. Had *he* been in command, he insisted, they'd have used slate shingles and sand-filled fire buckets would have been ready at hand. It was hard to find fault with Callaway's hindsight. Anyone could see now where mistakes had been made. Boone's friends wondered aloud why Callaway hadn't had all his grand notions while he'd been in command during Boone's captivity. Others tended to side with Callaway as he explained how Boone had come back just in time to mess things up. Probably in league with his old friend, Black Fish.

It was unkind and unfair, but it was human nature. Many a man had guilty memories of orders ignored and duties shirked. It was easier to agree it had been someone else's fault.

Joe Floyd and Margaret shared a damp

blanket with Mercy Bryan when Joe finished his shift at repairs and staggered inside to warm himself. He got under the blanket with the two girls and put an arm around them both, soaking up the warmth from their bodies.

Little Mercy held one of his hands between her knees to warm it and Margaret warmed the other by rubbing it. The girls were hungry but uncomplaining and as Joe told them the repairs were going well, Mercy brightened and said, "I heard Campbell's Virginian is due most any moment now."

Joe didn't answer. He was finding the constant rain tedious, but he knew it would stop all too soon. The powder both sides had would dry, and the Shawnee would be coming back before any fool militia figured on getting there.

25

Joe was right about the Virginia militia, but Britain's Indian allies had more than the little fort at Boonesburough to worry about that year. Far to the northeast another man named Joe was marching through the same rain, in the valley of the Mohawk River.

He was Major Joseph Bloomfield and he marched on one flank of Sullivan's Continental lines, leading a battalion of New Jersey militia.

They were hard men, the Jersey Devils, and they'd seen things in the last few weeks that had aged them years and left grim lines around their tight-set lips. They'd passed burned-out cabins and buried the bloated mutilated bodies of American men, women and children. The same ruthless Governor Hamilton who'd sent armed Shawnee down the Ohio Valley had sent painted Iroquois against the York State settlers under the bloody-minded Butler brothers and the twisted Simon Girty. George Washington himself had sent this punitive expedition to repay the People Of The Long House for tiny

nameless battles and for the terrible deaths of
frontier folk the history books would never record.

Joe Bloomfield, like Joe Floyd, was cold and
wet and grim of jaw that same rainy afternoon.
His men trudged silently behind him. Tough
iron miners from the Wachung Mountains. Char-
coal burners from the Jersey pine barrens.
Weathered market hunters from the swampy
Jersey meadows and many a stubborn Dutch
farmboy from the banks of the winding Passaic.
All they had in common was the name of their
new little state and a cold burning hatred for
anything in red skin and feathers.

Young Major Bloomfield stopped at the edge
of a clearing and stared out across the Mohawk
cornfield ahead. Rain dripped from his three-
cornered hat. As he saw the blue woodsmoke
above the Indian town beyond the corn, a junior
officer stood at his side to murmur, "Most of our
powder is wet, sir." Bloomfield said, "I know.
Have the men fix bayonets."

"Against Mohawk, sir?"

"Against the devil incarnate, mister! You saw
what they did to that baby we found back there
in the woods."

The ensign nodded and relayed the order
The grim snick of socket-bayonets being fitted
to musket barrels didn't carry far and the Indians hadn't posted lookouts. Since the legendary
Hiawatha had forged Mohawk, Oneida, Onon-
danga, Cayuga and Seneca into the dreaded Iro-

quois Confederacy, no enemy, red or white, had dared attack them on their home grounds. Most feared of all were the mighty Mohawk, who boasted of being one of few North American nations who ate human flesh.

So Major Bloomfield made no speeches as he prepared for his attack. His men knew who the Mohawk were. And they were enraged.

Bloomfield drew his sword and started forward, not looking back at the men he knew were following. The Jersey Devils fanned out as they left the tree line, bayoneted muskets held at waist level as they marched through and trampled the ripe corn. There was no battle flag. No fife and drum to keep time. The Jersey Devils didn't march in step. They just moved across the clearing as one man. One hard-eyed, hate-filled, grimly determined man. Or perhaps, this rainy day, something more than a man. Something meaner than a grizzly and ugly as a wolverine.

An Indian villager spotted them halfway across the cornfield. It didn't matter and they didn't care. Mohawk braves raised muskets to mow down the obviously insane strangers. But their powder was wet and, had they fired, it was doubtful the Jersey Devils would have wavered.

The Mohawk were brave. The toughest fighters of the eastern woodlands. They were angered by the trampling of their corn and mindful of the women and children in the long bark houses behind them. So they made the natural mistake of standing their ground with tomahawk and lance.

The result was quiet carnage. The Jersey Devils simply walked into them. No battle cries. No stirring bugles blowing the charge. It was silent, expert butchery as the white troops went to work with butt stock and bayonet, shoulder to shoulder and trained well at their grisly craft.

They moved as if on the muster field, following the silent drill of the sergeant. "Short thrust! Recover! Long thrust! Recover! Vertical butt stroke! Smash! Diagonal slash! Recover! Short thrust! Recover!" And so it went, mechanically, almost mindlessly, as shouting Indians died in almost every movement of the plodding line.

It had never happened before in the long verbal history they had of themselves, but the Mohawk began to fall back. These were not men they were fighting. This was something new. An enemy as frightening as the fever spirits who haunted the swamplands when the little flies were biting. A hero, painted with totem of his clan, tried to rally the Mohawk, shouting they were cowards. Then a bayonet drove into the painted turtle on his chest. As he fell the Cape May lad who'd killed him stepped on his face, wrenched the bayonet out with a sucking slurp and walked over him.

The militiamen came to the fence around the long houses. They walked over that too, flatten-

ing the cedar palings in the mud as they plodded
onward to the houses.

The houses were made of bark on willow
frames. Butt stocks smashed the flimsy walls as
the Jersey Devils moved on in line right through
them. A squaw rolled out from under a bear
skin, smiling and holding her deer-hide skirts
up to show she was a harmless friendly woman.
A man from the Oranges drove his bayonet into
her left breast and pitchforked her out of the
way. Another man from Crane's Town stepped
on her neck to make sure of her as the line
moved on.

In the clearing beyond, a Mohawk infant
wailed in terror by the blanket his fleeing mother
had dropped. One of the militiamen near Bloomfield wavered enough to ask, "What about this
baby, major?" When Bloomfield snapped, "It's
a *boy*, ain't it?" the man nodded and smashed
the infant into the mud like a crushed beetle.

They moved on to the far wall of trees, killing
everything living, including a Shanghai rooster
and two dogs. Then Bloomfield called a halt.
The Jersey Devils stood facing the silent dripping forest while a detail burned the village.
They burned everything inflammable and broke
every bit of pottery or glass they found. They
heated the barrels of dropped muskets and bent
them double around tree trunks. Then, when
they'd totally wiped out the Mohawk town, they
marched into the woods beyond to see if the
survivors wanted another fight.

There were no takers. Many of the Indians wouldn't stop until they got to Canada. Their descendents are still there.

That same raw afternoon, as Joe Floyd warmed himself between Margaret and Mercy and Joe Bloomfield hunted Iroquois like vermin, another angry American was moving northeast along the Ohio Valley. His name was George Rogers Clark and he didn't like Indians either.

Big John Floyd, Joe's cousin, was with young Colonel Clark and a hundred and fifty others. Big John was a scout. The men were mostly from Virginia or Kentucky. The Virginian, Clark, had been through the Cumberland Gap before Boone and was a founding father of Harrodsburg.

With them was Clark's younger brother, William, who would one day march with Meriwether Lewis in a longer-remembered expedition to the Pacific shore. Behind them, a British agent hung from a sycamore limb, his body cooling in the rain. The man had been on his way to the Cherokee with another message from Governor Hamilton. There'd been no trial. They'd simply relieved him of his dispatches and strung him up.

George Rogers Clark didn't know about the siege of Boonesburough, or the danger of his home in Harrodsburg. He wouldn't have swerved from his mission if he had. Clark didn't believe in fighting Indians from behind a barricade. He liked to go out and look for them.

A month before he'd taken and destroyed the British trading post at Kaskaskia, Missouri. Right now he was marching to attack the British frontier garrison at Vincennes, on the Wabash. He aimed to take it too, and if he had the men and ammunition left, he thought he just might go on up and take Detroit.

He wasn't as angry a man as Major Bloomfield to his north but, if anything, he was more dangerous. His men were not trained militia. They were rawboned frontier long-hunters who could show most Shawnee a thing or two about guerrilla war and frightfulness. They spotted Indian sign from time to time as they moved north—silent, buckskinned savages, one step removed from their redskin enemy. Clark didn't worry about encountering Shawnee in the swampy forests he marched through. He was too smart for them to ambush and too ornery for them to fight in the open. He'd heard Black Fish was prowling somewhere that summer, but if the sagamore knew what was good for him, he'd be well advised to stay clear of the column. Clark figured Vincennes was more important right now. But if Black Fish messed with him and the boys they just might take a side trip to that Shawnee town at Chillicothe and burn the rascals out.

Big John fell in beside his colonel as they hacked their way through another canebreak.

When John Floyd asked if they should maybe send a runner back to Kentucky with news of the Indian smoke talk they'd been seeing, Clark growled, "Forget it. The boys back home can handle any Injuns this fur south. Let's git on up to Hamilton's headquarters and cut the whole bush off at the roots!"

The long delayed autumn rains came down for a good three days and nights in the familiar pattern of American cyclonic storms. The settlers didn't call it that, of course. Those from the tidewater country called it a nor'easter and repeated the old bromide, "Winds from northeast, three wet days at least."

The less weather-wise simply wished it would stop, Indians or no.

The little Kentucky River was over its banks and lapping within yards of the gate as it carried torn-out sycamores, fence rails and dead Indians off to join the flooded Ohio beyond the horizon. The gully-washer uprooted the few stalks of corn the Indians had spared and swept the slopes clean of the debris of war. The earth was a sticky ankle-deep swamp inside the walls of Boonesburough, but as the men and boys worked on, the leaking roofs were repaired enough to matter and the women and girls dried blankets and clothing on lines stretched across fireplace openings.

In the blockhouse least battered by the enemy,

Dick Callaway and his younger kinsman Flanders risked their eyebrows if not their very lives in an attempt to dry the damp gunpowder. As Jemima carried trays of warm but flameless coals in from her hearth, the Callaway men stirred powder in skillets held gingerly above the dry heat. The jovial Boone had suggested they try the old frontier trick of pissing on damp powder and storing it to dry slow. Dick Callaway thought he was crazy. They were both partly right. Urine added nitrate salts to the undernitrated formula of the powder used at the times, thus making it quicker burning, damp or not. But Callaway was right when he maintained they hadn't time to wait for the powder to recrystalize at normal humidity. And so he worked on, trying not to think about the powder blowing up in his face as he nursed his suspicion of Boone into an explosive mixture in its own right.

The long cyclonic rain swept over the valley in sheets of near-tropical downpour, intervals of dry but overcast half-hours and longer periods of what some called a Scotch mist—a fine drizzle too thin to call rain and too wet to call fog. The mist cut the visibility to bare yards for the anxious marksmen manning the walls. It filtered through every chink in the cabins to hinder the drying and chill the flesh. It made bathing next to impossible, even had there been privacy left. The crowded cabins steamed with the reek of wet wool and unwashed flesh. Most frontier folk had a few lice under the best of circumstances.

By now everyone in Boonesburough itched, and most of the children dripped snot as they whined and whimpered underfoot. The older folk hawked and spat in the corners to clear their stuffy heads. Jemima showed Margaret and Mercy how to fight a head cold by dipping snuff. Little Mercy was getting right good at aiming a stream of tobacco juice between her front teeth. She'd never be able to pick a fly off the wall as Jemima could. But the trying helped to pass the weary time as they huddled cooped-up by the rains.

The last day it rained, Joe and Wolfgang risked stepping out through the wall while a trio of skilled rifle hands covered them from above. The Indians had carried away the dead from their frustrated night attack, but the ground outside was littered with scaling ladders and hooked poplar poles for pulling logs apart. As long as the river lapped almost at the gate, it seemed as good a time as any to let it carry away the abandoned siege gear. If the Indians aimed to hit again, after they'd dried their own powder, the rascals could just make new ladders and haul them this far under fire.

Opinion was divided about the silence of the wooded ridges all around. Dick Callaway wanted to send runners to the other settlements while it was so wet outside. He said a man with stout legs had a tolerable chance of getting through, since no trade musket was about to fire in such dampness. Boone pointed out the In-

dians still had tomahawks and likely some fair
runners out of maybe four hundred rested-up
pinesee.

Some of the single men had once more raised
the idea of striking out, every man for himself,
under cover of a midnight downpour. On this
the two bitter rivals for command were in agreement. Boone put it most gently by wondering
aloud why men who said "every man for himself" never seemed to have anyone but themselves to worry about. Dick Callaway just said
he'd shoot the first son of a bitch who went over
the wall.

As Joe and the Hessian swung the last ladder
out into the current of the swollen river, a distant
shot rang out across the valley. Joe and Wolfgang ran to the logs and snatched up their leaning weapons before they thought to look up the
slope in the direction of the sound.

Joe saw the gunsmoke drifting along the ridge-
line. Then he noticed three distant figures moving down the grassy slope from the direction
of the Shawnee camp.

The shot had brought the men and boys and
many of the women out and up on the wall.
Captain Boone called out, "Hold your fire, folks.
Looks like Black Fish wants another powwow!"

Callaway, a few yards down the wall, snorted,
"Damn it, Dan'l, I'm pure wore out with parley.
They've shown us they can't be trusted to
bargain in good faith."

"I know that, Dick. It gives us leeway to lie

our ownselves. We've been whittled down to a nub and ever' minute we can gain by jawing with the rascals is a minute we don't have to worry about our damp powder going off."

"I'll hear no more talk of aid and comfort to the enemy, Dan'l Boone!"

"Well then, stuff your fingers in your fool ears and you won't have to. I see no harm in promising Black Fish the surrender of Philadelphia, if we don't aim to deliver."

"I'll not be party to signing anything, Boone. And by God, I'll not lower the Stars and Stripes this time."

"Aw, Dick, why don't you stuff a sock in it and let me do the talking? I don't see no parley flag. I reckon they's being informal this time. I make out one as an Injun, wearing Cherokee rig. Other two look like white men. Scout in buckskins and a gent in the kit of The King's American Rifles. Must be a Tory officer."

Boone was right about the dress of the three approaching men, but wrong about their identity. As they got closer, a keen-eyed lad laughed and shouted, "By jimmies! It's old Simon Kenton! Simon and his Injun sidekick, Many Jackets!"

There was a glad shout along the wall and people started waving as the tall figure in buckskins waved back. Dick Callaway shouted, "Simmer down! There's something funny here! How come they's coming in from the Shawnee camp?"

But a lithe young girl in a tattered dress was

suddenly over the wall and running up the slope to her man, hair streaming and eyes brimming over with happy tears. She was Simon Kenton's woman and though Joe and Margaret hardly knew the shy and silent girl, Margaret at least knew how she felt.

The big scout handed his rifle to Many Jackets and swept his woman off her feet as the settlers cheered from the walls. Then the four of them came on in to be greeted with happy shouts and patted on their backs. By now Joe had recognized the man in British uniform. It was funny, but even Lieutenant Marvin, the spy, was being greeted like a long lost son. Joe noticed it seemed to make Marvin a mite nervous.

The three men were ushered into the ward room with Boone, Callaway, Joe and the other leaders. The door was politely but firmly shut in the faces of the milling crowd so Simon could bring them up to date. Only his woman was allowed to stay at Simon's side. She was sort of glued to his wet buckskins. It would have taken two men and a crowbar to pry her loose even had Simon wanted it.

Kenton pointed at the spy with his chin and said, "This here rascal is a straggler we picked up, boys. He had dispatches for Cornwallis on him. We figured you'd like to question him afore we string him up."

Marvin protested, "See here, gentlemen, I was captured in full uniform!"

A man growled, "Yep, you'll hang pretty as hell."

Joe went over to stand at Marvin's side and say, "Hold your fire, gents. I'll explain later why I don't think we should hang him. Right now I want to hear about the Shawnee!"

There was a murmur of approval. Simon Kenton grinned and said, "We just scouted their camp grounds. They've lit out. Ever' mother's son of 'em. This Tory rascal says Black Fish has heard about some fighting near his home town and the old bastard was fretted some by the news."

Marvin, feeling reassured by once more meeting up with the reasonable Joe Floyd, smiled wanly and said, "You might say the sagamore had a fit! First it turned out you really had a cannon down here after all. Then De Quindre's tunnel didn't work. When the news from the Mohawk Valley reached us, I decided it was no place for a white man to be. Unfortunately, these other gentlemen were between me and the Cumberland Gap. But I do seem less likely to be scalped at the moment, eh what?"

Someone said, "Sure, we only aim to hang you!" But Boone held up a hand for silence and asked, "What's going on? There ain't no Shawnee in the Mohawk Valley. That's Iroquois country, ain't it?"

Marvin said, "It used to be. Your General Sullivan seems to be running wild up in York State. He's savaged the Five Nations from German Flats to the Genesee. I gather Black Fish was impressed."

Boone grinned in disbelief and said, "Black Fish is impressed, you say? Hell, I'm fit to be switched! You don't mean to tell us Yanks have whupped Mohawk on their home ground! They's the toughest, meanest Injuns who ever drawed breath!"

Marvin nodded and insisted, "Sullivan has routed them. Black Fish was asking De Quindre to explain this when I last saw them. The five strongest Indian tribes on this front, led by British officers and armed with Brown Bess muskets by Governor Hamilton. Hamilton seems to be having trouble explaining it to His Majesty's red allies too. He's traded his civilian job for the military rank of brigadier and called in white regulars from eastern Canada. I gather he's somewhat disappointed in the way things have been going out here."

Marvin sniffed and added, with a thin smile, "I also gather the whites in Detroit are concerned about their own scalps at the moment. The Indians seem rather upset about their advice from the Great White Father in London. Your own Colonel Clark seems to have cut the southern tribes off from their northern allies. The Creeks under Mackintosh are taking a mauling from the Carolina and Georgia militia at the moment."

Many Jackets nodded and said, "Hear me. I brought down a Tory Cherokee scout a few nights ago. As we waited for him to die we talked. My Cherokee cousins are not happy about the way things have been going. I don't think they want to fight the Americans any more this year."

Simon Kenton grinned as he hugged his woman and said, "I figured you boys would like to hear it from the horse's mouth afore we hung him. Black Fish is off for Chillicothe, wet and mad as anything. I doubt if he'll be back this year."

Dick Callaway said, "He'll come back next summer. You can depend on that. By spring they'll be rested up and powwowed up for another go at us. We'll never have peace 'til we shove every tribe across the Mississippi and mebbe a mite further." He nodded at the Englishman and added, "You can write a letter to your kin afore we hang you if you like."

Before the pale-faced Marvin could protest, Joe Floyd said, "Wait a minute. I vote we turn him loose."

Even Boone seemed annoyed. He frowned and said, "Joe, the rascal is our enemy!"

Joe nodded and said, "I know. I've jawed with him some in the past."

"You mean you owe him for when you was captured by his side, Joe? I'll vote to just turn him over to Patrick Henry if he done you favors in the past."

Joe said, "Favors are one thing and war is another. Lieutenant Marvin is a damn fine spy and he's out to whup us if he can, but I still vote to turn him loose. I think we ought to let him report everything he knows to the other side."

"Have you been drinking, son?"

"No. I've been learning to play chess. You gents know there are two political factions in the British Parliament. Right now the Tories are running the king's army and navy. Marvin here is a Whig. His friends are out to whup the Tory party in the next election. I think we ought to help 'em. If we turn Marvin loose he'll go home to feed his friends voting ammunition. We all know Lord North and the Earl of Sandwich have made a mess of their war. I want Marvin to see the English know it too."

Boone stared thoughtfully at the captured spy and asked, "Is it your party's plan to help our cause, Marvin?"

The British officer swallowed and said, "Since I assume I'm with honorable men, I feel duty bound to inform you I'm a loyal subject of His Majesty. If my friends and I can possibly beat you rebels, we intend to."

Callaway muttered, "Hell, let's kill him."

But Joe held up his hand and insisted. "We're playing chess now, not checkers, dammit! From what I hear, the Whigs are more sensible enemies than the Tories. Our own leaders, Adams, Franklin and such, were Whigs themselves back in the days the Crown let us vote. We never would have had this fool war had the Whigs stayed in office."

Boone said, "I know why we named Pittsburgh after the Whig prime minister, son. But Marvin just said he aimed to whup us."

Joe argued, "He likely means it too. But once his party is back in power, they'll see they can't. It's too late for any notions of a British victory. They could have won her in '76, but German George sent over generals he played cards with. Or men like Howe, who hated Lord North worse'n we did. They messed around with fifes and drums and took real estate instead of General Washington, as sensible generals would have. Tories like Hamilton united every Yankee by buying the hair of Loyalist and Patriot alike. Last winter, while Washington whupped the Continentals into a trained army up in Valley Forge, the redcoats went to plays and held balls in Philadelphia. Now it's too late. We'uns are fighting back and winning on every front."

Callaway shrugged and said, "They're about to land a whole fresh army of redcoats in the Carolinas, boy. This war is a far piece from being settled."

Joe said, "We've won the fool war. England just doesn't know it yet. Cornwallis may land to open a southern front. He may win himself a few skirmishes, but he's stepping in the cow shit just the same. He's facing trained troops who outnumber him, three thousand miles from home. Marvin here likely thinks Clinton in New York can help Cornwallis with supplies from the north. Cornwallis is likely counting on it too. Just before we came out here, I read what we did to Clinton at the Battle of Monmouth. The redcoats in New York are bottled up good. The King's Writ just ain't any more. From Canada to the Spanish Floridas, our own now runs the country. There's at least four million of us, under a new flag and government. With the ocean betwixt us and whoever is in charge in London, Marvin's party will doubtless fume and fuss a mite. But we can leave that part to Doctor Franklin and the other politicians. No sensible British government is likely to risk another Saratoga. They got France and Holland closer if they want a serious war."

Boone nodded and said, "Joe's right. I vote we send this rascal home to tell the king he'd best leave us be."

Simon Kenton nodded and only Callaway and a few of his friends now voted to hang the captive. Boone said, "It's settled then. You'll sup with us tonight, Lieutenant Marvin. Come morning I'll issue you a pass and send you on your way. Simon, what do you think about Shawnee stragglers? How soon will it be safe for folks to leave these walls?"

Kenton shrugged and said, "We circled some. Didn't seem like any had hung back."

But Many Jackets said, "Hear me. The Shawnee are treacherous and men like Corn Burner count coup on easy scalps. Black Fish and the main party are gone for now. But it will not be safe to wander far until the first snows come.

I will scout the ridges. Simon knows my smoke talk. But be sure nobody leaves this place unarmed or in small numbers."

Boone nodded and said, "We'll make sure nobody goes out to hunt or gather unless they're escorted by some guns."

"If you are wise, Wide Mouth, you will not send anyone out to look for food before it snows."

"I hear my Cherokee brother's words. But Corn Burner's just a maybe. Going hungry is for sure! This damp spoiled such jerky as we had drying on the rooftops and the vegetation is all et. We're gonna have to nail and smoke at least a bear or two deer for every family here before we get snowed in for the winter. There may be roasting ears still fit to eat out there in the mud. There's hickory and hazel nuts all about. If we has to, we can make do with acorns, leached free of tannin in running water. It's too late in the year for bulbs or skunk cabbage shoots, but the cattails is in bloom and even if we don't gather much cattail pollen, there's always the roots."

The Indian shrugged. He knew white men worried more about their stomachs than his people. That was doubtless why the Shawnee had taken so few Cherokee scalps in the Grandfather Times when they were enemies.

As the meeting broke up, Joe stayed with Marvin and asked about Two Hearts. The spy said, "I assume she went back to Chillicothe with the others, Joe."

"You sure they didn't punish her for letting me get away?"

"Oh, was she supposed to be guarding you? Odd, but Running Wolf took the blame. They hazed him a bit about it, of course, but Black Fish let him regain his honor by leading the attack from the other side of the river."

Once again, Joe was struck by the ambivalence of war. He asked, "Did Running Wolf make it?"

"Hardly. That medicine gun of Boone's has become quite a legend, you know. They recovered the body about two miles downstream. Boone got him right between the eyes."

Joe started to tell him about Wolfgang's Hessian rifle. But he felt sick to his stomach and, what the hell, a little legend wouldn't do any harm once Marvin carried the tale to the British.

The spy was saying, "Two Hearts seemed quite upset about the death of Running Wolf. For some reason she seemed to blame herself."

"She's likely mad as hell at us, huh?"

"That would be an understatement. She's demanded the blood rights for his death. Running Wolf had no squaw and his mother is dead. Two Hearts vowed to avenge him the next time they took a white alive. I decided it was time to leave when Black Fish began to agree with the powahs that a white man was a white man, no matter where you found him!"

"Hmm, any chance Black Fish'll switch sides and turn on the British?"

"You never know with Indians, but I doubt it. They'll spend the winter rethinking their options. By spring the wounds will have healed and the young men will be demanding a chance to show their courage. Your sullen Mister Callaway is doubtless right about further Indian troubles for years to come. But I don't think Black Fish has his heart set on any more stand-up battles. From now on it should be a fire arrow in the night, or a lone settler picked off from the tree line. I must say you Yankees have shown the Indians you're rather dangerous to fight openly. Our little battle out here will probably be forgotten, next to Saratoga or Monmouth, but I intend to report it as another disaster for Lord North's depressing grand strategy. As a Loyalist, I hate to admit it, but you chaps won a victory here."

26

Many Jackets led Lieutenant Marvin safely out
of the valley as the rain let up the next morning.

The sun rose bright and hot as ever. The
soaked earth steamed while the river slowly
dropped back between its banks. The humidity
added to the discomfort of the heat, and mod-
esty made way for common sense. The smaller
children played naked in the drying mud. Men
worked shirtless and many of the women exposed more flesh than others thought seemly as
they worked with bodices open and skirts kilted
almost to their naked knees.

Little Mercy Bryan's tight hand-me-down
dress had shrunk from the damp and she bulged
most unseemly as she went about barefoot and
bareheaded, her hair in the braids of a child but
her budding figure drawing thoughtful glances
from the men she passed.

Wolfgang the Hessian liked Mercy well
enough but, like Joe, considered her a child.
Since they'd seen the young German in action
the few single maids of the community no

longer laughed at his broken English. If his legendary marksmanship would be attributed in the end to the famous Captain Boone, they and all the settlers knew better. And the brave Wolfgang's descendants would remember him well—albeit not as Wolfgang Rodenau from Frankenberg.

Wolfgang had decided, since he was now an American wanted for desertion, that it made sense to be known from now on as Wolfe Rogers. Mercy thought it was a fine name and Joe and Margaret managed not to smile when he announced it.

The humidity and semi-nudity added the spice of lechery to the dawning delight that they were all going to live after all. But in truth there was very little substance to the outburst of winking, tittering and stolen kisses in a corner. The community was too crowded for even the properly married to enjoy uninhibited sex.

In an age when adults of breeding covered their flesh from neckline to sole and even hid the natural color of their hair with powder or wig, the more casual dress occasioned by frontier living conditions aroused the youths and single men perhaps more than the female settlers intended. It was impossible to avoid accidental glimpses of a young girl furtively scratching an itchy crotch, or a pretty mother nursing a child with her bodice open. It was also nearly impossible to find a hidden corner where one could masturbate in peace. Hence many of the

requests for permission to go outside were moti-
vated by more than a desire to salvage what was
left of the harvest or see if the Indians had left
any blackberries along the tree line.

Boone was adamant. He hadn't stood off a
main Shawnee army for ten days only to lose a
man to some skulking pinesee who might be
waiting out there for just such an opportunity.
He lectured them about the time Jemima and
Fanny Callaway had been kidnapped from a
swimming hole within earshot of the gate. He
reminded them of children killed in sight of
their mothers and of boys who'd gone fishing
and had never been seen again. He lectured
them until many were heartily sick of it, whether
he was right or not.

Strangely, Joe and Margaret were more comfortable about their scandalous relationship now
that it had become almost impossible for them
to make love. Margaret had become reassured
about Joe's feeling for her. She'd recognized that
much of her apparent lust had been an instinctive drive to hold him to her. Now that he was
seldom from her sight, she saw he wasn't interested in the younger maids in the community.
She watched him tenderly, unselfishly. As long
as she'd live she'd never forget how he'd
shielded her from the final Indian attack with
his strong young body. She had no way of knowing how often her Joe's mind strayed to a tawny
blonde maid in smoke-cured Shawnee deerskins,
or how often, when they did manage a late-

night moment of privacy, her flesh invisible in the dark served as a substitute for the younger, firmer body of Two Hearts.

Simon Kenton and Many Jackets scouted the ridges around the settlement and uncovered no sign. If Black Fish had left any of his men behind, they were skilled skirmishers indeed. They left no cold fires or crushed grass where men might have bedded for the night. No signs of kneeling by the muddy shore of a forest spring. The birds and locusts once more sang in the sun-dappled glades and deer droppings or fresh racoon scat told the scouts the game was coming back, the battlefield sounds having faded from short animal memory.

So Boone let his people out, warning everyone to stay close to the fort and not to get out of sight of the lookouts on the tower. They burst forth like children who'd been kept after school. Grown men and women frolicked and rolled in the sweet-smelling grass. Others poked about for mementos, gathering spent musket balls, lost tomahawks or tattered feathered headbands washed free of blood and brains by the long rainstorm. A man suddenly dragged his blushing wife into a clump of elderberry, threw her down and, to her delight, ravaged her as brutally as any Shawnee might have, had things gone the other way.

The crops were nearly a total loss. There were a few taters, some bullet-riddled cabbages. Here and there the Indians and mildew had spared an ear of corn.

The remaining livestock was turned out to forage. The Indians had made short work of the hogs and cattle they hadn't rounded up before the siege. It was going to be a hungry winter.

But they still had timber and water. The rain had greened up the pasture and the waterfowl were migrating south. They had at least two months before the first frosts were likely. So some of the more optimistic drilled in radish and greens for luck while others dug and dried cattail root and arrowhead along the river bank. Some boys caught a snapping turtle and a string of blue-gill and also caught hell for fishing around the bend. Wolfgang, or Wolfe Rogers, brought in a poke of fat squirrel he'd barked off hickory limbs with his rifle and was rewarded with admiring glances from the girls.

It was going to be all right. Their troubles were over. Or so they thought.

27

Margaret was after Joe to sit down and seriously plan their future. And though he agreed to almost anything she said while in bed, he didn't feel the new world around him was quite real. He went about his chores as if in a dream, wondering what was wrong with him. He felt all right. There was nothing wrong with his head. He remembered killing his own father and he'd come to grips with it. He'd gotten over the awkwardness of bedding his own stepmother. Nobody else seemed to fret about it all that much. More than one of the Boone-Bryan-Callaway clan was living openly in what more polite society might call incest. At least a third of the couples out here hadn't gotten around to lawful weddings anyone remembered. And old Meg was a handsome woman. It wasn't as if there was anyone better to hanker after. Meg was as pretty as Jemima, even had Jemima been single and not carrying Flanders' papoose in her thickening young waist. Little Mercy was maybe put together a mite more exciting, but that was another what-the-hell.

The only girl Joe really wanted was one he'd never see again. It was no use fretting over Two Hearts. It hurt less not to think of her spread out on a bearskin in a smoke-filled wigwam with Corn Burner or some other buck on top of her. But he couldn't help wondering if she ever thought of him. He sure hoped she wouldn't moan like Meg when some durned old Injun was inside of her. He knew she would, of course. Human flesh was like that. He hadn't even *liked* the Hawkins gal back home, but he'd sure breathed some when they'd come together in that hayloft. Two Hearts would likely say all sorts of things she didn't mean to a man she was coming with. It was a tedious thing to think about. So he did his best to forget.

A few days later some men from the Holston Valley militia marched in to see if anyone was alive this far north. They reported no sign of the pesky Shawnee this side of the Ohio. And they brought other good news.

Virginia had recognized Kentucky as a western county and Harrodsburg had been named the seat of the new provisional government. At last the tattered Stars and Stripes above the battered little fort meant something real. The Continental Congress had extended the borders of the new United States to the Mississippi, save for the Spanish claims to New Orleans and the Floridas on the east bank. Spain had agreed to stay out of the war if the fierce long-hunters would be good enough not to invade the western lands Spain had gotten from France at the conclusion of the French and Indians Wars. The English, ignoring the Spanish and earlier French settlers along the Mississippi, had disdainfully built forts and armed the Indians on Spanish territory. So Spain along with France was now cautiously backing the Continental Congress, and it was all right with Madrid if the Clark brothers burned out Tories on either side of the border.

George Rogers Clark now held a military commission, if not a uniform. It had been signed by Governor Patrick Henry and Thomas Jefferson. If anyone ever caught up with him, wherever he was, they were supposed to tell him to stop scalping British officers.

The Holston Valley men had done more than re-establish communications with the eastern states. They'd brought along a brace of newspaper men from Richmond. One sketched pictures with a silver pencil. The other gathered stories for the sophisticated propaganda mill of the clever Doctor Franklin. The outside world, including Europe, had to be convinced the Americans were not only winning but winning with a certain style. The disorganized brawl at Saratoga was now a modern version of Marathon. The total confusion of that hot day at Monmouth, New Jersey, had been inflated to at least The Third Crusade, while, if cleverly presented, the drift of squatters through the Cumberland Gap could be likened to Hannibal crossing the Alps.

And so, as the artist sketched the tattered Kentucky folk as heroic-looking figures in bronze buckskin, the writer pestered the survivors for interviews. He found Joe too modest and truthful. Wolfgang, despite his new Anglo-Saxon identity, spoke terrible English, and Boone was too busy to trifle with such a foolish notion as the story of his life.

The two newsmen settled on Squire Junior, the occasional preacher and would-be inventor. The elder Boone was more than willing to help them with their frontier saga. If he got a few facts wrong, what matter? Squire Junior told a hell of a tale.

The fact that Dan'l's Tory wife had left him, at least for the moment, was forgotten in the rush to set it all on paper. Rebecca Boone was no longer a middle-aged Tory woman who dipped snuff and nagged her wandering man to settle down, for God's sake. Somehow Squire Boone had convinced himself his brave and beautiful sister-in-law had been at her husband's side during the battle, loading his long rifle that never missed.

Jemima and the other grown children of the Boone clan were suddenly brave little tykes, fighting at their young parent's side against thousands and thousands of desperate Shawnee.

Squire Junior didn't like Dick Callaway any

more than his brother did, so the Boone family, in his version, fought more or less alone to save the only town in Kentucky, aided modestly by a few faithful retainers and Boone's dog-like Cherokee blood brothers. Every Indian killed in the recent battle had, of course, been picked off by Dan'l or by one of the children.

The artist drew a picture of Captain Boone. Though Squire Junior pronounced it a perfect likeness, Boone himself snorted in disgust. Joe Floyd thought it was funny as hell.

"How come you got him standing there in Injun duds with that fool fur hat on his head?" asked Joe, adding, "The captain has a buckskin hunting jacket, but he favors broadcloth and none of us grown men wear Injun hats."

The artist explained that Doctor Franklin had worn a coonskin cap when he went to see King Louis in Paris and that the French court had been very taken by the "noble savages" of America.

Joe sniffed and said, "French Canucks and some of the young'uns wear coonskin caps now and again. You'll never see a serious long-hunter in such a fool rig."

"Why not? I thought the idea was to disguise one's head as a raccoon when you wanted to look over a log or something."

"That's what I mean. Would *you* want another hunter to take your head for a coon? Coons are right good eating."

"Ah, but Doctor Franklin explained the Indians might be fooled if they spotted a harmless raccoon in the distance rather than a white man's head."

"Shit, Injuns eat coon too. The idea isn't to make 'em think you're a critter. The idea is not to let the rascals see you at all! You publish that fool picture and everyone's going to think poor Dan'l is some fourteen-year-old playing Injun in his daddy's woodlot!"

But the picture would be reproduced back east in time, and the real Daniel Boone would take on the legendary lineaments of a tall youth with the face and figure of a Greek god and the costume of a half-breed Canadian trapper.

The writer read his description of the epic siege that night to those sitting on Squire Junior's doorstep or standing around to jaw with the interesting strangers. Joe, Boone and most of the others thought it was pretty amusing. But there were thoughtful frowns as many a man who'd fought hard and well found himself left out of the narrative or, worse, heard his efforts credited to another hero.

There'd been mutterings all along, for, in truth, the defense of Boonesborough had been a rather slipshod, improvised affair. Men forgot they'd ignored suggestions about the well any fool could now see should have been dug months ago. They remembered Boone's wife was a Tory, and wondered aloud about her leaving for the safety of the east just before the Shawnee attacked. They remembered Boone's curious relationship with the Indians. What sort of a man called a painted savage a brother or a father? They remembered how Boone had lowered the flag, and how they'd almost lost their scalps when they followed him out to parley with those Shawnee rascals Boone had said they could trust.

They remembered how he'd lived four months among the Shawnee, treated like an honored guest by Black Fish. Wearing Shawnee clothes and bedded with a Shawnee squaw some said he'd got with child. It was true he'd told them he'd "escaped" the Shawnee just in time to be in Boonesburough when his erstwhile friends closed in. Wasn't it a mite funny how he'd shirked strengthening the defenses after taking the command away from good old Colonel Callaway, who'd said they were in no shape to withstand a siege?

Oh, sure, old Dan'l had fought well enough at the last, with Black Fish likely sore at him for failing to get his friends to surrender, and with those same friends watching him for any last-minute treachery. Squire Junior and the other Boones in the fort were likely all right. That cannon had been a good notion and little Jemima had fought like a demon, for a gal. But Jemima was a Callaway. And everyone knew she wasn't really Boone's daughter. So it hardly counted.

They talked about it behind Boone's back and they talked about it to the militia officers from the other valley, who didn't know Boone all that well.

The next morning the militia captain found Boone chopping firewood. With a nervous glance at the ax in Dan'l's hand, he cleared his throat and said, "Captain Boone, I've orders to arrest you. We're, uh, sort of aiming to court martial you. The charge is treason. I purely hope you'll come quiet."

28

The court martial was held in the public square.
Everyone in the settlement wanted to attend it
and Boonesburough didn't have a town hall.
The militia court sat at an improvised trestle
table at the base of the tall pine flagstaff. A
barrel had been placed on the dry mud to serve
as the witness stand. The bewildered Boone sat
on it, facing the court as the charges were read.
From time to time the shadow of the fluttering
Stars and Stripes above them swept over the
rugged face of the accused. The wide generous
mouth was set in a bemused smile, but the innocent blue eyes held the expression of a friendly
pup who'd just been kicked and couldn't understand why.

The presiding officer had a sheet of yellow
foolscap and his voice droned like a bluebottle
fly in the hot sunlight as he read the charges.

"Number One: That Boone did take twenty-
six men to make salt at Blue Licks, and that the
Indians caught him, alone, down the Licking
River, and that Boone did then lead the Indians

405

to the other men and told them to surrender as said Indians would likely kill them. And that this surrender was voluntary and that no shots were fired."

"Number Two: That when a prisoner, he engaged with Governor Hamilton in Detroit to surrender the people at Boonesburough to be taken as captives to Detroit and to live there under British protection and jurisdiction."

"Number Three: That returning from captivity, in a manner never fully explained, he did encourage a scouting party to Paint Lick, thus weakening the garrison at a time when there was reason to expect an Indian attack."

At this, Boone suddenly cut in to shout, red-faced, "Now just a God damned minute! Me and the boys did spy Shawnee at Paint Lick, and we shot the shit outten them!"

From the sidelines, Simon Kenton yelled, "You tell 'em, Dan'l! I was with you at Painted Lick and, by God, we jumped the rascals, thanks to you! You remember that Shawnee you shot just as he was fixing to lift my hair?"

The presiding officer shushed Kenton and said, "The witnesses will speak in turn."

But Kenton said, "Aw, bullshit! Dan'l led us out on counter-patrol. We whupped a Shawnee raiding party and got back in time for the siege. We didn't lose nobody neither. If you ask me, Paint Lick was a right nice little fight!"

"The court ain't asking. The court is reading off the charges. So ever'body simmer down."

The man with the paper nodded and read, "Number Four: That preceding the attack on Boonesburough the accused did entice other officers of the fort out to parley with the enemy, out of range of the fort's guns, and that but for the grace of God, they'd have all been captured, and that it is further charged that Boone was party to this plan."

The presiding officer said soberly, "The accused has heard the charges read. How does he plead?"

Boone said, "Well . . ."

Then Joe Floyd was at his side and saying, "If it please the court, Captain Boone pleads not guilty and makes the countercharge that Dick Callaway is an idjet."

There was a rustle of laughter from the crowd. The militia officer frowned to ask, "May the court know who you are and if you've been appointed counsel for the defense?"

"My name is Joe Floyd and if any man here says I can't speak for the captain he'd best be bigger than me."

"That hardly seems possible. Is this young man your attorney of record, Captain Boone?"

Boone shrugged and said, "I reckon so. I don't see nobody but him and old Simon standing up for me."

But Many Jackets suddenly stepped out from the crowd and said, "Hear me. Wide Mouth is wrong. He has many to speak for him and I am one of them."

"Were you a witness to the events charged, uh, sir?"

"Only the one about Paint Lick. I was there. If Wide Mouth was a secret friend of the Shawnee at Paint Lick, he has peculiar ideas about friendship."

Many Jackets raised his hand and they saw it held a handful of dried human scalps. Many Jackets said, "I took these at Paint Lick with Wide Mouth and Simon Kenton. Colonel Callaway was not there. While we were killing Shawnee he was here with the women, writing down his lies. I have spoken." There was a murmur of approval.

The militia officer pounded for silence and said, "All right, we'll set that charge aside. But let's get to them in order and do this thing proper. How do you answer the first charge, Boone?"

Boone scratched his head and asked, "You mean when me and the other boys was captured last winter? Hell, they had the drop on us. We didn't know Hamilton had sicced the Shawnee on us. I didn't know Black Fish then. I mean, there I was, like a big-ass bird, and all these Shawnee stepped outten the bushes, grinning and pointing guns at me."

"But it says you led them back to camp, where the other men were boiling salt."

"I did. You would have too. I had a musket barrel stuck in each ear at the time. Besides, I knowed the salt boilers wasn't set up for no attack, and the Indians figured to kill 'em when they stumbled over the camp. I got to jawing with a neighborly Shawnee and he agreed not to lift no hair if the boys come quiet. I called out and a couple managed to slip away to carry the news to the fort. As to the men I talked into surrendering, the last I heard they was all still breathing."

"But as British prisoners of war."

"All but Andrew Johnson. He escaped afore I did. That made it harder for me and the others. As to them being prisoners right now, I still say they're better off alive than dead. The war can't last forever, but a man stays dead a right long time."

"How do you answer the charge you promised Governor Hamilton you'd surrender the fort if he let you go?"

Before Boone could answer, Joe said, "That charge is ee-relevant! In the first place Hamilton didn't let the captain go, so he likely thought Dan'l was lying. In the second place, Dan'l *was* lying. Promises don't count when a man's holding a gun on you. That's English Common Law. You can look it up."

Despite himself, the presiding officer chuckled. He was as much a frontier politician as a military man and he saw the looks and heard the remarks passed among the crowd around him.

He said, "All right, let's forget about Detroit.

How did you talk the Shawnee into letting you go after they brought you back down to Chillicothe, Captain Boone?"

Again, before Boone could answer, Joe said, "I can answer for that better than he can, sir. I was captured by Black Fish my ownself and he told me personally that Captain Boone escaped from the Shawnee. I got it from the horse's mouth that they chased him high and they chased him low. Black Fish was mad as hell about it too."

The militia men exchanged whispers and the presiding officer asked, "Are we to understand that you were with the Indians with Boone?"

"No, sir. I was taken in charge three. As to how I got away, I ran away. I suppose Dick Callaway suspicions *me* of being friends with the Shawnee now. But he's never run the gauntlet like me and the captain. So he has no call to talk about Injuns. He doesn't know the rascals the way we do."

From the crowd, Callaway shouted, "Fair is fair, Joe! I never said you was friends with the Shawnee. I seen you shoot too many, boy!"

"Well, I'll tell you something else, Dick Callaway. I'll credit you with being as brave as any man I know. But had you been with me up there in the Shawnee camp you'd have been as willing to smoke a pipe or share a bowl of succotash with Black Fish as me or Boone was. There's time for brave speeches and there's time to grin like a dog at the folks you hope might be willing to let you go on breathing another minute or two."

"God damn it, I would never knuckle under to a painted savage!"

"It's lucky for you they never captured you, isn't it?"

The presiding officer said, "Your point has been made, Mister Floyd. We'll accept Boone's escape at face value. That still leaves the very serious charge that the accused lured you and the others out to be tricked by the Shawnee."

Joe put a hand on Boone's shoulder to keep him quiet. He was surprised to feel the older man was trembling. It was strange to think a legend felt fear and rage the same as other men.

Joe said, "The captain was tricked as much as any of us. Before I went down, I saw him fighting like hell. If he was in on it, they were sure paying him back funny. Wolfe Rogers shot a Wyandot with a tomahawk right off Boone's back. I'll allow the captain might have been too trusting. I'll say right now that Dick Callaway saved the day by being suspicious as usual. But we're talking about something we can't pin down so's it's clear. The fort might have been saved the long hard fight we had if the Injuns had been acting in good faith. Black Fish told me personally they were, but we don't know for sure that they were. But if it was a trick, let's not forget it never worked. Not one of us got killed at the peace talk out there. The Injuns can't hardly boast the same. It doesn't matter if the captain trusted more than he should have. Nobody on our side was hurt and we shot the Injuns, sly as they might have studied to be."

Joe saw the militia men were buzzing at each other again. He kept talking. He said, "I got one thing more to say. You all know I admire and respect Captain Boone. I admire and respect Colonel Callaway too. I want it on record I think he's brave. He soldiered as good as any man could have when the fat was in the fire. I'll never forget the last night of the attack when he stood in the light of the fire blowing Injun after Injun away as he held like a rock betwixt them and his kin. Now, having said that, I have to say Dick Callaway is a mean-mouthed old biddy I'd be ashamed to have as a maiden aunt! This fool court martial is the spite work of a small-minded skunk, and like the Injuns say, I have spoken."

Pandemonium broke loose. The assembled crowd roared approval as the presiding officer pounded for silence. He saw he wasn't going to get any. So he shouted, "Aw, hell, case dismissed and who's got a jug? I'm thirsty from all this fool jabber in the hot sun."

Boone got up, his eyes moist, and took Joe's hand in both his own, murmuring, "That was neighborly of you, son."

Dick Callaway came over, scowling. But he held a hand out grudgingly and said, "I'm glad it's settled, Dan'l. I did what I thought I had to, but you won fair and square and we'll say no more about it."

Boone ignored the offer and turned away, stone-faced. Neither knew at the time that Colonel Richard Callaway had less than two years to live. But from the day of the court martial to Callaway's death under a tomahawk at Canoe Ridge not far away, the two men would never speak to one another again.

29

That weekend Joe went hunting with Simon Kenton. Not for Indians but for buffalo. A small herd had been spotted over by the Licking River and a single one meant more meat on the hoof than half a dozen deer. They took two of the older boys and a draft pony in case they had luck.

Closer to the fort and within sight of the lookout, Margaret and Mercy Bryan were gleaning taters from a hillside field the Indians and sheet erosion had partly spared. As the girls grubbed for the taters on their knees they were guarded by young Sam Collins, who sat on a stump with a loaded musket and tried not to feel guilty as he watched them work.

It was another hot September day. The dust clung grittily to their perspiring hands and forearms as they clawed the clods away with their fire-hardened digging sticks. They shared one trug basket between them and inched along on their knees. They dug a peck of dirt for every tater and many they uncovered had gone wormy.

Mercy chattered as they worked. Margaret mostly listened. She wasn't too clear as to how she and Joe had become the child's adopted parents, but Mercy seemed to assume it was settled. As soon as they repaired the cabins and Joe built the sleeping loft he'd mentioned, Mercy was moving in with them. She was sure she'd be no bother, since they had no young 'uns. She'd been living with Jemima and Flanders, sort of, but it was going to be pure crowded once Jemima had the baby and sometimes Flanders acted as if she were almost in the way.

Margaret muttered something noncommittal. She liked Mercy, but she knew how Jemima and Flanders probably felt. She'd been looking forward to the same sort of privacy with her Joe that the young Calloways wanted. And she was still concerned about Joe getting attracted to Mercy. She was a pretty little thing and almost old enough. If only that durned Wolfgang hadn't started sparking one of the McBride gals . . .

Margaret found a fair-sized tater free of blight or wormholes and dropped it in the trug basket. As she dug some more there was a funny whirring in the air. She thought it was some kind of locust. The sound ended with an odd thunk. From the nearby stump, Sam Collins said something very softly, and Margaret looked up at him. The boy sat facing her with an odd look in his eyes and a puzzled little smile on his lips. She asked what he'd just said and he didn't an-

swer. He was still smiling that way as he slowly
fell forward off the stump and flopped limply
across his musket. He lay face down in the grass.
She saw the feathered shaft standing upright
between his shoulder-blades. As she rose; she
ordered swiftly, "Mercy! Run!"

The young girl looked up, puzzled. Then, as
she saw Margaret moving towards the body and
the gun, Mercy sprang to her feet and started
running, not looking back as she screamed.
"You too, Meg! There's no time to tarry over
Sam!"

But Margaret wasn't trying to help the dead
youth. She'd known he was beyond help the moment she'd spotted the arrow in him. She darted
to him, rolled him a bit and tried to pull the
musket free as three grinning men with painted
faces stepped into view from the nearby tree
line.

She tugged at the musket, but the corpse was
too heavy for her to get it loose, so she gave up
and rose to run. Another arrow glinted in the
sunlight and Margaret gasped, "Oh!" as it took
her in one thigh. Again, she tried to run, ignoring the fire in her leg. Then another arrow
pierced her in the back, just below the ribs, and
she knew, in numb anger, they were toying with
her. She moved on a few more steps as, far down
the slope, Mercy was running like the wind, crying, "Injuns! Injuns!" and Margaret heard the
alarm triangle in the fort begin to clang.

Corn Burner saw he had no further time for

games. He sprang after the wounded woman like a catamount and grabbed her by the hair. He threw her on her back and the scalping knife in his hand ripped her open from chest to groin, spilling her insides as she screamed up at him with wide, disbelieving eyes.

As he sliced her right cheek to the bone, Corn Burner told her in a conversational tone, "I wish we had more time. You are pretty and we would like to fuck you."

Then he slashed her throat, cut off one breast and scalped her. His friend, Standing Elk, grunted, "Hurry! They are coming. Many!"

Corn Burner nodded. He forced the victim's mouth open, shoved the blood-dripping breast between her teeth and rose to follow the other two Shawnee into the shade of the sycamores. As they ran, Corn Burner laughed. A loud, mirthless, taunting laugh he knew would carry to the white men running up the slope.

Standing Elk had killed the one with the gun and was entitled to take that scalp. But Corn Burner had had all the fun.

30

The two bodies had been buried by the time Joe and the others got back from their fruitless hunt. The roughly gentle folk of Boonesburough tried to spare Joe's feelings making no mention of Margaret's mutilation. But Joe knew what they'd found on the hill as soon as Boone allowed it might have been the work of Corn Burner.

Boone and Kenton caught up with Joe as he marched out of the settlement alone, jaw set and musket double-charged with rusty nails.

Boone grabbed Joe's left arm, but it took Kenton holding the other to slow him down. Boone pointed his chin at the sky and said, "The evening star is out. It'll be dark afore you're outten this valley, son."

"I don't care. I'm out for Corn Burner and I'll do him dirty in sunshine or shadow. I'll get him if he runs for the north pole! This Earth ain't big enough for that murdering bastard to hide in now."

Boone insisted, "Joe, God damn it! I know just how you feel! I lost my eldest son the same way and I went a mite crazy too! You won't do poor Meg no favors by tearing through the woods at night like a bull with turpentine under his tail. You has to study on tracking Injuns, Joe."

Kenton added from the other side, "You can't cut even a careless white man's trail in the dark, Joe. You come on back and we'll help you track the bastard come sun-up."

Joe insisted, "Let me go! They might build a fire. They might be up at the old camp."

Boone tried to steady him, but Kenton suddenly released Joe's other arm. As he tore free, Kenton said softly, "Let him go, Dan'l. He ain't after Shawnee, he's after mights."

Joe whirled around and growled, "You take that back! I've a good notion to knock you on your ass, Kenton!"

Kenton smiled thinly and said, "You might be able to, Joe. But then I'd get back up and we'd be in a hell of a fix wouldn't we?"

Boone soothed, "You're riled at the wrong folks, damn it! We're on your side. Simon didn't mean to rile you."

But Kenton snorted, "The hell I didn't. I'd rather have him trying to whup me than running off to get scalped afore he's stopped acting like a durned little pup."

Joe took a step toward him and Kenton warned, "Don't try her unless you're good, Joe. I ain't like Dan'l. I hit back."

Boone got between them and said, "What

Simon is trying to tell you, Joe, is that you're going about it all wrong. Corn Burner is good as well as mean. He's made a pair of monkeys outten both Simon and Many Jackets and they been trying to cut his sign in daylight."

Kenton saw Joe's hesitation and said, "First thing we has to do is have a talk with Mercy Bryan. She's the only one alive who saw the rascals. We got to question her about their paint and feathers. For all we know it was Wyandot or some other tribe."

"What difference does it make? Whoever it was, I aim to kill 'em. Besides, I thought we'd agreed it was Corn Burner!"

Boone steered Joe back toward the gate as he explained, "We said it 'peared to be the ornery work of Corn Burner, son. But Corn Burner ain't the first and only ornery Injun who was ever birthed. We'd look like fools trying to cut Shawnee sign if we was after Cherokee."

"I don't see what difference it makes who did it, as long as I get 'em, damn it!"

Kenton said, "You still ain't cooled enough to think, Joe! Wyandot, Mingo or Shawnee would be headed north if they aimed to get away. A Cherokee would be headed south."

"What if they're not headed nowheres at all?"

"In that case they're as good as dead. We'll git 'em if they don't move their red asses fur and fast! If it was some stragglers aiming to carry easy hair home for the harvest dancing, they've been banking on us not knowing they was still about. Now they have their hair and we know to look for 'em. If I was Corn Burner or any other Injun I'd be headed home about now. From here on the game gets rougher for the rascals, and whoever it was don't strike me as a hero."

"But if we give them a whole night's march on us . . ."

"Joe, nobody figures to run all the way to the Ohio or the Tennessee. They'll be zigzagging and cutting back to double their trail. If they don't reckon anyone is right behind 'em, it's human nature they'll stop to rest up sooner or later."

Joe could see they had a plan after all. He hadn't counted on the help of the two best woodsmen in Kentucky when he first lit out in a rage. He said, "I'll go back with you. But I won't get a lick of sleep this night!"

Boone said, "I know. I told you they got my son Jim."

"Did you ever get the Injuns who killed him, captain?"

"No. Mebbe that's why me and Simon aim to help you get the ones who did in your stepmother and the Collins boy."

They returned to the fort and found Mercy with Jemima and Flanders. The girl had been crying all day and still blamed herself for running away and leaving Margaret to face the Indians alone.

Boone said, "You done right, missy. She told

you to run and you done it. Blubbering up ain't gonna help. The Injuns is likely sorry you got away too!"

Mercy looked up at Joe and sobbed, "Can you ever forgive me, Joe?"

"There's nothing to forgive, honey. The captain's right. I'd be twice as mad if they'd got you too."

"Oh, I feel so awful. Meg said I could come and live with you after Jemima has the baby. What ever will become of me now?"

Boone sat her on one knee and soothed, "Child, you're among kin. I'm your uncle, almost. If you want to do something useful, Mercy, I want you to think back on ever'thing you saw up there today."

"Oh no, I can't. I saw Meg laying there all bloody and dead and they . . ."

"Forget Meg and study on the they part, Mercy. What color paint was the rascals wearing? Was their heads shaved and roached or was they wearing braids?"

"They were striped red and black. Their heads were shaved save for a feathered tuft on top and, oh, one of 'em had painted the whole top of his head red, down to his brows. His eyes were painted black like a raccoon's mask."

"Did he have a turtle painted on his chest?"

"No. It was . . . more like zigzags of red and black with a sort of three-circle design at the top. I think he was the boss Injun."

Boone glanced at Joe and said, "I think so

too. Corn Burner is a member of the Thunder Society."

Kenton added, "We can forget about Cherokee. It's too bad. Many Jackets could find a Cherokee anywhere."

Boone insisted, "It's Corn Burner and two others. What we has to study now is where the rascals might be headed."

"What's wrong with Chillicothe? It's the main Shawnee town."

"I know, but Corn Burner knows we know. Besides, he and Black Fish ain't too fond of one another. He could decide to make for Point Creek to the east or even that British fort at Vincennes to the west."

Then he shrugged and said, "I'll sleep on her. Takes a clear head to study Shawnee. You want to bunk with me, Joe?"

Joe said, "No. I'm not afeared of ghosts. I'll stretch out on my own cot with a jug and . . ."

"Joe, you git drunk and me and Simon won't go with you. There's a time for drinking and there's a time for sober. Tracking Shawnee with a drunk is suicide."

Joe went to his cabin. The coals were cold on the hearth but it was too warm for a fire and he didn't feel the need for a candle. The cabin still smelled of damp scorch. Anyone could have been living there. Or it could have been abandoned long ago.

But the bedding was still haunted by Margaret's familiar scent. It didn't seem possible she lay buried in the damp soil out there. As Joe stretched out fully dressed atop the blankets he felt as if she'd just stepped outside for a moment. He wondered, if he went to sleep would he wake up to find her there with him? He wondered how he'd feel if it all turned out to be a dream. He'd been all mixed up about Meg while she was alive. Now that she was dead she still wouldn't let him go.

He heard the door open and stiffened in disbelief as he heard the rustle of petticoats and knew that what sat down there in the dark at the foot of his bed was a girl. He knew he couldn't have dreamed it all. But he didn't believe in haunts.

Mercy Bryan murmured, "Joe?" His heart was still pounding as he licked his lips and said, "What're you doing over here, Mercy?"

"I feel so bad about poor Meg. I thought mebbe we could comfort one another."

He said, "That's neighborly, honey, but does Jemina know you're over here with me?"

"I don't know. I don't reckon she'd mind, do you?"

"Mercy, I'm a man and you're almost a woman grown. I don't reckon they'd think it was seemly if we were to be found alone like this in the dark."

"Good gracious, Joe. I know about the birds and bees and such, but I reckon I can trust you!"

"You do, huh? Well, I don't know as I can trust me. You see, honey, there's things that just sort of creep up on folks when one is a man and the other is a gal and they're together in the dark."

"I don't reckon I'd want you to trifle with me that way, Joe. I'm still right upset. The last thing I'm looking for is a wrestle."

"I know. I don't want to wrestle neither. I'm trying to rest up for the morning hunt. Why don't you run along and try to get some sleep?"

"I don't know where I'd be more welcome, Joe. You and Meg was so kind to me. Can't I stay here and sleep with you?"

"Not hardly. I know what it is not to have a room of your own. You can bunk in here whilst I'm out on the trail with the others. If I don't come back, you can help yourself to such as there is."

"Meg said she was sort of your ma, and that after you all got this place fixed proper I could be sort of hers. That'd make you sort of my brother, wouldn't it?"

Joe wondered if she was funning him. She must have heard some of the gossip and she wasn't that young. Aloud he said, "Yep, I reckon it would."

"Well, if the durned Injuns kilt our ma, we can still be brother and sister, can't we?"

Joe smiled. "You can be my little sister. I just don't want you in my bed."

"But there's no harm in kin sleeping together. You and Meg slept here together, didn't you?"

"Maybe. I've given up sleeping with gals I

don't aim to marry up with. Life is complicated enough if you keep things simple."

As Joe and Mercy sorted out their provisional relationship, Daniel Boone was being pestered by another woman at another cabin. He and Jemima weren't in bed. They were sitting side by side on his doorstep sharing a pipe, and he'd just noticed she was getting the same nagging tone in her voice as her mother Becky had. Wherever the hell Becky was tonight.

Jemima repeated, "Flanders says you're a fool to go off hunting Shawnee at a time like this. He says the new government they're organizing over to Harrodsburg will be dealing new land titles. They're likely to rob us blind if we don't sent some men to the new county board. Flanders says you should be standing up for Boonesburough instead of chasing Injuns like a boy."

"Daughter, you helped sew Margaret Floyd in her shroud. Her son needs my help in tracking down her murderers."

"No, pa. You know Joe and Simon can do it without you. They got a Cherokee tracker and they're younger than you. Flanders says the old land surveys of the Transylvania Company are likely to be set aside, since Dick Henderson, the founder, was a Tory."

"Shoot, I've never been one for jawing with lawyers, honey. You and your man can speak for me if our title's clouded. Besides, I'll be back in a week or so, Lord willing."

She put a hand on his wrist and sighed, "Durn

it, pa. I do so wish you'd grow up. You'll never see forty again and I'm about to make you a granddaddy. Don't you never think on the future? What's to become of you if you just go on running wild through the woods like a boy hunting squirrel? You've been slickered outten ever'thing you've ever owned because you've never been about when the foxy ones with book larning came at us with law suits, bills for debts you never owed and such. Your land claims hereabouts is all you have to show for years of long-hunts. Flanders says if you don't get a lawyer and pay some attention to your affairs like a growed man, you'll likely wind up old and poor."

He took a drag on the pipe, passed it to her and said, "He may be right, honey. Your ma, God bless her, has said the same more'n once. She's sort of peeved at me right now, but I'll git her back when things settle down a mite. I always has."

"I know. Ma's a little childish too. Don't you want to provide for your old age, pa? Flanders says you'd die one of the richest men in Kentucky if you'd show some sense. He's filed on a couple of land sections for him and me. Dick Callaway's put in for a ferry franchise near Canoe Ridge."

"Hell, there's nobody needing a ferry over the Licking River yet."

"But there will be, pa. Once this war is over, Flanders says folks will flood out here and we'll all be in on the ground floor of a state as big as Virginia. But you've got to think ahead. You've been a boy in the woods long enough. It's time you settled down and studied on holding on to things."

"Mebbe. Your grandpa used to say it was time to move when you could see the smoke of a neighbor's cabin."

"I know. That's why you and poor Uncle Squire growed up barefoot. Me and Flanders aim to see our kids go to school wearing shoes. You got to quit this traipsing, pa. Goldurn it, you've seen the old woods!"

Boone sighed and said, "Not hardly, child. I've seen a few valleys and I've seen a few hills, but there's much more I've never laid eyes on. The Injuns tell me there's a range of shining mountains higher than the Blue Ridge somewhere out beyond the Sea of Grass. They tell of places further on that sound like Fairyland. Of painted cliffs ever' color of the rainbow, wild rivers no white man's ever named. They say there's a forest of stone trees, somewhere out beyond the sunset. They say there's an Injun trail clean out to the South Sea Ocean. I'd sure admire following it, if I could git some Injun to show it to me."

"Oh, pa, you'll soon be fifty. Can't you leave such dreams to the younger men like Joe Floyd, or the half-growed boys like Cousin Moses?"

He smiled sheepishly and said, "You git more like your dear mother ever' day. I know men who dream is hard on their womenfolk. You're lucky to have a sensible man like Flanders. It's my notion and some comfort to me that you'll likely be buried in a fine wood box with silver handles. As for me, it ain't that important. I'd rather leave my bones beside some uncharted stream no white man had ever seen afore than lie in a marble crypt in Philadelphia. We lives such a short mayfly time, Jemima, and in the end, all that matters is what we've seed and how much fun we had finding it."

She saw it was no use trying to make Dan'l grow up. So she switched to worries closer to home and asked, "Do you intend to be gone long on this hunt for Corn Burner, pa?"

"Don't know. He never left word where he was headed. Might have lit out for China. Might be up there on the ridge."

She put a hand on his knee and said, "I know why ma got so fretted at you, now that I'm a woman growed. Ever' time you light out through the trees, we wonder if we'll ever see you agin'."

Dan'l protested, "Don't I always come back sooner or later?"

"It's the later part that frets us so. One of these days . . . Well, I can see you're going. So I'll just wait and hope. If you let them lift your hair I'll never speak to you again."

He laughed. Then his face sobered and he said, "I never had much schooling, but I know what you want to know, Jemima. You're afeared

I'll git kilt afore we've ever had a chance to talk it out."

She looked away and didn't answer.

He said, "You're a married woman and about to be a mother. You likely heard some, well, talk about your birthing. Folks talk a mite about things they don't understand."

"I know, pa. But I've learned to live with it."

"It's not the sort of thing a man can talk about to a little gal, Jemima. But no matter what happens, I want you to know I've always loved you as much as I did the others."

She wiped at her eye with a finger and said, "If you're headed for who my real father might have been, I don't want to hear. You're all the pa I ever needed or wanted."

He put an arm around her and said, "Your mother was my wife, and that's good enough for me. Your mother is a good woman, Jemima. Right now she's sort of sulking over politics and my loose-footed ways, but you're never to be shamed of your birthing. You see, she thought I was dead. I'd been missing a while and there she was, a young widow woman in need of comforting."

"Didn't it make you sore, when you finally come home? Flanders said he'd be."

"Mebbe. You see, I've always loved your mother. And I've comforted a few widow women, too. So I was mebbe a mite more understanding. And, what the hell, she never left me for that other man, did she?"

"I reckon not. But Flanders says it sure sounds casual. Did you really bed down with that Shawnee squaw like they say, pa?"

"Well, I know it was weak and wicked, but it was February and it gits right cold sleeping alone in a wigwam. I was there four months. I know what I done was a sin, but so is self-abuse."

Jemina suddenly laughed and said, "Pa, you're an awful man. I purely love you."

He patted her and said, "I know. You must take after your ma. Soon as we finish off them pesky Shawnee, I aim to run back east and fetch old Becky. Since you're a growed and married woman I can tell you something else and we'll say no more about it."

"What's that, pa?"

"Your mother Becky Boone is the best I've ever bedded and I know she feels the same about me. We can fuss and fight and fool around on the side some. But sooner or later, come famine, flood or the seven plagues, we always wind up together again. Any man and woman can have fun together for a time. But if the magic ain't there, after a month or so it gets to be just another chore."

Jemina thought. "Flanders and me likely has some magic, pa," she said. "But you don't think ma is fooling around back east, do you?"

"It don't matter. I'm her man and she's my woman. Nobody else can ever come betwixt us permanent. Some folks go all their lives and never find the right partner, but when it happens they're just stuck, God help 'em. I don't hold with your mother's Tory family. She hates my way of living and sometimes she even hates me, but we both know all I need is a few minutes alone with her, just looking at her."

He chuckled fondly and added, "That's likely why she run off all the way to Carolina this time."

31

There were more volunteers the next morning than Boone was willing to take along. He told the angry men and boys their desire for revenge was only natural. Then he said, "You're needed here to protect the women and children in case there's another attack on the fort. We're headed after the rascals with three guns and an Injun scout, which gives us four men after three. Me, Joe and Simon are legged up better than most white men and Many Jackets can lope fifty miles at a clip. We aim to track Corn Burner quiet as well as sudden. A larger party is what the skunk is hoping we'll send after him."

As Joe fumed at the delay, Simon Kenton nudged Boone and growled, "Sun ball's almost riz, Dan'l. You can speechify about it when we gits back."

Boone agreed and the three whites headed out in the dawn mists after Many Jackets, who was already out ahead and almost invisible in the valley haze. Joe started to trot forward and Simon Kenton warned, "Slow and easy, Joe. The secret of a long-hunt is to move at a walk and keep moving. A man can walk sixty miles without stopping if he sets his mind to it. Running and jumping slows you down in the long haul."

They found Many Jackets kneeling up the slope where Margaret and the Collins boy had been killed. The Cherokee looked disgusted as he said, "Hear me. Your people are fools. Look at all the boot prints they left."

Boone said, "I'm surprised you even come up here. I could have told you there'd be no sign worth reading."

Many Jackets shook his head. "There is sign." He held up a tiny fluffy thing that might have been a dead insect. He said, "This was torn from an arrow feather. Arrow was not well-matched to the bow. It scraped threads off when they shot the boy."

"All right. We know they was Shawnee. So the bow was likely Shawnee and they got the arrow somewhere else. So?"

"Arrow was painted blue. It was made by one of the arrowsmiths of the western Algonquin nations. Maybe Arapahoe. Maybe Cheyenne. They now live beyond the Mississippi on the Sea of Grass. They no longer hunt by the Big Sweet Waters."

"Well, we know Black Fish had other tribes with his Shawnee. Hamilton's supplied ever' Injun he could find to fight us. You're not saying Corn Burner's headed across the Mississippi, are you?"

"No. He won't want to leave his own people. He'll be heading for someplace between Vincennes and Point Pleasant."

"I agree. So why are we jawing about the arrow fluff some fool Injun made out west?"

"I think maybe one of the men with Corn Burner is not Shawnee. I think they may split up."

Joe grimaced as he spied a dried clot of blood on a grass stem. He nudged Kenton. "How long do we stand here jawing like this? We're still in sight of the fort, God damn it!"

"You see where Corn Burner left us a note as to his whereabouts, Joe?"

"No, but damn it . . ."

"Shut up and listen, boy. You'll likely learn something."

Boone said, "Yep. If some western Injun tagged along with Corn Burner and another Shawnee, he might be having homesick thoughts at that. I don't like the idea of us splitting up though."

Many Jackets said, "A strange Indian would make for the falls of the Ohio. That's the crossing everyone knows. He would leave the others this side of the Licking River and follow the Licking northwest."

"Mebbe, but we ain't after him. We want Corn Burner."

"Hear me. I will leave now for Big Bone Lick. I will run the ridges and beat the stranger to the crossing by a day. He will be moving with

care to cover his tracks. I will be on the high
and dry ground and . . ."

"Damn it, we know how you head game off,
Many Jackets. Let's study on where we meet
again after."

"Hear me. I will catch the one alone and we
will talk as he is dying. I think you three should
follow the Warrior's Path toward Chillicothe."

"Hell, Corn Burner will be expecting that.
He'll never be on that trail even if he's headed
back to Black Fish."

Many Jackets nodded. "But if you follow it,
I will be able to rejoin you with any information
I can get. I think you should move directly for
the main Shawnee town until we know for sure
Corn Burner is not going there. If we all reach
the Ohio ahead of him . . ."

"You're right. It don't hardly matter where
he's aiming on the other shore if we can head
him off. Us three will cross the Licking and head
for the Little Miami, above the Ohio falls. Let's
move it out."

As the three whites started walking along the
ridge to the northeast, Many Jackets veered
away at an angle. He was in sight for some time
but out of earshot. Joe fell in beside Kenton and
demanded, "How come we think it's Chillicothe
after all? Last night I thought we agreed Corn
Burner and Black Fish didn't get along."

"They ain't that mad at one another and Corn
Burner has scalps to show off. We don't know
he's headed for the main camp, Joe. The idea is

to cover some ground while we study on it."

"This is crazy! I thought you tracked an Injun by finding his footprints."

Kenton spat and said, "They don't leave that many footprints, Joe. You've hunted deer, ain't you?"

"Sure. I'm fair at it too."

"All right. Let me ask you something. Does a deer paint arrows on the trees to show you where to find him, or do you sort of have to study on his whereabouts?"

"Well, you find some droppings, or maybe a hoofprint now and again."

"Deer ain't as careful as Shawnee. But you never caught a deer by walking up a line of hoofprints unless maybe it had just snowed recent. Tell me how you find a deer, Joe."

Joe shrugged. "You study the lay of the land. You figure where the brute's been browsing at night and where he might lay up to hide by daylight . . ."

"There you go. We knows where Corn Burner fed yesterday. Now we has to find his daytime cover. When you're after a deer, you search first in the nearest alder-hell. If he ain't there you beat through aspen or, if all else fails, a canebrake."

"I see. Chillicothe is the first alder-hell."

"Right. If he ain't headed there, he's making for Little Chillicothe or Vincennes. Mebbe Point Pleasant, up the river."

Boone had been listening as he swept the

ground ahead for sign. He said, "I don't like Vincennes. It's a mite too civilized for Corn Burner. He likes to be admired, and them English and French Canadian gals at the fort in Vincennes sort of wrinkle their noses at fresh scalps."

He thought some more. "More I study, the more I like Little Chillicothe."

Simon explained, "The English calls it Shawnee Town. It's a bit off from the main camp and capital city of the Shawnee. In Little Chillicothe he'd be close enough for politicking amongst the wilder Injuns and far enough from Black Fish and the English officers to stay outten their control."

"I see." Joe wondered, "Do you reckon the three of us will be enough to march into a town of wild Shawnee?"

Both older men laughed. Kenton said, "Not hardly. We has to cut the rascal off on this side of the Ohio or give it up."

"Give it up, hell! I'm following that bastard no matter where he goes."

"No you ain't, Joe. We wouldn't let you cross the Ohio even if you was dumb enough to want to. That's pure Injun country, all the way to the Great Lakes. That's why they calls it Indiana. Even Tory troops and traders has to mind their manners up there. There's a village ever' few miles. You'd lose your scalp afore your feet dried out if you was fool enough to ford the Ohio."

"But we can't just let the bastards get away, God damn it!"

"Simmer down. We ain't aiming to. We're just out to catch him sensible, on our side of the river."

Boone suddenly dropped to one knee and ran his finger over the packed earth of the natural ridge-trail. Joe asked what he'd found and Boone said, "Just a notion. These dead leaves here have been stepped on since they dried out after all that rain. See how the new crushed edges are sort of crisp?"

"You mean some Injun walked here, right?"

Boone shook his head. "I said *something* walked here. Might have been an Injun. Might have been a critter."

"Then why is it so important?"

"Might not be important, Joe. For all we know, we're headed the wrong way. Like Simon says, they seldom leave us a note tacked to a tree."

Boone led them to the crossing of the Licking River where the beaten path crossed over to Canoe Ridge. Joe could see the ridge was shaped like a long upside down canoe, but he couldn't see why the Shawnee might not have crossed somewhere else. Or, indeed, how Boone and Kenton knew Corn Burner had crossed at all.

On the river-bank, Boone knelt near the edge of the grass and studied a pebble. Kenton squatted beside him and grunted, "Yep. It's been turned over in the last few hours, Dan'l."

"Could have been a deer or bear, Simon."

"Or mebbe an elk. Buffalo would have left sign in that softer stuff behind us."

Joe asked, "For God's sake, what does it matter?"

Boone explained, "They didn't cross here. No injun would be careless enough to scuff pebbles with his moccasins."

"Then what are you so cheerful about?"

"We can move on up the ridge without scouting too careful for an ambush, son. Let's git on up to the crest and have us a look around."

Joe followed as the two older men legged it up the slope with the mile-eating pace he was finding harder on his own legs than he'd expected. In one way, the experienced long-hunters seemed to poke along. In another, since they never rested, they covered a mighty distance in a day. The sun was getting low in the west again. They'd been on the trail since sunrise. Boone hadn't rushed them. He'd almost sauntered along the wooded ridges or across one valley pasture after another. He'd commented on berry bushes someone, or some bear, had been at. He listened thoughtfully to bird cries and discussed the season for each sort of unseen flying critter with the laconic Kenton. And he'd never stopped walking.

They hadn't taken a rest break. They hadn't paused for a noonday meal. They'd just strolled along, and here they were, a good forty miles from Boonesburough with plenty of daylight left. It didn't seem possible even for a man Joe's age. He was starting to see why the Indians thought the captain had medicine. The old bastard was legged up like a cross between a mountain goat and a mule.

Boone strolled them up to the crest, not seeming to notice the incline, though Joe's tendons protested up and down his younger legs. Boone called a halt in a grove of poplar where their outlines were invisible against the skyline to anyone below. From the crest they could see for miles. A soft haze over the surrounding ridges glowed orange and purple in the gloaming. Boone said, "Jesus, ain't it pretty?"

Kenton pointed with his chin at a distant rising smudge and said, "Campfire. Small one. Mebbe ten miles out and to your left."

"I see her, Simon. It's about the right size for two men. There's a rock shelter over there, as I remember. Camped there one night myself, year or so ago."

Joe's voice was eager as he said, "Let's move in on that smoke!"

Boone shook his head and said, "Let's not, Joe. Our best bet is to follow this here ridge, cut through the canebrakes to the north and bed down for the night mebbe six or seven miles on. I remember a nice dry tanglewood on the high ground and it don't look like rain."

Exasperated, Joe waved his hand and said,

"Can't you see that Injun campfire right out there in front of us?"

"Let's go. We don't know whose fire it might be. If it's Corn Burner, we're cutting him off by moving north. If it's somebody else, we ain't wasting time creeping a good ten miles with the sun going fast."

As they started moving again, Kenton elaborated, "You try not to creep up on folks, Joe. It's better if you're forted up good somewhere and they is creeping up on you. It's even better if they don't know you're laying for 'em."

"Shit, we have three loaded guns to their two."

"You don't know that, Joe. You're guessing Many Jackets was right about 'em splitting up. There could still be two men with Corn Burner. There could be more. Mercy Bryan says she seen three Injuns. That don't mean she spied the whole party."

"I follow your drift, but this is a pure cautious way to hunt them sons of bitches if you ask me!"

Boone said drily, "You do git cautious after a while. Folks who don't hunt Injuns cautious gits dead! We ain't playing hide-and-go-seek with little fellers, Joe. Corn Burner is a master and this game is for keeps."

It was maybe four in the morning and Joe seemed to have just fallen asleep on the hard damp ground in the tanglewood when he felt

Kenton shaking him. It was black as pitch and he couldn't see the other two men, but Boone's voice was disgustingly cheerful as he said, "We're chawing some jerked buffalo for breakfast and then we have to git cracking, son."

Astonished, Joe said, "It's the middle of the night!"

"No it ain't. It'll be light enough to keep from walking through a tree by the time we chaw ourselves awake. I've studied about that fire we spotted last evening. I know a hidee-hole where we can mebba wait a spell. It's a long shot, but we won't be going outten our way for the meet-up with Many Jackets to our north, and there's a grain to the land that anyone who built that fire might follow if they're headed for the Ohio."

Kenton said, "I know the place you mean, Dan'l. It's that outcrop they call Trapper's Rock. I holed up there one weekend when the Wyandot was looking for me. It covers a branch of the Warrior's Path."

Boone said, "Yep. Let's eat."

Joe said, "I'm not hungry, but I'm purely dying for a smoke."

"Eat anyways, boy. There's no telling when you'll get another chance and buffalo sticks to the ribs all morning. You can chaw tobacco if you want to. I don't have to tell you why you can't light up, do I?"

"Hell, I said I wanted to smoke. I never said I was stupid enough to do it!"

They ate themselves awake and then Boone

led them through the dark woods in some manner Joe didn't understand. He decided the old man was likely part bat. He kept whipping himself across the face with wet branches until they stopped to water at some uncharted little spring. There it was light enough for Joe just to make out the white sand he was kneeling in. As they left, he noticed Kenton dragging a broken branch behind them to cover the tracks they'd made in that sand.

Trapper's Rock was a natural bowl of limestone boulders overlooking a bend in what might have been a game trail. The so-called Warrior's Path was simply a hazy corridor where the trees and bushes wouldn't trip a running man or brute. Most white people wouldn't have seen a trail at all. But Joe wasn't that green. He could see the natural ambush Boone had selected and it made him feel a little better as the light grew brighter.

Boone posted Joe with his musket trained in what Joe felt was the wrong direction. When he protested, Boone said, "They can come from any side, you know. I'll cover the trail. Simon will cover it from the other direction in case of unexpected company. You cover our backs. If I was leading a party in these parts, I'd scout these rocks afore I passed 'em like a bird on his way to the mill pond!"

Joe saw the sense of it, so he took up his position, which faced a totally uninteresting wall of alder. Even though he could see it was nearly impossible for Trapper's Rock to be approached from that side, he didn't comment. He could see why Boone had picked it.

The birds were singing now, and the light was good enough to make out the colors of the leaves. Kenton spat and muttered, "It's nigh sunup, Dan'l."

Boone nodded and replied, "We'd best be moving on."

Joe now protested, "I thought we had us an ambush here!" But Boone got up, stretched and said, "We did. It ain't no good. Whoever lit that fire we spotted ain't headed this way. The rascals have been up for hours if they're Injuns. If they ain't, it don't hardly matter. We're after Corn Burner, not some fool hide hunter."

As they started out again, Joe asked, "How far are we from where Many Jackets is supposed to meet up with us?"

Boone said, "Not more'n fifty miles."

Joe grimaced. "Another day like yesterday, right?"

"Wrong. We got to move slower from here on. If Corn Burner is ahead he may ambush us. If we're out in front we may get a crack at him. I figure two nice easy strolls with a night on the ground between."

Kenton said, "I been thinking 'bout the place they jumped you at Blue Licks, Dan'l."

"So have I. The Shawnee know the territory and they know they could ambush anyone on their trail. There too."

"If we was to git there fust, Dan'l . . ."

"Just what I been thinking. I know a rock cleft Corn Burner or us could sure cover the trail with. I know a knob of rock as dominates the site too. You reckon it's worth a try?"

"If we're ahead of them we'll never find a better place to trap 'em, Dan'l."

Joe asked, "What if they're ahead of us? They had a whole night's start on us. If they just lit out and never looked back . . ."

"They might have, Joe. In that case we'll never catch 'em this side of the Ohio. I'm counting on Corn Burner being more cautious."

"I met him. I think he's sort of hot-headed and foolish. He strikes me as the sort of cuss who'd just hit and run."

"You may be right, Joe. If you are, we'll have lost him."

"We can't lose him. He has to pay for what he did."

"He will, Joe, sooner or later. It ain't like he's about to retire to a farm in Connecticut, you know. If the English gave up and all went home this morning, we'd still expect the Shawnee to keep coming down to visit us from time to time. We're going to have trouble with Injuns 'til ever' tribe's across the Mississippi. It's a shame in a way. But there you have it. Their kind and ours just can't live close together."

Kenton said, "Many Jackets says his Cherokee and the other more civilized tribes figure to become an Indian State along the Tennessee when the war is over, Dan'l."

Boone shrugged. "It'll never work. Us and them just don't think the same. I've met Injuns I like. Sometimes I suspicion I understand 'em. But our heads ain't put together the same way. Try as we might, we has to have misunderstandings with Injun neighbors. Sometimes it'll be us at fault. Sometimes it'll be them not understanding a look or a gesture, and there the fur goes flying. We'll have to push 'em on toward the sunset iffen it's just or not. It's them or us. No way for both to come out on top."

Kenton frowned and said, "Durn it, Dan'l. I got Injuns friends I'm fond of, same as you."

"That you'd like to get more neighborly with? Trouble is it won't be up to folks like you an' me. Them politicians in Philadelphia ain't about to let this land out here lie fallow. Hell, those boys keep stealing it from *us!*"

They dropped the gloomy subject and just walked. It seemed to Joe they walked a hundred miles but it was more like ten when, a few hours later, Boone led them up the slope away from the stream and explained, "We'll circle in on the licks from northeast. You ain't been here afore, Joe. There's some salt water springs as comes outten the cliffs along the river. The cliffs are limestone and sort of melted into funny shapes by the rains of Time. We'll move in across the flat top of the plateau. You'll be moving through beech and juniper, sort of thick, so watch your step. There's sink holes et in the soft rock. When we get near the river agin' you'll find the land drops away sudden. The place they may have picked out for an ambush is where the cliffs hug the river and the country's tore up like busted crockery. I'm saying all this now 'cause there'll be no talking in the thickets as we moves in. You got questions, ask 'em now. The last few miles, I don't even want to hear you breathing."

Joe said he understood. They followed Boone away from the river and into the trees. Now that he had hopes of even spotting sign, Joe's fatigue had left him. He felt rather than saw the country change around them. It was more the type of vegetation he sensed and the smell of the forest that told him they were walking over ground something funny must have happened to a long time ago. He remembered stories of the big caverns under the Cumberlands, where men found dried-up Injuns and could drive a wagon in to gather saltpeter pure enough for making gunpowder. They said there were underground rooms big enough to build a frigate in and underground lakes deep enough to float one. The thought of walking over caves like that made a man mind his step.

There were places where the earth slumped down in shallow craters. Joe saw holes too big for a gopher to have dug. There was a salty tang to the air, as if they were walking near the distant sea instead of west of the mountains. Joe began to understand how Boone could get around so well in the dark. Once you knew the country, you could just about hear and smell your way. The birds in the beech saplings all around didn't sing like birds in pine, and neither sounded like the birds you heard in sycamores or along the riverside. Different flying critters likely built their nests according to what they fed on.

Joe stepped wide around a treacherous looking hole in the ground. Then, as if he'd opened a door, he was standing between two junipers and staring out over a dizzy drop to the river far below!

He stared down at the rain-rounded white boulders and stopped breathing as, beside him, Kenton whispered, "I see him. I make one Shawnee with his musket trained upstream. Hold on 'til we spot the other."

Joe sank to his haunches and studied the Indian down at the base of the cliff. It wasn't Corn Burner. It was a smaller man than the big sachem. Like other Shawnee he wore breech clout and fringed leggings. His upper torso was naked and painted with red dots, as was the shaved head facing away from Joe. The Indian crouched behind a cleft boulder, as motionless as a cat beside a mousehole. Only the feather of his scalplock moved from time to time in the vagrant breeze from the river.

Joe looked around for Boone, but the captain

had slipped away in the trees without a word to him or Simon Kenton. Joe raised his musket and trained the sights on the Indian's back. Simon made a slight warning hiss and Joe nodded. He wasn't going to fire until he knew where Corn Burner was either.

Time went by, then more time. A trinkle of sweat ran down Joe's nose. He wondered where Boone was and what in thunder was going on. His mouth was dry and it was worse than hunting any deer. The distant figure blurred in the musket sights and his finger trembled on the trigger.

He didn't know whether he wanted to pull the trigger or not. The stranger down there was a Shawnee, an enemy, but he wasn't Corn Burner. He wasn't anybody Joe knew. Joe wanted to hate him. He knew he likely should. The Shawnee had killed Meg and the rascal might have been the one who scalped her. But the stranger wasn't Corn Burner and having him in his sights didn't seem real.

And then they heard a shot and Boone yelled out, "Coming at you!"

Joe fired without thinking as Simon Kenton whirled and fired at a blur of motion in the trees behind them. Then, as he pulled his ramrod, Joe heard Boone again, shouting, "He was stalking from up here! Did you nail him, boys?"

Simon whipped the reloaded musket up and fired again from the hip before he yelled, "Not yet!" and charged out of sight through the brush.

Joe was totally confused. He rammed a fresh ball down his barrel. Through the drifting smoke he saw the man he'd shot, writhing below like a worm on a hot stove. He'd forgot he'd loaded with a double charge of rusty horseshoe nails.

Boone was at Joe's side now. He glanced down and muttered, "Finish him, boy! Corn Burner's lit out through the trees! I don't know how I missed him, but let's move!"

Numbly, Joe raised his musket, trained it on the ripped-up man down by the water and put a killing ball in his bloody back. Then Joe was up and running, following the sounds of crashing branches as he reloaded on the move.

A musket sounded in the trees ahead. Joe couldn't tell whether Boone or Kenton had fired. He tripped over a root and staggered. The unexpected move saved his life as a ball hummed past his ear. He'd clean forgot guns shot *both* ways! But he kept moving forward until he came upon Boone crouched behind a stump. The captain waved him to a halt and warned, "We'll wind up shooting one another in this brush, son. Simon's right on the rascal's tail!"

They crouched together, listening to distant crashes. Then, after a long interval of silence, Kenton called out, "Hey, Dan'l? Where you at?"

"Over here, with the boy! You git him, Simon?"

Kenton approached, biting a cartridge and wearing a disgusted look. He snorted, "He went down a sink hole like a rabbit! I throwed a rock down after him. He's in a cave. A big one."

Joe gasped, "Can't we go down after him?" Kenton snorted again. "Down a tunnel to who knows where, lit up from ahint? I wouldn't drop down that fool sink hole if he was only a bear!"

"Can't we head him off? Surely you know every entrance, captain!"

Boone looked mournful and said, "Nope. I only know a dozen or more. There must be hundreds. You remember me saying I knowed a place where a man could cover anyone waiting in ambush down below? Corn Burner knowed about it too! He was covering his sidekick from up here and we stumbled into one another about the same time. You likely know the rest."

Kenton asked, "Did you get the other Injun, Dan'l?" and Boone replied, "Joe here did. Looks like it was Standing Elk. I met him when I was visiting that time. He was might ornery, even for a Shawnee."

Kenton grinned at Joe and said, "There you go, Joe. You can count coup on one bad Injun."

"I didn't want him. I wanted Corn Burner. What do we do now?"

Boone scratched his head and said, "We'd best be moving on to meet up with Many Jackets. He might have found out something."

Joe frowned, "Move on? The son of a bitch is right under our feet somewhere!"

"It's that somewhere he's counting on, Joe. We'll never catch him chasing him through all these durned caves. He's likely expecting us to. With any luck, he won't come up for a look-see afore the sun goes down."

Joe grasped his meaning and said, "Oh, we get well out ahead and cut him off again, right?"

"Might work. Might not. He'll be expecting it and there's at least a hundred miles of Ohio he can cross."

"Then I vote we stay here and search some more. Maybe use some smoke."

Kenton said quietly, "You're outvoted, Joe. Let's move it on out. I'll take the point 'til we're out of these thick woods."

32

It took them two more days to meet with Many Jackets, another night and most of a day to reach the juncture of the Ohio and Little Miami. And another night and a morning for the Cherokee to reach them.

They were sheltered in a shallow limestone grotto opening on a flood terrace carved out by the river below. A thick canebrake shielded them from anyone approaching from downstream. Taking turns they could easily hold the one narrow path to the flood terrace from upstream. Kenton said he'd holed up there before and Many Jackets knew the place.

Many Jackets did. He'd had to circle some to get to them and he was tired, but the Cherokee was smiling as he flopped down to say, "Hear me. The man I killed was an Illinois. He did not die bravely. We spoke of many things while I was sitting on his chest."

Kenton grinned and asked, "Where's his scalp, old son?"

"I did not take it. First because my people are

less interested than Algonquin in such customs. Second because he cried. One does not count coup on a man who fights poorly and begs for his life. He said it was not his idea to kill my white friends. Then, after I worked on him with my knife a little, he decided to tell the truth when I asked questions that mattered."

"Did he know where the others was headed?"

"Yes. Little Chillicothe. Black Fish is holding a powwow there. The Shawnee don't want the English to hear them. The Illinois was frightened and wanted to leave the war even before Corn Burner killed our friends. The Americans are winning everywhere. They have burned out the Iroquois in the north. They have chased the Creek across the Black Warrior River in the south. The Great White Father in London didn't tell them this would happen. Black Fish is worried about his people."

Joe asked, "Do you reckon the Shawnee might switch sides?"

The Cherokee shook his head and said, "They can't. General Washington says it is wrong to use Indians against white enemies. He fought in the war against the French. He says Indian allies often kill the wrong people and refuse to follow orders they don't like."

Boone said, "Old George is larning. I thought he was a fool the way he let Howe outfox him back in '76. But he's purely starting to get the hang of it lately."

Many Jackets nodded and said, "Some of the powahs now say Washington, not the other George, may be the real Great White Father. Washington seems to have stronger medicine than the king across the Great Bitter Water, and Washington is closer. The man I caught at Big Bone Lick said Black Fish and the other sagamores must powwow about this before they make their next move."

Boone stared thoughtfully across the wide Ohio at the wooded shores of Indiana and muttered, "Poor old bastard. He's damned if he does and damned if he don't. I met the general once. He's a big red-headed rascal who can outcuss a drill sergeant and drink a muleskinner under the table. Folks in the tidewater country say he's a friendly neighbor, but if he don't like you, watch out!"

Boone shifted his pipe and added, "Washington has hated Injuns since he was a pup."

Joe Floyd cut in, annoyed. "What about Corn Burner? I'm not worried about Injun policy. I aim to kill that bastard!"

The other three exchanged thoughtful glances. Then Kenton shook his head and said, "He'll have crossed the river by now, unless he's just stupid. We've waited here a mite. He could have crossed anywhere upstream. He's long gone, Joe."

Joe pounded a fist on his own knee and snapped, "He may be gone but he's not forgotten! How do I get across this goddam river?"

Kenton said flatly, "You don't. That's Tory Injun country over there."

"I don't care if the Barbary pirates claim it as their own! I never came all this way just to give up. I'm going on into Indiana after him. Anybody hereabouts aiming to come along?"

There was a long mournful silence. Then Many Jackets said, "No. Hear me. You are talking with your heart and not your head."

Kenton said, "He's right, Joe. It's time we took it on back to the fort. From here on north it's nowhere."

"Damn it, I thought I was among friends."

"You are, Joe. But friendship has to stop short of suicide. If there was any chance at all we'd give her a try. But Corn Burner's in his own backyard by now. We done what we could. No man could do more."

Joe got to his feet and started walking, jaw set stubborn. He moved out along the path leading to the river's edge.

Boone motioned silently to the others to stay put and got up to follow. He caught up with Joe and fell in at his side. "You can't swim her, Joe," he said. "She's wider than she looks and the current would sweep you around the bend to the rapids below. Corn Burner will have picked a wide spot where the current slows and rafted hisself over on driftwood. You'll want to wait for sunset too. Bobbing out there like a daylit duck is asking for a bullet in the head."

"I thank you and I'll do it. Are you coming with me, captain?"

"Not hardly. But I've met fighting fools afore, so I know better than to try and stop you."

He knocked his pipe out on a sycamore, put it away and asked very quietly, "What's the matter, Joe? Didn't you love her?"

Joe stopped and frowned down at the older man. "What in hell is that supposed to mean?" he demanded.

"I lost a son to the Shawnee, boy. So I reckon I know the natural feelings of a natural grief. You got somethin' more powerful eating at your guts, Joe Floyd. You've been pushing it past hate into sick. You aim to tell me about it?"

Joe choked, "You know what Meg was to me."

"Heard some gossip. That ain't what's eating you. More than one man has been more than friendly with a sister or a daughter. Never seen one go alone into the Shawnee nation over it."

"Meg and I were lovers. Satisfied?"

"No. I ask you if the thing you're hiding from yourself is that you never really loved her. Thing like that could unsettle a man and you're mighty unsettled, Joe."

"Damn it, they killed her and they scalped her!"

"They did. They killed and scalped my son James. But I knowed how I felt about my son, so I never went crazy. You're driving yourself to give her in death what you could never give her in life. You feel it'd be disloyal to her memory not to push revenge past common sense. You ain't just out to punish Corn Burner, Joe. You're punishing yourself for, well, just being a natural man with a pretty gal."

"Maybe. It was more than just the things you likely heard. Meg and I shared more'n a bed. We had some awful secrets and . . ."

"Joe, the woman is dead and any hold she had on you should go with her to the grave. You come out here a boy. I've watched you grow to be a man. It's time to face up to the hurts like grown-ups do. Come home with us now and we'll get drunk and cuss it out. You'll git another crack at Corn Burner. They'll be coming south agin', once they get over the fright Clark and Sullivan just gave 'em."

Joe shook his head. He suddenly felt old and tired but rock-like in his determination as he said, very softly, "I have to avenge her, captain. You see, when I first heard she was dead . . . I felt sort of glad."

Boone whistled silently. Then he nodded and said, "Be sure you wait 'til nightfall and dry yourself good afore you move on. Don't try sneaking as fur as Little Chillicothe. You'll never make it past the young'uns hunting rabbit. There's English and Tory agents over there, so a white man on a path, looking innocent, might not draw fire."

"Thanks. I wouldn't have thought of that. How do I get to this Little Chillicothe?"

"It's to the northeast of here. Three days walk up the river. If they don't spot you for a Patriot, you can just ask for directions like a Tory would. Try to ask women or young boys. Shawnee men are sort of testy to any white man."

"What am I looking for, a stockade or just a wigwam camp?"

"Neither. Injuns like their comfort as much as we do. The Shawnee towns is regular settlements. Log cabins around a trading post or general store. They got a saloon in Little Chillicothe. Your only hope is to stroll in like a friendly Englishman or Yankee renegade and hope you spots Corn Burner afore him or one of his friends spots you. You was captured once by Black Fish, so a lot of 'em know you on sight. I'd go in after sundown and pray the light was poor."

"You're making it sound easier than I reckoned it might be. How do you figure the odds, fifty-fifty?"

"Shoot, if I thought the odds was that good I'd go with you! They're gonna lift your hair, son. I'm just passing on what I know to make 'em work a mite harder at it. Do you have any kin I should notify when you don't come back?"

"No. Mercy Bryan can have Meg's clothes. I told her she could bunk in our cabin whilst I was away."

"I'll look after her, Joe. No way I could talk you out of going on, I suppose?"

"No. I've been thinking about what you said about old guilts belonging in the grave. I've got to bury the past, captain. Even if it means I'm buried with it."

33

The sun had set, but the torchlight blazed in Little Chillicothe as if intended to hold the dark uncertain future at bay. Black Fish sat on a bearskin dais in front of the locked trading post. The Tory storekeeper had been sent away. The sagamore was making medicine and he didn't want white people near him right now.

At his side sat his adopted daughter Two Hearts, wearing the more seemly beaded deerskins of a Shawnee maiden. A powah sat at the end of the plank porch, singing softly in his buffalo-horned headdress as he beat a medicine drum. In the torchlit clearing before them, Corn Burner strutted up and down in his paint, waving aloft a long dark-braided scalp as he orated.

The Indians seated in a circle all around listened politely and waited for Corn Burner to finish. The big sachem was inclined to be long-winded even for a Shawnee, but many thought his words made sense.

"Hear me, my brothers!" he commanded. "While the rest of you sat here like old women

I was killing whites across the river. When Black Fish gave up the fight I did not dispute him even though we all know he is getting old. I helped you pack the ponies. I sent presents to the mourners of our dead. I did everything my father told me to do. And then, by Manitou, I went back."

He smiled scornfully at the sagamore and shook Meg's scalp as he continued, "Black Fish retreated with nearly four hundred young men. I attacked Boonesburough with two followers."

Black Fish frowned and asked, "Where are your followers, Corn Burner? Tonight the woman of Standing Elk wears black paint on her face."

"I have not finished. It is true I lost Standing Elk and my heart is heavy for his woman. But we killed two of them for one of ours. The Illinois ran away. When my father led us against the fort we lost more than one man. We lost many and we did not take the fort. I lost one and killed two enemy. This is true. Can anyone say I was less a leader?"

Two Hearts curled her lips and said, "Hear me! The scalp you hold so boastfully is that of a woman! No white man has such long hair. My father is a killer of men. He does not count coup on women and children."

Corn Burner flushed and said, "I did not know it was our custom for women to speak at council. Two Hearts is not a real Shawnee. Perhaps she thinks we are Iroquois? It is said the Mohawk women never shut up."

Black Fish saw his younger rival had committed a tactical error. The wiser sagamore took advantage of it by snapping, "It is true my daughter spoke out of turn. It is true the Shawnee do not take council with their women as the Iroquois do. But our Iroquois allies are brave men and good fighters. Does Corn Burner deny this?"

"Why should I? The Iroquois are nothing to me. I do not care what they do."

"Then you are not very wise, my son. I did not give up the siege to the south because I was afraid of those people. I did not give up because our powder was wet. As we speak the Yankee long knives are burning out the last of the dreaded Iroquois. Others have beaten the redcoats at Vincennes. I returned to our own lands to protect them. The enemy is coming at us from two sides and he is winning every fight."

"Does my father suggest we crawl to the sachem Washington, crying to be forgiven as if we'd been naughty children?"

"No. Washington is unforgiving and his thoughts of us are red thoughts. We have no choice but to go on fighting, but we must fight him our own way on our own ground. I am weary of the advice from London. I am weary of young men who boast of killing squaws. I need time to make medicine and pray for a vision from Manitou. My children are in terrible danger and I do not know what to do."

"Bah! Your words are the squaw-thoughts of a frightened old man!"

There was an intake of breath around the clearing, for the words of Corn Burner were killing words and Black Fish was rising slowly to his feet, his face turned to stone.

But before the older man could answer the taunt, a loud sound of struggle came from the darkness beyond the torchlight. Four shouting Shawnee were dragging a taller white man into view. The enemy was still trying to fight. They saw his face was bloody and his shirt was half torn off.

Two Hearts sprang to her feet with a strangled cry as the guards dragged Joe before the sagamore. Corn Burner laughed and said, "The spirits smile on us this night! I know this man! He is a friend of Boone! He is an enemy, and we have him!"

Black Fish held up a hand for silence and told Joe, "Stop fighting my young men, my son. Why have you come back to us? I thought you'd run away."

Joe gave up the struggle. The others held him anyway. He managed a tight defeated smile as he shrugged and said, "I was after Corn Burner. He owes me for that scalp there."

Two Hearts nudged the sagamore and tried to whisper something, but Black Fish said, "Silence. I know what is in my daughter's heart.

But this foolish young man was paid back for the life of Two Hearts. He comes here like a raging wolf cub after abusing my hospitality. Our debts to him are paid in full."

Staring gravely at Joe, the sagamore said, "You are in our power once more and I grow weary with the usual games. This war with your people has become a serious business. I hope you have sung your death song and are prepared to meet The Owl, my son."

Joe didn't answer. He'd done his best and it hadn't been enough. They'd jumped him from the dark as if he'd been a fool boy trying to steal green apples. And so now he was dead. But at least he'd tried.

Corn Burner said, "Hear me! This man is a friend of Boone. I say he should die as Boone would. I say he should die slowly. I would like to kill him in my own way for the ghost of Standing Elk."

Black Fish nodded with a thin smile and said, "I have heard my son's words and they make my heart soar. I agree Corn Burner should kill the captive, if he can."

Then he stepped forward, drawing a tomahawk from his belt. He held it out to Joe, telling the others, "Turn him loose. Corn Burner wants to fight him."

As Joe took the tomahawk, Corn Burner paled and gasped, "What is the meaning of this? Would my father arm a captive against his own sachem?"

"You said you wanted to kill him. You have been talking all evening about how brave you are. What troubles my son Corn Burner? Are you telling us now that you are afraid of one man?"

The old sagamore's face grinned wolfishly in the flickering torchlight as he purred, "Moments ago you called me an old woman. Moments ago you offered to lead our nation against the whole Continental Army. I think the young men would like to see how well you can do against one Yankee before they follow you into battle against hundreds."

Joe stepped clear of the Shawnee who'd been holding him, the tomahawk gleaming in his big right fist. Corn Burner backed away, shouting, "Hear me! This is madness! I never said we should give the enemy a fair chance! I said we should kill them, not play games with them!"

He turned to a pinesee standing in the surrounding crowd and called out, "Green Snake! You and I have counted coup together! Will you not help me?"

Green Snake drew the tomahawk from his belt and tossed it to Corn Burner, saying, "Now you have two blades. It should be a good fight to watch."

Two Hearts jeered, "He is afraid! Mighty Corn Burner whimpers like a camp cur when my father asks him to show us his manliness!"

There was a mutter of scornful agreement from the crowd. Corn Burner flushed almost as red as his paint. He yelled a wild war cry and rushed at Joe with an upraised tomahawk in each hand!

Joe grabbed the sachem's right wrist with his free hand and swung his own borrowed weapon as hard as he could. Corn Burner blocked it with his own tomahawk and the two blades shot sparks as they collided edge against edge. Neither wooden handle had been designed to take such a shock. The blades flew away leaving them with broken sticks in their hands.

Corn Burner stabbed at Joe with the jagged length of hickory. Had it been a knife, the fight would have ended on the spot. But the sharp wooden stake merely tore a shallow bloody gash across Joe's ribs. The Indian then twisted his remaining tomahawk free. He tried to stab again, but Joe had dropped his own useless stick and now he had Corn Burner by both wrists. The Indian went limp, fell backwards, then kicked upward and got a moccasin against Joe's belt buckle. Joe saw they were going down and over so he let go as Corn Burner's back hit the dirt and the Indian straightened the leg, vaulting Joe over him head first.

Joe landed on the back of his neck and shoulders, completed the somersault and sprang to his feet, twisting like a big cat to face the other way. Corn Burner bored in fast, slashing with his tomahawk as onlookers scattered out of their brawling path. Corn Burner backed Joe against a cabin wall and lunged at him, screaming like a demon. Joe avoided the blade by side-sliding and letting it thunk into the logs. Then he drove a fist into Corn Burner's middle, sending him back into the clearing, gasping.

Joe moved forward weaponless, his slitted eyes on his enemy. Corn Burner stood with upraised tomahawk, fighting for breath. Corn Burner saw the look on Joe's face and took a step backward as someone in the crowd jeered. Then Corn Burner grimaced with rage and came at Joe, swinging wildly.

It was not the best move he might have made.

Joe caught the descending blade on his forearm. Though it cut his elbow to the bone, he didn't feel the blow. He grabbed Corn Burner by the waistband and the scalplock on his head, lifted him high in the air, then threw him to the ground with a terrible thump. Corn Burner landed spread-eagle on his back and tried to roll aside. Joe dove on him. He landed with his full weight on the sachem, drove a knee into his groin then grabbed his head in both hands, a thumb in each of Corn Burner's eyes!

The Indian howled in agony. Joe thumped his head to the dirt, then drove in each thumb up to the knuckle and twisted the bloody eyeballs out of their sockets before he hammered the gore-spattered head unconscious against the hard earth. He broke Corn Burner's jaw as an afterthought. Then he slowly rose, pulling Meg's scalp free of the Indian's belt.

Green Snake stepped over to him, held out a

war club and suggested, "Finish him. It's your right. It is the only decent thing to do."

Joe ignored the offer. He limped over to where Black Fish stood with Two Hearts. He nodded and said, "I did what I came to do. You can do with me as you like."

"You haven't killed him."

"I know. I was about to. But it suddenly came to me what it would mean to be a warrior with no eyes, or to be a born bully who can't fight any more. I hope he lives to be a hundred now."

"My son, you have learned something about cruelty since we last met. I too think he should live to ponder the past. Have you eaten? The others will try to make Corn Burner comfortable. Let us go to my cabin and consider your own future."

"You mean I have one?"

"I do not know. I must think about it."

The morning sun was bright, but there was a hint of frost in the air and the leaves above them were losing their green as Joe, Two Hearts and Black Fish stood in the glade.

Joe's wounds had been daubed with birch tar, but his bones still ached. And though he'd listened to Black Fish most of the night, he knew he didn't understand the Indian and he knew the Indian would never really understand him.

Two Hearts was wearing a gingham dress from the trading post. The Tory merchant had been sent away but locked doors were made to be kicked open. Black Fish didn't want people laughing at his daughter. His eyes were moist as he stared down at her golden hair in the dappled sunlight. He murmured, "I have never seen you in the clothing of a white woman. You are beautiful to me either way. Are you sure you want this thing, my daughter?"

Two Hearts nodded and took the Indian's hand in both of hers. She murmured, "You named me well, my father. Part of me will always be Shawnee. But I know where I belong now."

"Hear me. Your children will be the enemies of my Shawnee grandchildren. I will always hold you in my heart. But when we cross the Ohio again, and we will . . ."

"I understand my father's words. They make my Shawnee heart heavy. But my other heart pulls me down a strange new path after this white brother you chose for me."

Black Fish scowled at Joe and snapped, "I chose him to be my son because he gave me back your life when it was in his hands. If I had known this would happen . . . And yet, it did. I am weary of trying to change things no man can."

Joe smiled at the sagamore and said, "Captain Boone said you were a real gent in your own way, Black Fish. I never expected you to be so neighborly. I purely thank you."

Black Fish neither smiled nor looked at Joe

as he muttered, "I heard a tale once about another Indian father who listened when his daughter pleaded for the life of a white captive. I think he was stupid too. He gave the white men his daughter and they took away his lands. I think her name was Pocahontas. Her father must have loved her very much."

"I understand, sir. But Two Hearts isn't an Injun gal. She's a white captive too."

Black Fish snorted and said, "Listen to him, my daughter! He says he understands. He understands nothing!"

Two Hearts said, "I have never been a captive, Joe. I have always been free to leave if I wanted to. I would not be following you to the world of my other heart if this were not so."

Black Fish nodded grimly and added, "You would not leave at all, white man, if my love for Two Hearts was not greater than my hatred of your kind. Last night I let you do me a small favor. Even two enemies may share an enemy. This does not make them friends."

He handed Joe his musket and said, "You must go. The others will be wondering why we have not come back from our morning walk. You saw last night I do not rule as your white leaders do. You white people speak much of every man doing as he thinks right. My people practice it. If friends of Corn Burner find you alone between here and the other side of the Ohio they will think it is right to kill you."

Joe put an arm around Two Hearts' shoulders

and said, "Don't worry, sir. I won't let 'em catch us."

Black Fish laughed harshly and asked Two Hearts, "Are you sure you want to be the woman of a crazy person, my daughter? He thinks he can get both of you safely away from here!"

"He has much to learn, my father, but I shall show him how to hide our tracks."

"Good. If he beats you, send word or come back to us. I think you had better go now. I have something in my eye and I want to lie down for a while."

Two Hearts raised the big brown hand and kissed it before she turned away and simply started walking, not looking back.

Joe held out his hand and said, "I'll take care of her, sir. Maybe when the war is over we can come back for a visit."

"By Manitou, I will never understand women. A whole nation of men to choose from and my daughter gives herself to a fool! Get her across the Ohio before I change my mind. When you see Big Turtle, tell him it was a good fight he gave us. Tell him we'll be back next summer for another."

"Does it have to be that way, Black Fish?"

"You know it does. Do not try to make me your friend. Take the woman we both love and go. I have spoken."

34

Joe would not have survived the trail back without Two Hearts. It was her idea to head northeast instead of making for the river. When Joe said the Ohio was to the south, she said, "I know. This path leads toward the British road between Point Creek and Detroit."

"But, honey, we have no business heading for Detroit. You and I are both Patriots now."

"The pinesee after us will think this too. By now they know my father let us go. They will be moving to cut us off from the Ohio. They will take some time to consider this trail. I am dressed like a white girl, almost. If we meet anyone, we will say we are a Tory couple fleeing from George Rogers Clark."

"Right. I'll tell English troops we meet we came from Vincennes. You can talk to any Shawnee."

"Oh, dear, my father was right, but my heart tells me I must go with you anyway. Don't you know *anything*, Joe? You've never been to Vincennes. You don't know anyone who lives there.

Any Englishman or Tory who had would trap you in a few minutes of friendly talk even if he was not trying. As for my speaking Shawnee, how could I speak Shawnee? I am not that white Shawnee girl they may be looking for! I am only a simple fur trader's woman. Do you not remember, Joe? You brought me here from upper Canada to buy furs from Black Fish. But he had no furs. So now we are going home."

"We are, huh? Where's our wampum?"

"Our what?"

"Wampum, trade goods, *some* damn thing. You may know more'n me about Injuns, but you got a lot to learn about my folks. I mean, our folks. Any whites we meet would wonder why we were so poor if we come down here to trade."

Two Hearts reached inside her bodice and drew out a little leather purse. She said, "I have some gold sovereigns my father gave me with this dress. He said it was enough to buy us a farm from whoever wins the war."

"My God, you mean Injuns use money, like everyone else?"

"What did you think we bought things with? No white trader would sell us powder and ball for wampum, Joe. About our home in Canada. I do not think we should live near any town. We might meet someone who knows any settlement we can name. I think we have a clearing near Lake Marie. The Canadians name every other lake, Marie. There is birch and maple around our cabin and the ground is granite gravel. Yes, that sounds like anywhere in upper Canada."

He laughed, stopped and swung her around to kiss her.

She responded warmly. Then she pulled away and said, "We can try to have a baby later, when it is dark and we are far from here. Why are you looking at me like that? I can't tell if you want to laugh or cry."

"I reckon I love you, Two Hearts. I mean, I'm getting used to you being pretty. It's coming to me what a hell of a little gal you are."

"Well, we talked last night about being in love. We'll talk about it some more when it gets dark. I think right now we should be thinking about getting away. By now they will have reached the river without cutting sign. They will be talking about it. Some will say we must be across the Ohio. They will want to go back to Little Chillicothe and eat. But there is always someone who will want to circle a bit and search further. We are only a mile or so from the town."

"Are you up to running some?"

"On a well-traveled trail in broad daylight, Joe? Only hunted people run on the trail. I do not understand how you've stayed alive so long."

He chuckled as he took her hand. Musket over the other shoulder, he walked with her along the sun-dappled path. He said, "I've got luck and you've got sly. Betwixt us, the world had best look out. I must say I'm surprised at how quick you changed sides. Yesterday morning, about this time, you were a Shawnee gal in deerskins. Here you are a blushing bride in calico. I've seen you as an Injun gal, and I still can't believe you're not a white gal birthed and raised. You're like one of those little lizards as can change its color to suit its surroundings."

"Of course. My father's people taught me. Even the Iroquois say the Shawnee are the best tricksters. Besides, if I am now your woman, I *am* a white girl now. You did mean all those things you said to me last night, didn't you? My father thinks you just want to trifle with me. He says white men tell Indian girls lies to take advantage of them."

"I know what your father was muttering about in Shawnee, but he was pure wrong about my feelings. He was right about some other things though. You do understand I'm against King George, and what Black Fish meant about us not being friends with the Shawnee any more?"

"Yes. It makes my heart heavy but I understood. Why do you think I'm trying to avoid my old friends right now? Do you think your friends will accept me if we manage to get away?"

"That blonde hair will help. We'll have to do something about the name though. You said when you were little your name was Joan or something, didn't you?"

"Joan, Jo-Anne, or maybe Jane. I think I would like to be Mary. There was a picture in the trading post of a white girl named Mary. She held a sweet little white child in her lap and the trader said she'd been a good person. Have you ever heard of the girl named Mary, Joe?"

"Yep. I forgot you weren't Christian. Mary it is, if the name suits your fancy. We'll talk some on the notions that goes with the name before I introduce you to folks."

"Do you think they'll like me? The Shawnee said I was a good person before they became my enemies."

"You'll likely get along with my friends. They put up with me and I'm not as pretty as you. But you sure do switch your sides with no shilly-shally, gal. Doesn't it bother you?"

"I told you it made my red heart heavy. But when you spoke of the medicine between us, and I felt it too, my white heart told me I had no choice. A woman must be on the side of her man. His people must be her people. She must bind his wounds and load his gun. And when they kill him, she must send her sons to collect the blood debts. This is true. I feel it with both hearts."

He kissed her hand without breaking stride and said, "I know what your white name is now. I aim to call you Ruth."

"Ruth? Ruth? It rolls well on the tongue. Was this Ruth a good person, Joe?"

"I'll tell you her story later. I see folks up ahead. Looks like a mess of 'em, heading south for the Ohio."

He paused and drew her to the side of the trail as they watched and waited. He spotted a flash of scarlet through the trees and muttered, "Oh-oh, British soldiers. Here's where we see how our fool story holds together, Ruth."

The British column was from Detroit, moving down to reinforce Hamilton's expedition on the Wabash. It was a company of the East Lancashire Light Foot, led by Canadian scouts. The Canadians wore buckskins and fur caps of the sort the artist had put on Captain Boone. The soldiers had discarded their white goat-hair wigs and patent leather helmets. They were more comfortably attired in cockaded tricorns and loose seaman's trousers. Their red greatcoats were a bit the worse for wear and they marched in a sensible route-step with each man's Brown Bess slung as its owner felt best. These were no green troops just off the boat. They were seasoned frontiersmen in their own right after three years of hard fighting on the northwestern front.

Joe and Two Hearts stood smiling as the redcoats approached. Joe assumed, correctly, they'd be questioned, at least for directions. The British captain in command held up a hand to halt his man and came over to the couple, putting a finger to his hat as he smiled a trifle warily. He said, "Captain Newton, East Lancs."

"I'm Joe Smith. This here's my woman, Ruth. We're traders. From Lake Marie, upper Canada."

"How'd you do, ma'am. We understand there's a Shawnee town with a tavern somewhere in the neighborhood, sir."

"That'd be Little Chillicothe, captain. It's about three miles further down and to your right. But I don't know if you really want to go there right now."

"Oh?"

"We came down to buy furs. The Shawnee took our gold and sent us packing. They're in a sort of surly mood for some fool reason."

"Hmm, so the Clark boys have been busy. You say the Indians robbed you?"

"Well, they said they just needed money to buy powder and ball and allowed they'd make it up to us next summer."

"That sounds like Shawnee all right. I must say you've taken it with surprising good grace, sir."

"We've traded with 'em before. They left us with our hair and gun. I don't reckon they're really sore at us. Just sort of sulky."

As they spoke, one of the men in Canadian dress was drifting over to join the conversation and Joe hoped he didn't hail from any Lake Marie.

Captain Newton was saying, "I think we just may make directly for the river and build our rafts behind a screen of pickets. If you'd be good enough to show me your pass I shan't detain you further."

"Uh, pass, sir?"

"I must insist. You know you're in the battle zone. The Yankee lines are just across the Ohio, a mile or so from here. Stupid formality and all that rot, but we can't take chances, eh?"

As Joe hesitated, the other man who'd joined them smiled thinly and said, "Well, Joe. We meet again."

And as Joe felt the blood drain from his legs, the red-coated captain asked, "Do you know these people, Lieutenant Marvin?"

The royalist agent nodded and said, "Yes. Our paths certainly seem to keep crossing of late, considering the size of this continent."

"He says they're Canadian fur traders."

"Does he? Well, my young friend has always been very enterprising."

Joe scowled and said, "Get it over with, Marvin. I can't stand a cat who gloats at mice."

Newton looked puzzled by the exchange. Marvin laughed and said, "I vouch for them, Captain Newton. He's Joe Floyd. The lady is . . . just what are you up to, Joe?"

"Her name is Ruth now, and we're looking for a preacher to marry us up."

Marvin bowed to the girl and said, "My congratulations, Ruth. I hope you know what a man you're getting. All of us can see, of course, what a lucky dog he is!"

Captain Newton frowned and said, "Damn my soul, I wish someone would tell me what the deuce is going on here! First he says his name is Smith and then you say it's Floyd, but

you say they're on our side and . . . Pon my
word, sir. I feel explanations are in order!"

Before Joe could put his foot in it, Marvin
nodded and said, "This young man has saved
my life on two occasions when I was on His Majesty's Service. I feel no further explanations are
required."

Newton suddenly brightened and winked at
Joe, saying, "Ah, a bit of slipping back and
forth across the lines, what? You were afraid
to tell me you were a spy. No doubt the charade
about having no money was occasioned by the
reputation some regulars have for being a bit
inclined to brigandry. I assure you the East
Lancs are gentlemen!"

Marvin asked, "Where were you young people headed, Joe? I thought I had you assigned
to Kentucky."

"I come up to marry Ruth here. We figured
we might start a new life up Canada way."

"I see. Are the Shawnee after you?"

"Some of 'em are. We have her daddy's bless-
ings."

"Hmm, you'll be safer traveling with a British
column. We have a chaplain with us. Perhaps
when we make camp down by the river he'll
be good enough to perform the ceremony."

Captain Newton grinned boyishly and said,
"By Jove, that will make for a cheerful break in
this bloody dull business! I have a spot of
brandy in my kit and we'll make a bit of a party
of it, what?"

Ruth was smiling prettily, but Joe's lips were numb as he said, "I'd say that was right neighborly of you all."

"I've got to move us on. Why don't you two march with Marvin? We'll have a jolly wedding after we make camp by the river."

As he motioned to the halted troops and resumed his march, Joe turned to Marvin and said, "I don't know how we'll ever thank you, sir."

Marvin shrugged and said, "Very few people have ever saved my life twice, Joe. Besides, I may be doing my king a service in the long run."

As the three of them fell in at the end of the British column, Joe said, "If you're trying to get me to be a double agent again, forget it. I'm a Patriot true and blue. Ruth here is a Yankee too, if I ever get her across the Ohio."

Marvin sighed and asked, "Don't you ever lie, son? I know what you are better than you do. You're a reasonable man, Joe. There aren't many of us on either side. This war won't last forever. No matter who wins, there'll be bitter scars it's going to take reason and common sense to heal. I know you'll go on fighting us, Joe. But you're no great danger to His Majesty with your musket and ridiculous little log fort. It's my hope that in the years to come you'll tell your sons we weren't all wearing horns and tails. I'd hate to go through this perishing business with you Yanks in my old age."

Joe laughed and said, "You're all right, Marvin. But we've got to quit this capturing each other, hear?"

"Ah, you see? We agree on some points already. You'll spend the night with us. If I know Newton and the other young officers, they'll give you a jolly wedding. I do wish you'd learn to be less truthful. Just keep quiet when I send you across the river on another mission for His Majesty. We don't want to confuse Newton again, so let's not have a speech about the rights of man as we send you to spy on the bloody Yanks for us. True Englishmen are not as far apart on the subjects of freedom and justice as the politicians would have us believe."

35

Six days later, Joe and Ruth Floyd topped a ridge and walked down the slope to Boonesburough. The lookout saw them coming and they were met at the gate by Kenton, Boone and all the others. Joe introduced his bride and little Mercy Bryan grinned and said, "Hot damn! Now I got me a big sister to go with my big brother!"

Joe had told Ruth about Mercy and so she put her arms around the child and kissed her. She didn't know what else to do. She felt awkward and confused to be among the white folk she'd last seen from the Shawnee campsite on the ridge above.

There was a little awkwardness on both sides. Moses Boone nudged his cousin Jemima and asked, loud enough to be heard, "Ain't she that Injun princess, Jemima?"

Jemima shushed him and held out a hand to the stranger, saying, "Howdy, Ruth Floyd. I bids you welcome and if anybody gives you trouble, just say the word and I'll snatch her bald-headed. You can likely see I'm expecting. But I can still whup any gal in town."

Ruth smiled warmly and said, "I think I must be going to have a baby too. We've been trying every night."

There was a roar of laughter and Boone said, "She sure smiles pretty as a picture, Joe. We've fixed your cabin up. Never expected to see you agin', but what the hell, it's too late in the year to work the fields."

Squire Junior looked wistful as he asked, "You folks is already married up, you say? I'm sort of a preacher, you know, and I thought . . ."

Joe punched him on his good shoulder and said, "We'll let you do her again, Squire. The British Army gave us a right nice wedding and the officers made us duck under their swords and all. Tory weddings might not be lawful in Kentucky though, so we'd be obliged if you'd tie us right."

Squire Junior brightened and said, "I got a prayer book somewheres. We'll do her proper afore bedtime. Don't want no sinning in the cabins, now that we're part of Virginee."

Boone took Joe and his bride on either arm and said, "These folks has walked a fur piece. They'll want to rest up afore we throw a proper brawl for 'em. Come on, Ruth Floyd, it's time you met your new home."

He led them to the cabin. As they went in he said, "I'll keep Mercy at my place tonight, but you seem to be stuck with her, Joe."

"Ruth here understands. She says she knows what it is to be an orphan. Besides, I see you rigged us up a closed-off sleeping loft. What do you think of the place, honey?"

The erstwhile Shawnee girl looked around and said, "It's lovely. You didn't tell me you were rich, Joe! We spoke only of the good medicine between us. I can't believe there's so much room for just three people."

"Well, we'll try and fill it up with young'uns. I've filed on a quarter section of land too."

Then Joe noted the expression on Boone's face and asked, "What's the matter, captain? You looked like I just said something stupid."

Boone said, "You go along and plow up all the land you want to, Joe. But don't plant no trees."

"You mean the Transylvania Company isn't in business any more?"

"Don't know what I mean, Joe. Some rascals was just out here from Richmond with survey chains and a map. They say our purchase from the Cherokee don't mean shucks. They say as soon as this war is over there's to be a proper re-something of the new western territories. Last time I went through this, over on the other side of the mountains, I found out I didn't hold a proper deed to the land I'd cleared."

"Aw, hell, Kentucky is ours by right of conquest, captain. We found it and we cleared it and we drove the Injuns from it."

"I know that, Joe. I've never understood the

way lawyers jaw things away from folks. But they won't be able to get the tamer folks out here 'til the last of the Injuns and other mean critters has been run across the Mississippi, so there's that. We'll git us a few crops outten the ground and have us some tolerable hunting afore it's time to move on."

Joe saw his wife was starting a fire in the hearth, not paying much attention. Jesus, she was pretty, kneeling there like that. He'd likely got himself the sort of woman a man would need out here on the edge of the new nation.

He put his musket on its pegs and asked Boone, "How long do you figure we got before the schoolmarms and lawyers come out here to pester us, captain?"

Boone said, "Long enough to clear the stumps. Not long enough for an apple orchard to bear fruit. That's why I suggested you plant no trees."

"Well, I don't know yet. I might just stay and fight to hold on. I can read and write. I can argue before a judge too."

"That you can. I remember my court martial. Dick Callaway's jawboned the provisional government into a ferry franchise. I sent a letter to Patrick Henry asking for a contract to widen the Wilderness Road. They never answered. They likely think a man who don't spell good can't be too handy with tools."

"God damn it, captain, you won this country

for the rascals with your ax and gun. I'll help you fight 'em with paper and pen."

"That's not my style, son. I'll be headed east to fetch my old woman Becky now that things has quieted. We'll be neighbors for a time. But my daddy always said, when you could see the smoke from a neighbor's cabin . . ."

"You're talking foolish. You're getting on in years and it's time you settled down and grew some roots."

Boone smiled down at the girl building the fire and said. "You sure sound married, Joe. My Becky talks the same way when we're on speaking terms. So does Jemima. I understand what you're saying and it makes a heap of sense. But you see, son, it's gonna take all sorts of men to build this new nation now that we got it. It'll take men like Jefferson to write the new laws. Men like Washington to see they's obeyed. It'll take farmers, engineers, artisans and just plain folk who don't mind hard work. And it's gonna take men like me, Simon Kenton and your Cousin John. Footloose men who can't stay put. Men whose wives complain a lot. Men the smart city slickers will never understand and will always consider fools."

"You mean you're thinking of moving further west."

"Not thinking. Knowing. We'll share us a few more hunting seasons here together, Joe. But, yep, I've been thinking of that Sea Of Grass across the Mississippi."

"The Spanish own it, captain."

"Shoot, what care I what it says on a fool map, son? The king of Spain needs white men out there to tame the Injuns and find the water. They say there's Shining Mountains no white man's ever explored. They say there's white-water streams as need to be named, beaver as need to be trapped, trees taller than a steeple as needs to be cut. We're gonna have us a lot to do, Joe!"

"Maybe. But in the end it'll all be surveyed and nailed down with titles, fences, roads and such. Men like you will find it. Men with lawyers will wind up owning it."

"I knows that, Joe. But, Jesus, it's so much fun to find it!"